DEEPER

RODERICK
GORDON

BRIAN
WILLIAMS

Chicken House
Scholastic Inc./New York

Text copyright © 2009 by Roderick Gordon and Brian Williams • Interior illustrations © 2009 by Brian Williams except "The Bridge" © 2009 by Roderick Gordon • www. tunnelsthebook.com • All rights reserved. Published by Chicken House, an imprint of Scholastic Inc., *Publishers since 1920.* CHICKEN HOUSE, SCHOLASTIC, and associated logos are trademarks and/or registered trademarks of Scholastic Inc. • www.scholastic.com • Published in the United Kingdom in 2008 by Chicken House, 2 Palmer Street, Frome, Somerset BA11 1DS. • www.doublecluck.com • No part of this publication may be reproduced, stored in a retrieval system, or transmitted in any form or by any means, electronic, mechanical, photocopying, recording, or otherwise, without prior written permission of the publisher. For information regarding permission, write to Scholastic Inc., Attention: Permissions Department, 557 Broadway, New York, NY 10012. • Excerpt from "The Hammers," by Ralph Hodgson, appears in *Collected Poems* © 1961 (New York: Macmillan), reprinted with permission. • Song lyrics by Lee Hazlewood from "These Boots Are Made for Walkin,'" © 1966 Criterion Music Corporation. Library of Congress Cataloging-in-Publication Data • Gordon, Roderick. Deeper / Roderick Gordon, Brian Williams. —1st American ed. p. cm. Summary: As Will Burrows continues to search for his lost archaeologist father in the strange underground world he has discovered, he stumbles across a sinister plot with terrible implications for the world above. ISBN-13: 978-0-439-87178-5 • ISBN-10: 0-439-87178-6 [1. Adventure and adventurers—Fiction. 2. Underground areas—Fiction. 3. Archaeology —Fiction. 4. London (England)—Fiction. 5. England—Fiction.] I. Williams, Brian James, 1958– II. Title. PZ7.G6591De 2008 [Fic]—dc22 • 2008013703 • 10 9 8 7 6 5 4 3 2 1 • 09 10 11 12 13 • Printed in the U.S.A. 23 • First American edition, January 2009 • The text type was set in Vendetta. • The display type was set in Squarehouse. • Book design by Leyah Jensen and Kevin Callahan

And I listened, and I heard
Hammers beating, night and day,
In the palace newly reared,
Beating it to dust and clay:
Other hammers, muffled hammers,
Silent hammers of decay.

from *The Hammers*
Ralph Hodgson (1871–1962)

PART 1

```
      C
      O
      V
BREAKING
      R
```

I

WITH A HISS and a clunk, the doors whisked shut, depositing the woman by the bus stop. Apparently indifferent to the whipping wind and the pelting rain, she stood watching as the vehicle rumbled into motion again, grinding the gears as it wound its way laboriously down the hill. Only when it finally vanished from sight behind the briar hedges did she turn to gaze at the grassy slopes that rose on either side of the road. Through the downpour they seemed to fade into the washed-out gray of the sky itself, so that it was difficult to tell where the one started and the other finished.

Clutching her coat tightly at the neck, she set off, stepping over the pools of rainwater in the crumbling asphalt at the edge of the road. Although the place was deserted, there was a watchfulness about her as she scanned the road ahead and occasionally glanced back over her shoulder. There was nothing particularly furtive about this — any young woman in a similarly isolated spot might have taken the same care.

Her appearance offered little clue as to who she was. The wind constantly flurried her brown hair across her wide-jawed face, obscuring her features in an ever-shifting veil, and her clothing was unremarkable. If anyone had happened by, they would most likely have taken her to be a local, perhaps on her way home to her family.

The truth couldn't have been more different.

She was Sarah Jerome, an escaped Colonist who was on the run for her life.

Walking a little farther along, she suddenly strode up the verge and hurled herself through a parting in the briar hedgerow. She alighted in a small hollow on the other side and, keeping low, spun around so she had a clear view of the road. Here she remained for a full five minutes, listening and watching and animal-alert. But other than the beat of the rain and the bluster of the wind in her ears, there was nothing.

She was truly alone.

She knotted a scarf over her head, then scrambled from the hollow. Moving quickly away from the road, she crossed the field before her in the lee of a loose stone wall. Then she climbed a steep incline, maintaining a fast pace as she reached the crest of the hill. Here, silhouetted against the sky, Sarah knew she was exposed and wasted no time in continuing down the other side, into the valley that opened out before her.

All around, the wind, channeled by the contours, was driving the rain into confused, twisting vortices, like diminutive hurricanes. And through this, something jarred, something registered in the corner of her eye. She froze, turning to catch a brief glimpse of the pale form.

A chill shot down her spine.

The movement didn't belong to the sway of the heathers or the beat of the grasses. . . . It had a different rhythm to it.

She fixed her eyes on the spot until she saw what it was. There, on the valley side, a young lamb came fully into view, prancing a chaotic gambol between the tussocks of fescue. As she watched, it suddenly bolted behind a copse of stunted trees, as if frightened. Sarah's nerves jangled. *What had driven it away? Was there somebody else close by — another human being?* Sarah tensed, then relaxed as she saw the lamb emerge into the open once again, this time escorted by its mother, who chewed vacantly as the youngster began to nuzzle her flank.

It was a false alarm, but there was little hint of relief, or of amusement, in Sarah's face. Her eyes didn't stay on the lamb as it began to scamper around again, its fleece fresh as virgin cotton wool, in marked contrast to its mother's coarse, mud-streaked coat. There was no room for such diversions in Sarah's life, not now, not ever. She was already checking the opposite side of the valley, scouring it for anything that didn't fit.

Then she was off again, picking her way through the Celtic stillness of the lush green vegetation and over the smooth slabs of stone, until she came to a stream nestled in the crook of the valley. Without a moment's hesitation, she strode straight into the crystal clear waters, altering her course to that of the stream and sometimes using the moss-covered rocks as stepping stones when they afforded her a faster means through it.

As the level of the water rose, threatening to seep in over the tops of her shoes, she hopped back onto the bank, which was carpeted with a springy green pad of sheep-cropped grass. Still she maintained the same unrelenting pace and, before long, a rusted wire fence came into view, then the raised farm track that she knew ran behind it.

She spotted what she'd come for: Where the farm track intersected the stream there stood a crude stone bridge, its sides crumbling and badly in need of repair. Her course beside the stream was taking her straight toward it, and she broke into a trot in her haste to get there. Within minutes she had arrived at her destination.

Ducking under the bridge, she paused to wipe the moisture from her eyes. Then she crossed to the other side, where she held completely still as she studied the horizon. The evening was drawing in and the rose-tinged glow of newly lit streetlamps was just beginning to filter through a screen of oak trees, which hid all but the tip of the church steeple in the distant village.

She returned to a point halfway along the underside of the bridge, stooping as her hair snagged on the rough stone above. She located an irregular block of granite, which was slightly proud of the surface. With both hands, she began to pry it out, levering it left and right, then up and down, until it came free. It was the size and weight of several house bricks, and she grunted with the effort as she bent to place it on the ground by her feet.

Straightening up, she peered into the void, then inserted her arm all the way to her shoulder and groped around inside. Her face pressed against the stonework, she found a chain, which she tried to pull down on. It was stuck fast. Tug as she might, she couldn't move it. She swore and, taking a deep breath, braced herself for another attempt. This time it gave.

For a second, nothing happened as she continued to pull one-handed on the chain. Then she heard a sound like distant thunder emanating from deep within the bridge.

Before her, hitherto invisible joints broke open with a spray of mortar dust and dried lichen, and an uneven, door-sized hole opened before her as a section of the wall lifted back, then up. After a final thud that made the whole bridge quake, all was silent again except for the gurgle of the stream and the patter of rain.

Stepping into the gloomy interior, she took a small key-ring flashlight from her coat pocket and switched it on. The dim circle of light revealed she was in a chamber some fifty feet square, with a ceiling that was sufficiently high to allow her to stand upright. She glanced around, registering the dust motes as they drifted lazily through the air, and the cobwebs, as thick as rotted tapestries, which festooned the tops of the walls.

It had been built by Sarah's great-great-grandfather in the year before he'd taken his family underground for a new life in the Colony. A master stonemason by trade, he'd drawn on all his skills to conceal the chamber within the crumbling and dilapidated bridge, intentionally choosing a site miles from anywhere on the seldom-used farm track. And as to why exactly he'd gone to all this trouble, neither of Sarah's parents had been able to provide any answers. But whatever its original purpose, this was one of the very few places she felt truly safe. Nobody, she believed, would ever find her here. She pulled off her scarf and shook her hair free.

Her feet on the grit-covered floor broke the tomblike silence as she moved to a narrow stone shelf on the wall opposite the entrance. At either end of the shelf were two rusty, vertical iron prongs, with sheaths of thick hide covering their tips.

"Let there be light," she said softly. She reached out and simultaneously tugged off both the sheaths to expose a pair of luminescent orbs, which were held in place on top of each prong by flaking red iron claws.

From these glass spheres no larger than nectarines, an eerie green light burst forth with such intensity that Sarah was forced to shield her eyes. It was as if their energy had been building and building under the leather covers and they now reveled in their newfound freedom. She brushed one of the spheres with her fingertips, feeling its ice-cold surface and shuddering slightly, as if its touch conferred some sort of connection with the hidden city where such orbs were commonplace.

The pain and suffering she had endured under this very light.

She dropped her hand to the top of the shelf, sifting through the thick layer of silt covering it.

Just as she'd hoped, her hand closed on a small polyethylene bag. She smiled, snatching it up and shaking it to remove the grime. The bag was sealed with a knot, which she quickly unpicked with her cold fingers. Removing the neatly folded piece of paper from inside, she lifted it to her nose to sniff at it. It was damp and fusty. The message must have been there for several months.

She kicked herself for not coming sooner. But she rarely allowed herself to check at fewer than six-month intervals, as this "dead mailbox" procedure held its dangers for all concerned. These were the only times that she came into contact, indirect as it was, with anyone from her former life. There was always a risk, however small, that the courier could have been shadowed as he'd broken out of the Colony and emerged on the surface in Highfield. She also couldn't ignore the possibility that he might have been spotted on the journey up from London itself. Nothing could be taken for granted. The enemy was patient, sublimely patient, and calculating, and Sarah knew they would never cease in their efforts to capture and kill her. She had to beat them at their own game.

She glanced at her watch. She always varied her routes to and from the bridge, and she hadn't allowed much time for the cross-country hike to the neighboring village where she would catch the bus for the journey home. She should have been on her way, but her craving for news of her family was just too great. This piece of paper was her only connection with her mother, brother, and two sons — it was like a lifeline.

She had to know what was in it.

She smelled the note again.

It was as if there was a distinctive and unwelcome smell to the paper, rising above the mingled odors of mold and mildew in the dank chamber. It was sharp and unpleasant — it was the reek of bad news.

With a mounting sense of dread, she stared deep into the light of the nearest orb, fidgeting with the piece of paper while she fought the urge to read it. Then, appalled with herself for being so weak, she grimaced and opened it up. Standing before the stone shelf, she examined it under the green-tinged illumination.

She frowned. The first surprise was that the message wasn't in her brother's hand. The childish writing was unfamiliar to her. Tam *always* wrote the notes. Her premonition had been right — she knew at once that something was amiss. She flipped the page over and scanned to the end to check the signature. "Joe Waites," she spoke aloud, feeling more and more uneasy. That wasn't right; Joe occasionally acted as the courier, but the message should have been from Tam.

She bit her lip in trepidation and began to read, darting through the first lines.

"Oh no!" she gasped, shaking her head.

She read the first side of the letter again, unable to accept what was there, telling herself that she must have misunderstood it, that it had to be some sort of mistake. But it was as clear as day; the simplistically formed words left no room for confusion. And she had no reason to doubt what it was saying — these messages were the one thing she relied on, a constant in her shifting and restless life. They gave her a reason to go on.

"No, not Tam . . . *not Tam!*" she howled.

As surely as if she had been struck, she sagged against the stone shelf, leaning heavily on it to support herself.

She took a deep, tremulous breath and forced herself to turn over the letter and read the rest, shaking her head vehemently and mumbling, "No, no, no, no . . . it can't be. . . ."

As if the first page hadn't been bad enough, what was on the reverse was just too much for her to take in. With a whimper, she pushed away from the shelf and into the center of the chamber. Swaying on her feet and hugging herself, she raised her head to look unseeingly at the ceiling.

All of a sudden she had to get out. She tore through the doorway in a frantic haste. Leaving the bridge behind her, she didn't stop. As she stumbled blindly by the side of the stream, the darkness was gathering rapidly and the rain was still falling in a persistent drizzle. Not knowing or caring where she was going, she slid and slipped over the wet grass.

She hadn't gone very far when she blundered straight off the bank and into the stream, landing with a splash. She lowered to her knees, the clear waters closing around her waist. But her grief was so all-consuming, she didn't feel their icy chill. Her head swiveled on her shoulders as if she was gripped by the most intense agony.

She did something she hadn't done since the day she'd escaped Topsoil, the day she'd abandoned her two young children and husband. She began to cry, a few tears at first, and then she was unable to control herself and they gushed down her cheeks in floods, as if a dam had been broken.

She wept and wept until there was nothing left. Her face was set in a mask of stone-cold anger as she rose slowly to her feet, bracing herself against the surging flow of the stream. Her dripping hands tightened into fists and she threw them at the sky as she screamed at the top of her lungs, the raw, primeval sound rolling through the empty valley.

2

"**NO SCHOOL** tomorrow, then!" Will shouted to Chester as the Miners' Train bore them away from the Colony, hurtling deeper into the bowels of the earth.

They erupted into hysterical laughter, but this was short-lived and they soon fell silent, happy just to be reunited. As the steam engine hammered along the rails, they didn't move from the bed of the massive, open-topped train car where Will had discovered Chester hiding under a tarpaulin.

After several minutes, Will drew his legs up in front of him and rubbed his knee, which still hurt from the rather haphazard landing on the train some miles back. Noticing this, Chester shot him a questioning look, to which Will gave his friend the thumbs-up and nodded enthusiastically.

"How did you get here?" Chester shouted, trying to make himself heard over the din of the train.

"Cal and me," Will yelled back, pointing over his shoulder to indicate the front of the train, where he'd left his brother. Then Will waved upward at the tunnel roof flashing over them, ". . . jumped . . . Imago helped us."

"Huh?"

"Imago helped us!" Will repeated.

"Imago? What's that?" Chester shouted even louder, cupping his hand over his ear.

"Doesn't matter," Will mouthed, shaking his head slowly and wishing that they could both lip-read. He gave his friend a grin and shouted, "Just brilliant you're OK!"

He wanted to give Chester the impression there was nothing to be worried about, although his mind was clouded with concern for the future. He wondered if his friend was even aware that they were headed for the Deeps, a place the people of the Colony spoke of with dread.

Will swiveled his head around to peer at the end panel behind him. From what he'd seen so far, the train and each of the freight cars it was pulling were on a scale several times larger than anything he'd ever encountered on the surface. He wasn't looking forward to the journey back to where his brother was waiting. Getting here had been no mean feat: Will knew that even the smallest misjudgment might have meant that he'd have slipped onto the track below and most probably been mashed by the giant wheels that ground and sparked on the thick rails. The thought alone was terrifying. He took a deep breath.

"Ready to go?" he shouted to Chester.

His friend nodded and rose uncertainly to his feet. Clinging to the end of the car, he braced himself against the incessant seesawing as the train wove around several bends in the tunnel.

He was dressed in the short coat and thick pants that were the usual garb in the Colony, but as the coat flapped open, Will was dismayed by what he saw.

Chester had been nicknamed Chester Drawers at school for his imposing physique, but, looking at him now, he seemed to have wasted away. His face was gaunter and his body had lost much of its bulk. Incredible as it seemed to Will right then, his formerly hefty friend now appeared to be almost frail. Will labored under no illusions as to how appalling the conditions in the Hold were. It wasn't long after he and Chester had first stumbled onto the subterranean world that they'd been caught by a Colonist policeman and thrust into one of the dark, airless prison cells. But Will had only been held there for about a fortnight — Chester had suffered a considerably longer ordeal. Months of it.

Will caught himself staring at his friend and quickly averted his eyes. He was racked with guilt, knowing that he was to blame for everything Chester had endured. He, and only he, had been responsible for dragging Chester into all this, driven by his impulsiveness and his single-minded determination to find his missing father.

Chester said something, but Will didn't catch a word of it, studying his friend under the illumination cast by the light orb in his hand as he tried to read his thoughts. Every exposed inch of Chester's face was pasted with a layer of filth from the sulfurous smoke constantly streaming past them. It was so thick that it looked like one big smudge broken only by the whites of his eyes.

From what little Will could see, Chester certainly wasn't a picture of health. In among the dirt mask were raised purple blotches, some with a hint of redness where the skin appeared to be broken. His hair, grown so long it was beginning to curl at the ends, was greasy and stuck to the sides of his head. And from the way Chester was looking back at him, Will assumed that his own appearance was equally shocking.

He self-consciously ran a hand through his white, dirt-streaked hair, which hadn't been cut for many months.

But there were more important things to attend to right now. Moving to the end panel of the car, Will was about to hoist himself up when he stopped and turned to his friend. Chester was extremely unsteady on his feet, although it was difficult to tell how much of this was due to the irregular swaying of the train.

"You up for this?" Will shouted.

Chester nodded halfheartedly.

"Sure?" Will shouted again.

"Yes!" Chester yelled back, nodding a little more vigorously this time.

But the process of crossing from car to car was a fraught undertaking, and after each one Chester needed to recover for longer and longer periods. Making the maneuver that much more difficult, the train seemed to be picking up speed. It was as if the boys were battling a force ten gale, their faces pulled back and their lungs filling with the putrid smoke whenever they drew breath. Added to this was the hazard of burning ash, pieces of which flared just over their heads like supercharged fireflies. Indeed, as the train continued to accelerate, there seemed to be so much of this carried in the slipstream that an orange glow pervaded the murky gloom around them. At least it meant Will didn't need to use his light orb.

As the two boys moved up the line of train cars, their progress was slow. Chester was finding it a challenge to keep on his feet, despite using the sides of the car to steady himself as he went. Before very long there was no hiding the fact that he couldn't cope. He dropped to all fours and it was all he could do to crawl sluggishly behind Will, his head hung low. Not about to stand by and let his friend struggle along like this, Will brushed aside Chester's protestations, forced an arm around his waist, and helped him up.

It took an enormous effort to manhandle Chester over the remaining end sections, and Will had to help him every inch of the way. Any miscalculation would have one or both of them falling under the massive wheels.

When he saw that they only had one more car to go, Will was beyond relieved — he sincerely doubted he had it left in him to lug his friend very much farther. As he held on to Chester, they both reached across to the end panel of the last car, grabbing hold of it.

Will took several deep breaths, preparing himself. Chester was moving his limbs feebly, as if he hardly had any control over them. By now Will was supporting Chester's full weight and barely managing. The maneuver was difficult enough in itself, but attempting it with the equivalent of a giant sack of potatoes slung under one arm risked trying too much. Will mustered all his remaining strength and hauled his friend along with him. With much grunting and straining, they eventually made it over, collapsing in a heap on the bed of the next car.

They were immediately bathed in copious light. Numerous orbs the size of large marbles rolled loosely around the floor. They had spilled out of a flimsy crate that had cushioned Will's landing when he'd first dropped into the train. Will had already tucked a number of these into his pockets.

But at present he had his hands full as he heaved his ailing friend to his feet. With his arm hooked around Chester, Will kicked at any orbs in his path so that he wouldn't lose his footing. These zipped around chaotically, leaving streaks of light in their wake and colliding with other spheres, which themselves were then set into motion, as if a chain reaction had been started.

Will heaved for breath, feeling the effects of the exertion as they covered the short distance they had yet to go. Even if Chester had lost a lot of weight, he was by no means an easy burden. Stumbling and tripping, and enveloped by the intense swirling light, Will looked for all the world like a soldier helping his wounded comrade back to the lines as an enemy flare caught them out in no-man's-land.

Chester seemed to barely register what was around him. The sweat poured from his forehead in rivulets, washing streaks into the grime coating his face. Will could feel his friend's body trembling violently against his as he panted short, shallow breaths.

"Not far now," he said into Chester's ear, urging him to keep going as they came to a section of the car where wooden crates were stacked. "Cal's just up here."

The boy was sitting with his back to them as they approached. He hadn't moved from between the splintered crates where Will had left him. Several years younger than Will, his newfound brother bore an uncanny resemblance to him. Cal was also an albino and had the same white hair and wide cheekbones they'd both inherited from the mother neither of them had ever known. But now Cal's head was hunched over and his features hidden as he tenderly rubbed the nape of his neck. He hadn't been quite as fortunate as Will when he'd fallen into the moving train.

Will helped Chester over to a crate, where his friend slumped down heavily. Approaching his brother, Will tapped him lightly on the shoulder, hoping he wasn't going to give him too much of a shock. They had been told by Imago to keep their wits about them, as there were Colonists on the train. But Will needn't have been concerned about alarming his brother; Cal was so preoccupied by his aches and pains that he barely reacted at all. It was only after some seconds, and a few inaudible grumbles, that he finally turned around, still kneading his neck.

"Cal, I found him! I found Chester!" Will yelled, his words all but drowned out by the noise of the train. Cal's and Chester's eyes met, but neither spoke, being too far apart for any sort of exchange. Although they had been introduced very briefly before, it had been under the worst of circumstances, with the Styx snapping at their heels. There had been no time for any niceties.

They looked away from each other and Chester lowered himself from the crate onto the freight bed, where he cradled his head in his hands. The trek he and Will had just made down the train had sapped all his remaining strength. Cal went back to massaging his neck. He didn't appear to be the least bit surprised that Chester was on the train. Or perhaps he simply didn't care.

Will shrugged. "What a pair of wrecks!" he said in a normal voice, so that neither of them would hear him above the mechanical roar. But as he began to think about the future again, his anxiety returned, as if something were gnawing away at his insides.

From all accounts, they were destined for a place that even the Colonists spoke of with a hushed reverence. Indeed, it was one of the worst punishments imaginable for a Colonist to be "Banished" and expelled there, into the savage wasteland known as the Deeps. And the Colonists were a phenomenally hardy race, who had endured the toughest living conditions for centuries in their subterranean world. So how were *they* going to fare? Will had no doubt that they were going to be put to the test again, all three of them. And there was no escaping the fact that neither his brother nor his friend was up to facing any challenges. Not right now.

Flexing his arm and feeling the stiffness in it, Will put his hand under his jacket to probe the bite on his shoulder. He'd been mauled by a stalker, one of the ferocious attack dogs used by the Styx, and even though the injuries had been tended to, he wasn't in great shape, either. He automatically glanced at the crates of fresh fruit around them. At least they had ample food to keep up their strength. But other than that, they were hardly well prepared.

The responsibility was immense, as if large weights had been placed on his shoulders and there was no way to shake free of them. He'd involved Chester and Cal in this wild-goose chase to search for his father, who even now was somewhere in the unknown lands they were nearing with every twist and turn of these winding tunnels. That was, if Dr. Burrows was still alive. . . . Will shook his head.

No!

He couldn't let himself think like that. He had to go on believing he'd be reunited with his father, and then everything would be all right, just as he dreamed it would. The four of them — Dr. Burrows, Chester, Cal, and him — working as a team, discovering unimaginable and wondrous things . . . lost civilizations . . . maybe new life-forms . . . and then . . . then what?

He hadn't the foggiest idea.

Will couldn't see that far ahead, see how all this would pan out. He just knew that, somehow, there would be a happy outcome, and finding his father was the key.

It had to be.

3

FROM DIFFERENT points around the floor, the sewing machines rattled and the steam presses hissed back their responses, as if they were trying to communicate with each other.

Where Sarah was sitting, the piping tones of a radio station, forever present in the background, were trying vainly to break through the mechanical din. Depressing the pedal with her foot, she whirred her machine into life, and it threw a thread into the fabric. Everyone on the floor was working flat out, as there was a rush on to get the clothes ready for the next day.

Sarah heard someone shouting and looked up — a woman was winding her way between the workbenches toward her companions, who were waiting by the exit. As she joined them, they chatted noisily, like a gaggle of overexcited geese, then pushed their way through the swinging doors.

As the doors flapped shut behind them, Sarah peered up at the dirty panes of the tall factory windows. She could see clouds gathering, making it as dark as early evening although it was only midday. There were still quite a number of other women on the factory floor, each of them isolated under a cone of illumination from their overhead light as they doggedly toiled away.

Sarah punched the button under her bench to turn off her machine and, snatching up her coat and bag, tore toward the doorway. She slipped through the swinging doors, then swept down the corridor. Through the window to his office, she could see the floor manager's plump back as he sat hunched over his desk, engrossed in his newspaper. Sarah should have told him she was leaving, but she had a train to catch and, besides, the fewer people who knew she'd left, the better.

Once outside, she scanned the sidewalks for anyone who didn't fit. It was an automatic gesture; she wasn't even aware she was doing it. Her instincts told her it was safe, and she forged down the hill, branching off the main road to take a far more circuitous route.

After so many years of moving from job to job every few months and varying her accommodation with similar regularity, she lived like a ghost, among the invisible people, the illegal immigrants and petty criminals. But although she was an immigrant of sorts, too, she was no criminal. Other than the several false identities she'd acquired over the years, she would have never dreamed of breaking the law, not even if she was desperate for money. No, that brought with it the risk of arrest and of being caught up in the system. Of leaving a trace that could be detected. And that was not an option, because the first thirty years of Sarah's life were not what would have been expected.

She'd been born underground, in the Colony. Her great-great-grandfather, along with several hundred other men, had been handpicked to work on the hidden city, swearing allegiance to Sir Gabriel Martineau, a man they believed was their savior.

Sir Gabriel had told his willing followers that, on an unspecified day in the future, the corrupt world would be wiped clean by an angry and vengeful god. All the people who inhabited the surface, the Topsoilers, would be exterminated, and then his flock, the pure people, would return to their rightful home.

And Sarah feared what her ancestors feared — the Styx. These religious police enforced order in the Colony with a brutal, single-minded efficiency. Years ago, against all odds, Sarah had escaped from the Colony, and the Styx would stop at nothing to capture and make an example of her.

She entered a square and walked a full circuit of it, checking that she hadn't been followed. Before she made her way back to the main road, she ducked behind a parked van.

It was a very different-looking person who stepped out from behind the van moments later. She had reversed her coat to change it from the green check to a dull gray fabric and had knotted a black scarf around her head. She covered the remaining distance to the train station, her clothes almost rendering her invisible against the grimy façades of the shops and office buildings she was passing, as if she were a human chameleon.

She looked up as she caught the first sounds of an approaching train. She smiled — her timing was perfect.

4

AS CHESTER and Cal slept, Will took stock of their situation.

Glancing around the train car, he realized that their first priority was concealment. He thought it highly unlikely that any of the Colonists would conduct any sort of search while the train was moving. However, if it did happen to stop, then he, Chester, and Cal had to be prepared. But what could he do? There wasn't much to work with; he decided that rearranging the undamaged crates would be their best bet. He set about dragging them around the slumbering forms of Cal and Chester, stacking them one upon the other, to build a makeshift blind with enough room for the three of them in the middle.

As he was doing this, Will observed that the car in front had higher sides to it than theirs — indeed, than any of the other cars he'd clambered over on his earlier expedition when he'd found Chester. Imago, whether by luck or design, had dropped them into a relatively sheltered spot where they had a degree of protection from the smoke and soot flung out by the engine up ahead.

Will hefted the last crate into place and stood back to admire his handiwork, his mind already moving on to their next priority: water. They could get by on the fruit, but they would really need something to drink before long, and it would also be good to have the provisions he and Cal had bought Topsoil. That meant someone was going to have to venture forward to retrieve their rucksacks from the cars up ahead where Imago had dropped them. And Will knew that someone would be him.

Balancing himself with his arms outstretched, as if he were on the deck of a ship in choppy water, he stared at the wall of iron he was going to have to climb. He raised his eyes to the very top of it, which was clearly silhouetted by the orange glow from the little pieces of burning ash racing overhead. He estimated it was about fifteen feet high — almost twice the height of the end sections he'd clambered over before.

"Come on, you wimp, just do it," he said, and then ran at full speed, hopping up onto the panel of the car he was in and catching hold of the higher wall of the next.

For a moment he thought he'd misjudged it and was going to slip off. With his hands gripping the car in front for all they were worth, he shuffled his feet until they were better positioned.

He allowed himself a split second of self-congratulation; it wasn't the safest of places to hang around for long. Both cars were rocking violently and jostling him about, threatening to dislodge him from his precarious position. And he didn't dare look down at the rails zipping beneath him, in case he lost his nerve altogether.

"Here goes nothing!" he shouted and, drawing on all the strength in his legs and arms, he hoisted himself over the edge.

He slid down the inside of the car and landed in a crumpled heap. He'd done it.

Taking out a light orb for a proper look around, he was disappointed to find that the car appeared to be empty except for small heaps of coal. He continued farther along, and offered up silent thanks when he spied the two backpacks lying at the opposite end. He picked up the rucksacks and carried them back. Then, with as much precision as he could muster, he hurled each of them over into the car behind.

As he returned to Chester and Cal, he found they were still soundly asleep. They hadn't even noticed the two backpacks that had miraculously appeared just outside their enclave. Knowing how weak Chester had become, Will wasted no time in organizing a sandwich for him.

When, after much shaking, Will managed to rouse Chester sufficiently to take in what was being offered to him, he fell upon the sandwich. He grinned at Will between mouthfuls, wolfing it down with some water from one of the canteens, then promptly went back to sleep.

And in the ensuing hours, that was how they occupied themselves — sleeping and eating. They put together bizarre sandwiches of chunky white bread with dried strips of rat jerky and coleslaw as filler. They even helped themselves to the rather unappetizing slabs of mushroom (the Colonists' staple diet — giant fungi known as "pennybuns"), which they stacked atop heavily buttered waffles. And to finish off each meal, they ate so much fruit that they'd very soon plundered everything from the shattered crates and were forced to pry open some new ones.

All the time the train roared along, sinking them deeper into the earth's mantle. Will realized that trying to communicate with the others was futile and instead lay back and studied the tunnel. It was a constant source of fascination for him as the train penetrated through the strata. He peered at the various layers of metamorphic rock they were passing through, studiously documenting his observations in his notebook in wobbly handwriting. This would be a geography report to end all geography reports. It certainly dwarfed his own excavations back in his Topsoil hometown of Highfield, where he'd barely scratched the surface of the earth's crust.

He also noted that the gradient of the tunnel itself varied considerably — there were stretches several miles long that were clearly man-made, where the train would descend more gently. Then, every so often, the track would level out and they would pass through naturally formed caverns, where they could see towering palisades of flowstone. The sheer scale of these structures took Will's breath away — he couldn't get over how much they resembled melted cathedrals. Sometimes these were surrounded by moats of dark water, which lapped over the railway track itself. Then there came the roller-coaster sections of tunnel that were so sheer that the boys, if sleeping, were rolled violently against each other and shaken awake.

Suddenly, as if the train had dropped off a ledge, there was a jarring crash. The boys all sat up and were looking around with startled faces when showers of water gushed from above. It was warm, flooding the car and drenching them as effectively as if they had been thrust under a waterfall. They waved their arms and laughed at each other through the torrents until, as abruptly as it had begun, the deluge ended, and they fell silent.

A light steam rose from the freight bed, then was immediately whisked away in the slipstream. Will had noticed how it was growing appreciably warmer as the train rocketed on its way. This was barely perceptible at first, but more recently the temperature had soared alarmingly.

After a while all three of them loosened their shirts and took off their boots and socks. The air was so fierce and dry that they took turns clambering onto the tops of the undamaged fruit crates in an effort to catch a little more of the breeze. Will wondered if this was how it was going to be from now on. Would the Deeps be unbearably hot, like blasts from an open furnace door? It was as though they were on the main line to hell itself.

His thoughts were soon interrupted as the brakes squealed with such intensity that the boys were forced to cover their ears. The train slowed, then jerked to a complete halt. Several minutes later, from somewhere up ahead, they heard a clanking, and then the resounding crash of metal upon rock. Will quickly pulled on his boots and went to the front of the car. He hoisted himself up to peek over the top and see what was going on.

It was useless — farther down the tunnel there was a dull red glow, but everything else was masked by lazy shrouds of smoke. Chester and Cal joined Will, craning their necks to see over the tops of the cars. With the engine ticking over, the noise level had now fallen off to almost nothing, and every sound they made, every cough or shuffle of a boot, seemed so remote and tiny. Although it was an opportunity for them to talk, they just glanced at each other, none of them really knowing what to say. In the end, Chester was the first to speak up.

"See anything?" he asked.

"You look better!" Will said to him. His friend was moving with more confidence and had hoisted himself up next to Will without any difficulty at all.

"I was just hungry," Chester muttered dismissively, pressing the palm of his hand against an ear as if he was trying to relieve the pressure in it from the unfamiliar quietness.

There was a shout, a man's deep voice booming from somewhere ahead, and they all froze. It was a salient reminder that they weren't alone on the train. There was, of course, a conductor — possibly accompanied by an assistant driver, as Imago had warned them — and a further Colonist in the guard's car at the rear. These men knew Chester was on board and it would be their job to send him on his way when they arrived at the Miners' Station, but Cal and Will were stowaways and most probably had prices on their heads. They couldn't be discovered, not at any cost.

The boys exchanged nervous glances, and then Cal pulled himself higher up on the end of the car.

"Can't see a thing," he said.

"I'll try over here," Will suggested, and, passing hand over hand, he moved himself to the corner of the car to try to get a better vantage point. Here he squinted down the side of the train, but he couldn't make out anything more through the smoke and darkness. He returned to where the two other boys were perched. "Do you think they're doing a search?" he asked Cal, who merely shrugged and looked anxiously behind them.

Without the slipstream to cool them, the heat was almost unbearable. "Man, it's sweltering," Chester whispered, blowing through his lips.

"That's the least of our problems," Will murmured back.

Then the engine juddered to life again, lurching forward in a series of fits and starts until it was once more under way. The boys remained where they were, hanging doggedly on to the side of the high car, and were soon resubmerged in the thrashing tumult of noise and the soot-heavy smoke.

Deciding they'd had enough, they jumped down and returned to their blind, although they continued to keep watch from over the tops of the crates. It was Will who spotted the reason why the train had stopped.

"There!" he shouted, pointing as the train chugged along. Two huge iron doors were opened back against the tunnel walls. They all stood up to see.

"Storm gates!" Cal yelled at him. "They'll be shut again after us. You'll see."

Before he'd finished speaking, the brakes squealed and the train began to decelerate. It came to another juddering halt. There was a pause, then they heard the cranking noise again, this time from behind them. It culminated in a percussive thud that made their teeth rattle together and the whole tunnel quake as if there had been a small explosion.

"Told you, didn't I?" Cal declared smugly in the lull. "They're storm gates."

"But what are they for?" Chester asked him.

"To stop the full force of the Levant Wind from reaching the Colony."

Chester looked at him blankly.

"You know, the windstorms blowing up from the Interior," Cal answered, adding, "kind of obvious, isn't it?" He rolled his eyes as if he thought Chester's question was absurd.

"He probably hasn't seen one yet," Will intervened quickly. "Chester, it's like a thick dust that blows up from where we're going, from the Deeps."

"Oh, right," his friend replied, and turned away.

Will couldn't help but notice the look of irritation that flicked across his face.

As the train began to move at speed again, the boys resumed their positions among the crates. Over the next twelve hours, they went through many more sets of these storm gates. Each time, they kept on the lookout in case one of the Colonists got it into his mind to come back and check on Chester. But no one came, and after each interruption the boys settled back into their routines of eating and sleeping. Aware that sometime soon they would reach the end of the line, Will began to get ready. On top of all the loose light orbs he'd already squirreled away in the two rucksacks, he packed in as much fruit as he could. He had no idea where or when they'd find food once they were in the Deeps, and was determined they'd take all they could with them.

He'd been in a deep sleep when he was rudely awoken by the sound of a clanging bell. In a state of groggy confusion, his first thought was that it was his alarm clock waking him to get ready for school. He automatically groped over to where his bedside table should have been, but instead of the alarm clock, his fingertips encountered the grit-covered floor of the freight bed. The mechanical urgency of the bell hammered him fully awake, and he jumped to his feet, rubbing the sleep from his eyes. The first thing he saw was Cal frantically putting on his socks and boots as Chester watched him bemusedly. The harsh ringing kept going, echoing off the walls and down the tunnel behind them.

"C'mon, you two!" Cal bawled at the top of his lungs.

"Why?" Chester mouthed to Will, who could see the haunted look on his friend's face.

"This is it! Get ready!" Cal said, securing the flap on his backpack.

Chester looked at him questioningly.

"We've got to bail out!" the younger boy yelled at him, gesturing at the front of the train. "*Before* the station."

ON A TRAIN very different from the one carrying her two sons, Sarah was on her way to London. She didn't allow herself to sleep, but for much of the time feigned it, half closing her eyes in order to avoid any contact with the other passengers. The car became increasingly crowded as the train made frequent stops on the final stretch. She felt distinctly uneasy. A man with a mangy beard had boarded at the last of these stops, a wretch in a tartan overcoat, clutching a motley collection of plastic bags.

She had to be careful. *They* sometimes passed themselves off as tramps and down-and-outs. All the hollow-cheeked countenance of the average Styx required was several months' growth of facial hair and a generous pasting of filth and it became indistinguishable from those poor unfortunates that can be found in the corners of any city.

It was a clever ruse, allowing them to man surveillance posts around the busier train stations for days on end, monitoring the passengers passing through. Sarah had lost count of how many times she'd seen vagrants loitering in doorways, and how, from under matted hair, their glassy eyes would probe her with all-seeing black pupils.

But was this tramp one of them? She watched his reflection in the windows as he produced a can of beer from a grubby shopping bag. He popped it open and began to drink, slopping a good measure of it down his beard. She caught him looking directly at her, and she didn't like his eyes — they were jet-black, and he squinted as if he wasn't quite used to daylight. All ominous signs. But she didn't move to another seat on the train. The last thing she wanted was to draw attention to herself.

So she gritted her teeth and sat still until the train finally drew into St. Pancras station. She was among the first passengers to disembark and, once through the turnstile, she strolled unhurriedly over to where the kiosks were located. She kept her head bowed to avoid the security cameras dotted around the place, holding a handkerchief to her face when she thought she might be in range of any of them. She stopped and hovered by a shop window, observing the tramp as he crossed the main concourse.

If he *was* a Styx, or even one of their agents, far better she remain in a crowd. She weighed her options for escape. She was debating whether she should jump on an outgoing train when, just a few feet away from her, he stopped to fumble with his bags. Then, swearing incoherently at a man who happened to brush against him, he started toward the main doors of the station in a stumbling gait, his arms outstretched as if he were pushing an invisible shopping cart with a bum wheel. He left through the main entrance of the station.

By now Sarah was almost certain he was a genuine tramp, and she was eager to be on her way. She picked a direction at random, headed off through the crowd, and then slipped out of the station by a side exit.

Outside, the weather was fine and the London streets were full. Just the way she liked it. It was better to have a healthy throng of people milling around her — safety in numbers. The Styx were less likely to pull anything in front of multiple witnesses.

She set off at a fair pace, heading north toward Highfield. The rumble of the busy traffic seemed to coalesce into a single continuous beat, which was conducted through the pavement to the soles of her feet, until she could almost feel it resonating in the pit of her stomach. Strangely enough, it put her at ease. It was a comforting and constant vibration, as if the city itself were alive.

She looked at the new buildings as she went, turning her head away whenever she spotted one of the many security cameras mounted on them. She was astounded by how much had changed even since her first time in London. *What was it, almost twelve years ago?*

It is said that time heals. But that depends on what has happened since.

For so long, Sarah's life had been a featureless and forlorn plain: She felt she hadn't been really alive. Her flight from the Colony was still painfully vivid in her mind.

Walking the Topsoil city streets now, she found that she couldn't stem the rush of memories as they flooded back. She began to relive the crushing self-doubt that she'd escaped from one nightmare only to be cast into another, into this alien land where the glare of the sunlight was agonizing and everything was so unfamiliar. Worst of all, she'd been torn apart by the guilt at leaving her children, her two sons, behind.

But I had no choice, I had to go. . . .

Her baby, barely a week old, had developed a fever, a horrible, consuming fever that racked the tiny thing with violent shivering fits as it succumbed to the illness. Even now, Sarah could hear its interminable crying and remember how she and her husband had felt so helpless. They'd pleaded with the doctor for some medicine, but he said he didn't have anything he could give them from his black valise. She'd become hysterical, but the doctor merely shook his head dourly, avoiding her eyes. She knew what that shake of his head meant. She knew the truth. In the Colony, medicines such as antibiotics were in permanent short supply. The little that had been stockpiled was for the sole use of the ruling classes, the Styx and maybe a very select band of elite within the Board of Governors.

There had been another alternative: She'd suggested buying some penicillin on the black market and wanted to ask her brother, Tam, to get hold of some for her. But Sarah's husband was adamant. "I cannot condone such actions" were his words as he stared bleakly at the hapless infant that was growing weaker with every hour. Then he had blathered on about his position in the community and how it was their duty to uphold its values. None of this mattered one jot to Sarah; she just wanted her baby to be well again.

There was nothing else to do but continually swab the shining red face of the howling infant in an attempt to lower its temperature, and pray. Over the next twenty-four hours, the baby's crying quieted to pathetic little gasps, as if it was all it could do to breathe. It was useless trying to feed it; it made no effort to draw milk. The baby was slipping away from her and there was nothing, absolutely nothing, she could do.

She thought she might go mad.

She went into fits of barely suppressed fury and, backing away from the crib into a corner of the room, she would try to hurt herself by frenziedly scratching at her forearms, biting her tongue lest she cry out and disturb the semiconscious child. At other times, she slumped to the floor, overcome by such a deep despair that she prayed she might also die with her child.

In the final hour, its pale little eyes became glazed and list-less. Then, sitting by the crib in the darkened room, Sarah had been roused from her desolation by a sound. It was like a tiny whisper, as if someone were trying to remind her of something. She leaned over the cot. She knew instinctively that she'd heard the final breath leak from the baby's dry lips. It was still. It was over. She'd lifted the child's tiny arm and let it fall back against the mattress. It was like touching some exquisitely made doll.

But she didn't cry then. Her eyes were dry and resolute. At that very instant, any loyalty she had felt for the Colony, her husband, and the society in which she'd lived her whole life evaporated. And in that instant, she saw everything so clearly, as if a spotlight had been switched on in her head. She knew what she must do, with such conviction that nothing was going to get in her way. She must spare her other two children from the same fate, whatever the cost.

That same evening, as the body of the dead baby, the child that had no name, lay cooling in its cot, she had thrown a few things into a shoulder bag and grabbed her two sons. While her husband was out making arrangements for the funeral, she left the house with both her boys, heading toward one of the escape routes her brother had once described to her.

As if the Styx knew her every move, it had very quickly gone wrong and become a game of cat and mouse. While she'd struggled through the warren of ventilation tunnels, they were never far behind. She recalled how she'd stopped for a moment to catch her breath. Leaning against the wall, she cowered in the darkness with a child held under each arm. In her heart of hearts, she knew she had no choice but to leave one of them behind. She wasn't going to make it, not with both of them. She recalled her tortured indecision at the time.

But shortly afterward, a Colonist, one of her own people, had stumbled across her. In the frantic tussle that ensued, she had fought the man off, stunning him with a wild blow. Her arm had been badly hurt in the struggle, and there was no question about it anymore.

She knew what she had to do.

She left Cal behind. He was barely a year old. She'd gently laid the twitching bundle between two rocks on the grit floor of the tunnel. Etched indelibly into her memory was the image of the child's cocoonlike swaddling, smeared with her own blood. And the noise he was making, the gurgling. She knew it wouldn't be long before he was discovered and returned to her husband, and that he would care for him. A scant consolation. She had resumed her flight with the other son and, more by luck than skill, had somehow eluded the Styx and broken out onto the surface.

In the small hours of the morning, they had walked down Highfield's Main Street, her son on the pavement beside her, a toddler still unsteady on his legs. He was her eldest child and he was called Seth. He was nearly three years old. He had turned this way and that as he gaped at the strange surroundings with wide, frightened eyes.

She had no money, nowhere to go, and before long the realization hit her that it was going to be a struggle to look after even the one child.

Hearing people in the distance, she led Seth away from the main thoroughfare and down several side streets until she spied a church. Seeking refuge in its overgrown graveyard, mother and son sat on a mossy grave, smelling the night air for the very first time in their lives and looking with awe at the sodium-soaked sky above. Sarah just wanted to shut her eyes for a few minutes, but she feared if she rested for too long, she might not ever get up again. With her head spinning, she summoned all her remaining strength and got to her feet with the aim of finding some food, some water, somewhere they could hide.

She had tried to explain to her son what she intended to do, how soon she'd be back, but he just wanted to come with her. Poor little confused Seth. The expression on his face, the pure, heartrending incomprehension, was all she could bear as she hastily walked away from him. He clung to the railings around the most commanding tomb in the graveyard, which, strangely enough, had two small stone figures at its apex wielding a pickax and a shovel. Seth called out to her as she went, but she couldn't turn to look back, her every instinct raking at her, telling her not to go.

She left the churchyard, heading she knew not where, all the while fighting the dizziness that, with each step, made her feel as though she was walking on rolling pins.

Sarah didn't remember much after that.

She'd regained consciousness as something prodded her awake. When she opened her eyes, the light was unbearable. It was so blindingly bright, she could barely make out the face of the concerned woman who stood over her, asking her what was wrong. Sarah found she'd passed out between two parked cars. Shielding her eyes with her hands, she pulled herself to her feet and ran.

She'd eventually found her way back to Seth, but stopped as she saw figures milling around him, dressed in black. Her first thought had been that they were Styx, but then, through her watering eyes, she had been able to read the word POLICE on the car. She'd slunk away.

Since that day, she had tried to tell herself a million times that it had been for the best, that she'd been in no condition to care for a young child, let alone go on the run from the Styx with one in tow. But that did nothing to dispel the image of the small boy's tear-filled eyes as he reached out a tiny hand and called for her over and over again as she'd slipped into the night.

The tiny hand wavering in the light of the streetlamps, reaching for her. . . .

Something hurt recoiled in her head, like a badly injured animal rolling itself into a ball.

Her thoughts were so vivid that, as a passerby on the pavement threw a glance at her, she wondered if she'd been talking out loud.

"Pull yourself together," she urged herself. She had to stay focused. She shook her head to dispel the image of the little face from her mind. Anyway, it was so long ago now and, like the buildings around her, everything had changed, changed irreparably. If the message for her in the dead mailbox was true — something she couldn't yet bring herself to believe — then Seth had become *Will*.

He had become someone else altogether.

After several miles, Sarah came to a busy street, with shops and a brick-built monolith of a supermarket. She grumbled beneath her breath as she was forced to stop at a crosswalk in the midst of a small crowd, waiting for the lights to change. She was uncomfortable, and huddled tightly inside her coat. Then, with a beeping, the green man lit up and she crossed the road, forging ahead of the people burdened by their shopping bags.

It began to rain, and people scurried for cover or back to their cars, leaving the streets less busy. Sarah carried on, unnoticed. She heard Tam's voice, as clearly as if he was walking beside her.

"See, but don't be seen."

It was something he had taught her. As young children, in brazen disregard of their parents' instructions, they had often sneaked out of the house. Disguising themselves by donning rags and wiping burnt cork on their faces, they had taken their lives in their hands and gone deep into one of the roughest, most dangerous places you could find in the whole of the Colony — the Rookeries. Even now she could picture Tam as he was then, his grinning, youthful visage streaked with black and his eyes shining with excitement as the two of them hared away after yet another close scrape. She missed him so much.

She was pulled once more from her thoughts. A loud exchange in a language she couldn't understand had caught her attention. Several shops down, two workmen were leaving a café, its steamy windows illuminated by the striplights inside. She made a beeline for it.

She ordered a cup of coffee, paid for it at the counter, then took it over to a table by the window. Sipping the thin, tasteless liquid, she slipped the creased note from her pocket and slowly reread the artless handwriting. She still couldn't bring herself to accept what it said. *How could Tam be dead? How could that be?* As bad as things were in this Topsoil world, she'd always been able to draw small comfort from the knowledge that her brother was still alive and well in the Colony. It was like a flickering candle at the end of an incredibly long tunnel, the hope that one day she might see him again. And now even that had been taken away from her; now he was dead.

She flipped over the note and read the other side, then read the entire letter again, shaking her head.

The note must be wrong; Joe Waites must have been mistaken when he wrote it. How could her own son, Seth, her firstborn, who was once her pride and joy, have betrayed Tam to the Styx? Her own flesh and blood had effectively murdered her brother. *And if it really was true, how could Seth have been corrupted like that? What could have driven him to do it?* There was equally shocking news in the final paragraph. She read the lines over and over again, about how Seth had abducted her youngest son, forcing Cal to go with him.

"No," she said out loud, shaking her head, refusing to accept that Seth was responsible. And there it was again: Her son was *Seth*, and not *Will*, and he couldn't be capable of any of this. Perhaps someone had tampered with the note. Perhaps someone knew about the dead mailbox. But how, and why? None of it made any sense.

She realized her hands were trembling. She rested them hard against the table, crumpling the letter in her palms. Then she cleared a small circle in the condensation on the inside of the café window and peered through. It was still too early, too light, so she decided to bide her time a while longer, drawing with the corner of a paper napkin in some coffee slopped on the scratched red melamine of the tabletop. As the coffee evaporated, she simply stared down at her front, as if she'd fallen into a trance. When, several moments later, she came to with a small start, she noticed a button on her coat hanging by a thread. She tugged at it and it came away in her hand. Without thinking, she dropped it into her empty cup and then just gazed blankly at the steamed-up windows, at the vague shapes of people hurrying by.

Finally the owner ambled over, giving the empty tables a casual swipe with his grimy dishcloth and straightening the chairs on the way. He stopped by the window and joined Sarah in looking out, then, in an offhand tone, asked if he could get her anything else. Without acknowledging him, she simply got up and made straight for the door. Angered, he snatched up her empty coffee cup and spotted the discarded button sitting in the bottom of it.

That did it. She wasn't a regular, and she'd hogged his table, spending next to nothing.

"Ch . . . !" he started to yell, but only managed the first letters of "Cheapskate" before the word shriveled on his lips.

He'd happened to glance down at the tabletop. He blinked and shifted his head, as if the light were playing tricks on his eyes. There, staring back at him from the red melamine, was a surprisingly accomplished image.

It was a face, some five inches square and built up from layer upon layer of dried-out coffee, as if it had been painted with tempera. But it wasn't the artistry that stopped him cold, it was the fact that the face had its mouth wrenched open in a jaw-breaking rictus of a scream. He blinked again; it was so unnerving that for several seconds he didn't move, simply stared at the image. He found it impossible to associate the quiet, mousy woman who had just left his café with this shocking portrayal of anguish. Quickly he covered it with his dishcloth as he set about wiping it away.

Back out on the street, Sarah tried not to walk too quickly. Before she entered Highfield, she broke her journey to book a room in a bed-and-breakfast. There were several on the same street, but she chose one, a shabby Victorian terraced house, at random. That is how she had to be if she wanted to survive.

Never the same twice.

Never twice the same.

If she fell into any sort of routine or pattern, the Styx would be on her in a flash.

Giving a false name and address, she paid cash in advance for a single night. She took her key from the manager, a wrinkled old man, and on the way to her room checked the location of the fire escape. *Just in case.* Once in her room, she locked the door, wedging a chair under the handle. Then she pulled the sun-faded curtains closed and perched on the end of the bed while she attempted to gather her thoughts.

She opened the *Highfield Bugle,* a newspaper she'd taken from the reception desk. As she always did, she took out a pen and went straight to the classifieds, circling the advertisements for short-term employment that might suit her. Then she flicked her way back through the rest of the paper, perusing the articles without much interest. But one item caught her eye:

THE BEAST OF HIGHFIELD?

By T. K. Martin, Staff Reporter

Another sighting of the mysterious doglike animal took place on Highfield Common over the weekend. Mrs. Croft-Hardinge of the Clockdown Houses was out walking her basset hound, Goldy, on Saturday evening when she spotted the beast in the lower branches of a tree.

"It was chewing the head off something I thought was a children's plush toy until I realized it was a rabbit and saw the blood everywhere," she told the *Bugle*. "It was huge with horrible eyes and nasty-looking teeth. When it noticed me, it just spat out the head, and I could have sworn it was looking straight at me."

Reports of the animal are confused, some describing it as a jaguar or puma, similar to the sightings of a large cat at Bodmin Moor, which began in the eighties, while others say it is more doglike in appearance. The Inspector of Parks for Highfield, Mr. Kenneth Wood, recently supervised a search after a local man claimed that the beast made off with his miniature poodle, tearing the leash from his hands. Other residents from the Highfield area have reported that their dogs have gone missing in recent months.

The mystery continues. . . .

With aggressive jabs, Sarah began to doodle in the margin by the article. Although she was only using an old ballpoint, before long she had drawn an intricately detailed picture of a moonlit cemetery, not that different from the one in Highfield where she had taken refuge when she'd first escaped to the surface. But there the similarities ended, as she sketched a large, blank headstone in the foreground. She stared at it for a while before, using his Topsoiler name, she eventually wrote:

Will Burrows?

Sarah frowned. The anger welling up inside her from her brother's death was so powerful, she felt as if she were being swept along on a wave. And when she arrived wherever it was taking her, she needed someone to blame. Of course, at the root of it there were the Styx, but now she allowed herself to think the unthinkable: If it really was true about Seth, then he was going to pay, and pay dearly.

Still staring at the sketch, she tensed her hand and the pen snapped, sending slivers of clear plastic shooting over the hotel bed.

WITH GRIM FACES, the boys clung to the side of the railroad car, the tunnel wall flashing past them in a terrifying blur even though the train was decelerating as it negotiated a sharp bend.

They had already thrown the backpacks out, and Chester had been the last to hoist himself over the side and join the other two. He let his feet scrabble down until they found a ledge, then held on for all he was worth. Will was just about to shout to the other two boys when his brother beat him to the punch.

"JUMP!" Cal yelled, and let loose a howl as he thrust himself off. Will watched as he vanished into the darkness.

Will had no option but to follow his brother. He gritted his teeth and then pushed himself off, twisting around as he did so. For a split second he seemed to hang in the wind. Then he landed on his feet with a bone-jarring jolt and pitched forward into a helter-skelter sprint, running at a crazy speed with his arms outspread as he tried to keep his balance.

Everything was a confusion of acrid smoke as the enormous wheels ground just feet away from him. But he was going impossibly fast and had hardly covered any distance when his own feet tripped him up. He went flying, falling first onto one knee, and the next instant flipping onto his chest. He skid along, his body plowing up dust in its wake. Coming to a halt, he slowly rolled over onto his back and then sat up, coughing out a mouthful of dirt. The huge train wheels continued to trundle past, and he thanked his lucky stars that he hadn't fallen under them. He pulled a light orb from his pocket and began to look for any sign of the others.

After a while he heard a loud groaning coming from farther up the track. As he watched, Chester emerged from the smoke-ridden darkness, crawling on all fours. He raised his head like an ill-tempered tortoise and, spying Will, sped up.

"All right?" Will shouted at him.

"Oh, just brilliant!" Chester shouted as he plunked himself next to Will.

Will shrugged, rubbing the leg that had taken all the impact of his fall.

"Cal?" Chester asked.

"Dunno. Better wait for him here." Will couldn't tell if Chester had heard him, but his friend didn't seem inclined to go and look for the boy, anyway.

Some minutes later, as the train continued its relentless passage past them, Will's brother emerged through the smoky gloom with a rucksack on each shoulder, strolling jauntily, as if he didn't have a care in the world. He squatted next to Will.

"I got the bags. You all in one piece?" he yelled. There was a large scrape on his forehead, and little droplets of blood were collecting and running down the bridge of his nose.

Will nodded and looked past Cal. "Get down! The guard's car!" he warned, pulling his brother close to him.

Tucked into the tunnel wall, they watched the light looming toward them. It was streaming from the windows of the guard's train car, forming broad rectangles on the walls as it went. It shot past them, blasting them with a split second of illumination. As the train sped into the tunnel ahead and the light receded, growing smaller and smaller until there was nothing of it still visible, Will had an overpowering sense of finality.

In the unaccustomed silence, he got up and stretched his legs. He'd grown so used to the rocking of the train that it was a novelty to be back on terra firma again.

Will sniffed and was just about to say something to the other two boys when the train whistle blew in the distance.

"What does that mean?" he said eventually.

"It's coming up to the station," Cal answered, his eyes still on the darkness where they had last seen the train.

"How do you know that?" Chester asked him.

"My . . . our uncle told me."

"Your uncle? Can he help us? Where is he?" Chester fired the questions at Cal in rapid succession, his face filled with anticipation at the thought that there might be someone who could come to their rescue.

"No," Cal snapped, frowning at Chester.

"Why not? I don't understand —"

"No, Chester," Will interjected, shaking his head urgently. His friend could tell he needed to keep his mouth buttoned.

Will turned to his brother. "So what happens now? They'll find out Chester's gone when they unload the train. What then?"

"Then nothing." Cal shrugged. "Job done. They'll just think he's bailed out. They know he won't survive for long on his own. . . . After all, he's only a Topsoiler." He laughed humorlessly and kept on talking, as if Chester weren't there. "They won't send a search party or anything."

"How can you be so sure about that?" Will quizzed his brother. "Wouldn't they assume he'd head straight back to the Colony again?"

"Nice idea, and even if he did happen to make it all the way — on foot — the Blackheads would just pick him off as soon as he showed up," Cal said.

"Blackheads?" Chester asked.

"Styx — that's one of the names the Colonists call them behind their backs," Will explained.

"Oh, right," Chester said. "Well, anyway, I'm never going back to that foul place again. Not on your life!" he added firmly to Cal.

Cal didn't respond, instead putting on his backpack as Will picked up the other one by its straps, testing its weight. It was heavy, stuffed to the brim with their equipment and the extra food and light orbs. He lifted it onto his back, wincing as the strap dug into his injured shoulder. The poultice Imago had applied to the wound had done wonders, but any pressure was still incredibly painful. Will tried to adjust the rucksack so that most of the weight was on his good shoulder, and they set off.

Before long, Cal sped onward at a fast trot, leaving Will and Chester to watch his bobbing silhouette advance into the murky gloom. The two of them strolled between the enormous metal girders of the train tracks. There was so much they wanted to say to each other, but now that they were alone, it was as if neither knew where to begin. Finally Will cleared his throat.

"We've got some catching up to do," he said awkwardly. "Stuff happened — crazy stuff — while you were in the Hold."

Will began to speak about his family, his *biological* family, whom he had met for the first time in the Colony, and what life had been like with them. Then he recounted how he and Uncle Tam had planned Chester's escape. "It was awful when it went wrong. I just couldn't believe it when I saw Rebecca was with the St —"

"That little brat!" Chester exploded. "Didn't you ever think there was something seriously wrong with her? All those years you were growing up together?"

"Well, I thought she was a bit strange, but then I thought all sisters were like that," Will said.

"A bit strange?" Chester repeated. "She's a certifiable nut-case. You must have known she wasn't your *real* sister."

"No, how could I? I . . . I didn't even know *I* was adopted or where *I'd* come from."

"Don't you remember when your parents first brought her home?" Chester said, sounding a little amazed.

"No," Will replied thoughtfully. "I would have been about four, I suppose. Do *you* remember much from when you were that old?"

Chester made a noise as if he wasn't wholly convinced, but Will went on with the chain of events. Trudging along beside him, Chester listened intently. Will finally came to the discussion with Imago, when he and Cal had had to decide whether they were going to return Topsoil or travel down into the Deeps.

Chester nodded.

"And that's how we came to be on the Miners' Train with you," Will finished, reaching the end of the story.

"Well, I'm glad you did." His friend smiled.

"I couldn't leave you behind," Will said. "I had to make sure you were OK. That's the least I —"

Will's voice broke. He was attempting to articulate his emotions, his remorse, for everything Chester had been put through.

"They beat me, you know," Chester said abruptly.

"Huh?"

"After they caught me again," he said, so quietly that Will could hardly hear him. "They threw me back in the Hold and whacked me with clubs . . . tons of times," he continued. "Rebecca would come to watch."

"Oh no," Will mumbled.

They were both silent for a few paces as they picked their way over the massive railroad ties.

"Did they hurt you badly?" Will eventually asked, dreading the answer.

Chester didn't reply right away. "They were really angry with us . . . with you mostly. They were shouting about you a lot as they hit me, saying you'd made them look like fools." Chester cleared his throat weakly and swallowed. His speech became confused. "It was . . . I . . . they . . ." He took in a sharp breath. "The beatings never went that far, and all I could think was that there was something much worse in store for me." He paused as he wiped his nose. "Then this old Styx sentenced me to Banishment, which was even more frightening. I was so scared, I completely fell apart." Chester's gaze dropped to the ground, as if he'd done something to be ashamed of.

He continued, a tone of the coldest controlled fury creeping into his voice. "You know, Will, if I could have, I would have *killed* them . . . the Styx. I wanted to, so much. They're evil . . . all of them. *I would have killed them, even Rebecca.*" He stared at Will with such intensity that Will shivered — he was seeing a side of Chester he hadn't known existed.

"Oh, I'm so sorry, Chester."

But something equally important occurred to Chester, deflecting his thoughts. He stopped short, teetering on the spot, as if he'd been slapped in the face. "What you were saying about the Styx and their . . . what are they called . . . their people up on the surface?"

"Agents," Will helped him.

"Yes . . . their *agents* . . ." He narrowed his eyes. "Even if I could get back above ground again, I couldn't go home, could I?"

Will stood before him, not knowing what to say.

"If I did, my mum and dad would be abducted, like that family you mentioned, the Watkinses. The dirty, rotten Styx wouldn't just be after me. They'd grab my parents and turn them into slaves, or murder them, wouldn't they?"

Will could only return Chester's stare, but that was enough.

"And what could I do? If I tried to warn Mum and Dad, or even the police, do you think they'd believe me? They'd think

I'd lost my mind or something." His head sagged forward and he sighed. "All the time I was locked up in the Hold, all I 'thought about was you and me getting home. I just wanted to go *home*. It kept me going for all those months." He broke into a cough, which might have masked a sob — Will couldn't tell. Chester grasped Will's arm and stared straight into his eyes. His expression was one of the deepest despair. "I'm never going to see daylight again, am I?"

Will remained silent.

"One way or another, we're stuck down here for good, aren't we? There's nowhere for us to go, not now. Will, *what* are we going to do?" Chester said.

"I'm so sorry," Will said again in a strangled voice.

Cal's excited cries echoed from up ahead. "Hey!" he was calling repeatedly.

"No!" Will yelled back in frustration. "Not now!" He waved his light in a gesture of irritation. He needed more time with his friend. "Just wait!"

"Found something!" Cal hollered even more loudly, either not hearing Will's response or choosing to ignore it.

Chester glanced to where the younger boy was and declared, "It'd better not be the station. I am *not* going to get caught again." He took a step forward along the tracks.

"Hold up, Chester," Will started, "hang on a second. I want to say something."

Chester's eyes were still red-rimmed with fatigue. As they stood there, Will fidgeted with the light orb in his hands, and from its illumination Chester could easily read the turmoil in his friend's filth-covered face.

"I know exactly what you're going to say," he said. "It's not your fault."

"But it is!" Will cried. "It *is* my fault. . . . I didn't mean to get you into all this. You've got a *real* family, but . . . I've . . . I've got no one to go back to. I've got nothing to lose."

Chester tried to reply, reaching a hand forward, but his friend went on, growing more incoherent as he attempted to give voice to the emotions and regrets that had been knocking around in his head for the past months.

"I never should have gotten you into this . . . you were just helping me. . . ."

"Look . . . ," Chester said, trying to calm his friend.

"My dad will be able to fix everything, but if we don't find him . . . I—"

"Will—" Chester tried to interrupt once again, then allowed him to continue.

"I don't know what we're going to do, or what's going to happen to us . . . we might never . . . we might die. . . ."

"Just forget it," Chester said softly as Will's voice fell to a whisper. "Neither of us knew it would turn out like this, and besides"—Will saw a broad grin ease itself into place on his friend's face—"it really *can't* get any worse, can it?" Chester punched Will playfully on the shoulder, unknowingly hitting the precise spot that had been so horribly injured by the stalker dog in the Eternal City.

"Thanks, Chester," Will gasped, clenching his teeth to stop himself from crying out from the fresh wave of pain.

"Hurry up!" Cal's shouts came again. "I've found a way through here. Come on!"

"What's he ranting about?" Chester asked.

Will tried to pull himself together. "He's always doing this, running off," he said, rolling his eyes.

"Oh really? Remind you of anyone?" Chester said, arching an eyebrow.

Slightly abashed, Will nodded. "Yeah . . . a little." He managed to return Chester's smile.

They caught up with Cal, who was positively vibrating with excitement, babbling something about a light.

"Told you! Look down there!" He was jumping up and down, pointing into a large passage that led away from the train tunnel. Will peered down it and saw a soft blue glow, flickering as if it was quite some distance away.

"Keep up with me," Cal ordered and, without waiting for either Will or Chester to react, raced off at a furious pace.

Will tried to shout after him, but Cal didn't stop.

"Who does he think he is?" Chester said, looking at Will, who just shrugged as they both followed Cal's lead. "Can't believe I'm being told what to do by a pesky midget," Chester complained under his breath.

The temperature suddenly seemed to soar, making them pant. The air was so searingly dry and arid that their sweat was whisked off their skin the moment it appeared.

"Man, it is *sweltering* down here. It's like Spain or something," Chester complained, undoing several shirt buttons and scratching his chest.

"Well, if you believe the geologists, the temperature should rise one degree for every seventy feet you get closer to the earth's core," Will said.

"What does that mean?" Chester asked.

"It means we should be *toast* by now."

As Will and Chester followed Cal, wondering what exactly they were getting themselves into now, the light grew in intensity. It seemed to pulse, sometimes bathing the jagged walls around them, and then gradually diminishing so that there was only a bluish haze ahead.

They caught up with Cal just as he reached the end of the passage. A large space opened up before them.

A single flame, about six feet high, sprouted from the central point in the space. With a loud hissing, the flame grew, the blue plume elongating until it had quadrupled in height, spearing up and licking into a circular opening in the roof above it. The heat from the flame was too much to bear, and they were forced to back away and cover their faces with their arms.

"What is it?" Will asked, but neither Cal nor Chester answered, all three boys bewitched by its sheer beauty. For at the base of the flame, as it emerged from the blackened rock,

it was almost transparent, but it transformed through a spectrum of colors, into shimmering yellows and reds, to a staggering range of greens, until it became the deepest magenta at its apex. But the overall light, the summation of these colors, was the blue that it cast around them, and which had led them here. They stood together, their eyes reflecting the iridescent display, until the hissing subsided and the flame shrank back down again.

As if they had all snapped out of a spell at the same instant, they turned to see what lay around them. They could make out a number of shadowy openings in the walls of the chamber.

Will and Chester made for the nearest of these. As they cautiously entered it, the light from the orbs in their hands mingled with the blue of the residual flame to reveal man-sized bundles leaning against the walls, two or three deep in places.

Wrapped in dusty cloth, each was bound several times around its girth with some type of twine. A few of the bundles appeared to be more recent than others, encased in a less soiled and stained cloth. But the older ones were so dirty as to be almost indistinguishable from the rock behind them. Closely followed by Chester, Will went over to one of these and held up his light to it. Strips of material had rotted and fallen away, allowing the boys to see what was inside.

"Ohmygosh," Chester said, so quickly it sounded like a single word.

Desiccated skin was drawn tightly across a skeletal face, which stared back at them from its empty eye sockets. Here and there the dull ivory of clean bone poked through cracks in the dark skin. As Will moved his light, they could see other parts of the skeleton: Ribs protruded through the fabric, and a spiderlike hand rested against a hip covered with skin as tightly stretched as a piece of ancient parchment.

"I suppose these must be dead Coprolites," Will mumbled as he and Chester followed the wall around, surveying the other bundles.

"Oh. My. God," Chester repeated, slowly this time. "There are hundreds of them."

"This has to be some sort of burial ground," Will spoke in a subdued voice, as if showing these amassed bodies respect. "Just like the American Indians. They left their dead on wooden platforms, on mountainsides, rather than bury them."

"So if this is some type of holy place, shouldn't we get the heck out of here? We don't want to upset these people, the Cupcakes or whatever they're called," Chester said urgently.

"Coprolites," Will corrected him.

"Coprolites." Chester pronounced the word carefully. "Right."

"And another thing," Will said.

"What?" Chester asked, turning to him.

"The name *Coprolites*," Will continued, barely suppressing a grin. "That's just what the Colonists call them. If you ever meet a Coprolite, don't use that name, OK?"

"Why?"

"It's not very flattering. It's dinosaur droppings. It means fossilized *dinosaur poo*." Will smirked as he walked a little farther along the wall of mummified bodies, until his attention was caught by one whose shroud had all but disintegrated.

He played his light on the corpse, passing the beam slowly down its length to its feet and then back up to its head again. Although the body was taller than either Will or Chester, it was so shrunken that it looked very small, and nothing at all like the cadaver of a fully grown adult. It had a thick golden bracelet around its bony wrist, in which were inset chunky rectangular gemstones of red, green, dark blue, and a few with no color at all. Their matte surfaces glinted dully, like old cough drops.

"I bet that's gold, and I reckon those stones could be rubies, emeralds, and sapphires . . . and even diamonds," Will said with bated breath. "Isn't this just incredible?"

"Yeah," Chester replied, without conviction.

"I must take a picture of this."

"Can't we just get out of here?" Chester urged as Will shrugged off his rucksack and extricated his camera from it. Then Chester noticed Will was extending a hand toward the braceleted wrist.

"Just what do you think you're doing, Will?"

"I need to move this slightly," Will said, "for a better shot."

"Will!"

But Will wasn't listening. He had taken hold of the bracelet between his thumb and forefinger and was gently rotating it.

"Don't, Will! Will, c'mon! You know you shouldn't . . ."

The whole body quaked and then simply collapsed to the floor, throwing up a plume of dust.

"Oops!" Will said.

"Yeah, oops! That's great! Just great!" Chester gulped as they both took a hasty step backward. "Look at what you've done!"

As the cloud settled, Will peered shamefacedly at the small mound of bones and grayish ash before him — it resembled a pile of old branches and twigs left over from a bonfire. The body had simply disintegrated.

"Sorry," he said to it. With a shiver, he realized he still had the bracelet in his fingers; he dropped it on top of the heap.

Any thoughts of taking pictures now abandoned, Will squatted down by his pack to put away his camera. He had just secured the side pocket when he noticed he'd picked up some dust on his hands in the process. Right away he began to inspect the ground on which he and Chester now stood. Making a face, Will quickly stood up and wiped his hands on his pants.

They were treading on several inches of dust and bone fragments from decomposed cadavers.

They were tramping in the remains of many dead bodies.

"Let's go back a bit," Will suggested, not wanting to upset Chester even more. "Away from these."

"Works for me," Chester answered gratefully, without inquiring why. "This is all way creepy."

They both stepped back a distance, pausing as Will regarded the silent ranks against the walls.

"Thousands of them must be buried here. Generations," he said thoughtfully.

"We should really —"

Chester stopped in midsentence, and Will reluctantly tore his eyes from the mummified corpses to focus on his friend's anxious face.

"Did you see where Cal went?" Chester asked.

"No," Will said, immediately concerned.

They raced back into the central chamber, paused to peer into its corners, then edged around so they could see to the far end, past the flame, which once again was beginning to hiss loudly and stretch its wispy apex toward the roof.

"There he is!" Will exclaimed in relief as he spotted the lone figure making its way determinedly into a distant corner. "Why does he never stay put?"

"You know, I've only known your brother for . . . what . . . forty-eight hours, and I have to tell you I've already had enough of him," Chester complained, watching Will's reaction carefully to see if he was offended.

But Will didn't seem to mind in the slightest.

"Maybe we could tether him to something?" Chester smiled wryly.

Will hesitated for a second. "Look, we'd better go after him. He must have found something . . . maybe another way out," he said, starting after his brother. Chester glanced sidelong into the chamber containing the massed ranks of bodies. "Good idea," he muttered and, giving an involuntary groan, took off after Will.

They ran at a trot, giving the flame a wide berth as it peaked at its full height again and radiated its intense heat. They could just about see Cal as he left the farthermost reaches of the central chamber and passed under a large, roughly hewn archway. They followed him through this and found themselves on an area of ground the size of a soccer field, with a high canopy above it. Cal had his back to them and was clearly looking at something.

"You can't keep running off by yourself," Will reprimanded him.

"It's a river," Cal said, oblivious to his brother's irritation.

Before them was a broad channel, the water sweeping quickly past and throwing up a fine, warm spray. They could feel it on their faces even from the bank.

"Hey! Look there!" Cal directed Will and Chester.

Jutting out over the water was a pier some sixty feet in length. It was constructed from rusting metal girders, which looked irregular and handmade. Although it didn't appear to be well built, the pier felt solid enough underfoot. They didn't hesitate to go to the very end, where a circular platform edged with a railing fashioned from odd pieces of metal was suspended.

As their lights, which barely reached across to the opposite side of the river, picked out the white flecks of spume in the otherwise unbroken sheet of speeding black water, their minds played tricks on them and they felt as if *they* were racing along. Occasional splashes drenched them as the fast-flowing water dashed against the stanchions on the platform's underside.

Cal leaned forward over the railing as he spoke.

"Can't see the bank, or . . . ," he began.

"Careful," Will warned him. "Don't fall in."

". . . or anywhere to cross it," he finished.

"No!" Chester immediately spoke out. "I, for one, am *not* putting a foot anywhere near that. The current looks really strong."

Nobody disagreed, and the three of them stood there for a moment, welcoming the warm spray on their faces.

Will shut his eyes and listened to the sound of the water. Behind his calm exterior, he was grappling with his emotions. A part of him said he should be insisting that they cross the river, even though they had no idea how deep it was or what lay on the other side, just to keep forging ahead.

But what was the point? They had no idea where they were going, and there was nowhere they had to be. At this very moment he was deep in the earth's mantle, farther down than anyone from the surface had probably ever been, and why? Because of his father, who, for all he knew, was already dead. Difficult as it was for him, he had to consider the possibility that he might be wasting everyone's time chasing a ghost.

Will felt a light breeze ruffle his hair and opened his eyes. He looked at his friend, Chester, and his brother, Cal, and saw their bright eyes gleaming in their grubby faces, entranced by the vision of the underground river before them. He hadn't ever seen either of them look more alive. Despite all the hardships they had suffered, they appeared to be happy. The doubts fell from his mind, and he felt in control of himself again. He knew it all had to be worth it.

"We're not going to cross the river," he announced. "Let's just go back to the railway track."

"Yes," Chester and Cal both immediately answered.

"Fine. That's decided, then," Will said, nodding to himself as the threesome turned together and walked side by side by side back down the pier.

SARAH STROLLED casually down Main Street, in no particular hurry. She couldn't explain it to herself, but there was something deeply reassuring about returning to the place where she had first broken out to the surface.

It was as if by coming back, she was reaffirming that the specter she'd been running from for so very long now, the Colony hidden down below, really *did* exist. There'd been occasions in the past when she'd actually wondered if she wasn't just imagining the entire thing, if the whole basis of her life wasn't some elaborate self-delusion.

It was just after seven in the evening and the interior of the rather uninspiring Victorian building that proclaimed itself to be the Highfield Museum was in darkness. Farther along from the museum, she noticed with some surprise that Clarke Brothers, the greengrocers, appeared to have closed up shop. The shutters, painted with many coats of a treacly pea-green gloss, were firmly sealed. They must have been that way for some time, since a thick crust of fliers covered them, the most prominent advertising some recently reunited boy band and a New Year's used car sale.

Sarah drew to a halt and stared at the shop. For generations, the population of the Colony had relied on the Clarkes for regular consignments of fresh fruit and vegetables. There were other Topsoil suppliers, but the brothers and their forebears had been trusted allies for as long as anyone could remember. Short of the possibility that they had both died, she knew they would have never closed shop, not voluntarily.

She contemplated the sealed shutters of the storefront one last time, then moved on. The closing of Clarke Brothers bore out what the note from the dead mailbox had said: The Colony was subject to a lockdown, and the majority of the aboveground supply links had been severed. It underlined just how far things must have gone down below.

Several miles later, Sarah rounded the corner onto Broadlands Avenue. As she approached the Burrowses' house, she saw that its curtains were drawn and there was no sign of life anywhere in the place, either. Quite the opposite: A discarded packing crate under the lean-to, and the unkempt front garden, spoke to her of months of neglect. She didn't slow as she walked past it, glimpsing in the corner of her eye an uprooted real estate agent's sign in the long grass behind the chain-link fence. She continued along the row of identical houses to the end of the avenue, where an alleyway took her through to the Common.

Sarah put her head back and flared her nostrils, drawing the air into her lungs, a mix of city and countryside smells. Exhaust fumes and the slightly sour scent of massed people fought with the wet grass and fresh vegetation around her.

Sarah kept to the perimeter path for several hundred yards and then ducked into the foliage, pushing her way through the trees and shrubs until she could see the backs of the houses on Broadlands Avenue. Moving stealthily from one to another, she observed the occupants from the ends of their gardens. In one, an elderly couple sat stiffly at a dining table, drinking soup. In another, an obese man in a vest and underpants was smoking while he read the paper.

The inhabitants of the subsequent two houses were lost to her, as both had their curtains pulled, but in the next, a young woman was standing by the windows and playing with a baby, bouncing it up and down. Sarah stopped, compelled to watch the woman's face. Feeling her emotions and her sense of loss begin to rise within her again, Sarah tore her eyes away from the mother and child and moved on.

Finally she reached her destination. Sarah stood on the very same spot behind the Burrowses' house where she'd stood so many times before, hoping to catch the smallest glimpse of her son as he grew up, and away, from her.

After she'd been forced to leave him behind in the church graveyard, she'd searched high and low for him all over Highfield. For the following two and a half years, wearing sunglasses until she became acclimatized to the painful daylight, she'd combed the streets and hovered outside the local schools at the end of classes. But there was absolutely no sign of Seth anywhere. She'd widened her search radius, venturing farther and farther afield until she was wandering around the neighboring London boroughs.

Then, on a day shortly after her son's fifth birthday, she happened to be back in Highfield again when she caught sight of him outside the main post office. He was steady on his feet, running around wildly with a toy dinosaur. Already he was quite different from the child she'd left behind. Nevertheless, she had recognized him immediately; he was unmistakable with his unruly shock of brilliant white hair, precisely the same as hers, although she was now forced to use dyes to mask it.

She'd followed Seth and his new mother home from the shops to find out where they lived. Her first impulse had been to snatch him back. But it was just too dangerous with the Styx still after her. So, season after season, Sarah came back to Highfield, even if just for part of a day, desperate for the briefest sighting of her son. She'd stare at him over the length of the garden, which was like some untraversable abyss. He grew taller and his face filled out, becoming so much like hers that sometimes she thought it was her own reflection she was seeing in the glass of the French doors.

And on those occasions she yearned to call out over the tantalizingly short distance, but she never did. She couldn't. She'd often wondered how he would have reacted if she'd walked across the garden and into the house and, there, had clasped him to her. She felt her throat close up as the imagined scene unfurled before her like a preview of some television melodrama, their eyes filling with tears as they looked upon each other with startled mutual recognition. He would be mouthing the words *Mother, Mother,* over and over again.

But all that was history now.

And if the message from Joe Waites was to be believed, the child was now a murderer, and had to pay for his crimes.

As if she were on a rack, Sarah was torn between the love that she had known for her son and the hollow hatred that simmered at its borders, the two extremes pulling remorse-lessly at her. They were both so powerful that, caught in the middle, she was plunged into a state of confusion and an utter, overpowering numbness.

Stop it! For the sake of all that's holy, snap out of it! What was happening to her? Her life, for years so controlled and disci-plined, was slipping into disarray. She had to get hold of herself. She raked the nails of one hand over the back of the other, then did it again, and yet again, each time pressing harder, until she broke the skin, the stinging pain bringing a bitter relief of distraction.

Her son had been christened Seth in the Colony, but Topsoil somebody had renamed him Will. He had been adopted by a local couple called Burrows. While the mother, Mrs. Burrows, was a mere shadow of a woman, who spent her life ensconced in front of the television, Will had evidently fallen under the spell of his adoptive father, who worked as the curator of the local museum.

Sarah had followed Will on numerous occasions, trail-ing behind as he went off on his bicycle, a gleaming shovel strapped across his back. She would watch as the lonely figure, a baseball cap pulled low over his distinctive white locks, toiled in the rough ground at the edges of town or by the local dump. She observed him digging some surprisingly deep holes with guidance and encouragement, she assumed, from Dr. Burrows. *How very, very ironic,* she thought. Having eluded the tyranny of the Colony, it was as though her son was trying to return to it, like a salmon swimming upstream to its spawning ground.

But though his name had been changed, what had happened to Will? Like her and her brother, Tam, he had Macaulay blood in him; he was from one of the oldest founding families in the Colony. How could he have changed so much for the worse in those years on the surface? What could have done that to him? If the message in the dead mailbox was correct, then it was as though Will had gone insane, like some insubordinate cur that turns on its master.

A bird screeched somewhere above her and Sarah flinched, crouching defensively behind the low branches of a conifer. She listened, but there was just the wind sifting through the trees and a car alarm sounding intermittently several streets away. With a last check of the Common behind her, she edged cautiously along the end of the Burrowses' garden. She stopped abruptly, thinking she'd seen light coming from between the closed curtains of the living room. Satisfied that it was just a stray beam of early moonlight poking its way through the clouds, she peered at the upstairs windows, one of which she knew had been Will's bedroom. She was pretty sure the place was deserted.

She slipped through the gap in the hedges where a garden gate had once hung and crossed the lawn to the back door. She paused again to listen, then kicked over a brick at the side of the doormat. She wasn't in the least bit surprised to find the spare key still there — Dr. and Mrs. were a careless couple. She used it to enter the house.

Closing the door behind her, she raised her head and sampled the air, which was fusty and undisturbed. No, nobody had been living there for months. She didn't turn on the lights, even though her sensitive eyes were struggling to make out anything in the shadowy interior. Lights were just too risky.

She stole down the hall to the front of the house and entered the kitchen. Feeling around with her hands, she discovered the work surfaces were clear and the cupboards emptied. Then she backtracked into the hall again and went into the living room. Her foot knocked against something: a roll of Bubble Wrap. Everything had been removed. The house was completely empty.

So it *was* true: The family *had* been broken up. She'd read how Dr. Burrows had stumbled upon the Colony under Highfield and been transported to the Deeps by the Styx. Most likely he would have perished by now. Nobody penetrated very far into the Interior and survived. Sarah had no idea where Mrs. Burrows or her daughter, Rebecca, had gone, and she didn't much care. Will was her concern, very much her concern.

Something caught her eye on the floor by the front door, and she crouched down to feel around. She found a pile of letters scattered on the doormat and immediately began to gather them up and cram them into her shoulder bag. Halfway through doing so, she thought she heard noises . . . a car door slamming . . . a muted footfall . . . and then the faintest suggestion of a low voice.

Her nerves fired like electrical short circuits. She held absolutely still. The sounds had been muffled — she couldn't tell how far away they'd been. She strained to hear anything more, but now there was only silence. Telling herself that it must have been somebody passing the front of the house or maybe just one of the neighbors, she finished collecting the last of the letters. It was high time she left.

She hurried back through the dark hall and, stepping through the back door, had just turned to pull it shut when a man's voice sounded not inches from her ear. It was confident and accusatory.

"Gotcha!" it announced.

A large hand clamped on her left shoulder and heaved her away from the door. She jerked her head around to catch a glimpse of her assailant. In the scant light, she saw a triangle of lean, well-muscled cheek and a flash of white collar.

Styx!

He was strong and had the advantage of surprise, but her reaction was near-instantaneous. She swung her arm against his, sweeping his hand from her shoulder, then looped her arm around his in one skillful move that put him in a painful lock. She heard his sharp intake of breath: This wasn't going the way he thought it would.

As she arched her body to intensify the hold on him, he tried to push himself forward to relieve the pressure on his elbow joint. This brought his head within easy reach, and he'd just opened his mouth to cry out for help when Sarah silenced him with a single blow to the temple. He slumped unconscious onto the patio tiles.

She had disabled her attacker with savage precision and blistering speed, but she wasn't about to stick around to admire her handiwork; there was more than an even chance of other Styx in the area. She had to get away.

She tore across the garden, delving in her shoulder bag for her knife. As she arrived at the opening in the hedges, she thought she was in the clear and was already planning her escape across the Common.

"WHAT DID YOU DO TO HIM?" came a furious shout, and a large shadow loomed in her path.

She pulled the knife out of her bag, and the letters that she'd taken from the house came with it, flying through the air in a hail. But something whipped across her hand, sending the knife spinning from her grip.

In the moonlight she saw the silver glint of the insignia, the numbers and letters on the man's uniform, and realized far too late that these weren't Styx. They were policemen — Topsoil policemen. And she'd already knocked one out for the count. Too bad. He had gotten in her way, and her self-preservation was paramount. She probably wouldn't have done anything differently, even if she'd known.

She tried to dodge away from the man, but he moved quickly to block her. She immediately lashed out with her fist, but he was ready.

"Resisting arrest," he growled as he swung something at her again. A billy club! She saw it the instant before it made contact. It struck her a glancing blow to the forehead, filling her vision with cascading pebbles of bright light. She didn't fall, but the club was quick to come again, swiping across her mouth. This time she folded to the ground.

"Had enough yet, you crazy hag?" he seethed, his contorted mouth spitting the words into her face as he leaned over her. She did her best to throw another punch at him. It was pathetically weak, and he fended it off with ease.

"Is that all you've got left?" He laughed caustically, then fell on her, pinning her down with his knee on her chest. It felt as if an elephant were using her as a footrest.

She tried to worm her way out from under him, but it was no use. She felt a numbness descending over her as she teetered on the edge of consciousness. Everything was going into a lopsided kaleidoscope: the trace of the club against the indigo sky, the hazy circle of the moon eclipsed by the officer's face, a ghastly pantomime mask. She thought she was going to pass out.

No!

She couldn't give up. Not now.

From the patio, the injured policeman moaned, and Sarah's attacker was momentarily distracted. His arm poised above him for the next blow, he glanced quickly over at his partner.

The crushing weight shifted for the briefest instant, enabling her to swallow a mouthful of air and regroup her senses.

Her hands scrambled over the ground for her knife, a rock, a stick, anything she could use as a weapon. All she found was the long grass. The policeman's attention was back on her again; he was shouting and cursing, raising the club even higher. She braced herself, prepared for the inevitable, knowing it was all over.

She was beaten.

All of a sudden, something formless and blurred with speed attached itself to the man's arm. Sarah blinked, and the next instant his arm was gone, his weight lifted. There was the oddest silence; he didn't seem to be shouting anymore.

It was as if time had ground to a halt.

She couldn't understand it. She wondered if she'd lost consciousness. Then she glimpsed two massive eyes and a blaze of teeth like a stockade of sharpened stakes. She blinked again.

Time restarted. The policeman let out a piercing scream and slid off her. He struggled clumsily to his feet, one arm hanging uselessly at his side as he tried to defend himself with the other. She couldn't see his face. Whatever was attacking him had wrapped itself around his head and shoulders in a storm of claws and hairless limbs. She saw long, sinewy hind legs raking furiously. The policeman fell flat on his back like a bowling pin as the onslaught continued.

Fighting her dizziness, Sarah sat up. She pushed her blood-soaked bangs from her eyes and squinted, trying to see, trying to make out what was happening.

The clouds parted, allowing the weak moon to cast its light on the scene. She caught an outline.

No, it couldn't be!

She looked again, not believing what she was seeing.

It was a Hunter, a type of large cat specially bred in the Colony.

What in the world was it doing here?

With the most immense effort, she crawled over to a nearby gatepost and used it to drag herself up. Once on her feet, she felt so groggy and confused, she waited for several moments as she tried to collect her wits.

"No time for this," she chastised herself as the reality of the situation came back to her. "Pull yourself together."

Ignoring the groans and stifled pleas of the policeman as he continued to roll with the Hunter on top of him, she tottered unsteadily up the garden to where she thought her knife had landed. Retrieving it, she also gathered up the letters. She was determined not to leave anything behind. Feeling a little steadier on her feet, she turned to check on the first policeman. He lay unmoving on the patio tiles where she'd dropped him, clearly not posing any sort of threat.

Back at the end of the garden, the second policeman was on his side, his hands pressed to his face as he moaned horribly. The Hunter had detached itself and was sitting next to him, licking a paw. It stopped as Sarah approached, coiling its tail neatly around its legs, and regarded her intently. It flicked its massive eyes across to the groaning man, as if it had had nothing to do with his condition.

The fact that both policemen were injured and needed help was neither here nor there to Sarah. She felt no pity or regret at what had happened to them; they were a casualty of her own survival, nothing more, nothing less. She went over to the conscious policeman, stooping to unhook the radio from his jacket.

With a speed that took her by surprise, he grabbed her wrist. But he was weak. She broke his grip without much effort and then tore off the radio — he made no move to stop her. She threw the radio down and stamped her heel into it with a crunch of broken plastic.

With some nervousness, she took a step toward the Hunter. Although they were born killers, it was rare for them to attack people. There had been stories of them going rogue, turning on their masters and anyone else who happened to cross their paths. She had no way of knowing if this Hunter could be trusted after what it had done to the policeman. From the appearance of its bare skin stretched over its ribs, it was badly malnourished and hardly in the best condition. She wondered how long it had been fending for itself up here.

"Where did you come from?" she asked it softly, keeping a safe distance.

The animal angled its head toward her, as if trying to understand, and blinked once. She ventured closer, tentatively reaching out her hand, and it leaned forward to sniff at her fingertips. The top of its head was almost on a level with her hips — she'd forgotten just how big these animals were. Then it suddenly leaned toward her. She tensed, but it merely rubbed its head affectionately against her palm. She heard the deep rumble of a purr kick in, as loud as an outboard engine on a dinghy. That was uncharacteristically friendly behavior for a Hunter. Either it had been slightly unhinged by its Topsoil life or it thought, for some reason, that it *knew* her. But she didn't have time to ponder that now — she needed to decide her next move.

She had to get as far away as she could and, as she rubbed the rather flaky and scabbed skin under the cat's incredibly wide muzzle, she recognized that she owed the animal a debt of honor. She would have almost certainly been caught if it hadn't come to her rescue. She couldn't leave it behind.

"Come on," she said to the cat, and made for the Common. Her bruised head began to clear slightly as she saw the open path ahead. They ran together toward the metal arch that marked the entrance.

Sarah was crossing the road in the direction of Main Street, but drew to a halt once she happened to glance back to make sure the cat was still with her. It was sitting on the pavement by the gate, looking down the road that branched to the right, as if it was trying to tell her something.

"Come on! This way!" she said impatiently, thrusting a finger in the direction of the town center and her hotel. "We don't have time for this . . . ," she trailed off, realizing just how difficult it was going to be to get the animal through the streets and into her room without being noticed.

The Hunter remained steadfastly facing off to the right, just as it would have done when alerting its handler that it had scented quarry. "What is it? What's there?" Sarah said, jogging back toward it and feeling a little ridiculous attempting to converse with a cat.

She looked at her watch, weighing her options. It wouldn't be long before someone discovered the scene back at the Burrowses' house, and then the Common and the whole town of Highfield would be bristling with police. But she took consolation from the fact that nightfall had only just begun.

She was in her element; she could use the darkness to her advantage. She had to put as much distance between her and the house as she could, and taking the busier streets might prove to be a mistake. Not to mention that her battered face would make her stick out like a sore thumb.

She tried to see what lay in the direction the cat was pointing: Perhaps it wouldn't do any harm to set down a false trail, and, if necessary, take a more roundabout route back to the hotel. As she debated with herself, the Hunter pawed the pavement, eager to be on the move again.

"All right — have it your way," she said, suddenly making up her mind. She could have sworn the cat grinned at her before it bounded off so quickly that she struggled to keep up.

Twenty minutes later, they entered a street she didn't know and, from a signpost, she saw that they were heading toward the municipal dump. The cat hung back briefly by an entrance at the end of a long line of billboards, then turned into it. As Sarah followed, she could dimly make out an area of rough ground, overrun with weeds.

The cat galloped past a derelict car and toward one of the corners. It seemed to know precisely where it was going. It skidded to a halt and stuck its nose into the air to sniff as Sarah fought to catch up.

She wasn't far behind it when caution urged her to swing around and make sure nobody was following them. But when she turned again to where the cat had been, it was nowhere to be seen. As good as her night vision was, she had absolutely no idea where the animal had gone. All she could see were small clumps of bushes sprouting from the muddy soil.

She took her key-ring flashlight from her bag and played it before her. Several yards away from where she was searching, she spotted the cat's head as it popped rather comically from out of the ground.

It ducked down again, disappearing from view. She went over to investigate and found there was some kind of trench there, much of which was covered by a sheet of plywood. She stuck a hand in to try to feel what lay below — there seemed to be a sizable hollow there. She heaved the sheet aside, groaning from her aching ribs as she made the opening just large enough for her to get in.

Stretching a leg tentatively into the darkness, she completely lost her footing on the loose soil. Her arms flailed helplessly as she tried to grab something to stop her rapid descent, but nothing presented itself. She fell almost twenty-five feet and landed in a sitting position with a loud crunch. Cursing quietly, she waited for the pain to subside, then switched on her flashlight again.

To her astonishment, she found she'd fallen into a pit filled with what appeared to be a mass of bones. The floor was thick with them, all picked clean of flesh and shiny white under her light. Scooping up a handful, she selected a tiny femur and examined it. And as she looked around her, she spotted several small skulls. All bore teeth marks and, from their size, could have been rabbit or squirrel. Then she noticed a much larger skull with pronounced canines.

"Dog," she said, identifying it immediately. Stuck to the skull was a chunky leather collar, darkened with dried blood.

She was in the cat's lair!

The newspaper article she'd read in the hotel suddenly came back to her.

"So you're the one who's been snatching dogs!" she said. "*You're* the beast of Highfield Common," she added with an amazed chuckle, addressing the darkness where she could hear the cat's regular breathing.

She got herself up, the skeletons cracking and splintering beneath her feet, and began down the gallery that led off the bone pit. Its sides were battened with timbers that to her practiced eye didn't look too sound — there were signs of wet rot and the green of excessive dampness on them. Worse still, there weren't enough of these props to brace the roof, as if someone had been randomly removing them without any thought for what effect it might have. She shook her aching head. She certainly wasn't in the safest of places, but she needed somewhere to recover from her injuries.

The gallery took her lower, and then she emerged from it into a larger area. She glimpsed some duckboarding on the ground, its surface covered with spreading tendrils of white rot. On this was a pair of dilapidated armchairs positioned side by side. In one of these, the cat was sitting perfectly still, as if it had been waiting for her for some time.

She shone the light around her and gasped with surprise. At its widest point, the earthen chamber was approximately fifty feet across, but at the back end the wall had evidently collapsed, a drift of spoil reaching almost as far as the armchairs. Water dripped steadily from the roof and, as she edged around the wall, she stepped straight into a puddle. It was deceptively deep, and she lost her balance.

Cursing, her foot drenched in muddy water, she grabbed at the nearest thing she could to steady herself, one of the roof props. Her hand came away with a clutch of soggy splinters and she fell against the wall, her leg slipping even deeper into the pool. Worse still, as the prop she'd grabbed shifted, a gap opened in the bowed timber planks supporting the roof. A torrent of soil cascaded over her.

"For heaven's sake!" Sarah fumed. "What *stupid fool* built this place?"

She stepped out of the pool, wiping the soil from her eyes. At least she'd managed not to drop her flashlight, which she now used for a more detailed examination of her surroundings. She made her way carefully around the excavation, assessing the props, all of which appeared to be in various states of decay.

Pursing her lips, and asking herself what had possessed her to come down here, she turned to the cat, which hadn't as much as moved a muscle while she'd been flailing around. It was sitting patiently in the armchair, its head held high as it studied her. She could have sworn that there was something about its expression — as if it was quietly amused by her antics.

"Next time you try to take me anywhere, I'll think twice about it!" she said angrily.

Careful! She held her tongue, reminding herself what she was dealing with. Although the cat looked placid enough, Hunters, especially if they turned feral, could be volatile, and she shouldn't do anything that might alarm it. She edged closer to the empty armchair, taking care not to make any sudden movements.

"Mind if I sit down?" she asked in a gentle voice, holding up her muddy palms to the cat as if to show she meant it no harm.

As she lowered herself into the seat, a thought began to nag at her. She was looking around the excavation, trying to work out exactly what it was that was bothering her, when the cat made a small lunge toward her. Sarah drew back, then relaxed as she saw it was merely rubbing its muzzle against the armchair.

Sarah noticed something draped there, and slowly reached across to take it in her hands. It looked like a piece of damp fabric. Sitting in the armchair, she spread it open. It was a mud-soaked rugby shirt of black and yellow stripes. She sniffed at it.

Despite the heavy odor of rot and damp that pervaded the air, a single smell could be perceived. Just the faintest trace. She sniffed it again to make sure she wasn't mistaken, and then looked intently at the cat. Her brow furrowed as a notion began to take form. It gathered momentum and, like a bubble rising to the surface of water, it suddenly burst into the open.

"This was *his*, wasn't it?" she said, holding the shirt in front of the cat's scarred muzzle. "My son, Seth, wore this . . . and so he . . . he must have dug this place! Goodness, I never knew he'd gotten quite this far down!"

For a few seconds, she peered around the excavation with renewed interest. But then she was thrown once more into a tumult of conflicting emotions. Before the note, she'd have been in raptures about being here in her son's excavation, as if it brought her closer to him. But now, she couldn't enjoy the discovery — indeed, she felt uneasy in the place, uneasy about the hands that had created it.

Another thought exploded in her mind. She turned to the animal, which hadn't once averted its unwinking eyes from her. "Cal? Were you Cal's Hunter?"

At the mention of the name, the cat twitched a cheek, drops of moisture on its long whiskers sparkling in her light.

She raised her eyebrows at the animal. "You *were*, weren't you?" she spluttered.

With a frown, she sank deep into thought for a few seconds. If this cat was indeed Cal's, then it might substantiate what Joe Waites had written in his note: that Seth had forced Cal to go with him Topsoil before dragging him down to the Deeps. That would explain the cat's presence here — it had accompanied Cal when he had escaped to the surface.

"So, somehow, you got out of the Colony with . . . with Seth?" she said, thinking out loud. "But you know him as *Will*, don't you?" She carefully enunciated the name again, watching for a reaction from the cat. But this time there was no sign of recognition.

She fell silent. *If it was true that Cal had been on the surface, then was everything else true about Seth?* The implications were too much for her. It was as if all her love for her eldest son was slowly being sucked out of her to make room for something ugly and vengeful.

"Cal," she said, wanting to see the animal's reaction again. It cocked its head toward her, then slid its eyes back to the entrance of the excavation.

Wishing the cat were able to answer all the hundreds of questions knocking around her confused mind, she let her head sink back against the chair. She found herself gradually succumbing to sheer fatigue. Hearing the shifting and groaning of the timbers around her and the occasional patter of falling soil, she briefly took in the various roots dangling from the roof above, before her eyelids grew too heavy. As her finger slipped from the button on her flashlight, the chamber was plunged into darkness, and she was almost at once asleep.

THE BOYS retraced their steps past the flickering blue flame and back into the railway tunnel. In a little more than twenty minutes, they reached where the train had come to a stop.

Crouched by the guard's car, its dust-filmed windows now dark, they looked down the locomotive's long line to where the engine sat. But nobody was in evidence — it seemed the train was completely unattended.

Then they moved their attention to the rest of the space. From what they could see, the cavern before them was at least several hundred feet from side to side.

"So this is the Miners' Station," Will said under his breath, focusing on the area to the left of the cavern, which was dotted with a line of lights. It didn't look like much, consisting of a row of rather ordinary, single-story shacks.

"Not exactly platform nine and three-quarters, is it?" Chester muttered.

"No . . . I thought it would be far bigger," Will said in a disappointed voice. "Hardly remarkable," he added, using the phrase his father would utter when unimpressed by something.

"Nobody sticks around here for long," Cal said.

Chester looked distinctly uncomfortable. "I don't think we should, either," he whispered nervously. "Where is everybody? The guard and the train driver?"

"Inside the buildings, probably," Cal told him.

There was a noise, a muted rumbling like distant thunder, and then a huge clattering began.

"What's that?" Chester exclaimed with alarm as they all shrank back into the tunnel.

Cal was pointing above the train. "No, look, they're just loading up for the return journey."

They saw large chutes poised above the higher-sided train cars. At least the diameter of an average trash can, they were cylindrical and appeared to be made from sections of sheet metal riveted together. Something was gushing from their mouths at great speed and hitting the metal beds of the freight cars with a massive clamor.

"Now's our chance!" Cal urged the others. He got up and, swooping around the back of the guard's car, belted down by the side of the train before Will could object.

"There he goes again," Chester moaned, but just the same he and Will took off after the younger boy, keeping to the lee of the train like Cal was doing.

They ran down the line of lower cars, passing the one in which they had spent the journey, then continued beside their higher-sided counterparts. Dust and debris sprayed over their heads, and they had to pause several times to wipe it from their eyes. It took the boys a full minute to travel the length of the train, enough time for the loading to be completed. A few remaining scatters of whatever the material was fell from the row of chutes, and the air was laced with a gritty dust.

Uncoupled from the train, the steam engine was farther along the track, but Cal had tucked down beside the last of the higher cars. As soon as Will and Chester caught up with him, Will lashed out, cuffing his brother around the head.

"Oi!" Cal yelped, raising his fists as if about to retaliate. "What was that for?"

"That was for running off again, you stupid little spod," Will chided him in a low, furious voice. "If you keep doing things like that, we're going to get caught."

"Well, they didn't see us . . . and how else could we get through here?" his brother defended himself vehemently.

Will didn't answer.

Cal blinked slowly, as if to say his brother was being tedious, and simply turned his head away to look into the distance. "We need to go down th—"

"No way," Will said. "Chester and I are going to check first before any of us does anything. You just stay put!"

Cal obeyed reluctantly, flopping onto the ground with a bad-tempered groan.

"You all right?" Will asked Chester as he heard a loud snuffling noise behind him. He twisted around to look.

"This stuff gets everywhere," Chester complained, then proceeded to blow his nose by clamping each nostril in turn with his fingers to clear them of the dust.

"That's disgusting," Will said under his breath as Chester pinched a dangling skein of snot and flicked it to the ground. "Do you *have* to do that?"

Taking no heed of his friend's distaste, Chester squinted at Will's face, then examined his own hands and arms. "We're certainly well camouflaged," he observed. If their faces and clothes had been filthy before from the continuous stream of carbon-black smoke on the train, they were even filthier now after being showered during the loading of the freight cars.

"Yeah, well, if you're quite finished," Will said, "let's recce the station."

On their elbows, he and Chester edged around the front of the car until they had an uninterrupted view of the buildings. There was absolutely no sign of any activity.

Making not the slightest effort to keep his head down, Cal disobeyed Will's orders and joined them. He couldn't seem to stay still, positively vibrating with impatience. "Listen, the railwaymen are in the station, but they're going to come out soon. We *have* to get out of this place before they do," he insisted.

Will considered the station buildings again. "Well, OK, but we all stick together and only go as far as the engine. Got that, Cal?"

They moved swiftly from the cover of the car, running half crouched until they came alongside the massive engine. Every so often it vented hissing jets of steam, as if it were a dragon in deep slumber. They could feel the warmth that still emanated from its giant boiler. Chester foolishly placed his hand on one of the massive plates of pitted steel that formed its slab-sided base and retracted it quickly. "Ow!" he said. "It's still really hot."

"You don't say," Cal muttered sarcastically as they skirted around to the front of the massively proportioned machine.

"It's awesome! Looks exactly like a tank," Chester said in schoolboy wonder. With its huge interlocking armor plates and giant cowcatcher, it certainly did resemble a military vehicle of some kind, an old battle tank.

"Chester, we really don't have time to admire the choo-choo!" Will said.

"I wasn't," he mumbled in response, still ogling the engine.

They began to debate their next move.

"We should go down there," Cal said forcefully, indicating the direction with his thumb.

"Blah, blah, blah," Chester mocked under his breath, giving Cal a disdainful stare. "Here we go again."

Will studied the area of the cavern his brother had pointed to. Across a stretch of about fifty yards of open ground was what could have been an opening in the cavern wall, metal ramps descending on either side of it from some structure above. Will couldn't see enough in the murkiness to be sure if it was a way out.

"I can't tell what's there," he said to Cal. "Too dark."

"That's exactly *why* we should go there," his brother replied.

"But what if the Colonists come out before we reach it?" Will asked. "There's no way they can miss us."

"They're on a break," Cal replied, shaking his head at Will. "We'll be OK if we go right now."

Chester chimed in. "We could always back off . . . into the tunnel again and wait until the train's gone."

"That could be hours. We've got to go *now*," Cal said, his voice brimming with irritation. "While we've still got the chance."

"Hang back," Chester immediately countered, turning to Cal.

"Go now," Cal insisted tetchily.

"No, we —" Chester came back at him, but Cal raised his voice and didn't let him finish.

"You don't know anything," he sneered.

"Who died and made you boss?" Chester swiveled around to his friend, looking for support. "You're not going to listen to this, are you, Will? He's just a stupid brat."

"Shut up," Will hissed through gritted teeth, his eyes on the station.

"I say we —" Cal declaimed loudly.

Will shot out his hand and clapped it roughly over his brother's mouth. "I said shut it, Cal. Two of them. Over there," he whispered urgently into Cal's ear, then slowly took his hand away.

Cal and Chester sought out the two railwaymen, who were standing under a portico that ran along the front of several of the station buildings. They had just emerged from one of the shacks, and strains of bizarre music filtered across to the boys through the open door.

They were wearing bulky blue uniforms and some type of breathing apparatus over their heads, and as the boys watched they lifted these up so they could drink from the large tankards each of them had in his hands. Even from where the boys were positioned, they could hear the men's grumbling tones as they stepped a few paces forward and stopped, idly perusing the train, and then turned to point out something in the gantry high above it.

After several minutes, they turned on their heels and went back inside the shack, slamming the door behind them.

"Right! Let's go!" Cal said. He chose to look only at Will, studiously avoiding Chester.

"Cut it out," Will growled. "We go when we all decide. We're in this together."

Cal started to reply, his upper lip lifted in an aggressive snarl.

"This isn't some children's game, you know," Will shot at him before he could speak.

The younger boy huffed loudly and, rather than continue to challenge Will, turned on Chester, glowering fiercely.

"You . . . you Topsoiler!" Cal spat.

Chester was completely unfazed by this and, raising an eyebrow, gave Will a small shrug.

So they remained there, Will and Chester carefully watching the frontage of the station while Cal drew pictures in the dirt that had a remarkable resemblance to Chester, with squarish bodies and blocky heads. Every so often he chuckled evilly to himself and wiped them over, only to begin drawing again.

After five minutes with no further sign of the railwaymen, Will spoke. "Right, I reckon they've settled in. I say we should go now. Happy, Chester?"

Chester gave a single nod, looking distinctly unhappy.

"At last," Cal said, leaping to his feet and rubbing his hands together to shake off the dust. In an instant he was in the full glare of the lights on the open ground, striding cockily away.

"What's his problem?" Chester said to Will. "He's going to get us all killed."

In the darkness by the cavern wall, they stepped between the pair of ramps and discovered that there was indeed a way through, a sizable cleft in the rock. Cal had struck it lucky with his suggestion and wasn't going to let this go unnoticed.

"I was r —" he started.

"Yeah, I know, I know," Will interrupted. "This time."

"What are those?" Chester said, noticing a number of structures as they entered a new stretch of tunnel. They were almost buried by large drifts of silt along one side of the wall. Some were like huge cubicles and others were circular in shape. Odd pieces of metal and debris lay discarded around them. The boys approached one of the structures, which, close up, looked like a giant honeycomb built of gray brick. As Will was wading through the silt to get closer, his foot flipped something over. He stooped to retrieve whatever it was. Hard, flat, and with undulating edges, it fit the palm of his hand. He kept hold of it as he went up to the honeycomb structure.

"There'll be a hatch down here," Cal said, pushing past his brother. He cleared the accumulated silt away at the base of the structure with his boot. Sure enough, there was a small-ish door, about a foot and a half square, which, as he squatted down and yanked it open a little, squealed loudly on dry hinges. Dark ash spilled out.

"How did you know that?" Will asked.

Rising to his feet, Cal snatched the object from his brother's grip and rapped it hard against the rounded surface of the structure beside him. The object gave off a dull but slightly glassy sound, and fragments broke from it. "This is a piece of slag." He swung his foot at a pile of dirt, sending it flying. "And I'm willing to bet there'll be some charcoal under all this."

"So?" Chester inquired.

"So these are furnaces," Cal replied confidently.

"Really?" Will said, bending to peer in through the hatch.

"Yes, I've seen these before, in the foundries in the South Cavern of the Colony." Cal lifted his chin and regarded Chester truculently, as if he had proved his superiority over the older boy. "The Coprolites must've been smelting pig iron here."

"An age ago, by the looks of it," Will said, gazing around the place.

Cal nodded, and, there being nothing else worthy of note, they trooped along the tunnel in silence.

"He's a smart aleck," Chester said when Cal was far enough ahead to be out of earshot.

"Look, Chester," Will replied in a low voice, "he's probably scared stiff by this place, like all the Colonists are. And don't forget, he's a lot younger than either of us. He's just a kid."

"That's no excuse."

"No, it's not, but you have to make a bit of an allowance," Will suggested.

"That's no good down here, Will, and you know it!" Chester blurted. Noticing that Cal had heard his outburst and turned to look at them curiously, Chester immediately dropped his voice. "There's no room for anyone to mess up. What, do you think we can ask the Styx for a second chance, like having another life in some stupid video game? Get real, will you?"

"He won't let us down," Will said.

"Are you willing to bet your life — your one life — on that?" Chester asked him.

Will just shook his head as they continued to plod along. He knew that there was nothing he could say to change his friend's opinion, and maybe Chester was right.

Away from the furnaces and the mounds of silt, they found the floor of the tunnel compacted, as if many feet had trodden it into a firm surface. Although they kept to the main tunnel, every so often smaller passages spun off from it. Some of these were high enough to stand in, but the majority were mere crawlways. The boys had no intention of leaving the main thoroughfare, and they eventually came to a place where the tunnel split.

"So, which way now?" Chester asked as he and Will neared Cal, who had come to a stop. The boy had spotted something lying at the base of the wall and went over to it, nudging it with his toe cap. It was a signpost of bleached, splintery wood with two "hands" affixed to the top of a broken-off stake, their fingerlike extensions pointing in opposite directions. Cal picked up the stake and held it so Will could read the barely legible writing carved into each.

"This says *Crevice Town*, which must be the tunnel to the right. This . . . ," he faltered, "I can't quite make it out . . . the end's been chewed off. . . . I think it says *The Great* something or other?"

"The Great Plain," Cal volunteered immediately.

Will and Chester regarded him with not a little surprise.

"Heard my Uncle Tam's friends talk about it once," he explained.

"Well, what else did you hear? And what's this town like? Is it a Coprolite place?" Will asked him.

"I don't know."

"Come on, should we go there?" Will pressed him.

"I really don't know anything more," Cal replied indifferently, letting the sign slide to the ground.

"Well, I like the sound of the town. Bet my dad would have gone there. What do you think, Chester, do we go that way?"

"Whatever," Chester answered, still staring distrustfully at Cal.

But as they ambled along, it became evident in only a few hours that the route they'd chosen wasn't a main thoroughfare like the tunnel they'd left behind. The floor was rougher and loosely packed, with large chunks of stone strewn across it, suggesting that it wasn't used very often. And, even worse, they were forced to climb over large falls of rock where the roof or walls had partially collapsed.

Just as they began to deliberate whether to turn back, they rounded a corner and their lights cut a swath through the darkness to reveal a structure barring their path. It was regular and clearly man-made.

"So there *is* something here after all," Will said with a gush of relief.

As they neared the obstruction, the tunnel ballooned into a larger cavity. Their lights revealed a tall, fencelike structure with two towers, each about thirty feet in height, which formed a gateway of sorts. Stretching high between the towers, a metal panel proclaimed **CREVICE TOWN** in crude cut-out letters.

Crunching on the cinders and gravel, they ventured cautiously forward. On either side, the tall fence ran uninterrupted, completely blocking the width of the cavern. There was nowhere else to go but under the open gateway. Nodding at one another, they crept through it.

"Looks like a ghost town," Chester said, observing the rows of huts arranged on either side of the central avenue where they were now walking. "There can't be anyone living here," he added hopefully.

If any of the boys had been nursing the illusion that the huts might be occupied, this was dispelled as soon as they saw the condition they were in. Many had simply collapsed in on themselves. Of those that were still standing, their doors were open or missing altogether, and every single window was broken.

"Just going to check inside this one," Will said. With Chester waiting nervously behind him, he negotiated his way through a pile of timber in the threshold, gripping the doorjamb to steady himself. The whole structure groaned and heaved ominously.

"Be careful, Will!" Chester warned, moving a safe distance back in case the hut came crashing down. "Looks a bit dodgy."

"Yeah," Will muttered, but he was not going to be deterred. He ventured farther inside and shone his light around as he threaded his way through the debris scattered across the floor.

"It's full of bunk beds," he reported back to the others.

"Bunk beds?" Cal echoed inquiringly from outside while Will continued to nose around the interior. There was a splintery crash as his foot went through the floor.

"Blast!" He extricated his foot, and began to carefully reverse out again. He'd seen enough, given the parlous condition of the floor. "Nothing here," he shouted, and returned outside.

They continued down the central avenue until Cal broke the silence.

"Can you smell that?" he asked Will suddenly. "It's sharp, like —"

"Ammonia. Yes," Will cut in. He played his light on the area in front of his feet. "It seems to be coming from . . . from the ground. It feels sort of damp," he observed, grinding the ball of his foot into the cavern floor and then squatting down. He took a pinch of the soil and held it under his nose. "Phew, it *is* this stuff. It stinks! Looks like dried bird droppings. Isn't it called *guano*?"

"Birds. That's OK," Chester said in a relieved voice, recalling the harmless flock they'd encountered in the Colony.

"No, not birds, this is different," Will immediately corrected himself. "And it's sort of fresh. It feels really squidgy."

"Oh crikey," Chester sputtered, looking frantically in all directions.

"Yuck! There are things in it," Will observed, adjusting his weight from one leg to the other as he remained squatting.

"What things?" Chester all but jumped into the air.

"Insects. See them?"

Shining their lights by their feet, Chester and Cal saw what Will was talking about. Beetles the size of well-fed cockroaches crawled ponderously over the slimy surface of the amassed droppings. They had creamy-white carapaces, and their similarly colored feelers twitched rhythmically as they went. Other, darker insects were around them, but these were harder to observe, apparently more sensitive to the light, since they scuttled rapidly away.

As the boys watched, just within their pooled circle of light a large beetle flapped open its carapace. Will chuckled with fascination as its wings hummed into life with the sound of a clockwork toy and it took to ungainly flight. Once in the air, it weaved erratically from side to side until it vanished from view, into the gloom.

"There's a complete ecosystem here," Will said, engrossed by the variety of insects he was finding. As he scratched around in the droppings, he uncovered a large, engorged, pale-colored grub as big as his thumb.

"Grab that. We might be able to eat it," Cal said.

"Ewwww!" quivered Chester, stamping his feet. "Don't be gross!"

"No, no, he's being serious," Will said flatly.

"Can we just get going again?" Chester begged.

Will reluctantly pulled himself away from the insects and they resumed their walk down the central avenue. They were at the last of the huts when Will beckoned them to a halt again.

"Feel that breeze? I think it's coming from up there," Will observed. "This whole area has some type of netting over it. Look at the holes."

They peered above the tops of the huts, where they could see a layer of mesh. Weighed down with debris, in some places it sagged so much it almost touched the roofs of the huts, while in others the mesh was absent altogether. They tried to shine their lights up through one of these openings, past the torn strands of the mesh and into the void high above. But the orbs weren't strong enough, and only revealed an ominous darkness.

"So could that be the crevice this place was named after?" Will pondered aloud.

"HEY!" Cal hollered at the top of his voice, making the other two start. Vague echoes of his shout reverberated across the void. "It's big," he said unnecessarily.

Then they heard a noise.

Gentle to begin with, similar to the sound when pages of a book are being fanned through, it was growing louder at an alarming rate.

Something was stirring, waking.

"More beetles?" Chester asked, hoping that was all it was.

"Uh, no, I don't think so," Will said, scanning the space above their heads. "That shout might not have been such a great idea, Cal."

Chester immediately turned on the younger boy. "What have you done now, you little jerk?" he said in an urgent whisper.

Cal made a face.

All of a sudden, from holes in the mesh up above the boys' heads, dark shapes dipped down, swooping at them. Their wingspans were huge and their screeches echoed off the walls like unearthly, high-pitched feedback, hitting the very limits of the boys' hearing.

"Bats!" Cal yelled, recognizing the sound right away. Chester howled in panic as he and Will remained rooted to the spot, mesmerized by the spectacle of the hurtling mammals.

"Run, you idiots!" Cal bawled at them, already taking to his heels.

Within seconds, the air was thick with the flying animals. They flicked past so quickly that Will couldn't keep track of any single one.

"This isn't good!" he exclaimed as leathery wings thrummed currents of dry air around their heads. The bats began to plunge at the boys, swerving aside just at the last moment.

Will and Chester raced down the avenue after Cal, not thinking, not caring, where they were going as long as they got away from the onslaught of airborne monsters. They were driven by a single thought, almost a primordial fear: to escape from these screeching, oversized beasts.

As if in answer to their plight, a house loomed out of the darkness ahead. At two stories high, its austere façade towered over the low huts. It appeared to be constructed of a light-colored stone, and all its windows were shuttered.

"Quick! Over here!" Cal cried as he spotted that the front door was slightly ajar.

In the midst of all this nightmarish confusion, Will glanced behind just in time to see a particularly large bat hurtle straight into the back of Chester's head. He heard the soft thud as it struck. The size of a soccer ball, its body was black and solid. The collision sent Chester sprawling. Will raced over to help his friend, while trying to protect his own face with his arm.

Shouting, he pulled Chester to his feet. And with the boy slightly dazed and running unsteadily, Will guided him toward the strange house. Will was lashing out in front of himself, trying to ward off the beasts, when one careened into his ruck-sack. He was knocked sideways but managed to keep his balance by hanging on to the still-befuddled Chester.

Will saw that the bat had dropped to the ground, one of its wings twisted and flapping uselessly. In an instant another bat was on it. A second one flicked down, alighting next to the first. Then yet more, until the injured animal was almost completely hidden from sight by clambering bats. As the felled creature struggled futilely to get away, trying to crawl from under the others, Will saw them snapping at it, their tiny pinlike teeth colored scarlet with its blood. They attacked mercilessly, nipping at its thorax and abdomen as it began to squeal in pain.

Ducking and stumbling with Chester beside him, Will continued along the remainder of the avenue. They staggered up the front steps of the house, under the porch, then through the door. Cal slammed it shut behind them. Several bangs followed as bats dashed against it, then others brushed their wings over its surface. This fracas soon died down, leaving only their strange piping calls.

The boys found they were in an imposing hallway replete with a large chandelier, its intricate design gray and furred with dust. A pair of elegantly curving staircases, which swept up to a landing, flanked this foyer. The place appeared to be empty; there was no furniture and just the odd tatter of curling wallpaper hung on the dark walls. It looked as though it had been uninhabited for years.

Will and Cal began to wade through the dust, which was nearly as thick as driven snow. Chester, still shaken, leaned over by the front door, panting heavily.

"Are you all right?" Will called back to him, the sound of his voice quiet and muffled in the strange house.

"I think so." Chester straightened up and stretched his head back, rubbing his neck to alleviate the soreness. "Feels like I was hit with a basketball." As he inclined his head forward again, he noticed something.

"Hey, Will, you should see this."

"What's up?"

"Looks like someone broke in here before us," Chester replied nervously.

9

THE SMALL FIRE pirouetted on the scraps of timber, filling the earthen chamber with flickering light. Sarah was rotating a makeshift spit over the flames, on which two small carcasses were skewered. The sight and smell of the gently browning meat made her realize how hungry she was. The cat must have felt the same way, if the necklaces of milky drool dangling from its muzzle were anything to go by.

"Good work," she said with a sidelong glance at the animal, which hadn't needed any encouragement to go out and forage food for both of them. In fact, it had seemed relieved to do what it was trained for. In the Colony, its role as a Hunter would have been to trap vermin, particularly eyeless rat, which was considered a rare delicacy.

In the light of the fire, Sarah had an opportunity to inspect the cat more thoroughly. Its bald skin, like an old, partially deflated balloon, was crisscrossed with lacerations and, around its neck, a number of these were a livid purple and had clearly been recently inflicted.

Across one of its shoulders was a nasty-looking gouge, flecked with spots of sickly yellow. The injury was bothering the cat, since it kept trying to clean the wound with its forepaw.

Sarah knew she'd have to attend to the injury before long — it was badly infected. That was, if she wanted the animal to live. But considering the possibility of some kind of link with her family, she felt she couldn't just desert it.

"So who did you actually belong to? Cal or my . . . my . . . *husband*?" she asked, finding it difficult to utter the word. She gently stroked the cat's cheek as it continued to stare fixedly at the roasting carcasses. It wasn't wearing a collar with any form of identification, but this didn't surprise her. It wasn't common practice in the Colony, as Hunters were expected to move through narrow passages and crawlways, and a collar might catch on rocks and hinder the animal in the chase.

Sarah coughed and rubbed her eyes. It wasn't an entirely satisfactory arrangement to have a fire burning underground; the kindling, which was too damp to begin with, had to be kept aloft from the pools of water on the chamber floor by a platform she'd fashioned from a pile of rocks. And, since there was nowhere for the smoke to go, it was filling the chamber so thickly that her eyes kept weeping.

Above all else, she hoped that they were far enough away from anybody that the smell of cooking wouldn't be detected. She consulted her watch. It was nearly twenty-four hours since the incident, and any searches, particularly using dogs, would be unlikely to extend as far as the wasteland above. The police would be concentrating their efforts on the immediate area of the crime scene and on the Common itself.

No, she didn't think it at all likely that she would be discovered here — in any case, none of the police would have the finely developed sense of smell that most Colonists possessed.

It occurred to her how remarkably safe she felt down here in the excavation — and being underground again probably played no small part in this. The earthen hollow was a home away from home.

She took up her knife and dug the tip into each carcass.

"Right, dinner's ready," she announced to the cat at her side. It was rapidly switching its expectant gaze from her to the food and back again, with all the regularity of a metronome. She slipped the first carcass, the pigeon, from the spit and onto a folded newspaper in her lap.

"Careful. Hot," she warned, dangling the still-impaled squirrel in front of the cat. But she was wasting her breath: The cat lunged forward, snapping its jaws around the carcass and snatching it off. It immediately scurried away into a dark corner where she could hear it eating noisily, all the time purring furiously.

She juggled the pigeon from one hand to the other, blowing on it as if it were a hot potato. When it had cooled sufficiently, she quickly started on one of the wings, nipping at the meat with her teeth. As she moved on to the breast, tearing off slivers and devouring them appreciatively, she began to assess her situation.

Her cardinal rule for survival was never to stay put for any longer than she had to, particularly when the heat was on. Although her face was a mess from the fight with the policemen, she'd cleaned off the blood and done her best to mask the worst of the bruises. She'd used her makeup kit for this, something she carried with her wherever she went, since her lack of pigmentation, her albinism, forced her to use a blend of sunscreen and foundation cream to protect herself from the sun. So she felt confident that her appearance wouldn't attract attention if she decided to set foot outside the dugout.

Sucking thoughtfully on a tiny bone, she remembered the papers she'd taken from the doormat in the Burrowses' house. She wiped the grease from her hands with a handkerchief and pulled out the clutch of letters from her bag. There were the usual fliers for plumbing services and freelance house painters, which she examined one by one under the light from the dying fire before she fed them to the flames. Then she came across something that looked far more interesting, a manila envelope with a badly typed label. It was to the attention of *Mrs. C. Burrows,* and the return address was the local social services agency.

Sarah wasted no time tearing it open. As she read it, somewhere in the shadows there was a sharp snapping noise: The cat cracked open the squirrel's skull between its jaws, then licked greedily at the animal's exposed brain with its rasping tongue.

Sarah looked up from the letter. Suddenly her path had become clear.

10

WILL AND CAL waded back through the dust to the front door and directed their lights where Chester was pointing. He was right — the edge of the door had been broken off, and not so long ago, if the lighter-colored wood that had been exposed was anything to go by.

"Looks new to me," Chester noted.

"We didn't do that, did we?" Will asked Cal, who shook his head. "Then we should give this place the once-over, just to make sure," he said.

Keeping together, they moved down the hallway until they reached a pair of large doors, which they flung open. The dust rose up in waves ahead of them, like a visual premonition of their every move. But even before it had begun to settle, they were taking in the size of the room and its impressive features. The depth of the skirting and the elaborate ceiling moldings — an intricate lattice of plasterwork interlacing above them — hinted at its former grandeur. It could have been a ballroom or a formal dining room, given its dimensions and position in the house. As they stood around in the middle of the room, they couldn't help but chuckle because the whole scenario was so unexpected and inexplicable.

Will sneezed several times, irritated by the dust. "I'll tell you something," he said, sniffing and wiping his nose.

"What?" Chester asked.

"This place is a disgrace. It's even worse than my bedroom back home."

"Yep, the maid definitely missed this room!" Chester laughed. As he made the motions of pushing a vacuum cleaner around the floor, he and Will completely cracked up, howling with laughter.

Shaking his head, Cal gave them a look as if they'd taken leave of their senses. The boys resumed their exploration, padding gently through the dust and checking the adjoining rooms. They were mostly small utility rooms, all similarly bare, so they retraced their steps to the hallway, where Will pushed open a door at the foot of one of the staircases.

"Hey! Books!" he said. "It's a library!"

Except for two large windows that had their shutters closed, the walls were covered with shelf upon shelf of books, all the way up to the high ceiling. The room was some one hundred feet square, and toward its farthest end was a table, around which a couple of chairs lay toppled over.

All three of them spotted the footprints at the same time: They were difficult to miss in the otherwise perfect carpet of dust. Cal placed his boot inside one, measuring it for size. There were a couple of inches between his toes and the front of the imprint. He and Will caught each other's eye, and Will nodded at him, then began to peer nervously into the shadowy corners of the room.

"The tracks go over there," Chester whispered. "To the table."

The footprints led from the door where the boys now stood, over to the shelves, and then circled around the table several times, disappearing into a jumbled confusion behind it.

"Whoever it was," Cal observed, "they went back out again." He was stooping to examine another, less obvious set of tracks that went past a wall of shelves, then meandered back toward the door.

Will had stepped farther into the room and was holding up his light to inspect the corners. "Yeah, it's empty," he confirmed as the others joined him by the long table.

They fell silent, listening to the occasional fluttering and high-pitched call from the bats on the other side of the shutters.

"I'm not going back out there, not until those bloodsucking beasties have gone away again," Chester said as he leaned against the table. His shoulders sagged as he blew wearily through his lips.

"Yes, I think we should stop here for a while," Will agreed, heaving off his rucksack and placing it on the table next to Chester.

"So are we going to check out the rest of the house or not?" Cal pressed Will.

"Don't know about you two, but I need something to eat first," Chester cut in.

Will noticed how, quite suddenly, Chester's speech had become slurred. All the walking they'd done, and the attack of the bats, had obviously taken it out of him. Will reminded himself that his friend was probably still suffering from the aftereffects of the rough treatment he'd received in the Hold.

Making his way toward the door, Will turned to Chester. "Why don't you keep an eye on things here while Cal and I . . . ," he said, trailing off as the books on the shelves caught his eye. "These bindings are awesome," he said, scanning his light over them. "They're pretty old."

"Really," Chester said disinterestedly. He undid the flap on Will's pack and fished out an apple.

"Yeah. This one's interesting. It's called *The Rise and Progress of Religion in the Soul* by . . . " He wiped away the dust and then leaned in to peer at the rest of the gilt lettering on the dark leather spine. "By Reverend Philip Doddridge."

"Sounds gripping," Chester commented through a mouthful of apple.

Will gently slid the book out from between the other grand-looking tomes and flipped it open. Fragments of the pages spewed up into his face, the rest of the paper reduced to a powdery residue that seeped onto the floor by his feet.

"Blast!" he said, holding up the empty book cover with an expression of pure disappointment on his face. "What a shame. Must be the heat."

"Looking forward to a good read, were you?" Chester chuckled as he lobbed the apple core over his shoulder and then began to root around in the rucksack for more food.

"Ha-ha. Very funny," Will retorted.

"Let's just get on with it, shall we?" Cal said impatiently.

Will ventured upstairs with his brother to check that the rest of the house was indeed unoccupied. Among all the empty rooms, Cal came across a small washroom. This consisted of a limescale-encrusted tap protruding from the tiled wall over an old copper bowl set into a wooden shelf. He pushed back the lever at the top of the tap. There was a faint hiss of air and then, after several seconds, an almighty knocking sound that seemed to come from the walls themselves.

As the racket continued, transforming into a low, whining vibration, Will bounded out of the room he'd been investigating and down the long corridor that led back to the landing. He paused to look over the splintered balustrade to the hall below, then dashed into the corridor where Cal had gone. Calling his brother's name, he stuck his head through each doorway until he found him.

"What's going on? What have you done?" Will demanded.

Cal didn't answer. He was staring fixedly at the tap. As Will watched, a dark molasseslike fluid oozed from it, and then the whining noise ceased altogether. Nothing happened at first; then clear water flowed from the spout with a huge gush, much to the boys' delight.

"Do you think it's safe to drink?" Will asked.

Cal shoved his mouth under the flow to sample it.

"Ahhh, beautiful. Nothing wrong with that! Must be from a spring."

"Well, at least we've solved our water problem," Will congratulated him.

Having gorged himself on food, Chester slept for several hours atop the library table. When he finally awoke and learned of the washroom discovery from Will, he slipped out to have a look for himself and didn't reappear for some time.

When he finally did come back, the skin on his face and neck was red and blotchy where he'd evidently aggravated his eczema in an attempt to scrub .off the ingrained dirt, and his hair was wet and slicked back. The way he looked now, in his cleaned-up state, reminded Will of how they'd once been. It brought back memories of less troubled times before they stumbled upon the Colony, of their life back in Highfield.

"That's better," Chester mumbled self-consciously, avoiding the others' gazes. Cal, who had been taking a nap on the floor, propped himself up and, still not fully awake, regarded Chester with a kind of bleary amusement.

"Why'd you do that?" he asked wryly.

"Smelled yourself lately?" Chester fired back at him.

"No."

"I have," Chester said, wrinkling his nose. "And it's not very pleasant!"

"Well, I think washing up's a great idea," Will instantly spoke out to spare Chester any further embarrassment, but Cal's comments seemed not to bother him in the slightest. Chester was totally preoccupied by something on the end of his pinkie finger, which he'd just been using to pick away energetically at his ear.

"And I'm going to do just the same," Will proclaimed as Chester started on his other ear, ramming a finger repeatedly into it.

Will rummaged around in his rucksack for some clean clothes, then took a second to examine his shoulder, wondering whether it was time to change the dressing on the wound. Through the rends in his shirt, he gingerly probed the area around the bandage, then decided he needed to remove the shirt altogether in order to see what state it was in.

"Will, what happened to you?" Chester said, forgetting his ear for the moment and turning quite pale. He'd caught sight of the large patch of dark crimson showing through the bandage on Will's shoulder.

"From the stalker attack," Will told him. He bit his lip, then groaned as he lifted the dressing to look underneath. "Yuck!" he exclaimed. "I definitely could do with a new poultice." He turned to his pack and hunted through the side pockets for the spare bandage and the small parcels of powder that Imago had given him.

"I didn't realize it had been that bad," Chester said. "Want any help?"

"No, really . . . feels better now, anyway," Will replied, lying through his teeth.

"OK," Chester said, his face still displaying his squeamishness as he tried to smile but only managed a grimace.

And, despite his initial reaction at Chester's efforts to clean himself up, Cal, too, took the opportunity to slip out of the room and wash himself in the tepid water once Will had returned.

The hours seemed to pass more slowly within the house, as if it was somehow isolated from everything outside. And the absolute hush that pervaded the interior gave the impression that it was itself asleep. This stillness affected the three boys;

they made not the least effort to talk and instead took catnaps on the long library table, using the backpacks as pillows.

But eventually Will began to feel restless and found that he couldn't sleep. To pass the time, he resumed his investigation of the library, wondering who had lived in the house. He went from shelf to shelf, reading the titles on the ancient hand-tooled spines, which mostly had esoteric religious themes and must have been written centuries ago. It was an exercise in frustration, because he knew all the pages inside would be nothing more than confetti and dust. Nevertheless, he was fascinated by the obscure names of the authors and the ludicrously long titles. It had almost developed into a contest to try to find a book he'd actually heard of when he came across something curious.

On a lower shelf, a set of matching books appeared to have no titles at all. After wiping off the grime, Will could see they had covers of deep burgundy, and that the tiniest gilt stars were picked out at three equidistant points on each of their spines.

He tried to take out one of the volumes, but unlike the other books, which had disappointed him with the usual avalanche of silt from their disintegrated pages, this one resisted, as if it was somehow stuck in place. Even more strange, the book itself felt solid. He tried again but it wouldn't move, so instead he selected another in the series and attempted to lever that one out, with the same result. But he noticed that the entire series, which occupied about a foot and a half of the shelf, had shifted ever so slightly as he'd applied more force. He felt a flush of elation that, at last, he'd found something he might be able to actually read and, puzzled as to why the books seemed to be glued together, used both hands to pull at them.

They slid out all in one block, all the volumes together, and Will placed them on the floor by his feet. They felt heavy, and the pages even appeared to be intact. But he couldn't pry away any of the individual books. He felt the tops of the pages, picking at them with a fingernail to see if they would part. Then he rapped a knuckle against them. They gave a hollow sound — and it dawned on Will that the books weren't made of paper, but of wood, carved very precisely to resemble the roughly cut leaves of old volumes. He felt around the back and found a catch, which he pushed open. With a creak, the top flipped up. It was a lid with an invisible hinge. These weren't books at all. This was a box.

With a rush of excitement, he hastily plucked out the layer of tattered cloth he found inside and peered in. The dark oak interior contained odd-looking objects. He lifted one out.

It was obviously a lamp. It had a cylindrical body, approximately five inches in length, to which was attached a circular housing with a thick glass lens inside. At the rear of the cylinder was some form of sprung arm, and there was also a switch of sorts behind the lens.

It was highly reminiscent of a bicycle light, but it was sturdily made — from brass, Will guessed, given the green patches that he observed on its surfaces. He tried the lever, to no avail, and pulled at one end of the cylinder where there were two slight indentations. With a pop, the end came off, revealing a small cavity inside. If it was indeed a light, then it would need batteries, but even so, Will couldn't work out how such a small battery could power it, or where the wires were.

Stumped, he called over to his brother. "Hey, Cal! Don't suppose you know what this is? Probably just a piece of junk."

Cal ambled groggily over, but his face lit up as soon as he saw the object. He snatched it from Will's hands.

"Hey, these are brilliant!" he said. "Got a spare orb on you?"

"Here," Chester offered, swinging his legs over the edge of the table and climbing off.

"Thanks," Cal said, taking the orb. First he removed all the dust from the device, turning it upside down and tapping it, then blowing inside.

"Watch this."

He dropped the orb into the cavity and pushed down until it clicked.

"Pass me the top."

Will handed it to him and Cal pushed the end of the cylinder back on. Then he rubbed the lens on his pants to clean it.

"You move this lever," he told Chester and Will, "to adjust the aperture and focus the rays." He held it so they could see as he tried to move what appeared to be a lever behind the lens housing. "It's a little stiff," he said, applying as much pressure as he could with both his thumbs. Then, as the small lever gave, he grinned. "Got it!"

Light leaped from the lens, an intense beam that Cal played around the walls. Although the room was already quite well illuminated from the light orbs they'd placed at various points on the bookshelves, they could see how bright the lantern's beam was in comparison.

"That's awesome," Chester said.

"Yep. They're called Styx Lanterns — pretty rare, really. This is the best thing about them," Cal said, and, pulling open the spring-loaded flap of brass at the back of the light, slotted it over his shirt pocket. He took his hands away and moved his chest from Will to Chester, the lantern clamped firmly in place as its beam flashed in their faces.

"Hands free," Will observed, blinking.

"Absolutely. Very useful when you're on the move." Cal leaned over to look at the contents of the box. "More of them! I can rig up one for each for us."

"Cool," Chester said.

"So . . . ," Will began as the thought occurred to him, "so this house — all the way down here — was for the Styx!"

"Yes," Cal answered. "I thought you knew that!" He made a face, as if it had been blindingly obvious all along. "They would have lived here. And Coprolites would have been kept in the huts outside."

Will and Chester exchanged glances.

"Kept? What for?" Will asked.

"As slaves. For a couple of centuries they were made to mine stuff the Colony needed. It's different now — they do it in exchange for food and the light orbs they need to live. The Styx don't force them to work like they used to."

"That's nice of them," Will said drily.

11

MRS. BURROWS was in the dayroom of Humphrey House, an establishment that purported to be a haven of recuperation, or "a respite from your day-to-day worries and strife," if you believed the brochure. The dayroom was her domain. She had commandeered the largest, most comfortable chair and the only footstool in the place, and, to sustain her for the afternoon's television viewing, had stuffed a bag of hard candy down the side of the chair. One of the orderlies in the home had been persuaded to pick these up for her on a regular basis from the town, but they were rarely shared with any of the other patients.

As *Oprah* came to an end, she flicked through the other channels in a frantic haste. She ran through them all several times, only to find there was nothing on that remotely interested her. Thoroughly frustrated, she stabbed at the mute button to silence the television and leaned her head back against the chair. She missed her extensive video library of films and favorite shows much as a normal person might mourn the loss of a limb.

She sighed a long and forlorn sigh and the irritation receded, leaving in its place a vague sense of helplessness. She was humming the theme from *Murder, She Wrote* in a mournful and desperate way when the door thumped open.

"Here we go again," Mrs. Burrows muttered under her breath as the matron breezed into the room.

"What, dear?" inquired the matron, a rake-thin woman with her gray hair tightly pulled back into a bun.

"Oh, nothing," Mrs. Burrows replied innocently.

"There's someone here to see you." The matron had made a beeline for the windows and now heaved back the curtains to flood the room with daylight.

"Visitors? For me?" Mrs. Burrows said unenthusiastically as she shielded her eyes from the glare. Without leaving the chair, she attempted to get her feet into her slippers, a tawdry pair of stained, fake suede moccasins with the backs trodden

down. "Hardly likely to be family — not that there are many of them left, not now," she said, a little soulfully. "And I don't imagine Jean has stirred her stumps to bring my daughter all the way here. . . . Haven't heard a squeak from either of them since before the New Year."

"It's not family —" the matron tried to tell her, but Mrs. Burrows carried on regardless.

"And as for my other sister, Bessie, well, we're not on speaking terms. . . ."

"It's not *family*, it's a lady from social services," the matron managed to make herself heard, before opening one of the casement windows with incantations of "That's better."

Mrs. Burrows gave no reaction to this piece of news. The matron rearranged the flowers in a vase on the window ledge and gathered up some fallen petals before turning to her. "And how are we today?"

"Oh, not so good," Mrs. Burrows answered, laying it on thick with a whining, despondent tone and finishing her sentence with a small groan.

"I'm not surprised. It's not healthy being cooped up indoors all day — you ought to get some fresh air. Why don't you go for a walk on the grounds after you've seen your visitor?"

The matron stopped and swiveled back to the window, scanning the garden beyond as if she was looking for something. Mrs. Burrows immediately took notice, her curiosity piqued. The matron spent her every waking hour tirelessly organizing people or things, as if her calling in life was to impose some sort of order over an imperfect world. A human dynamo, she did not stop — in fact, she was the complete antithesis to Mrs.

Burrows, who had put the struggle with the last mutinous slipper on hold for the moment to watch the matron's atypical inactivity.

"Is something the matter?" Mrs. Burrows asked, not able to keep silent any longer.

"Oh, it's nothing really . . . just that Mrs. Perkiss swears she saw that man again. Quite beside herself, she was."

"Ah." Mrs. Burrows nodded knowingly. "And when was this?"

"This morning, first thing." The matron turned back into the room. "Can't figure it out myself. She seemed to be getting on so well, and, all of a sudden, these strange episodes started." Frowning, she looked at Mrs. Burrows. "Your room is directly under hers — you haven't spotted anyone out there, have you?"

"No, and I'm not likely to."

"Why's that?" the matron asked her.

"Bit bloomin' obvious, isn't it?" Mrs. Burrows replied bluntly, finally succeeding in ramming her foot home into her slipper. "It's the person we all fear, deep down . . . the final curtain . . . the big sleep . . . whatever you want to call it. That Perkiss woman has had the sword of Damocles hanging over her for a long time . . . poor cow."

"You mean . . . ," the matron began, as she caught on to what Mrs. Burrows was suggesting. She gave Mrs. Burrows a gentle "pah" just to emphasize what she thought of her theory.

Mrs. Burrows wasn't deterred in the slightest by the matron's reaction. "Mark my words, that'll be it," she said with total conviction, her eyes drifting back to the silent television screen as it occurred to her that *Millionaire* could be about to start any moment now.

The matron exhaled skeptically.

"Since when has *death* been a man in a black hat?" she said, and reassumed her usual businesslike manner, glancing at her watch. "Is that the time? I must be getting on." She fixed Mrs. Burrows with a stern glance. "Don't keep your visitor waiting, and then I want you to go for that brisk walk on the grounds."

"Of course," Mrs. Burrows agreed, nodding vigorously, but inwardly finding the whole suggestion of exercise quite distasteful. She hadn't the slightest intention of taking a "brisk walk," but would make a big show of getting ready to go out, then merely promenade once around the house before ducking into the kitchen to lie low for a while. If she was lucky, she might even get a cup of tea and some shortbread biscuits out of the cook.

"Tickety-boo," the matron said, checking the room for anything else that wasn't in its place.

Mrs. Burrows smiled sweetly at her. She'd learned very soon after arriving that if she played along with the matron and her staff, she could get her own way, well, most of the time, anyway, particularly since she wasn't much trouble in comparison with many of the other inpatients.

These were a mixed bunch, and Mrs. Burrows viewed them all with equal disdain. Humphrey House had its fair share of "Snifflers," as she called them. There was a barrel-load of these miseries who, if left to their own devices, positioned themselves all over the place like lost, lonely waifs, usually in corners where they could mope away the hours uninterrupted. But Mrs. Burrows had also witnessed the quite startling change that this breed could go through, more often than not in the evenings. Without warning, they would undergo some form of transformation after "lights out," like a caterpillar wrapping itself in a duvet cocoon only to emerge as a completely different creature, a "Screamer," in the small hours of the morning.

Then this normally nonviolent breed would howl and wail and break things in their rooms until members of the staff came to placate them or administer a pill or two. And, usually, they'd miraculously metamorphose back into Snifflers again by sunup.

Then there were the "Zombies," who shuffled around as if they were clueless extras on a film set, not knowing what they were supposed to be doing or where they were meant to be going, and certainly never remembering their lines (they were mostly incapable of any rational exchange). Mrs. Burrows largely ignored them while they stumbled around the place on their random, senseless paths.

But the very worst for her had to be the "Bagmen," horrible specimens of middle-aged, male professionals who had burned out from their overpressured careers in accountancy or banking or, as far as Mrs. Burrows was concerned, similarly inconsequential occupations.

She loathed these pinstripe casualties with a passion — sometimes, she thought, because their mannerisms and blank expressions reminded her so much of her husband, Roger Burrows. She'd seen the little danger signs that he was going that way just before he had upped and offed, disappearing who knows where.

For Mrs. Burrows hated her husband with a passion.

Even in the first years of their marriage, things hadn't gone smoothly. Their inability to have children together had soon cast a pall over the relationship. And all the rigamarole associated with adopting meant she couldn't concentrate on her own job and she'd been forced to pack it in: Another dream stymied. After they had been successful in their applications to adopt two young children, a boy and a girl, she had struggled to give them everything she'd had in her own childhood, all the trappings, such as nice clothes and mixing with the right people.

But it was impossible; after years of trying to make her family something it could never be — not on Dr. Burrows's fleabite salary — she gave up. Mrs. Burrows had closed her eyes to her surroundings and her situation, seeking solace in the worlds on the other side of the television screen. In this blinkered, unreal state, she'd abdicated motherhood, handing the responsibility of the house, the washing, the cooking, everything, to her daughter, Rebecca, who took it all on with surprising ease, considering she had been only seven years old at the time.

And Mrs. Burrows felt no remorse or guilt about doing this, because her husband hadn't upheld his part of the bargain when they had first married. And then, to cap it all off, Dr. Burrows, the chronic loser, had had the gall to walk out on her, taking away what little she did have.

He had ruined her ruined life.

She loathed him for this. And all this loathing fermented away inside her, never far below the surface.

"Your visitor," the matron prompted her again.

Nodding, Mrs. Burrows tore her eyes from the television and rose wearily from her chair. She shuffled out of the room, leaving the matron rearranging some boxes of puzzles on the sideboard. Mrs. Burrows didn't want to see anyone, least of all a social worker who might bring unwanted reminders of her family and the life she'd left behind her.

In no hurry to reach her destination, she slid her slippers lethargically over the highly buffed linoleum as she passed "Old Mrs. L," who, at twenty-six, was ten years Mrs. Burrows's junior, but had shockingly little hair. She was in her habitual pose, fast asleep in a corridor chair. Her mouth was open so wide that it looked as though someone had tried to saw her head in two, her prominent larynx and tonsils displayed in their full glory for all to see.

The woman let go an almighty rush of air from her gaping mouth, with a sound somewhat akin to air escaping from a slashed truck tire. "Disgraceful!" Mrs. Burrows declared, continuing down the corridor. She came to a door with a crude plastic label in black and white proclaiming it to be the Happy Room and pushed it open.

The room was at the corner of the building and had windows on two of its walls that looked out onto the rose garden. Some bright spark on the staff had come up with the idea of encouraging patients to paint murals on the other two walls, although the final result hadn't been quite as anticipated.

A five-foot-wide rainbow composed of brown strands of varying hues arched over a strange assortment of human-oid figures. One end of the rainbow curved down into the sea, where a grinning man stood on a surfboard, his arms outstretched in some form of clownish greeting, as a large shark's fin cut a circle through the water around him. In the sky above the dun rainbow, seagulls wheeled, painted in the same naïve style as the other pictures. They had a certain charm to them, until one noticed the droppings shooting from their rear ends in broken lines, much as a child might draw gunfire in a battle scene, which strafed the heads of a group of figures with bloated human bodies and the heads of mice.

Mrs. Burrows didn't feel at ease in the room, as if the fractured, mysterious images were trying to communicate hidden messages. For the life of her, she couldn't imagine why it was used to receive guests.

She turned her attention to her unwanted visitor, staring disdainfully at the woman in nondescript clothes, who had a folder on her knees. The woman immediately got to her feet and looked at Mrs. Burrows with her very pale eyes.

"I'm Kate O'Leary," Sarah said.

"I can see that," Mrs. Burrows said, looking at the visitor's badge clipped to Sarah's sweater.

"Pleased to meet you, Mrs. Burrows," Sarah continued, unperturbed, forcing a perfunctory smile as she offered her hand.

Mrs. Burrows murmured a hello but made no move to shake it.

"Let's sit down," Sarah said as she took her seat again. Mrs. Burrows looked around at the plastic chairs and intentionally didn't pick the one closest to Sarah, but chose another by the door, as if she expected she might want to make a quick exit.

"Who are you?" Mrs. Burrows asked bluntly, sliding her eyes over Sarah. "I don't know you."

"No, I'm from social services," Sarah answered, briefly holding up the letter she had retrieved from the doormat in the Burrowses' house. Mrs. Burrows craned her neck to try to read it. "We wrote to you on the fifteenth about this meeting," Sarah said as she quickly put the creased letter on top of the folder on her lap.

"Nobody told me anything about a meeting. Let me see that," Mrs. Burrows demanded as she went to get up, one hand extended toward the letter.

"No . . . no, it doesn't matter now. I expect the manager here forgot to inform you, and it won't take long, anyway. I just wanted to make sure everything's OK for you and —"

"Not about the fees, is it?" Mrs. Burrows cut in as she settled back in her chair, crossing her legs. "As far as I know, the health insurance pays a top-up on the government's contribution and when the insurance runs out, the money from the house sale will cover me."

"I'm sure that's right, but it's not my department, I'm afraid," Sarah said with another transient smile. She opened the folder on her knees, took out a pad of paper, and was just slipping the cap off her pen when she caught sight of the painting of a coffee-colored teddy bear on the wall a little way above Mrs. Burrows. Around the bear were carefully painted dice, all in bright colors such as red, orange, and royal blue, and all showing different numbers. Sarah shook her head and turned her attention to Mrs. Burrows again, her pen poised above a clean sheet of paper.

"So tell me, when were you admitted here, Celia? Do you mind if I call you Celia?"

"Sure, anything. It was November last year."

"And how have you been getting on?" Sarah asked, pretending to take notes.

"Very well, thank you," Mrs. Burrows said, and then added somewhat defensively, "but I've still got some way to go after my . . . er . . . trauma . . . and I'm going to need much more time here. More rest."

"Yes," Sarah agreed noncommittally. "And your family? Any news of them?"

"No, none at all. The police say they're still investigating the disappearances, but they're hopeless."

"The police?"

Mrs. Burrows answered in a forlorn monotone. "They even had the gall to come to see me yesterday. You probably heard what happened a couple of days ago . . . the incident at my house?" She flicked her eyes lethargically at Sarah.

"Yes, I read something about it," Sarah said. "Nasty business."

"Certainly was. Two policemen on the beat surprised a gang outside my house and there was one heck of a fight. Both officers got a bad hiding, and one of them even had a dog set on him." She coughed, then tugged a grimy handkerchief from where it was tucked inside her sleeve. "I suppose it was those horrid squatters. They're worse than animals!" Mrs. Burrows pronounced.

If only she knew, Sarah thought. She nodded her head to show she was in total agreement with Mrs. Burrows, the image of the policeman lying senseless on the patio after she'd knocked him out cold flashing through her mind.

Mrs. Burrows blew her nose at great volume and tucked the handkerchief back into her sleeve. "I really don't know what this country's coming to. Anyway, they picked the wrong place this time. Nothing left there to steal . . . it's all in storage while the property's being sold."

Sarah nodded her head again as Mrs. Burrows went on.

"But the police aren't much better. They just won't leave me be. My counselor tries to stop them from coming, but they insist on interviewing me, time and time again. They act as if I'm to blame for everything . . . my family's disappearances . . . even the attack on the policemen . . . I ask you, as if I could've had anything to do with that — I'm here under twenty-four-hour watch, for heaven's sake!" She uncrossed her legs and shifted in her chair before crossing them again. "Talk about getting some rest! This is all very unsettling for me, you know."

"Yes, yes, I can quite understand that," Sarah agreed quickly. "You've been through enough already."

Mrs. Burrows gave a small nod and lifted her head to gaze through the windows.

"But the police haven't given up looking for your husband and son?" Sarah inquired softly. "Hasn't there been any news about them at all?"

"No, nobody seems to have the faintest idea where they've gone. I'm sure you're aware my husband walked out, then my son vanished from the face of the earth," she said desolately. "There've been various sightings of him — a couple right back in Highfield. There was even some security-camera footage from the tube station of someone who looked vaguely like Will, with another boy . . . and a large dog."

"A large dog?" Sarah put in.

"Yes, an Alsatian or something like that." Mrs. Burrows shook her head. "But the police say they can't verify any of it." She sighed self-indulgently. "And my daughter, Rebecca, is at my sister's, but I haven't had a squeak from her for months." Mrs. Burrows's voice fell to a whisper, her face blank and unreadable. "Everyone I know goes away. . . . Maybe they all found better places to be."

"I can only say how truly sorry I am," Sarah responded in a gentle, consolatory voice. "Your son — do you think he went off to search for your husband? I read that the investigating officer considered it a possibility?"

"I wouldn't put it past Will," Mrs. Burrows said, still gazing outside, where someone had made a halfhearted effort to tie some unhealthy-looking climbing roses to the cheap plastic pergola not far from the window. "I wouldn't be surprised at all."

"So you haven't seen anything of your son since . . . when was it . . . November?"

"No, it was before then, and no, I haven't," Mrs. Burrows exhaled.

"What was he . . . what state of mind was he in, before he left?"

"I really can't tell you — I wasn't too good myself at the time, and I didn't . . . ." Mrs. Burrows stopped herself in mid-sentence and switched her gaze from the rose garden to Sarah. "Look, you must have read my case file, why are you asking me all this?" All of a sudden, her whole manner transformed, as if a spark had been ignited. Her voice reverted to its usual rather impatient and snappy tone. She pulled herself up in her chair, squaring her shoulders as she regarded Sarah with a fierce intensity.

The change wasn't lost on Sarah, who immediately broke off eye contact, pretending instead to consult the meaningless notes she'd made on the pad of paper. Sarah waited a few seconds before she resumed, her voice as level and calm as she could make it.

"It's quite simple, really. I'm new to your case and it's very helpful to have some background information. I'm sorry if this is painful for you."

Sarah could feel Mrs. Burrows's eyes boring into her as they analyzed her like twin X-ray beams. Sarah slowly sat back. Her outward appearance was relaxed, but inwardly she braced herself, ready for an onslaught.

"O'Leary . . . Irish, hmmm? You don't have much of an accent."

"No, my family moved to London in the sixties. But I go back for the odd holiday to —"

Mrs. Burrows, her face animated and her eyes sparkling, didn't let her finish.

"That's not your natural hair color; your roots are showing," she observed. "They look white. You dye your hair, don't you?"

"Uh . . . I do, yes. Why?"

"And is there something wrong with your eye — is that a bruise? Also your lip — it looks a bit puffy. Someone take a pop at you?"

"No, I tripped down some stairs," Sarah replied tersely, injecting equal measures of indignation and exasperation to make her reaction sound credible.

"That old chestnut! If I'm not mistaken, you're wearing heavy makeup over what I would say is a very pale complexion?"

"Um . . . I suppose," Sarah flustered. She was staggered by Mrs. Burrows's powers of observation. Sarah's disguise was being slowly but surely dismantled, like petals being torn from a flower one by one to reveal what lay within.

She was just wondering how she could deflect Mrs. Burrows's interrogation, which showed no sign of abating, when she caught sight of a clump of balloons painted on the wall just above the other woman's left shoulder. A swipe of blue sky was washed over the balloons, almost completely obscuring and swallowing them up, turning their vibrant colors into dullness. Sarah took a shallow breath and cleared her throat, then said, "I need to ask you just a few more questions, Celia." She coughed to mask her unease. "I do think you are getting a little . . . um . . . personal. . . ."

"A little personal?" Mrs. Burrows laughed drily. "Don't you think all your idiot questions are *a little personal*?"

"I need . . ."

"You have a very distinctive face, Kate, however hard you try to disguise it. Come to think of it, you have a very *familiar* face. Where might I have seen you before?" Mrs. Burrows frowned and inclined her head, as if trying to remember. There was more than a little of the theatrical about her — she was enjoying herself.

"This doesn't have anything to do with —"

"Who are you, Kate?" Mrs. Burrows cut her off sharply. "No way are you from social services. I know the type, and you're not it. So who *exactly* are you?"

"I think perhaps that's enough for now. I should go." Sarah had made up her mind to call a halt to the meeting and was gathering her papers and replacing them in the folder. She'd hastily gotten to her feet and was retrieving her coat from the back of the chair when Mrs. Burrows sprang up with surprising speed and stood before the door, barring Sarah's way.

"Not so fast!" Mrs. Burrows exclaimed. "*I* have some questions for *you* first."

"I can see I've made a mistake coming here, Mrs. Burrows," Sarah said decisively as she put her coat over her arm. She took a step toward Mrs. Burrows, who didn't budge an inch, and so they stood, face-to-face, like two prizefighters sizing each other up. Sarah was beginning to tire of the pretense — and Mrs. Burrows clearly didn't know anything more than she did about Will's whereabouts. Or if she did, she wasn't telling.

"We can finish this another time," Sarah told her, flashing a sour smile and turning sideways as if she meant to squeeze between Mrs. Burrows and the wall.

"Stop right where you are," Mrs. Burrows ordered. "You must think I'm gaga. You come here with your shabby clothes and your second-rate performance and expect me to swallow it?" Her eyes, narrowing to two vicious slits, flashed with the satisfaction of *knowing*.

"Did you really think I wouldn't figure out who you are? You have Will's face, and no amount of hair dye or stupid playacting"— she swatted the folder in Sarah's arms with the back of her hand —"is going to hide that." She nodded slyly. "You're his *mother*, aren't you?"

"I don't know what you're talking about," Sarah answered as coolly as she could.

"Will's biological mother."

"That's absurd. I . . ."

"What hole did you crawl out of?" Mrs. Burrows sneered sarcastically.

Sarah shook her head.

"Why did it take so long for you to come back? And why now?" Mrs. Burrows continued.

Sarah didn't say anything, staring daggers at the red-faced woman.

"You abandoned your child. . . . You gave him up for adoption. . . . What gives you the right to come sniffing around here?" Mrs. Burrows demanded.

Sarah let out a sharp breath. She could knock this rather flabby, lazy woman out of her way with so little effort, but chose to do nothing. They stood there, under a pounding silence, one Will's adoptive mother and the other his birth mother, inexorably linked and both instinctively knowing who the other was.

Mrs. Burrows broke the silence. "I take it that you're looking for him, or you wouldn't have shown up here," she simmered. She raised her eyebrows like a TV detective making a vital deduction in a case. "Or maybe *you* were responsible for his disappearance?"

"I had nothing whatsoever to do with his disappearance. You're insane."

Mrs. Burrows snorted. "Oh . . . insane, you say. . . . Is that why I'm in *this* awful place?" she said in a hammy, melodramatic way, rolling her eyes like a terrified heroine in a silent film. "Dear me!"

"Let me through, please," Sarah asked with resolute politeness, taking a small step forward.

"Not just yet," Mrs. Burrows said. "Perhaps you decided you wanted Will back?"

"No —"

"Perhaps *you* were the one who snatched him?" Mrs. Burrows accused her again.

"No, I —"

"Well, I bet you're involved in some way. You bloody keep your bloody nose out of my affairs. It's *my* family!" Mrs. Burrows scowled. "Look at the state of you. You're not fit to be *anyone's* mother!"

Sarah had had enough.

"Oh yes?" she retorted through tightly clenched lips. "And what did *you* ever do for him?"

A wave of triumph swept across Mrs. Burrows's face. She'd flushed Sarah out into the open. "What did *I* do for him? I did my best. You were the one who dumped him," she answered angrily, unaware that Sarah was struggling with an almost irrepressible urge to kill her. "Why didn't you come to see him before? Where've you been hiding all these years?"

"You bitter, vindictive hag!" exploded Sarah, revealing the scorn and resentment she felt for the other woman, her face erupting with all the violence of which she was capable.

But Mrs. Burrows wasn't put off by this, not in the least. She stepped back from the door, not in retreat, but to place her hand over the large red panic button on the wall. Sarah now had a clear passage out of the room and went to the door, twisting the handle to open it a fraction. As she did so, the sound of a commotion echoed down the corridor — a tremendous clattering and hysterical shouts. Mrs. Burrows knew immediately that one of the Screamers' body clocks must have gone awry. That was odd — they usually saved their histrionics for the small hours.

For the briefest moment, Sarah was distracted by the noise, then she focused her full attention back on Mrs. Burrows, who remained with her hand poised over the button.

Sarah looked fiercely at her, shaking her head. "You don't want to do that," she threatened.

Mrs. Burrows laughed unpleasantly. "Oh, don't I? What I really want is for you to get out—" she said.

"Oh, I'm going all right," Sarah snarled, cutting her short.

"— and never set foot in here again. Ever!"

"Don't worry . . . I've seen all I need to," Sarah replied caustically, wrenching the door fully open so that it crashed back against the wall with the bizarre murals and rattled the window casements. She took a step, but hesitated in the doorway, realizing she hadn't said all she wanted to, now that the gloves were off. And, in the heat of the moment, she was finally able to admit to herself what she had been trying so hard to suppress — that Joe Waites's message could be true.

"Tell me what you did to Seth—"

"Seth?" Mrs. Burrows interrupted sharply.

"Call him what you want, Seth or Will — it doesn't matter. *You* made him into something twisted, something evil!" she screamed in Mrs. Burrows's face. "Into a filthy murderer!"

"A murderer?" Mrs. Burrows asked, looking a great deal less certain of herself. "What on earth are you saying?"

"My brother's dead! Will killed him!" Sarah howled, tears filling her eyes. It was as if this meeting with Mrs. Burrows had provided her with a piece of a jigsaw puzzle, which, once completed, would show the vilest scene imaginable. And Sarah's outburst carried with it such complete conviction, such rawness of emotion . . .

Mrs. Burrows began to shake — for the first time she was completely thrown off her stride. Why was this woman accusing Will of murder? And what was this about him being called Seth? It didn't make sense. Her face was a picture of confusion as she took her hand away from the panic button and held it supplicatingly toward Sarah.

"Will . . . murdered . . . your brother? What . . . ?" Mrs. Burrows spluttered.

But Sarah merely gave the woman a final withering glance and flew from the room. She was bolting down the corridor as two heavyset orderlies thundered past her in the opposite direction.

They were heading toward the source of the high-pitched wailing but skidded to a halt when they saw Sarah in flight, uncertain whether they should intercept her instead.

Sarah didn't give them a chance to make up their minds. She hared around a corner in the corridor, her shoes slipping and squealing as they fought for purchase on the overwaxed linoleum. She wasn't going to stop for anyone or anything. The orderlies shrugged at each other and continued toward their original destination.

Sarah pulled open the glass door to the foyer. As she entered, she spotted a security camera on the wall — trained directly on her. *Curses!* She tucked her head down, knowing it was too late. There was nothing she could do about it now.

The receptionist behind the desk was the same one who had signed Sarah in. She was on the telephone but immediately dropped it as she called out.

"Are you all right? Miss O'Leary, what's wrong?"

With the receptionist still shouting after her to stop, Sarah sprinted across the parking lot and then down the driveway to the road. She didn't let up until she was on the main street. A bus drew up and she quickly boarded it. She had to get clear of the area in case the police had been called.

Sitting well away from the other passengers in the rear of the vehicle, Sarah was finding it difficult to get her breathing under control. She was in a seethe of thoughts and emotions. Never, in all her years of being Topsoil, had she revealed so much of herself to anyone, let alone to *Mrs. Burrows*, of all people! She should never have let her cover drop. She should have kept her cool. It had gone so horribly wrong. What *had* she been thinking?

The whole incident made her heart thump in her ears as she replayed it in her mind. She was at once infuriated with herself for her lack of self-control and deeply upset at the exchange with the ridiculous, ineffectual woman who had been such a large part of her son's life . . . who had had the privilege of watching him grow up . . . and who had to take responsibility for turning him into what he'd become. She'd said things to Mrs. Burrows that before she hadn't allowed herself to believe: that Will could indeed be a traitor, a turncoat, and a killer.

Once back in Highfield, she couldn't stop herself from breaking into a trot for the last stretch to the waste ground. She'd regained a measure of composure by the time she pulled aside the plywood trapdoor and jumped down into the entrance pit, with the usual comforting crunch of little bones to greet her.

She fished in her pocket for her flashlight but, having found it, didn't turn it on, choosing instead to feel her way through the enveloping darkness of the tunnel until she came to the main chamber.

"Cat, are you there?" she said, finally flicking on the light.

"Sarah Jerome, I presume," came a voice as the chamber burst into a dazzling brilliance, much more than was merited by Sarah's small beam. She shielded her eyes, half blinded and reeling at what she thought she'd glimpsed.

She desperately tried to focus on the source of the voice.

"Who . . . ?" she said, beginning to draw back.

What was this?

A girl of perhaps twelve or thirteen reclined in one of the armchairs, her legs primly crossed and a coquettish smile on her pretty face.

The girl was dressed as a Styx.

A large white collar over a black dress.

A Styx child?

And standing beside the girl was a Colonist, a big, surly brute. He had a strangle leash around the cat's neck and was holding the straining animal back.

Instinct replaced thought as Sarah wrenched open her bag, and in an instant her knife was out and flashing in the bright light. She dropped the bag, brandishing the knife, crouching and edging farther back. Looking frantically around her, she saw where all the light was coming from. Many light orbs — how many, she didn't know — were held aloft around the chamber walls, held by other Colonists. These squat, heavily muscled men lined the space like unmoving statues, like guardians.

Hearing the scratchy and indecipherable language of the Styx, she shot a glance at the tunnel she'd come down. A rank of Styx, in their uniform of black coats and white shirts, had moved across it behind her, sealing off her only means of escape. Talk about a full house — the White Necks were here in force, too.

She was completely surrounded. She wasn't going to be able to fight her way out of this one. It was an impossible situation. She'd been in too much of a hurry — her mind had been elsewhere as she'd carelessly entered the excavation without taking the usual precautions.

You stupid, stupid fool.

And now she was going to pay for her mistake. Dearly.

Dropping her flashlight, she raised the knife and held the blade hard against her own neck. There was time. They couldn't stop her.

Then the girl spoke again in her gentle voice.

"You don't want to do that."

Sarah croaked something unintelligible, her throat constricting with fear.

"You know who I am. I'm Rebecca."

Sarah shook her head, her eyes stricken. A remote corner of her brain wondered why the Styx girl was using a Topsoiler name. Nobody ever knew their real names.

"You've seen me at Will's house."

Sarah shook her head again, then froze. There was something familiar about the child. Sarah realized she must have been passing herself off as Will's sister. *But how?*

"The knife," Rebecca urged, "put it down."

"No," Sarah tried to say, but it came out as a groan.

"We have *so* much in common. We have a common interest. You should hear what I've got to say."

"There's nothing to say!" Sarah cried, finding her voice again.

"Tell her, Joe," the Styx girl said, half turning.

Someone stepped from the wall. It was the man who had written the note, Joe Waites, one of her brother Tam's gang. Joe had been like family to her and her brother, a loyal friend who would have followed Tam to the ends of the earth.

"Go on," Rebecca commanded him. "Tell her."

"Sarah, it's me," Joe Waites said. "Joe Waites," he added hastily, as she didn't show any sign that she recognized him. He inched forward, his trembling palms turned to her and his voice cracking with hysteria as he delivered a tumble of words. "Oh, Sarah," he pleaded, "please . . . please put it down . . . put the knife down . . . do it for your son's sake . . . for Cal's sake. . . . You must've seen my message. . . . It's true, it's the God's own . . ."

Sarah pressed the blade deeper into the flesh over her jugular and he stopped dead on the spot, his hands still raised, his fingers spread out, his whole body shaking violently. "No, no, don't, don't, don't . . . Listen to her . . . you have to. Rebecca can help."

"Nobody's going to make a move on you, Sarah. You have my word," the girl said calmly. "At least hear me out." She raised her shoulders in a small shrug, setting her head at an angle. "But you go ahead if you want to . . . cut your throat . . . I can't do anything to stop you." She let out a long sigh. "It would be such a waste, such a stupid, tragic waste. And don't you want to save Cal? He needs you."

Turning one way, then the other, gasping for breath like the cornered animal she was, Sarah's wide eyes stared at Joe Waites, blinking uncomprehendingly at the old man's unmistakable face under its tight-fitting skullcap, a lone tooth protruding from its top jaw.

"Joe?" she whispered hoarsely at him, with the quiet resignation of someone who was ready to die.

She twisted the blade deeper into her throat. Joe Waites flapped his arms frantically and cried out as the first drops of blood trickled down the paleness of her neck.

"Sarah, please!" he screamed. "Don't! Don't! DON'T!"

12

WILL HAD VOLUNTEERED to take first watch so the others could get some more rest. He tried to write in his journal but found it difficult to concentrate and, after a while, put it to one side. He paced around the table, listening to Chester's steady snoring, and then resolved to use the time to explore the house more thoroughly. Besides, he was dying to try out his new lantern. He proudly hooked it over his shirt pocket as his brother had shown him, and adjusted the intensity of the beam. With a last look at his sleeping comrades, he quietly left the library.

His first stop was the room on the opposite side of the hall, which he and Cal had only investigated briefly on their earlier excursion. He tiptoed through the dust and, nudging the door open, he went in.

It had the same dimensions as the library but was completely devoid of any furniture or shelves. He walked around the edge of the room, peering down at the deep skirting where there were small strips of a lime-green paper, which had obviously once adorned all the walls.

He went over to the shuttered windows, fighting the impulse to open them, and instead strolled around the floor several more times, the spotlight beam slashing through the darkness before him. Seeing nothing of interest, he was just on his way out when something caught his eye. He hadn't noticed it before, when all he and Cal had were the luminescent orbs, but now, with his brighter light, it was difficult to miss.

Scratched into the wall by the door, at about head height, were the following words:

I STAKE THIS HOUSE AS MY FIND.
SIGNED DR. ROGER BURROWS

Then, following a day with a number next to it that meant nothing to Will, was:

P.S. WARNING—LEAD ON WALLS
HIGH RADIOACTIVITY OUTSIDE?!

In wonder, Will reached out and ran his hand over some of the words, which reflected his light as if they had been gouged into metal.

"Dad! Dad's been here!" he began to shout. He was so elated that he forgot they had all been trying to be quiet. "My dad has been here!"

Chester and Cal, both wakened by his shouting, came tearing into the hallway.

"Will? What is it, Will?" Chester cried from the doorway, concerned for his friend.

"Look at that! He's been here!" Will was babbling, overcome with excitement.

They began to read the inscription, but Cal didn't seem to be impressed, almost immediately slouching against the wall. He yawned, rubbing the sleep from his eyes.

"I wonder how long ago he did that," Will said.

"Incredible!" Chester exclaimed as he finished reading the message. "That's just wild!" He grinned widely at Will, sharing his friend's euphoria. But then a suggestion of a frown wrinkled his brow. "So do you think they were *his* footprints in the library?"

"Bet they were," Will said breathlessly. "But isn't it just too weird? Talk about a coincidence — we chose exactly the same route as him."

"Like father, like son." Chester gave Will a pat on the back.

"But he's not his father," said a resentful voice from the shadows behind Chester. Cal was shaking his head. "Not his *real* father," he said disagreeably. "And he didn't even have the guts to tell you that, did he, Will?"

Will didn't react, not allowing his brother to take away from the moment. "Well, we can't hang around this area for long, if *Dad's* right about the radioactivity" — he carefully emphasized the word without looking at Cal — "and the walls are all coated with lead. I think he was right — feel here." He touched the surface of the wall under the message, and Chester did likewise. "Must act as shielding."

"Yeah, feels cold, like lead, all right. So I suppose the rest of the house must be the same," Chester agreed, glancing around the room.

"That's obvious. I told you the air's bad in the Deeps, you dolts," Cal said contemptuously and stamped his way back through the dust, leaving the two of them standing there.

"Just when I'm beginning to think he's not such a brat," Chester grumbled, shaking his head, "he goes and ruins everything."

"Just ignore it," Will said.

"He may look like you, but that's as far as it goes," Chester fumed. He was irked by the younger boy's behavior. "The little midget only cares about one person, and that's himself! And I know what his game is, always trying to wind me up. . . . He eats with his mouth wide open just to . . ." Chester stopped in midflow as he noticed the faraway look on his friend's face. Will wasn't listening; he stared at the writing on the wall, totally absorbed by thoughts of his father.

The boys spent the next twenty-four hours taking it easy, sometimes sleeping on the library table, sometimes roving through the large house. As Will looked around the other rooms, it made him uncomfortable to think the Styx had once lived here, even though it had been a long time ago. However, despite his searching, he didn't find any further evidence of his father and was becoming impatient to get going again — fired up by the notion that Dr. Burrows might still be in the area and desperate to catch up with him. With every hour, Will grew more restless, until he could bear it no longer. He rallied Chester and Cal together, telling them to pack their things, and then left the library to wait out in the hallway.

"I don't know what it is, but there's something about this place," Will said as Chester joined him by the front door. Will had opened it a fraction, and they were shining the focused beams of their lanterns at the dismal forms of the squat huts as they waited for Cal. After his outburst about Will's father, he'd been moody and uncommunicative, and both Will and Chester had largely left him to his own devices.

"It makes me feel . . . feel kind of uneasy," Will continued. "It's all those little huts out there and the thought that the Styx made the Coprolites live in them, like slaves. I bet they were treated so badly."

"The Styx are the worst type of scum," Chester said, then hissed sharply through his teeth and shook his head. "No, Will, I don't like it here, either. It's strange that . . . ," he pondered.

"What?"

"Well, just that this building's been empty for years, maybe centuries, until your dad broke in. Just locked up, like nobody's *dared* to put a foot in it."

"Yes, that's right," Will said thoughtfully.

"Do you think people stay away because things were once so awful here?" Chester asked him.

"Well, the bats are definitely carnivorous — I saw them attacking an injured one — but I don't think they're too much of a danger," Will replied.

"Huh?" Chester said apprehensively, his face draining. "*We're* made of meat."

"Yeah, but I would guess they're more interested in the insects," Will began. "Or animals that can't fight back." He shook his head. "You're right—I'm sure it isn't just the bats that have kept people away from this place," he agreed.

As Will had been talking, Cal had stomped sullenly through the dust, thrown down his rucksack, and sat himself on top of it.

"Yeah, the bats," he butted in sulkily. "How are we going to get past them?"

"There's no sign of them at the moment," Will said.

"Wonderful," Cal snarled. "So you don't have a plan at all."

Will responded evenly, refusing to be ruffled by his brother's criticism. "Right, then: This time we dim our lights, we don't make any noise, or *shout*—got that, Cal? And, as a precaution, I've got some firecrackers ready if they do come. Should scare off the freaky things." Will tugged open the side pocket of his pack, in which there were a couple of Roman candles left over from the batch he'd set off in the Eternal City.

"That's it? That's the plan?" Cal demanded aggressively.

"Yes," Will said, still trying to keep his cool.

"Foolproof!" Cal grunted.

Will gave him a look that could kill and warily pulled the door farther open.

Cal and Chester both edged out, with Will bringing up the rear, a pair of firecrackers in one hand and a lighter poised in the other. Every so often they heard the screeches of the bats, but they came from far enough away not to cause any real alarm. The boys moved silently and quickly, using the minimum of light to show them the way. In the shadows around their feet the tiny scuttlings and scrabblings tested the limits of their resolve, their imaginations running riot with thoughts of what was there.

They had left the gateway behind them and then back-tracked a good distance down the main tunnel when Cal stopped and pointed at a side passage. True to form, he had wandered ahead by himself, and now did not say anything as he continued to point.

"Is the midget trying to tell us something?" Chester asked Will sarcastically as they approached the resentful boy. Will stepped closer, until his face was inches from Cal's.

"For goodness' sake, grow up, will you? We're all in this together."

"A sign," Cal merely said.

"From heaven?" Chester asked.

Unspeaking, Cal moved aside to allow them to see a wooden post that rose a few feet from the ground. It was ebony-black, with the surface cracked as if it had been badly charred, and at the top it had a carved arrow pointing into the passage. They hadn't spotted it on the way down because it was tucked just inside the mouth of the passage.

"I reckon this could be a good way to get through to the Great Plain," Cal told Will, studiously avoiding Chester's belligerent glare.

"But why would we want to go there?" Will asked him. "What's so special about it?"

"It's probably where your *dad* went next," Cal replied.

"Then we follow it," Will said, and turned away from his brother, entering the passage without a further word.

Their journey through the passage was relatively easy — it was quite sizable, and its floor level, but the heat grew stronger with every step. Following Chester's and Cal's example, Will had removed his jacket, but he still felt the sweat soaking his back under his rucksack.

"We *are* going in the right direction, aren't we?" he said to Cal, who for once was not straying ahead of them.

"I hope so, don't you?" the boy replied insolently, then spat on the ground.

The change was immediate. There was a flash of illumination, far brighter than the glow issuing from the lanterns all three boys had hooked on their shirt pockets. It was as if all the faces of the rocks, and even the very ground itself, were radiating a clean yellow light. And it wasn't just limited to where they stood, but surging in pulses along the passage in both directions and illuminating everything as surely as if a switch had been flicked on, lighting the way for them.

They were stunned.

"I don't like this, Will," Chester gibbered.

Will pulled his jacket from where it was draped over the top of his rucksack and rummaged in it for his gloves.

"What are you doing?" Cal asked.

"Just a hunch," Will replied, stooping to pick up a brightly glowing rock the size of a golf ball. He closed his gloved hand over it, the creamy efflorescence shining through the gaps between his fingers. Then, balancing the rock on his open palm, he examined it carefully.

"Look at this," he said. "See that it's covered with a growth of some sort, like lichen?" Then he spat on it.

"Will?" Chester exclaimed.

The rock shone even more keenly. Will's mind was working overtime. "It feels warm. So moisture activates whatever this organism is — possibly bacteria — and it gives off light. Except for the stuff you find in some oceans, I've never heard of anything quite like this." He spat again, but this time on the wall of the passage.

Sure enough, where spots of his saliva had landed, the wall glowed that much more fiercely, as if luminous paint had been flicked at it.

"C'mon already, Will!" Chester said urgently, his voice low with fear. "It could be dangerous!"

Will ignored him. "You can see what water does to it. It's like a seed that's dormant . . . until it gets wet." He turned to the other two boys. "Better not get any on your skin — wouldn't like to think what it might do to it. Might suck all the moisture . . ."

"Thank you, Professor Smarty-Pants. Now let's get out of here ASAP, shall we?" Chester said, exasperated.

"Yep, I'm done," Will agreed, tossing the rock aside.

The rest of the journey was uneventful, and it was many hours of monotonous trudging before they left the passage and came out into what at first Will took to be another cavern. But as they moved forward, it soon became apparent that the space was something altogether different from any of those they'd been in before.

"Hold up, Will! I think I can see lights," Cal said.

"Where?" Chester asked.

"There . . . and more over there. See them?"

Both Will and Chester peered into the seemingly unbroken blackness.

To catch sight of them, they had to look just off center — attempting to view the lights directly blotted the dimly blinking specks from view.

In silence, they turned their heads slowly from one side to the other as they took in the tiny points, which were spaced at random intervals across the horizon. The lights seemed so far away and vague as to be gently pulsing and shifting through a haze of colors, similar to stars on a warm summer's night.

"This'll be the Great Plain," Cal announced all of a sudden.

Will took an involuntary step backward. It had begun to sink in that the expanse ahead was truly vast. It was daunting. The darkness made his mind play tricks on him, so he couldn't tell if the lights were in the extreme distance or, indeed, much closer by.

Together, the boys edged forward. Even Cal, who had spent his life in the immense caverns of the Colony, had never before encountered anything with dimensions like this. Although the roof remained at a relatively constant height, fifty feet or so from the floor, the rest — a yawning, endless gap — wasn't visible even with their lanterns set to full beam. It stretched before them, a slice of continuous blackness unbroken by a single pillar, stalagmite, or stalactite. And, most remarkably, gentle gusts of air wafted around, cooling them down a degree or two.

"It does look massive!" Chester put into words what Will was thinking.

"Yeah, goes on forever," Cal rejoined indifferently.

Chester turned on him. "What do you mean, *forever*? How big is it, really?"

"About a hundred miles across," Cal answered flatly. Then he strode off, leaving the other two standing side by side.

"A hundred miles!" Will repeated.

Chester suddenly blew his top. "Why doesn't your brother just tell us everything he knows? This place doesn't 'go on forever.' He's such a jerk! He either exaggerates everything or never gives us the whole story." With the sourest of expressions, he leaned his head to one side and then the other as he mimicked Cal. "This is Crevice City . . . blah, blah . . . here is the Great Plain . . . blahbiddy-blah . . . ," he spat, his words clipped through his anger. "You know, Will, I keep getting the feeling that he's holding things back just so he can get one up on me."

"On *us*," Will said. "But can you believe this place? Mind-blowing." Will was doing his best to change the subject and knock Chester off a course, which, it was clear, would eventually lead to a violent collision with his brother.

"Yeah, it's sure blown my mind," Chester replied sarcastically and began to probe the darkness with his lantern, as if trying to prove that Cal was wrong.

But it did seem as though the space stretched on forever. Will immediately began to theorize about how it could have been formed. "If you had pressure against two loosely bonded strata from . . . from a tectonic movement," he said, overlaying one hand on the other to demonstrate it to Chester, "then it could be possible for one to just ride up over the other." He arched the top hand. "And, bingo, you could get this sort of feature. Like wood grain splitting when it gets damp."

"Yes, that's all great," Chester said. "But what if it closes up again? What then?"

"I suppose it could — after many thousands of years."

"Knowing my stinking rotten luck, it'll probably be today," Chester muttered dolefully. "And I'll be squashed like an ant."

"Nah, come on, the chances of that happening right now are pretty small."

Chester grunted skeptically.

13

IN A CLEVERLY disguised entrance in the empty cellar of an old almshouse up in Highfield, not far from Main Street, Sarah stepped into an elevator. She slung her bag down by her feet and, hugging herself, made herself as small as she could. Backing into one of the corners, she looked miserably around the interior. She loathed being confined in the constricted space, with no means of escape. The sides and roof of the elevator were panels of heavy iron trelliswork, and the interior had been coated with a thick pasting of grease, the remaining traces of which were spiky with dirt and dust.

She heard a brief, muffled exchange between the Styx and Colonists hanging back in the brick-walled chamber outside the elevator, and then Rebecca entered, unaccompanied. The girl didn't give Sarah as much as a glance as she swiveled sharply around on her heels, one of the Styx ramming the gate shut behind her. Rebecca pushed and held down the brass lever by the side of the gate and, with a lurch and a low grinding noise from above, the elevator began to descend.

As it went, the heavy trellis cage creaked and rattled against the sides of the shaft, this din punctuated occasionally by the grating squeal of metal on metal.

They were being slowly lowered to the Colony.

However much she tried to contain it, a new sensation was building in Sarah, pushing up against her fear and anxiety. It was anticipation. She was returning to the Colony! Her birthplace! It was as though she had suddenly been given the ability to go back in time. With each foot the elevator dropped, the clock was speeding in reverse, regaining hour after hour, year after year. Never in her wildest dreams had she imagined she'd ever see her homeland again. She'd dismissed the possibility so irrevocably that it was hard for her to grasp what was now happening.

Taking several deep breaths, she unclenched her arms and straightened her back.

She'd heard about the existence of these elevators, but had never actually seen, let alone ridden in, one before.

Sarah rested her head against the trelliswork and, as the cage bumped its way down, watched the side of the shaft. The glow from Rebecca's light illuminated it, revealing that it was pocked with innumerable regular henpeck gouges. These were a testament to the work gangs who had dug their way down to the Colony almost three centuries ago, using only rudimentary hand tools.

As the different rock strata flashed by, giving up their brown, red, and gray hues, Sarah thought about the blood and sweat that had gone into establishing the Colony. So many people, generation upon generation, had toiled for all their natural lives to build it. And she had rejected it all, fleeing to the surface.

At the top of the shaft, now several hundred feet above her, the sound from the winch raised in pitch as it shifted up a gear, and the elevator accelerated in its descent.

This mechanical means in and out of the Colony was a world away from the one she had taken for her escape twelve years ago. Then, she had been forced to climb the entire way, using a stone staircase that spiraled up a huge brick-built shaft. It had been long and arduous, especially because she'd been hauling young Seth after her. The worst part had been her final emergence into the open air onto a rooftop via the inside of an age-old chimney stack. As she had scrambled to get some sort of bearing on the crumbling, soot-coated sides, all the while dragging the crying and confused boy behind her, it had taken every last drop of her strength to hold on and stop them both from slipping and tumbling down into the well below.

Don't think about that now, Sarah scolded herself, shaking her head. She realized how utterly spent she was from the day's events, but she had to get a grip. The day was far from over. *Focus,* she urged herself, glancing at the Styx girl traveling with her.

Facing away from Sarah, Rebecca hadn't moved from where she stood just inside the gate. Occasionally scuffing her shoe against the steel plate that formed the floor of the rattling cubicle, she was clearly impatient to reach the bottom.

I could deal with her right now. The thought suddenly forced itself into Sarah's head. As the Styx girl didn't have her escort, there would be nothing to stop Sarah. The notion gathered momentum, and Sarah knew she didn't have much time before they arrived at the bottom.

The knife was still in Sarah's handbag — for some reason the Styx hadn't taken it away. She regarded the bag where it lay by her feet, gauging how long it would take her to retrieve the weapon. *No, too risky. Much better, a blow to the head.* She balled her hands into fists and then opened them again.

No!

Sarah checked herself. Allowing her to be alone with the girl was a demonstration of the Styx's trust. And everything Sarah had been told seemed to fit together, to be true, so she'd decided to go along with them for the time being. She tried to calm herself, taking some more deep breaths. She raised a hand to her neck, tentatively probing the swelling around the self-inflicted wound.

It had been a close call — she'd started to push the knife into her jugular with the desolate intent of sinking it up to the hilt. But with Joe Waites screaming and pleading like a madman, she'd stayed her hand. She'd been prepared to go through with it: She'd lived with the certainty that at some point the Styx would catch up to her. She had rehearsed her suicide in one form or another a thousand times before.

With the knife poised and the silent audience of Styx and Colonists lining the walls around her, she'd listened to what Joe and Rebecca had to say, telling herself that a few more seconds wouldn't make any difference to someone who was already dead.

But then, the story they told her bore out what was written in the note. After all, the Styx could have executed her there and then in the excavation. So why go to all that trouble to save her?

Rebecca had recounted what had happened on the fateful day Tam lost his life. How the Eternal City had been blanketed in an impenetrable fog and the viperous Will had set off pyro-technic devices to attract the Styx soldiers. In all the confusion, Tam was drawn into the middle of an ambush and, mistaken for a Topsoiler, had been killed. Worse still, Rebecca said there was a strong possibility that Will himself had wounded Tam with blows from a machete in order to leave him behind as a decoy for the Styx soldiers. Sarah's blood boiled at this. Whatever had happened, Will had saved his own worthless skin, forcing Cal to go with him.

Rebecca also said Imago Freebone, a childhood friend of Sarah's and Tam's, had been present at the incident. According to Rebecca, he had since gone missing, and she could only pre-sume that Will had something to do with this as well. Sarah saw tears in Joe Waites's eyes as Rebecca spoke about this. As a member of Tam's little gang, Imago had been Joe's friend, too.

Sarah couldn't begin to comprehend Will's callous lack of regard for his own brother's life, let alone his murderous behav-ior. What sort of devious, conniving animal had he become?

Once Rebecca had finished telling her the chain of events, Sarah had asked for a moment alone with Joe Waites, and the Styx girl, much to Sarah's amazement, had granted it. Rebecca and the complement of Styx and Colonists dutifully withdrew from the underground cavern, leaving them together.

Only then had Sarah lowered her knife. She sat in the empty armchair next to Joe. The two of them had talked rap-idly while Rebecca and her escort waited in the tunnel leading to the bone pit. Joe retold the tale in rushed whispers, cor-roborating everything in the note he'd left and the version of events Rebecca had just given. Sarah needed to hear it again from start to finish, from someone she knew she could trust.

When Rebecca returned, she made Sarah a proposal: If Sarah was prepared to join forces with the Styx, she would be provided with the means to track down Will. She would be given the opportunity to right two wrongs: to avenge her brother's murder and to rescue Cal.

It was an offer Sarah couldn't ignore. Too much was left undone.

And, now, here she was, in a metal cage with her avowed enemy, the Styx! What had she been thinking?

Sarah tried to imagine what Tam would have done if faced with the same situation. But it didn't help, and she became agitated, picking at the clot on her neck, not caring in the least that it might cause the cut to open up and start bleeding again.

Rebecca half turned her head but didn't look toward Sarah, as if she could sense her turmoil. She cleared her throat and asked softly, "How are you doing, Sarah?"

Sarah stared at the back of the Styx girl's head, at the raven-black hair that spilled over the immaculate white collar, and spoke, her voice finding a new aggression.

"Just dandy. This sort of thing happens to me all the time."

"I know how difficult this is for you," Rebecca said soothingly. "Is there anything you want to talk about?"

"Yes," Sarah replied. "You insinuated your way into the Burrows family. You were in the house with my son for all those years."

"With Will—yes, that's right," Rebecca said without any hesitation, but ceased the constant scuffing of her shoe on the iron floor.

"Tell me about him," Sarah demanded.

"What will grow crooked, you can't make straight," the Styx girl said, letting the phrase hang in the air as they trundled downward. "There was something a little strange about him, right from the word go. He found it difficult to make friends and became even more withdrawn and distant as he grew older."

"No question he was a loner," Sarah agreed, recalling the times she had watched Will as he went about his digs.

"You don't know the half of it," Rebecca said in a slightly tremulous voice. "He could be really scary."

"What do you mean?" Sarah asked.

"Well, he expected everything to be done for him: his laundry, his meals . . . everything, and he'd fly off the handle at the smallest thing that wasn't just as he wanted it. You should've seen him—one moment he was fine, and the next he'd completely flip out and go into a horrible rage, screaming like a madman and smashing up the place. He was forever getting into trouble at school. In a fight he had last year, he beat up some of his classmates *really* badly. They hadn't done anything to him! Will just lost it and laid into them with his shovel. Several had to be taken to the hospital, but he wasn't the slightest bit sorry for what he'd done."

Sarah remained silent, absorbing what she'd just been told.

"No, you have no idea what he was capable of," Rebecca said softly. "His adoptive mother knew he needed help, but she was too bone idle to do anything about it." Rebecca slid her hand over her forehead as if the memories were causing her pain. "Perhaps . . . perhaps Mrs. Burrows was the reason he was like he was. She neglected him."

"And you . . . what were you there for? To keep tabs on him . . . or to catch me?"

"Both," Rebecca answered dispassionately as she twisted at the waist to regard Sarah with a steady gaze. "But the priority was to get you back. The Governors wanted you stopped — it's been bad for the Colony to have you unaccounted for. A loose end. Messy."

"And you've managed to pull it off, haven't you? You even got me alive. They'll be delighted with you."

"It's not like that. Anyway, it was your decision to come home." There was nothing in Rebecca's manner to suggest she was gloating over her success. She turned back to the gate again. Every so often, bright illumination from the entrances to other levels flashed before her, reflecting in the lustrous sheen of her jet-black hair.

After a pause, she spoke again. "It was quite something to survive for all that time, always keeping one step ahead of us and rubbing shoulders with the Heathen day in, day out." She was silent for several seconds. "It must have been hard for you, away from everything you knew?"

"Yes, sometimes," Sarah replied. "They say freedom has its price." She knew she shouldn't be opening up to the Styx girl, but she felt a grudging respect for her. Because of Sarah, Rebecca had been thrust into the alien place that was Topsoil. And at such a tender age. Almost the whole of the girl's life had been spent on the surface as she lived in the Burrows household; to say they had something in common would be a rank understatement. "What about you?" Sarah asked her. "How did you get by?"

"It was different for me," Rebecca replied. "Living in exile was my duty. It was a bit like some sort of game, but, all through it, I never forgot where my loyalties lay."

Sarah shivered. Although it seemed to have been uttered without reproach, the comment was like a blow, striking at the very kernel of her guilt. She slumped back into the corner of the elevator and wrapped her arms across her chest again.

For a while, neither of them spoke. The creaking and rattling descent of the elevator continued.

"Not far now," Rebecca eventually announced.

"I have one last question," Sarah shot back.

"Sure," Rebecca replied distractedly as she glanced at her watch.

"When this is all over . . . when I've done what I have to . . . will you let me live?"

"Of course." Rebecca spun daintily around and turned her bright eyes on Sarah. She smiled broadly. "You'll be back in the fold again, back with Cal and your mother. You're important to us."

"But why?" Sarah frowned.

"*Why?* Isn't it obvious, Sarah? You're the *prodigal daughter.*" Rebecca smiled even wider, but Sarah couldn't reciprocate. Her mind was awash with confusion. Maybe she just wanted to believe what the girl was saying a little too much. A voice of caution nagged her insistently, setting her nerves on edge. She didn't try to stifle it. She'd learned from bitter experience that if anything seemed too good to be true, then it almost certainly was.

Finally the elevator cage thumped against its stops at the bottom of the shaft, jolting its two occupants. Shadows moved outside. Sarah glimpsed a black-sleeved arm as it drew back the trellis door, and Rebecca strode purposefully out.

Is this a trap? Is this it? hammered through Sarah's mind.

Sarah remained within the car, peering down the metal-lined corridor at the two Styx who held back in the darkness. They were positioned on either side of a thick metal door, thirty or so feet away. Rebecca raised her light and beckoned for Sarah to follow, motioning toward the door. The only way out of the corridor, it was covered in glossy black paint with a large zero roughly daubed on it. Sarah knew they were at the bottom level and that on the other side of the door would be an air lock, then a final door, and then the Quarter.

This was it, the final step: If she crossed through that air lock, she was back, and well and truly in their clutches again.

His ankle-length leather coat creaking as he moved, one of the two Styx stepped into the light and took the edge of the door with his thin white fingers, pulling it back so that it clanged against the wall behind. No one spoke as the sound echoed around them. The Styx's black hair, drawn back tightly over his head, had traces of silver at the temples, and his face had a distinctly yellow hue to it and was deeply wrinkled. There were such uncomfortably deep creases on each of his cheeks that it looked as though his face were about to fold in on itself.

Rebecca was watching Sarah, waiting for her to enter the air lock.

Sarah hesitated, her instincts screaming at her not to go through the door.

The other Styx was more difficult to observe, as he remained in the shadows behind the girl. When the light did catch him, Sarah's first impression was that he was much younger than the other man, with clear skin and hair of the purest black. But as she continued to look, she could see that he was older than she'd first thought; his face was lean and drawn to the point that his cheeks were slightly hollowed, and his eyes were like mysterious caverns in the dim light.

Rebecca continued to watch her. "We'll go on. You come when you're ready," she said. "OK, Sarah?" she added softly.

The elder of the two Styx exchanged glances with Rebecca, and gave her the merest of nods as the three of them passed into the air lock. Sarah heard their feet clunk on the ridged floor of the cylindrical room, followed by a hiss as the seal on the second door was broken. She felt the gush of warm air on her face.

Then all was silent.

They had gone into the Quarter, a series of large caverns linked by tunnels, where only the most trusted of citizens were selected to live. And a handful of these were, under the supervision of the Styx, allowed to trade with Topsoilers for the basic materials that couldn't be grown or mined in the Colony or the layer below, the dreaded Deeps. The Quarter was something akin to a frontier town, and the living conditions weren't very wholesome, with the ever-present risk of cave-ins and floods of Topsoil sewage.

Sarah tilted her head to squint into the darkness of the elevator shaft above. She realized she was kidding herself if she thought she had any alternative. There was nowhere to run. Her destiny had been taken away from her and placed in the hands of the Styx the moment she'd taken the knife from her throat. At least she was still alive. And what was the worst they could do? Kill her, after they had subjected her to one of their more horrible tortures? The outcome would be the same in the end. *Dead now, or dead later.* She had nothing to lose.

She swept her eyes over the elevator cage for a last time, then started toward the dusky interior of the air lock. It was approximately fifteen feet long and oval in shape, with deep corrugations along its walls. Using the sides to brace herself as her feet slid on the greasy metal furrows beneath them, she slowly stepped to the open door at the other end, her apprehension mounting.

She leaned out. She caught the abhorrent language of the Styx — reedy, staccato words that ceased as soon as the trio saw her. They were waiting a little distance away on the other side of the large tunnel. As far as the light in Rebecca's hand permitted Sarah to see, the tunnel was empty, with an expanse of cobbled road and then a strip of stone pavement where Rebecca and the other Styx stood. There were no houses; it was a highway tunnel, perhaps connecting to one of the warehouse caverns that were dotted around the periphery of the Quarter.

Slowly she lifted one foot, then the other, over the lip of the air lock doorway and planted them on the shiny-damp cobblestones. She couldn't believe she was actually back in the Colony. She hesitated. Glancing over her shoulder, she looked at the wall that swept up in an elegant arc to where it would join the similarly built opposing wall, although the apex was obscured from sight in the gloom. She reached out a hand to touch the wall by the door, pressing her palm against one of the huge rectangular blocks of precisely cut sandstone. She felt the faint thrumming from the massive fans that circulated air around the tunnels. So very different from the vibrations in the Topsoil city above, it was a constant rhythm and gave her such comfort, like a mother's heartbeat.

She drew the air deep into her lungs. The scent was there, the characteristic mustiness, a distillation of all the people living in the Quarter and the larger area of the Colony beyond it. It was so distinctive, and she hadn't smelled it for so very long.

She was home.

"Ready?" Rebecca called, breaking into her thoughts.

Sarah's head jerked around to the three Styx.

She nodded.

Rebecca snapped her fingers and from the shadows a horse-drawn carriage rolled into view, its iron wheels rattling over the cobbles. Black and angular, and pulled by four horses of the purest white, these carriages were not an uncommon sight in the Colony.

It drew up next to Rebecca, the horses stamping their hooves and thrusting their noses in the air, eager to keep moving.

The austere hansom rocked as the three Styx climbed into it, and Sarah slowly made her way across. A Colonist sat in the driver's seat at the front of the cab, an old man wearing a battered trilby, who fixed his hard little eyes on Sarah. As she passed before the horses, she became self-conscious under the severity of his gaze. She knew what he'd be thinking: He probably didn't know *who* she was, but it was enough that she was dressed in Topsoiler clothes and had a Styx escort — she was the enemy, the hated.

As Sarah stepped onto the pavement, he cleared his throat in a coarse, exaggerated way and leaned over to spit, only just missing her. She stopped, and very purposefully stepped on the mess he'd coughed up, grinding the ball of her foot into it as if she were squashing an insect. Then she looked up at him, defiantly returning his stare. Their eyes locked together, long seconds passing. His flared with anger, but then he blinked and averted his gaze.

"OK, so let it begin," she said out loud, and climbed into the carriage.

14

"**WANT A DRINK?**" Will proposed. "I'm parched."

"Good idea." Chester grinned, his mood lightening. "Let's catch up with Boy Scout over there."

They were closing in on Cal, who was still striding quickly along in the direction of one of the distant lights, when he turned to them. "Uncle Tam said that the Coprolites live *in* the ground . . . like rats in burrows. He said they have towns and food stores that are dug into —"

"Watch out!" Will cried.

Cal stopped himself short just in time, at the edge of a stretch of darkness where the ground should have been. He teetered and then fell back on the loose floor, his feet scattering dirt over the ledge in front of him. They heard splashes of water as it landed.

While Cal picked himself up, Will and Chester cautiously approached the ledge and peered over. By the light of their lanterns they could see there was a drop of ten feet or so, and then inky, rippling water that reflected their lantern beams, sending circles of light back at them. The water flowed gently along, with nothing like the speed of the rushing stream they'd encountered earlier.

"This is man-made," Will observed, pointing at the regularly cut slabs forming the ledge. He leaned out as far as he dared to examine what lay below. The side of the canal was also lined with slabs, right down to the water's surface. And as far as they could see, the opposite bank was of identical construction.

"Coprolite-made," Cal commented quietly, as if to himself.

"What did you say?" Will asked him.

"The Coprolites built this," Cal said in a louder voice. "Tam told me once that they have giant canal systems to shift the stuff they mine."

"Useful piece of information to have known . . . *beforehand,*" Chester complained under his breath. "Got any more surprises for us, Cal? Any words of wisdom?"

To forestall a throw-down between the two, Will quickly intervened, suggesting they stop for a rest. They made themselves comfortable by the canal side, leaning on their rucksacks and sipping from their canteens. As they surveyed the canal that stretched on either side of them, all three were thinking the same thing: There was nowhere to cross. They'd just have to follow alongside and see where it took them.

They'd been sitting in silence for some time when a gentle creaking stirred them into activity again. They rose nervously to their feet, peering into the pitch-black and fixing their lanterns on the point from which the noise had emanated.

Like a ghost, the prow of a boat drifted into the far limits of their combined illumination. It was so eerily quiet, except for the odd gurgle of water, that they blinked, wondering if their eyes were deceiving them. As it glided into view, they could make out more of the vessel — it was a barge, rusted brown and unfeasibly wide, and sitting deep in the water. Heavily laden, its midsection was piled high with some organic matter.

Will couldn't believe how long the barge was — it just kept on coming and coming. The distance from the bank where the boys were standing to the side of the vessel — just a few feet — was such that they could have easily jumped aboard if the whim had taken them. But they were frozen to the spot by a mixture of fascination and fear.

The stern came into view, and they saw a stubby funnel from which wisps of smoke were issuing. Next they detected the deep and muted *thump-thump* of an engine. The noise was gentle, like an accelerated but regular heartbeat, sounding from somewhere below the waterline. Then they saw something else.

"Coprolites," Cal whispered.

Three lumbering forms stood stock-still in the stern, one with the shaft of the tiller in its hand. The boys watched, mesmerized, as the unmoving forms drew nearer. Then, as they drifted past, the boys could see every detail of the bloated, grublike caricatures of men, with their round bodies and globular arms and legs. Their suits were ivory in color and absorbed the light into their dull surfaces. Their heads were the size of small beach balls, but the most remarkable thing about them was that where their eyes should have been, lights shone like twin spotlights. The direction of these eye-beams revealed precisely where the strange beings were looking.

The boys couldn't help but gawk, while the three Coprolites seemed not to take the blindest bit of notice of them. With

their lanterns blazing, the boys' presence on the bank was unmistakable, so there was absolutely no way the Coprolites could have missed them.

But there was no sign whatsoever that they were paying the boys any attention. Instead, the Coprolites moved very slowly, their eye-beams creeping around the barge like lazy lighthouses, never once alighting on them. Two of the strange beings turned ponderously, their lights creeping down the port and starboard sides of the barge, then both coming to rest on the prow, where they stayed.

But suddenly the third Coprolite twisted around to face them. He moved with greater speed than either of his companions; with some urgency his eye-beams flicked backward and forward over the boys. Cal caught his breath, then murmured something as the Coprolite ran a plump hand over his eyes, the other hand raised as if in a salute or perhaps a wave. The strange being's head bobbed from side to side as though he was trying to get a better view of the boys, all the while sweeping his eye-beams over them.

This silent connection between the boys and the Coprolite was brief, the barge continuing its steady, undeviating passage into the penumbra. The Coprolite was still facing them, but the increasing distance and wisps of smoke from the funnel made the twin spots of his eyes hazier and hazier, until they were finally lost in the darkness.

"Shouldn't we get away from here?" Chester asked. "Won't they sound the alarm or something?"

Cal was dismissive. "No, no way. . . . They don't take any notice of outsiders. They're stupid. . . . All they do is mine and then trade it with the Colony, for things like the fruit and light orbs that were on the train with us."

"But what happens if they tell the Styx about us?" Chester pressed him.

"I told you . . . they're stupid, they don't talk or anything," Cal replied wearily.

"But *what* are they?" Will asked.

"They're men . . . sort of. . . . They wear those dust suits because of the heat and bad air around here," Cal answered.

"Radioactivity," Will corrected him.

"Sure, if you want to call it that. It's in the rock in this place." Cal waved his hand expansively. "That's why none of my people hang around for long."

"Oh, this just gets better and better," Chester complained. "So we can't go back to the Colony, and now we can't stay here, either. Radioactivity! Your dad was right, Will, and we're going to fry in this forsaken place."

"I'm sure we'll be OK for a while," Will said, trying to allay his friend's fears, but without much confidence.

"Great, great, and freakin' great," Chester growled, then stomped over to where they'd left the rucksacks, still grumbling to himself.

"Something wasn't right back there," Cal said confidentially to Will, now that they were alone.

"What do you mean?"

"Well, you saw the way that last Coprolite was watching us?" Cal said, shaking his head with a confused expression.

"I did, yes," Will said. "And you just told us they don't take any notice of outsiders."

"I'm telling you . . . they don't. I've seen them a thousand times back in the South Cavern and they never do that. They never, ever look straight *at* you. And he was moving strangely . . . too fast for a Coprolite. He didn't act normal." Cal paused to scratch his forehead. "Maybe it's different down here, because it's their land. But it's weird, all the same."

"I guess it is," Will said thoughtfully, little knowing how close he'd just come to his father.

15

DR. BURROWS stirred, thinking he'd heard the soft chiming sound, the wake-call that rang without fail every morning in the Coprolite settlement. He listened intently for a while, then frowned. There was nothing but silence.

"Must have overslept," he decided, rubbing his chin with a look of some surprise as he encountered the stubble on it. He'd grown fond of the straggling beard he'd sported for so long, and found he missed it now that he'd shaved it off. Something within his psyche had been very comfortable with the image it presented. He'd promised himself that he would regrow it for his glorious return, his eventual emergence back out on the surface again — whenever *that* was going to be. He'd cut an impressive figure on the front pages of all the newspapers. The imagined headlines loomed before him: "The Robinson Crusoe of the Underworld"; "The Wild Man of the Deeps"; "Dr. Hades . . ."

"That's quite enough," he said out loud, putting a stop to his self-indulgence.

He pulled aside his coarse blanket and sat up on the straw-stuffed mattress. It was too short even for an average-sized man, as he was, and his legs hung over the edge by nearly two feet.

He put on his spectacles, scratched his head. He'd attempted to cut his hair himself and hadn't made a terribly good job of it; in some places it was almost down to the scalp, while in others there were tufts about an inch long. He scratched even more vigorously, working his way around his head and then across his chest and armpits. Scowling with displeasure, he gazed in an unfocused way at his fingertips.

"Journal!" he said suddenly. "I didn't make an entry yesterday." He'd arrived back so late that he'd completely forgotten to record the day's events. Clicking his tongue against his teeth as he retrieved his book from under his bed, he opened it at a page that was blank except for the heading:

DAY 141

Under this he began to write, whistling a random and disjointed tune all the while:

Scratched myself half to death during the night.

He paused and thoughtfully licked the end of his pencil stub, then continued:

The lice are simply unbearable, and they're getting worse.

He glanced around the small, almost circular room, some twelve feet from side to side, and up to the concave ceiling.

The texture of the walls was irregular, as if the drying plaster or mud or whatever it was constructed from had been applied by hand. As for the shape, it gave him the impression that he was inside a large jar, and it amused him that he knew now how a genie trapped in a bottle might feel. This impression was heightened by the fact that the only way in or out was below him, in the center of the floor. It was covered by a piece of beaten metal that resembled an old trash can lid.

He glanced at his dust suit, hanging from a wooden peg on the wall like the shucked-off skin of a lizard but with a light coming from the eye holes where the luminous orbs were inserted. He should be putting on the suit, but he felt duty-bound to complete the entry for the previous day first. So he continued with his journal:

I sense the moment has arrived for me to move on. The Coprolites . . .

He hesitated, debating whether to use the name he had devised for these people, assuming they were a distinct species from *Homo sapiens*, something he hadn't been able to ascertain yet. "*Homo caves*," he said, then shook his head, deciding against it. He didn't want to confuse matters before he had his facts straight. He began to write again.

The Coprolites are, I believe, trying to communicate to me that I should leave, although I know not why.

I don't think it has anything to do with me or, more specifically, with anything I've done. I might be mistaken, but I am certain the mood has changed in the encampment. During the last twenty-four hours, there has been more activity than I've seen in the past two months. What with the additional food stores I saw them laying down, and the restrictions on the womenfolk and children from venturing outside, they are almost acting as if they are under siege. Of course, these could merely be precautionary measures that they put into practice every so often—but I do believe something is about to happen.

And so it seems it is time for me to resume my travels. I shall miss the Coprolites in no small measure. They have accepted me into their gentle society, one in which they seem perfectly at ease with each other, and, strangely enough, with me. Maybe it's because I'm not a Colonist or a Styx, and they recognize that I pose no risk to them or their progeny.

In particular, their offspring are a constant source of fascination, almost adventuresome and playful. I have to keep reminding myself the young are not a completely different species from the adults.

He stopped whistling to allow himself a chuckle, reminiscing how at first the adults wouldn't even hold his stare when he tried, fruitlessly, to communicate with them. They would avert their rather small gray eyes, their body language one of awkward submission. Such was the difference in temperament between him and these unassuming people that at times he pictured himself as the hero from a Western, the lone gunslinger who had trekked across the prairies to a town of cowed farmers or miners or what have you. To them, Dr. Burrows was a powerful, all-conquering, he-man hero. *Hah! Him!*

"Get on with it, will you," he told himself, and resumed his writing:

All in all the Coprolites are such a gentle and chronically reticent people, and I can't claim that I have gotten to know them. Perhaps the meek have inherited the earth, after all.

I shall never forget their act of mercy in rescuing me. I have written of it before, but now that I am to leave, I have been thinking much about it again.

Dr. Burrows stopped and looked up, staring into the middle distance for several moments, with the air of someone who is trying to remember something but has forgotten why he is trying to remember it in the first place.

Then he flicked back through the pages of his journal until he found his first entry on arriving in the Deeps and read it to himself.

The Colonists were unfriendly and uncommunicative as they led me a merry dance away from the Miners' Train and into what they said was a lava tube. They told me to continue along it toward the Great Plain, and that what I wanted to see was on the way. When I tried to ask them some questions, they became quite hostile.

I wasn't about to get into an argument with them, and so did what they told me. I walked away, at a brisk pace to start with, but then stopped once I was out of sight. I wasn't convinced I was going in the right direction. I was suspicious that they were trying to get me lost in the maze of tunnels, so I backtracked and . . .

At this point Dr. Burrows clicked his tongue against his teeth again and shook his head.

. . . in the process, I became completely lost.

He whisked the page over as if he was still annoyed at himself, then scanned his description of the empty house that he'd discovered, and the surrounding huts.

He moved past the entry as if it didn't interest him much, to a smeary, dirty page. His handwriting, never very legible at the best of times, was even worse here, and his hastily written sentences ran across the page at an array of different angles, blissfully ignoring the ruled lines. In places, his sentences were even written on top of one another, in a kind of literary pick-up sticks. At the bottom of three successive pages, the word *LOST* was scrawled in large, increasingly more erratic capitals.

"Messy, messy," he admonished himself. "But I was in a bad way."

Then a passage in the entry caught his eye, and he read it out loud.

I can't truthfully say for how long I have roamed through this hotchpotch of passages. At times all hope has deserted me, and I have begun to resign myself to the fact that I might never emerge from them, but it has all been worth it now. . . .

Directly below it, a subheading proudly announced *THE STONE CIRCLE.* On the next pages were sketch after sketch of the stones comprising the underground monument he'd stumbled across. He'd not only recorded the positions and shapes of the stones themselves, but on each page had drawn circles in the corners, like the view through a magnifying glass, recording in painstaking detail the symbols and the strange inscriptions chiseled into their faces. His spirits had soared at the discovery, despite his increasing hunger and thirst. Not knowing how long he had to make his supplies last, each day he'd been forcing himself to consume as little as he could.

A self-satisfied grin played on his face as he inspected these pages, admiring his labors.

"Perfect, perfect."

Then he stopped as he came to the next page, pursing his lips with an unuttered "Ohhhh!" as he read the heading:

THE TABLET CAVES

He'd written a couple of lines below this:

After finding the stone circle, I thought my luck was in. Little did I realize I was to find something that, in my opinion, is of equal or greater importance. The caves were filled with tablets, scores of them, all with writing not dissimilar to that cut into the menhirs of the Stone Circle.

Dozens of pages with drawings of the tablets followed, skillful pictures of the writing carved on their faces, all meticulously copied. But, as he turned the pages, they became less carefully drafted, until it looked as if a young child had been drawing them.

I HAVE TO KEEP WORKING was written so forcibly under one of the final, slapdash sketches that the pencil lines, pressed deep into the page, had even torn the paper in places.

*I MUST DECIPHER THIS WRITING! IT
IS THE CLUE TO WHO LIVED DOWN HERE!
I HAVE TO KNOW, I HAVE TO . . .*

With a finger, he felt the impressions of his words in the journal, trying to recall his state of mind at that instant. It was hazy. The food had all gone, and he had continued to work feverishly, with scant regard for his water supplies. When he found they, too, had run out, it had taken him completely by surprise.

Still trying to remember, he looked at the note he'd scrawled in a neater, almost despairing way, in the middle of an outline of a stone tablet he had never finished drawing:

I must keep working. My strength is deserting me. The stones become heavier and heavier as I lug them from the piles to examine them. I live in fear that I might drop one. I have to st

It ended there. He had no recollection of what had happened next, except that in a kind of delirium he had staggered off in search of a spring and, not finding one, had somehow managed to get himself back to the Tablet Caves.

After a blank page there was *DAY?* and the words:

Coprolites. I keep debating whether I'd still be alive if the two youngsters hadn't chanced upon me and fetched the adults. Probably not. I must have been in a bad way. I have a mental picture of the

STRANGE figures leaning over my journal, their lights crisscrossing as they peered at the pages on which I'd drawn my sketches, but I'm not sure if I really saw this or if it's just my mind telling me what might have happened.

"I digress. This is no good," he said sternly to himself, shaking his head. "Yesterday's entry! I must finish *yesterday's* entry." He fanned through the pages until he found the one where he'd started, and put pencil to paper once more:

In the morning, after I'd suited up, I was making my way down to the food stores to collect my breakfast, through the communal area where a group of the coprolite children were playing a game somewhat akin to marbles. Must have been a dozen or so of the youths, of varying ages, squatting down and rolling these large marbles, made from what appeared to be polished slate, across a clear-swept area of ground. They were trying to knock over a carved stone bowling pin that vaguely resembled a man.

Taking turns, they flicked the marbles at it, and when they had all had their goes the pin was still standing. One of the smaller children handed me a marble. It was lighter than I expected, and I dropped it a few times to start with (still not used to the gloves) and then, with some difficulty,

I finally managed to manipulate it into position between my thumb and forefinger. I was just rather clumsily trying to aim it when — imagine my surprise! — the gray sphere suddenly came to life! It uncurled and scurried over my palm! It was a huge wood louse, the likes of which I've never seen before.

I have to say, I was so astounded, I dropped it again. It had similarities to an Armadillidium vulgare, a pill wood louse, but on steroids! It had multiple pairs of articulated legs, which it used to great effect, scuttling away at a rate of knots as several of the children followed in hot pursuit. I could hear the others giggling away in their suits; they thought it was hilarious.

Later that day I saw a couple of the more senior members of the encampment preparing to leave. They were touching the heads of their dust suits together, quite possibly conversing with each other, though I have never heard their language. For all I know, it might be English.

I followed them and they didn't seem to mind — they never do. We climbed out of the encampment, somebody rolling the boulder back behind us to block the entrance after we exited. The fact that their encampments are excavated into the floor of the

GREAT PLAIN AND the side PASSAGES leading off it, OR SOMETIMES EVEN cut into its ROOF, RENDERS them almost invisible to the CASUAL obSERVER. I tagged Along behind the two COPROLITES for SEVERAL hours until we left the GREAT PLAIN, taking A PASSAGE that dipped steeply down. As it leveled out, I found WE WERE IN SOME TYPE of PORT AREA.

It WAS substantial, with large-gauge railway tracks running Alongside a basin of WATER. (I believe that the COPROLITES WERE RESPONSIBLE for the construction of the track for the MINERS' TRAIN AND for digging the CANAL system, both TREMENDOUS undertakings.) At the quayside, three CANAL boats WERE docked, and I WAS delighted when the COPROLITES boarded the NEAREST ONE. It WAS fully laden with RECENTLY mined COAL. The vessel WAS POWERED by A STEAM ENGINE — I watched AS they shoveled coal into A furnace and lit it with A tinderbox.

WHEN sufficient PRESSURE had built up, WE SET off, traveling out of the basin AND Along mile after mile of enclosed WATERWAYS. WE stopped several times to operate the locks AS WE CAME to them — here I WAS Able to step off the boat AND onto the bank AND watch AS they hand-cranked the lock gates.

As we went, I thought much on how these people and the colonists rely on each other, a sort of slipshod symbiosis, but I would say that the fruit and light orbs are little recompense for the vast tonnage of coal and iron ore that the colony receives in return. These people are master miners, laboring with their heavy, steam-driven digging equipment (see Appendix 2 for my drawings).

We went past some of the areas of intense heat I've described before, where lava must flow close behind the rocks. I dread to think what temperature it was outside my dust suit. We eventually emerged back onto the Great Plain, making good speed now that the furnace was roaring, and I was beginning to feel rather exhausted (these suits are intolerably heavy after prolonged use) when we saw a group of what I can only assume were colonists on the canal side.

They categorically weren't Styx, and I believe we may have startled them. There were three, a motley crew from what I could tell, looking a bit lost and nervous. Couldn't see very much, since the combination of my glasses and the light orbs around the eyepieces of the suit produces such a glare, it impairs my vision somewhat.

They didn't look like full-grown Colonists, so I haven't the foggiest what they were doing so far away from the train. They gawped at us, though the two Coprolites accompanying me typically took no notice whatsoever. I tried to wave at the trio, but they didn't acknowledge me. Perhaps they, too, had been Banished from the Colony, just as I would have been if I hadn't actually wanted to go into the Interior.

Dr. Burrows reread the last paragraph, then his eyes glazed over as he began to dream again. He imagined his battered journal, open at this very page, in a glass case in the British Library or perhaps even the Smithsonian.

"History," he said to himself. "You are making *history*."

Finally he'd put on his suit and, moving the trash-can-lid door aside, climbed down the steps carved into the wall. At the bottom, as he stood on the well-raked dirt floor, he peered around, his breathing loud in his ears.

His hunch that change was in the air had been right.

The settlement was uncharacteristically dark.

And completely deserted.

In the center of the communal area, a single, flickering light burned. Dr. Burrows began walking toward it, keeping the wall to his side and glancing up at the roof spaces above him. The twin beams from his suit revealed that all the hatches to the other living spaces were open. The Coprolites never left them like that.

The encampment had been evacuated while he slept.

He approached the light. It was an oil lamp suspended above a tabletop of polished "snowflake" obsidian, which was set into a rusty iron frame. Like a mirror, the highly polished black surface, dappled with diffuse white patches, reflected the flame, and he could see that something was on it, eerily lit by the shifting light. Rectangular packets, neatly wrapped in what appeared to be rice paper, were arranged on the table in a row. He picked up one of these, weighing it in his hand.

"They left me some food," he said. Moved by an unexpected swell of emotion for the gentle beings he'd spent so long with, he went to wipe away the tears forming in his eyes. But his gloved hand encountered the glass lenses of the bulbous helmet he was wearing.

"I shall miss you," he said, his wavering voice reduced to a murmur through the thick layers of the suit. He shook his head quickly, ending the moment. He was distrustful of such outpourings of sentimentalism. If he gave in to them, he knew he would begin to feel pangs of guilt about the family he'd deserted, about his wife, Celia, and his children, Will and Rebecca.

No. Emotion was a luxury he couldn't afford, not now. He had his *purpose* and nothing was going to deflect him from it.

He began to gather up the packages. As he lifted the last of these, cradling them in his arms, he saw that a scroll of parchment had been left between them. He quickly replaced the packages on the table and opened the scroll.

It was a map, drawn up in bold lines and with stylized symbols dotted around it. He rotated the parchment first one way and then the other, trying to work out where he was. With a triumphant "Yes!" he recognized the settlement he was now in, and then traced a fingertip around the heaviest outline on the map, the border of the Great Plain. From the edge of this, tiny parallel lines ran on, evidently marking tunnels that ran off it. Next to their courses were many more symbols that he couldn't immediately understand. He frowned, totally engrossed.

These quiet, self-effacing creatures had given him what he needed. They'd shown him the *way*.

He clasped his hands together and held them up in front of his face, wringing them in a prayer of gratitude.

"Thank you, thank you," he said, his mind already buzzing with thoughts of his onward journey.

PART 2

THE HOMECOMING

16

SARAH HOOKED the leathery blind to one side to peer through the small window in the door of the cab. The journey took the carriage along a succession of darkened tunnels, until finally it turned a corner and she spotted an illuminated area ahead.

In the light shed by the streetlamps, she saw the first of many ranks of terraced houses. As they sped past, she noticed that some of the doors were open, but she couldn't see a single person in evidence, and the small lawns to the front of each home were overrun with tall clumps of black lichen and self-spored fungi. What had been the contents of the houses now littered the pavements; pots and pans and pieces of broken furniture lay discarded there.

The cab slowed to negotiate a cave-in. It was a serious one: Part of the tunnel had collapsed, and the massive blocks of limestone had tumbled down on top of a house, smashing in the roof and almost completely crushing the building.

Surprised, Sarah glanced at Rebecca, who was sitting across from her.

"This stretch is to be filled so we can cut the number of Topsoil portals. That's some of the fallout from your son's break-in to the Colony," Rebecca said matter-of-factly as the carriage accelerated again, jostling them from side to side with its motion.

"This is all because of Will?" Sarah asked, imagining how the people would have been cruelly forced to leave their houses.

"I told you — he doesn't care who he hurts," Rebecca said. "You have no idea what he's capable of. He's a sociopath, and someone has to stop him."

The old Styx beside Rebecca nodded sanguinely.

Through the twisting tunnels and cobbled tracks they went, lower and lower. As they began the final descent toward the Colony, there was no longer anything to see, and Sarah sat back. Feeling awkward, she lowered her eyes to her lap. One of the wheels rode over something and the carriage tipped precariously, throwing its passengers violently across the wooden seats. Sarah shot a look of alarm at Rebecca, who gave her one of those comforting smiles as the cab righted itself with a crash. The two other Styx remained impassive, just as they had been for the whole journey. Sarah stole furtive glances at them and couldn't suppress a shudder.

Imagine.

The enemies she had reviled with every fiber of her soul were a hairsbreadth away from her. They were her traveling companions. So close she could smell them. She wondered for the millionth time what they really wanted from her. Perhaps they were simply going to throw her into a cell when they reached their destination, and then Banish or execute her. But why go through with this charade if that were the case?

The urge to escape was building irrepressibly in her once more. Her mind screamed at her to flee, and she began to calculate how far she might get. She was looking at the door handle, her fingers fidgeting, when Rebecca stretched out a hand and placed it on hers, stilling their movement.

"Not far now."

Sarah tried to smile and then, in the flash of light from a passing lamppost, she noticed the old Styx was looking straight at her. His pupils weren't quite jet-black, as they were with the rest of the Styx, but appeared to have an additional tinge to them, the slightest glimmer of a color she couldn't classify — between red and brown — that, to her, was darker and deeper than black itself.

And as his gaze rested momentarily on her, she felt an intense uneasiness, as if somehow he knew precisely what she was thinking. But then he was looking out the window again and didn't move his eyes from it for the rest of the journey, not even when he began to speak. It would be the only time he did so during the entire trip. His manner was that of someone wise with years; it was not the vengeful ranting Sarah was accustomed to hearing from senior members of the Styx. He seemed to weigh his words carefully, as if balancing them against each other before he let them past his thin lips.

"We are not that different, Sarah."

She jerked her head toward him. She was spellbound by the web of deep lines at the corners of his eyes that sometimes curled as if he were about to smile — although he never did.

"If we have a failing, it is that we do not recognize that a handful of people down here, the very few, are not that different from us, the Styx."

He blinked slowly as they passed a particularly large lamppost that shone into the cab so brightly it lit up all its corners. Sarah saw then that neither of the other two in the carriage were looking at the old Styx or, indeed, at her, as he went on.

"We set ourselves apart and, every so often, somebody like you comes along. You have a strength that singles you out; you resist us with the passion and fervor we expect from our own kind.

"You are merely striving for recognition, fighting for something you believe in — it matters not what — and we do not listen." He paused to take a long, considered breath.

"Why? Because we've had to dominate the people of the Colony for so many years — for the common good — and we tend to treat you all the same. But you are *not* all from the same mold. Although you are a Colonist, Sarah Jerome, you are passionate and committed, and not the same . . . not the same at all. Maybe you *should* be tolerated, for your spirit alone."

Sarah continued to stare at him long after he'd stopped speaking, wondering if he'd been inviting a response from her. She had no idea what message he'd been giving. Was he trying to show compassion toward her? Was this some kind of Styx charm offensive?

Or was he making some bizarre and unprecedented invitation for her to *join* the Styx? That couldn't be. That was unthinkable. That *never* happened. The Styx and the Colonists were races apart, the oppressors and the oppressed, as the old Styx had implied. And never the twain shall meet . . . and that was how it had always been and always would be, world without end.

A further possibility surfaced. Were his words simply an admission of the Styx's failure, a belated apology for the way she had been treated over her dying baby?

She was still pondering all this as the hansom drew to a halt before the Skull Gate.

She'd passed through it only a dozen or so times in her life, accompanying her husband on some official matter or other in the Quarter, where she had been left to wait outside in the street or, if actually allowed into the meeting, had been expected to remain silent. This was the way in the Colony: Women were not considered to be equal to men and could never hold positions of any level of responsibility.

She'd heard rumors that things were different with the Styx. And wasn't the living proof of it sitting across from her right now, in the shape of Rebecca? Sarah found it hard to believe that this mere child seemed to hold such sway. She'd also heard talk, mostly from Tam, that there was an inner circle, a kind of royalty at the top of the Styx hierarchy, but this was pure speculation. The Styx lived apart from the people of the Colony, and so nobody knew for sure what went on, although rumors of their bizarre religious rituals were bandied about in the taverns in low whispers, growing more and more exaggerated with each telling.

As she looked from the girl to the old Styx and back again, Sarah caught herself thinking that they could be related in

some way. If the hearsay was to be believed, the Styx didn't
have traditional family units, the children instead being taken
away at an early age and raised by designated guardians or
headmasters in their private schools.

But Sarah felt that there was definitely a bond between the
two of them as they sat there in the dark. She sensed some
sort of connection that went beyond the Styx's allegiance to

each other. Despite his advanced years and his inscrutable face, there was the vaguest hint of the avuncular about the old Styx's manner toward the young girl.

Sarah's thoughts were interrupted by a single knock on the door of the hansom cab. It flew open. A blindingly bright lantern shone rudely in, the glare making Sarah shade her eyes. Then came an exchange, in reedy clicks, between the younger Styx by her side and the lantern bearer. The light withdrew almost immediately, and Sarah heard the clanking of the port-cullis as the Skull Gate was raised. She didn't lean over to the window to watch, but instead pictured the pig-iron gate as it retreated into the huge carved effigy of a skull above it.

The gate's purpose was to keep the inhabitants of the huge caverns in place. Of course, Tam had found myriad ways around this main barrier. It had been like a game of Chutes and Ladders to him; each time one of his smuggling runs was discovered, he always managed to find an alternative route to get Topsoil.

Indeed, she herself had used a route he'd told her about to make good her escape, through an air-ventilation tunnel. With another pang of loss, Sarah smiled at the memory of the scene as the big man, with his bearlike hands, had painstak-ingly sketched her an intricate map in brown ink on a square of cloth the size of a small handkerchief. She knew that par-ticular route was useless now — with typical Styx efficiency it would have been closed off in the hours after she'd fled to the surface.

The carriage surged forward, moving at an incredible rate, descending deeper and deeper. Then came a change in the air, and a burning smell filled her nostrils, and everything began to vibrate with a pervasive low rumble. The carriage was passing the main fan stations. Hidden from sight in a huge excavated space high above the Colony, massive fans churned away, day and night, drawing off the smog and stale air.

She sniffed, inhaling deeply. Down here, everything was more concentrated: the smoke and fumes from fires; the smell of cooking, of mildew and rot and decay; and the collective stench of the huge number of human beings segregated in several interlinking, albeit quite large, areas. A distilled essence of all life in the Colony.

The carriage made a sharp turn. Sarah gripped the edge of the wooden seat so she wouldn't slide along its worn surface and into the younger Styx at her side.

Closer.

She was getting closer.

As they continued down, she leaned expectantly forward to the window.

She looked out, no longer able to stop herself from gazing at the twilight world that had once been the only one she knew.

From this distance, the stone-built houses, workshops, storefronts, squat places of worship, and substantial official buildings of which the South Cavern was composed looked very much the same as when she'd last seen them. She wasn't surprised. Life down here was as constant as the pale light of the orbs that burned twenty-four hours a day, week in, week out, for the last three centuries.

The hansom cab raced off the bottom of the incline and through the streets at breakneck speed, people stepping out of the way or pushing their handcarts quickly against the curbs so as not to be mown down.

Sarah saw Colonists regarding the speeding carriage with bewildered expressions. Children pointed, but their parents pulled them back as they realized that the hansom was carrying Styx. It wasn't done to stare at members of the ruling class.

"Here we are," Rebecca announced, swinging the door open even before the carriage had come to rest.

Sarah recognized the familiar street with a jolt. She was home. She hadn't marshaled her thoughts yet; she wasn't ready for this. Shakily she got up to follow Rebecca as the girl nimbly skipped straight from the carriage step to the sidewalk.

Sarah was reluctant to leave the cab, lingering on the brink.

"Come along, then," Rebecca said gently. "Come with me."

She took Sarah's hand, guiding the quaking woman out into the dimness of the cavern. As she allowed herself to be led, Sarah lifted her head to look at the immense span of rock that stretched over the subterranean city. Smoke rose lazily from chimneys in vertical plumes, as if streamers had been hung from the stone canopy above, rippling slightly as the enormous vents around the walls fed fresh air into the cavern.

Rebecca kept Sarah's hand clasped in hers, drawing her on. There was a clattering and another hansom cab drew up behind the one from which they had just dismounted. Sarah stopped, resisting Rebecca and turning to look back at it. She could just make out Joe Waites through the carriage window.

She swung back to view the uniform row of houses stretching along the street. It was completely empty, which was unusual at this hour. Her unease grew again.

"I didn't think you'd want people gaping at you," Rebecca said, as if she knew what was in Sarah's mind. "So I had the area cordoned off."

"Ah," Sarah said quietly, "and *he's* not here, is he?"

"We've done exactly as you requested."

Back in the cat's chamber in Highfield, Sarah had insisted on one condition: She couldn't face seeing her husband, even after all this time. Whether it was because it would bring back memories of the dead baby or because she couldn't cope with her own betrayal and abandonment of him, she didn't know.

She still hated him and, when she allowed herself to be brutally honest, still loved him, in equal measures.

She walked as if she was in a dream. The appearance of her house was unchanged, as if she'd left it only yesterday and the last twelve years had never happened. After all that time on the run, living hand to mouth like some sort of animal, Sarah was home.

She touched the deep cut on her throat.

"It's all right, it doesn't look too bad," Rebecca said, squeezing Sarah's hand.

There it was again: a Styx child, spawn of the worst filth imaginable, trying to comfort her! Holding her hand and acting like she was her *friend*. Had the world gone mad?

"Ready?" Rebecca asked.

The last time Sarah had seen the house, her dead baby had been laid out — in that room there — her eyes flicked up to the master bedroom, where she'd sat by the cot on that dreadful night. And down there—she turned her attention to the living-room window—flashes of her past life came back: mending her sons' clothes; emptying the grate in the morning; bringing her husband tea as he read the paper; and smiling at her brother Tam's deep voice, as if heard from another room, his laughter soaring as glasses clinked together. *Oh, if only he was still alive. Dear, dear, dear Tam.*

"Ready?" Rebecca asked again.

"Yes," Sarah replied decisively. "I am."

They went slowly up the path, but as they reached the front door, Sarah shrank back.

"It's OK," Rebecca cooed soothingly. "Your mother's waiting." She pushed through the door and Sarah followed her into the hall. "She's through there. Go and see her. I'll be outside."

Sarah looked at the familiar green-striped wallpaper upon which hung the stern pictures of her husband's ancestors, generations of men and women who had never seen what she'd seen: the sun. Then she touched a smoky-blue shade on a lamp on the hall table, as if making sure that everything was real, that she wasn't in the throes of some bizarre hallucination.

"Take as long as you want." With that Rebecca whirled around and, in prim steps, exited the house, leaving Sarah standing alone.

She drew a deep breath and, walking stiffly as an automaton, made her way into the living room.

The fire was lit and the room looked as it ever did, maybe a little more worn and discolored by smoke, but still warm and welcoming. She padded quietly over to the Persian rug and the winged leather armchairs, edging slowly around until she could see who was sitting there. She still thought that at any moment she'd wake and all this would be over, dimming in memory like any dream.

"Ma?"

The old lady raised her head feebly, as if she'd been dozing, but Sarah knew she hadn't when she saw the tears on her wrinkled cheeks. Sarah felt her body go limp with all the emotions that were sweeping through her.

"Ma." Her voice gave out and all she could manage was a croak.

"Sarah," the old lady said, and stood up with some difficulty. She raised her arms to Sarah, who saw she was still crying and couldn't stop herself, either. "They said you were coming, but I didn't dare hope."

Her mother's arms were around her but the embrace felt frail, not the strong grip she remembered. They stood, holding each other, until her mother spoke.

"I need to sit," she gasped.

As she did so, Sarah kneeled down before her chair, still holding her mother's hands.

"You look well, my child," her mother said.

Sarah fumbled for something to say in response, but was too overwrought to speak.

"Life up there must suit you," the old lady went on. "Is it really as wicked as they tell us?"

Sarah started to answer, but once again words failed her. She couldn't begin to explain and, at that moment, it really didn't matter to either of them, anyway. It was being together, being reunited, that counted.

"So much has happened, Sarah." The old woman hesitated. "The Styx have been good to me. They've been sending someone to help me to services every day so I can pray for Tam's soul." She lifted her eyes to the window as if it was too painful to look at her daughter. "They told me you would be coming home, but I didn't dare believe them. It was too much to hope that I might see you again . . . one last time . . . before I die."

"Don't talk like that, Ma, you've got a good few years in you yet," Sarah said ever so softly as she shook her mother's hands in a gentle reprimand. As her mother turned her head back toward her, Sarah looked deep into her eyes. It was heartrending to see the change, as if a light had gone out. There'd always been a vibrant sparkle to them, but now they seemed lackluster and vacant. Sarah knew that time alone had not been responsible. She knew that she was partly to blame, and felt she had to account for her actions.

"I've been the cause of so much, haven't I? I split the family. I put my sons in danger . . . ," Sarah said, her voice trembling. She took several rapid breaths. "And I have no idea how my husband . . . John . . . feels."

"He looks after me now," her mother said quickly. "Now that there's nobody else."

"Oh, Ma," Sarah croaked, her speech becoming broken. "I . . . I didn't mean for you to be left alone . . . when I went . . . I'm so sorry—"

"Sarah," the old lady interrupted, the tears flowing freely down her lined face as she squeezed her daughter's hands. "Don't torture yourself. You did what you thought you had to."

"But, Tam . . . Tam's dead . . . and I just can't believe it."

"No," the old lady said, so softly as to be barely audible against the crackle of the fire, and bowed her grief-stricken face. "Neither can I."

"Is it true . . ." Sarah hesitated in midsentence, then asked the question she had been dreading to ask. "Is it true that Seth had a hand in it?"

"Call him *Will*, not Seth!" her mother snapped, her head jerking toward Sarah, who jumped at the outburst. "He is not Seth, he is not your son anymore," her mother said, her swift anger tightening the sinews in her neck and making slits of her eyes. "Not after all the harm he's done."

"Do you know that for sure?"

Her mother became incoherent. "Joe . . . the Styx . . . the police . . . everyone knows it for sure!" she spluttered. "Don't *you* know what happened?"

Sarah was torn between needing to know more and not wanting to upset her mother any further. "The Styx told me Will led Tam into a trap," Sarah said, pressing her mother's hands consolingly. They were tensed and rigid.

"Just to save his own worthless hide!" the old woman spat. "But how could he?" Her head sagged, but her eyes remained fixed on Sarah. The anger seemed to desert her for that instant and was replaced with an expression of mute incomprehension. For a moment she was closer to the person Sarah remembered, the kindly old lady who had spent her whole life working so hard for her family.

"I don't know," Sarah whispered. "They say he forced Cal to go with him."

"He did!" In an instant, her mother had resumed the vengeful, ugly mask, hunching her already rounded shoulders in a show of anger and snatching her hands away from Sarah. "We welcomed Will back with open arms, but he'd become a foul, loathsome Topsoiler." She thumped the arm of the chair, her teeth clenched. "He fooled us . . . all of us, and Tam died because of him."

"I just don't understand how . . . why he did that to Tam. Why would any son of mine do that?"

"HE'S NOT YOUR SON!" her mother wailed, her small chest heaving.

Sarah recoiled — she'd never heard her mother yell before, not once in her whole life. And she feared for her mother's health. She was in such a state of distress, Sarah was worried that she might do herself harm.

Then, becoming quiet again, the old woman pleaded, "Whatever you do, you must save Cal." She leaned forward, tears streaming down her wrinkled face. "You'll get Cal back, won't you, Sarah?" her mother said, a hard, steely edge creeping into her voice. "You are going to save him — promise me that."

"If it's the last thing I do," Sarah whispered, and she turned to stare into the hearth.

This moment of meeting her mother again, of which she'd dreamed so many times for so long, had been desecrated by Will's duplicity. The depth of her mother's conviction that he was responsible banished any reservations she'd had. After a span of twelve long years, Sarah's strongest connection with her mother was their overwhelming need for vengeance.

They listened to the crackle of the fire. There was nothing to be said, and neither felt like talking anymore, consumed by the pure hatred they shared for Will.

Outside the house, Rebecca watched the horses champing impatiently and rattling their harnesses as they shook their heads. She was leaning against the door of the second carriage, in which Joe Waites sat nervously, hemmed in by several Styx. He stared at Rebecca through the small carriage window, his face taut and strained, a sheen of unhealthy sweat on his forehead.

A Styx appeared at the door of the Jerome house. It was the same Styx who'd been sitting next to Sarah for the coach journey to the Colony and, unbeknownst to her and her mother, had stolen in through the back of the house so he could monitor their conversation from the hallway.

He raised his head high to Rebecca. She nodded back once in acknowledgment.

"Is that good?" Joe Waites asked quickly, edging closer to the carriage window.

"Sit down!" Rebecca hissed with all the vehemence of a disturbed viper.

"But, my wife, my daughters?" he said hoarsely, his eyes pathetic in their desperation. "Do I get them back now?"

"Maybe. If you're a good little Colonist and continue to do as you're told," Rebecca sneered at him. Then, in the clicking, nasal language of the Styx, she addressed his escort in the carriage: "After we're finished here, put him in with his family. We'll deal with them all together when the job's done."

Joe Waites watched apprehensively as the Styx by his side acknowledged Rebecca, then gave her a sardonic grin.

Rebecca strolled back to the first coach, swaying her hips in a way that she'd seen precocious teenage girls do when she'd been Topsoil. It was her victory walk; she was reveling in her success. It was so close now, she could almost taste it, her mouth filling with a gush of sticky saliva. Her father would be so proud of her. She'd taken two problems, two strands, and was setting one against the other. The best outcome would be if they neutralized each other, but even if one remained at the end of the play, she could snuff it out so easily. *Ah, the elegance!*

She came alongside the first carriage, where the old Styx sat.

"Progress?" he asked.

"She's swallowing it, hook, line, and sinker."

"Excellent," the old Styx said to her. "And what about the loose end?" he queried, tilting his head at the carriage behind.

Rebecca smiled that gentle smile she had used to such effect on Sarah.

"When Sarah's safely on the Miners' Train, we'll shred Waites and his family and spread them over the fields in the West Cavern. Compost for the pennybun crops."

Sniffing, she made a face as if she'd smelled something distasteful. "And the same for that useless old crone in there," she added, jabbing her thumb toward the Jerome house.

She chuckled as the old Styx nodded approvingly.

17

"**F**ᴏᴏᴅ . . . no doubt about it . . . it's food," Cal said, tilting back his head and flaring his nostrils with a heavy inhalation.

"Food?" Chester reacted immediately.

"Nah, can't smell a thing." Will looked at his feet as they dawdled along, not really knowing where they were going, or why. All they knew was that they had been following the canal for miles and had not yet come across anything that even vaguely resembled a track.

"I got us fresh water, in the old Styx house, didn't I? Now I'm going to find us some fresh supplies," Cal declared with his usual cockiness.

"We've still got some left," Will replied. "Shouldn't we be heading for that light ahead or finding a road or something, not going where there might be Colonists? I say we should try and get down to the next level, where my dad's probably already gone."

"Exactly!" Chester agreed. "Especially if this wasted place is going to make us glow in the dark."

"Now," Will said, "*that* would be really useful."

"Don't be daft." Chester grinned at his friend.

"Sorry, I don't agree," Cal said, cutting across their banter. "If this is some sort of food store, we may be close to a Coprolite village."

"Yeah, and . . . ?" Will challenged.

"Well, your *so-called* father . . . he's going to be on the lookout for food, too," Cal reasoned.

"True," Will agreed.

They walked a little farther, their feet kicking up dust, until Cal announced in a singsong voice: "It's getting stronger."

"You know, I think you're right. There *is* something," Will said as they drew to a halt, sniffing.

"Hmmm, a fast-food place, maybe?" Chester suggested wistfully. "I'd give my little finger for a supersized Mac Meal right now."

"It's like something . . . sweet," Will said, a look of intense concentration on his face as he took a further succession of deep sniffs.

"Whatever it is, let's not bother," Chester proposed. He became nervous, darting cautious glances around him so that he appeared a little like a strutting pigeon. "I really don't want to meet those Coprolite things."

Cal turned to him. "Look, how many times do I have to tell you? They're completely harmless. People in the Colony say you can take what you like from them, if you can find them in the first place."

Since Chester didn't make any sort of response, Cal continued. "We have to investigate anything unusual. If we've noticed it, Will's *father* might've, too, and that's what we're sort of here for, isn't it?" he finished sarcastically. "In any case, we had to stay on this side of the canal because you didn't want to get your feet wet." Cal bent to pick up a stone, which he threw aggressively. It hit the water with a loud *splash*!

"You never let up, or shut up, do you?" Chester groaned.

"Oh yeah?" Cal replied.

"Well, it's funny, but I didn't see *you* stripping off and jumping in the canal headfirst." Chester glared at the younger boy. "What's the saying — *lead by example?*"

"What do you mean, *lead*? We don't have a leader; we're all in this together, remember?"

"Could've fooled me."

"C'mon, guys," Will pleaded. "Knock it off. We don't need this."

The trio lapsed into an aggrieved silence as they set off again, the bickering between Cal and Chester suspended for the moment.

Then Cal peeled away from Will and Chester, taking a route perpendicular to the canal.

"It's coming from over here."

He stopped as the beam of his lantern caught a rocky outcrop. Next to this was an opening, a naturally formed slit in the ground, like a large letterbox.

As the other two peered into the opening, Will happened to catch sight of a cross staked into the earth by the side of the outcrop. The cross was fashioned from two pieces of wood, bleached as white as bone and somehow bound together.

"What does that mean?" he asked, pointing it out to Cal.

"Bet it's a Coprolite marker," his brother replied, nodding enthusiastically. "If we're in luck, there could be a settlement down there, and they're certain to have some food. We can help ourselves to all we want."

"I'm not too sure about this." Will shook his head.

"Will, let's just forget it and keep going," Chester urged his friend, staring into the hole apprehensively. "I don't like the look of it, either."

"You don't like the look of *anything*," Cal spat at him. "Why don't you stay here while I take a look," he said, and scuttled down into the opening. After a few seconds, he shouted up to them that he'd found a passageway.

Will and Chester were too weary to say anything to stop him, knowing full well they'd get into another fight. With reluctance, they both followed him in. Clambering down, they found themselves in a horizontal gallery. Cal hadn't waited for them and was already some distance farther into it. They went after him, but it wasn't easy going. As the gallery pinched down to a small passageway, Will was forced to dump his backpack, next to where Cal had already shed his.

"I hate this," Chester groaned. Both he and Will were breathing hard as they pulled themselves along, sometimes dropping onto their chests to squeeze through the places where the passage ceiling lowered.

Chester was struggling. Will could hear his friend's labored breathing as he wormed his way along. He still hadn't recovered from the months of incarceration in the Hold, despite the brief rests on the Miners' Train and at the old Styx house.

"Why don't you turn around? We'll meet you back at the entrance," Will suggested.

"Nah, it's OK," Chester puffed, grunting with the effort as he forced himself through a particularly narrow gap. "Got this far, haven't I?" he added.

"OK. If you're sure."

After a couple of minutes, Will was relieved to find that the height of the ceiling was increasing, and they were able to stand once again.

And there was Cal, some fifty feet away, poised before the entrance to another long cavern. As Will and Chester stretched their limbs, he waved to them. Then he was off, brandishing his lantern before him. Will and Chester watched him go.

"He's fast, I'll give him that. I reckon he's got some rabbit in him," Chester said, breathing more steadily.

"Are you feeling better?" Will asked him, noticing the pained way Chester was rubbing his arms and how the perspiration was running down his face.

"Sure."

"We'd better catch up to him, then," Will said. "I don't like this smell at all. Really sickly," he added, wrinkling his nose.

They came to the spot where Cal had been standing and looked in.

They could feel the dryness in the air and the smell had become even more intense. It wasn't pleasant; there was an insubstantiality to it, and warning bells were beginning to ring in Will's head. He knew instinctively there was something false about it, something saccharine.

Cal was now exploring an area of the floor that was dotted with many large, rounded boulders. On these were clusters of pipelike structures protruding upward, some reaching several feet in height. Each cluster had a few larger pipes in its center, each about five inches in diameter, and around these were groupings of smaller ones, all radiating outward.

The pipes were slightly lighter in color than the rocks on which they stood, and from where he was standing, Will could see that the outsides of these pipes had definite rings circumscribing them every inch or so. To his eye, this suggested that the extensions secreted their casings as they grew. He also observed that they were anchored to the boulders by some sort of resinous secretion, like an organic glue.

They were living creatures.

Fascinated, he took a step closer.

"Will, do you think this is safe?" Chester said, grabbing his arm to hold him back.

Will just shrugged, and was peering back into the cavern when they both saw Cal lose his footing. He grabbed at the top of one of the tubes to steady himself, but withdrew his hand quickly. There was a sound, as if someone had snapped their fingers, but sharper. Cal recovered his balance and straightened up.

"Ouch," he said quietly, looking at his hand with a mystified expression.

"Cal?" Will called.

For a heartbeat the boy stood there, his back to them, still examining his hand.

Then he simply crumpled to the ground.

"CAL!"

Will and Chester exchanged frantic glances, and Will started to move forward but found Chester was still gripping his arm.

"Let me go!" he said, trying to detach himself.

"No!" Chester shouted at him.

"I have to!" Will said, struggling.

Chester released him, but Will halted after a few steps.

"What the . . . ?" Chester gasped.

They could hear it. More snaps, growing louder and more frequent. Muted, dry-sounding clicks, getting faster and faster until they merged into one resounding barrage. The terrified boys turned this way and that, trying to figure out where the throbbing percussive cacophony was coming from. But they couldn't tell; nothing appeared to have changed in the cavern where Cal lay.

"We have to get him out!" Will yelled, and started forward.

They both rushed to Cal's side. Chester eyed the columns around them with caution as Will squatted down to roll the boy over onto his back. He was limp and unresponsive, his eyes open and staring.

At first they thought he had just been stunned, but even as they watched, livid purple lines, accenting the network of capillaries beneath his skin, spread from under each of his eyes, much as ink permeates through water. With terrifying rapidity, the bruises grew larger, until they were encroaching upon his cheeks. It looked as though he had two huge black eyes.

"What's going on? What's wrong with him?" Will shouted, his voice hoarse with panic.

Chester looked blank. "I don't know," he said.

"Did he bang his head on something?" Will yelled.

Chester examined Cal's head, running his hand over his crown and down to the nape of his neck. There was no sign of any injury. "Check his breathing," he muttered to himself, trying to recall first-aid procedures. Tilting back Cal's head, he leaned forward so his ear was over the boy's nose and mouth, and listened. He pulled back slightly, vexed. Then he leaned forward again, forcing Cal's jaw farther down to check that his airway wasn't blocked by an obstruction, and once again cocked his head to one side to listen. Blowing through his lips, Chester sat back on his haunches and placed his hand on the boy's chest.

"Will! I don't think he's breathing!"

Will grabbed his brother's limp arm and shook him.

"Cal! Cal! Come on! Wake up!" he cried.

He placed two fingers on the boy's neck, feeling for the artery and frantically trying to find a pulse.

"Here . . . No . . . Where is it? . . . Nothing . . . WHERE IS IT?" he yelled. "Am I doing this right?" He looked at Chester, his eyes wide with the wrenching, screaming awareness that he couldn't find a heartbeat.

That his brother was dead.

At that very moment, the clicks were replaced by another sound. A soft popping similar to that of champagne corks going off, but gentler, as if heard through a wall.

A streaming, fluxing whiteness instantly filled the air. The deluge engulfed the boys, catching in the beams of their lights and clogging the space. These particles, like a million tiny petals, spewed forth in torrents. They could have been coming from the tubes, but it was so dense it was impossible to tell.

"No!" Will shrieked.

With a hand clapped over his nose and mouth, he began to heave his brother by his arm, trying to drag him toward the entrance of the cavern. But Will found he couldn't draw breath; the particles were like sand, blocking his mouth and nostrils.

He arched his back and swallowed a little air, enough for him to shout a few words at Chester. "Get him out!" he cried over the incessant popping.

Chester didn't need to be told, but was floundering under the onslaught, blinking and shielding his eyes as the dry, snow-like material continued to spurt forth. The air was so thick and impenetrable that, as he waved at Will, his arm left swirling eddies behind it.

Will slipped and fell to the ground, coughing and choking. "Can't breathe," he wheezed with what little air he had left in his lungs. Lying on his side, he struggled to fill them again, cursing inside as he thought of the gas masks he and Cal had used in the Eternal City. They'd dumped them, figuring they would be of no further use. They'd been wrong.

With his hand held over his face, Will stayed on his side, panting, unable to do anything. Through the deluge he saw Chester hauling Cal along, the boy's body leaving tracks behind it in the whiteness.

Will forced himself to crawl, his lungs aching from lack of oxygen, his head spinning. He couldn't think about his brother; he knew *he* was going to succumb if he didn't get out of the cavern. His throat and nostrils were blocked as if he'd been buried in flour. With a supreme effort he staggered to his feet and managed a few steps. Chester, his back to Will, was still pulling and heaving Cal's lifeless body.

Will launched himself forward, propelling himself only a couple of paces before collapsing to the ground again. It was enough. He was away from the worst of the swirling maelstrom of whiteness and able to suck in some clean air.

He continued at a slow crawl but hadn't gone very far when he doubled up and coughed so much he was sick, uncontrollably so. To his horror, his vomit was awash with the minute pale particles and small slugs of blood. With the single thought of survival in his mind, he forced himself down the passageway on his hands and knees, pulling himself blindly through the narrow stretch, and didn't stop until he'd reached the letterbox opening.

He heaved himself back out onto the Great Plain and lay coughing and spluttering and throwing up a mottled fluid. But his ordeal wasn't over yet. Where the white specks had stuck to the exposed skin of his neck and face, they began to irritate it, the irritation very quickly transforming into the most excruciating burning sensation. He tried to scratch off the particles, but this just seemed to make things worse: As the white specks came away, they took the skin with them. Soon blood was smeared all over his fingers.

Not knowing what else to do, he grabbed handfuls of dirt and scrubbed furiously at his face and neck. This seemed to do the trick, the intolerable itching and pain easing a little. But his eyes were still on fire, and it took him some minutes to wipe them clean using the inside of his shirtsleeve.

Then Chester appeared. He scrambled up through the opening, staggering around blindly. As he fell on all fours and coughed and retched, Will saw that he had been dragging something behind him. Through his watering eyes, he thought it was Cal. But his heart sank as he realized it was just the rucksacks.

Chester howled, clawing at his face. He was completely covered in the white particles, his hair matted with them and his face furred where they had stuck in his sweat. He howled again, scratching violently at his neck as if he were trying to tear off his own skin. "It burns!" he cried in a strangled, tortured wail.

"Use the dirt, rub it off!" Will yelled.

Chester immediately did so, seizing handfuls of soil and scouring his face with it.

"Make sure it's out of your eyes!"

Chester rummaged in his pants pocket and, bringing out a handkerchief, dabbed urgently at his eyes. After a short while his movements became less frantic. Snot streamed from his nose, and his eyes were still watering and rimmed bright red. His face was a mixture of streaked dirt and blood, as if he were wearing some ghastly mask. He looked at Will with a haunted expression.

"I couldn't take it any longer," he croaked. "I couldn't stay in there . . . I couldn't breathe." He broke into a racking cough.

"I've got to get him out," Will said, starting toward the opening. "I'm going back in."

"No, you're not!" Chester snapped, leaping to his feet and seizing hold of him.

"I have to!" Will protested, trying to pull away.

"Don't be stupid, Will! What if those things get you, and I can't get *you* out!" Chester shouted.

Will grappled with his friend, struggling to break loose, but Chester was determined not to let him go. In sheer frustration, Will made a halfhearted attempt to punch Chester, and then began to sob. He knew what Chester was saying made sense. His whole body went limp, as if all his strength had suddenly deserted him.

"OK, OK," Will said in an unsteady voice, holding his hands up to Chester, who released him. He coughed, then threw back his head as if looking for the sky, even though he knew it was hidden from him by many miles of the earth's mantle. He sighed a sigh that shook his whole body as the realization sank in.

"You're right. Cal's dead," he said.

Chester fixed his eyes on Will, nodding once.

"I'm sorry, Will, I really am."

"He was just trying to help. He was trying to find us some food . . . and now look what happened." Will's shoulders sank and he bowed his head.

As his raw skin continued to burn, Will rubbed his neck, his hand touching and unconsciously closing around the jade pendant that hung there. It had been given to him by Tam minutes before he was slaughtered by the Styx. "I promised Uncle Tam I'd take care of Cal. I gave him my word," he said bleakly, turning away. "What are we doing here? How did all this happen?" He coughed, and then spoke in a small voice. "Dad's probably dead somewhere just like that, and we're idiots and we're going to die, too. I'm sorry, Chester — game over. We're done for."

Leaving his lantern behind, he walked away from Chester, stumbling toward a boulder. There, in the dark, he sat down and stared into the nothingness before him, as it stared back into him.

18

WITH A LOUD LASH of the whip, the carriage left the Jerome house. It passed through the cordon as a barricade was hurriedly pulled aside by some policemen. A small crowd had gathered farther down the road, and Colonists were doing their best to appear to be going about their everyday business. They failed miserably, craning their necks toward the cab in a bid to see who was inside, as indeed did many of the policemen.

Sarah gazed vacantly through the window, oblivious to the faces and their curious stares. She was utterly exhausted from the reunion with her mother.

"You do realize you're somewhat of a celebrity," Rebecca said as she sat by the old Styx, the younger one having remained behind at the Jerome house.

Sarah gave the girl a glassy-eyed stare before turning to the window again.

The carriage rattled through the streets to the farthermost corner of the South Cavern, where the Styx compound stood. The compound was encircled by a thirty-foot wrought-iron fence, and within it was a huge, forbidding building. Its seven stories were carved from the very rock itself, and it had two square towers at either end of its frontage. The building, known as the Styx Citadel, was functional and stark, its rough stone walls without a single decorative feature to relieve its geometric simplicity. No Colonist had ever set foot in it, and nobody knew exactly what went on inside or quite how big it was, since the structure penetrated so deep into the actual bedrock. There had been talk that the Citadel was linked to the surface by various tunnels so the Styx could make their way up whenever they wanted.

Also within the compound, to the side of the Citadel, was a large but far squatter building, with ranks of small and regularly spaced windows dotted through its two stories. Referred to as the Garrison, it was generally thought to be the center of the Styx's military operations. Unlike the Citadel, Colonists were permitted into this building and, indeed, a number worked there in the service of the Styx.

And it was to this building, the Garrison, that the carriage went. Disembarking, Sarah unquestioningly followed Rebecca to the entrance, where a policeman in a sentry box touched his cap respectfully, his eyes averted. Once inside the Garrison, Rebecca handed Sarah over to a Colonist and promptly left.

Sarah, her head hanging with fatigue, managed a glance at the man. His shirtsleeves were rolled up to reveal massively powerful forearms, and he was deep-chested and stocky, like many of the men of the Colony. He wore a long black rubber apron upon which was centered a small white cross insignia. His scalp was almost clean-shaven, with the odd stubble of white hair beginning to show through, and his enormous brow overhung two perfectly pale blue but rather small eyes. With similar coloration to Sarah herself, he was a "pure stock," to use the local term for the albinos, the descendants of some of the original founders of the Colony. He, like the policeman, had acted very deferentially toward Rebecca, but now he kept stealing glances at Sarah as she trailed listlessly behind him.

He led her up a flight of stairs and through several corridors, their footsteps clacking on the polished stone floors. The walls were plain and unadorned, interrupted only by the numerous dark iron doors, all of which were closed. He came to one of these and swung it open before her. The stone floor continued in, and she saw that a bed mat lay in the corner under a slit window set high into the wall. There was a white enamel bowl beside the bed, filled with water, and by it were a similarly enameled mug and some slices of pennybun fungus, stacked neatly on a plate. The simplicity and bareness of the room gave it the feel of a monastery or some sort of religious retreat.

She stood on the threshold but did not make a move to go in.

The man opened his mouth as if to speak, then closed it. He did this several times, like a beached fish, and then seemed to summon up enough courage.

"Sarah," he said, ever so gently, as he inclined his head toward hers.

She looked slowly up at him.

He checked up and down the corridor, making sure no one was close enough to overhear. "I shouldn't speak to you like this, but . . . don't you recognize me?" he asked.

She crinkled her eyes as if trying to focus on him, and then a startled look of recognition came over her.

"Joseph . . . ," she said in a whisper. They were of the same age, and as teenagers had been close. She had lost contact with him when his family had fallen on hard times and been forced to relocate to the West Cavern, to work the fields there.

He gave an uneasy grin, at odds with his great ham of a face and strangely all the more tender for it.

"You should know everyone understands why you went, and . . . we . . ." He fumbled for the right words. "We never forgot you, some of us . . . me."

A door slammed somewhere in the building, and he glanced anxiously over his shoulder.

"Thank you, Joseph," she said as she touched his arm, then shambled into the room.

Joseph muttered something and closed the door softly behind her, but none of it registered with Sarah, who dropped her bag on the floor and crumpled onto the bed mat. She stared at the burnished stone of the wall where it joined the floor, seeing in it the outlines of many fossil forms, mostly ammonites and other bivalves, their subtle traces appearing as if some divine designer had drawn them in with a china marker.

As she tried to organize her different thoughts and emotions into some semblance of order, the massed remains of the fossils, caught for all time in their frozen attitudes, almost made sense to her. It was as if she suddenly understood them, as if she could read a pattern in their chaotic arrangement, a secret key, which helped to explain everything. But then the moment of clarity passed and, in the abounding silence, she drifted into a dead slumber.

19

THE FIRST RAYS of the sun tipped over the horizon, suffusing a narrow strip of sky with a dawn palette of reds and oranges. Within minutes, its nascent light was stretching low across the rooftops, pushing back the night and marking the start of the new day.

Below in Trafalgar Square, a trio of black cabs jostled away from traffic lights as a lone cyclist weaved recklessly between them. Beyond the far corner of the square, a convoy of red double-deckers came into sight, pulling up at the bus stops. But very few passengers could be seen getting on or off at that time in the morning. The rush hour was yet to come.

"The early bird catches the worm," Rebecca laughed mirthlessly, scanning the sidewalks below as she picked out the odd pedestrian walking there.

"I think not of them as worms; they are worse than senseless things," the old Styx proclaimed, contemplating the scene with his glittering eyes, which were every bit as alert as Rebecca's.

In the growing light, his face was so pale and unyielding it could have been carved from a block of ancient ivory. And with his ankle-length leather overcoat and his hands clasped behind his back, he resembled a conquering general as he stood by Rebecca on the very edge of the roof of Admiralty Arch. Both of them showed not the slightest fear at the sheer drop immediately before them.

"There are those who would oppose us and the measures we are to take," the old Styx said, still regarding the square. "You have begun to cleanse the Deeps of renegades, but it does not end there. There are reactionary factions both here on the surface and in the Colony, in the Rookeries, of whom we have been far too tolerant for far too long. You have brought your late father's plans forward and, now when they are so finely poised, we cannot allow a fly in the ointment."

"Agreed," Rebecca said, giving no clue that the decision had been taken there and then to kill several thousand people.

The old Styx closed his eyes, not because the gathering Topsoil light bothered him, but because he had been struck by a thought that was tiresome.

"That Burrows child . . ."

Rebecca opened her mouth to speak, but held her tongue as the old Styx continued.

"You and your sister did well to pull in the Jerome woman and neutralize her. Your father was not one for unfinished business, either. Both of you have his instinct," the old Styx said, so softly that it could have been construed as affection.

His tone resumed its usual hardness. "That being as it is, we have scotched the snake, not killed it. Will Burrows is contained for the moment, but he may yet become a false idol, a figurehead, for our enemies. They might seek to use him in their opposition of us and the measures we intend to take. He cannot be allowed to continue to roam unchecked in the

Interior. He must be flushed out and stopped." Only then did the old Styx swivel his head slowly toward Rebecca, who continued to gaze down on the scene below. "And the boy might yet piece together what we're doing and sideline our plans. This is to be avoided . . . at all costs," he stressed.

"It will be dealt with," Rebecca assured him with unerring conviction.

"Make sure of it," the old Styx said and released his hands from behind his back, swinging them in front of him and clapping them together.

Rebecca took her cue from the gesture. "Yes," she said, "we should get under way." Her long black coat billowed open in the breeze as she half turned to the troop of Styx waiting quietly behind her.

"Let me see one," she ordered as she left the roof edge and strode imperiously toward the rank of shadowy men. There were perhaps as many as fifty of them in a perfectly straight line, and from this a single Styx snapped obediently to life, breaking from the formation. He kneeled down to slip his gloved hand under the lid of one of a pair of large wicker baskets that he and every one of the Styx on the rooftop had by their feet. From the basket came the soft sounds of cooing. He plucked out a pure white dove and closed the lid again. As he passed the dove to Rebecca, it tried to flap its wings, but she took it firmly in both hands.

She held the bird on its side to inspect its legs. There was something around both of them, as if the bird had been ringed, but these were more than mere metal bands. Made from an off-white fabric, they sparkled dimly as the light caught them.

Each band had tiny spheres embedded in it, which had been designed to degrade upon several hours' exposure to ultraviolet light and shed their load. The sun itself was the timing mechanism, the trigger.

"They are ready?" the old Styx asked as he came alongside Rebecca.

"They are," another Styx confirmed from farther down the line.

"Excellent," the old Styx said as he began to stroll along the rank of men, each one melding with the next in the weak light as they stood shoulder to shoulder, all wearing identical black leather greatcoats and breathing apparatus.

"My brothers," the old Styx addressed them. "We're done with hiding. It's time to take what is rightfully ours." He was silent for a moment, allowing his words to sink in. "Today will be remembered as the first day of a glorious new epoch in our history. It is a day that will mark our eventual return to the surface."

Drawing to a halt, he punched his fist into the palm of his hand. "In the last hundred years we have made the Topsoilers atone for their sins by unleashing the germules they call *influenzas*. The first was in the summer of nineteen eighteen." He gave a sour laugh. "The poor fools called it the Spanish Flu, and it took millions of them to their graves. Then we gave them further demonstrations of our power in nineteen fifty-seven and nineteen sixty-eight with the Asian and Hong Kong variants."

He punched his palm with even greater force, the slap of his leather gloves resounding around the rooftop.

"But those epidemics amount to nothing more than common colds compared to what is to come. The Topsoilers' souls are rotten to the very core — their morality is that of the insane — and they ruin our promised lands with their excessive consumption and greed.

"Their time is drawing to a close, and the Heathen shall be purged," he growled like a wounded bear, scanning from one end of the rank to the other before he began to walk again, his boot heels clicking on the lead flat of the roof.

"For today we test a reduced strain of *Dominion*, our holy plague. And through the fruits of our labors, we will confirm that it can be spread throughout this city, throughout this country, and then to the rest of the world." He raised his hand, splaying his fingers at the sky. "Once our birds take flight, the sun will see to it that the air currents carry our message to the evil masses, a message that will be written in blood and pus across the face of this earth."

Reaching the last man in the rank, he swung around to return down it again, silent until he neared the midpoint of the line.

"So, my comrades, the next time we find ourselves here, our cargo will indeed be deadly. Then our foes, the Topsoilers, will be laid low, just as it is decreed in the *Book of Catastrophes*. And we, the true heirs to the earth, shall regain what is rightfully ours."

He came to a dramatic halt and addressed the Styx in a lower, more intimate tone. "To work."

There was a flurry of activity as the troop got ready.

Rebecca took over. "On my mark . . . three . . . two . . . one . . . go!" she commanded, pitching her dove high into the air. The Styx immediately heaved open the baskets by their feet and the birds took to the wing, a white swarm flapping from between the amassed men and lifting from the rooftop.

Rebecca watched her dove for as long as she could, but the hundreds of others caught up with it, and it was soon lost in the flock, which seemed to linger for a second over Nelson's Column before dispersing in all directions, like a cloud of pale smoke fanned by the wind.

"Fly, fly, fly!" Rebecca called out after them, laughing.

PART 3

DRAKE
AND
ELLIOTT

20

"IT'S JUST TERRIBLE," Chester kept saying over and over again as the enormity of what had happened sank in. "But there wasn't anything we could do. He didn't have a pulse."

Chester was remonstrating with himself, laden with a mounting sense of guilt. He believed that he was partly to blame for Cal's death. Perhaps, by being so critical of the boy, he had goaded him on, provoking him into being so reckless and entering the cavern by himself.

"We couldn't go back in . . . ," Chester babbled on to himself.

He was rocked to the very core. He'd never seen anybody die, not before his very eyes. It took him back to the time he had been in the car with his father and they'd driven past the aftermath of a bloody motorcycle accident. He didn't know if the twisted body by the roadside was dead — and he'd never found out. But this was different. This was someone he knew, who had died while he'd actually been watching. One minute Cal was there, the next he was just a limp body. *A dead body.* It was so absolute, and so brutally final; it was as if he'd been talking to someone on the telephone and they'd been cut off, never to speak again. Chester just couldn't come to terms with it.

After a while he lapsed into silence and he and Will walked side by side, their boots scuffling in the dust. Oblivious to his surroundings, Will placed one foot mechanically in front of the other like a sleepwalker, as the canal continued for mile after monotonous mile.

Chester watched him with concern. If Will didn't pull through this, he didn't know how they would be able to go on. The Deeps weren't the sort of place that gave you any leeway; you had to have all your wits about you if you wanted to stay alive. The grim spectacle of Cal's demise chillingly confirmed that hard truth. All Chester could do now was keep them on course by the side of the canal, which had altered direction and seemed to be taking them directly toward one of the flickering points of light. With every hour, the light grew brighter and brighter, like a guiding star. Guiding them to what, he didn't know.

On the second day, they came close enough to the light to make out the unsteady illumination it was shedding on the curving rock wall around it. They were evidently at the limits of the Great Plain. As Chester crept stealthily, Will just ambled along behind, not giving his surroundings the slightest attention.

They arrived at the source of the light. A metal arm, about a foot and a half long, sprouted from the rock wall with a blue-tinged flame dancing at its end. It hissed and spluttered in the breeze as if disapproving of the boys' presence there. Under this gaslight, the canal continued undeterred, straight into an opening in the wall so perfectly round that it had to be man-made, or at least Coprolite-made. But there was no ledge, or anything else that would afford them a way beside it.

"Well, that's that," Will articulated miserably. "We're snookered."

He backed away from the canal, totally disregarding a small stream issuing from the wall beside it. Water was trickling out of a fissure at about chest height and had worn a smooth groove down the cavern wall. It ran into an overflowing basin of water-polished rock. From there it flooded over the lip and down several small plateaus until it drained into the canal. The passage of water had left a brownish stain around its path, but this didn't deter Chester from sampling a mouthful.

"It's good. Why don't you try some?" he called over to Will. It was the first time he'd attempted to speak directly to him in nearly a day.

"Nope," Will replied morosely, flopping down on the ground with a forlorn sigh. He hugged his knees to his chest, rocking gently, and lowered his head so his face was hidden from Chester.

His frustration building to bursting point, Chester resolved to snap his friend out of it, and stomped over to him.

"OK, Will," he said in a level, carefully controlled voice, so much so that it didn't sound natural at all and alerted Will to what was coming next. "We'll just sit here until you make up your mind you want to do something again. Take your time. I don't care if it's days or even weeks. Take as long as you want. That's fine with me." He blew through his lips. "In fact, if you want to just stay here until we *rot*, that's fine with me, too. I'm very sorry about Cal, but it doesn't change the reason why we're here . . . why you asked for my help to find your dad." He didn't speak for a moment, hovering over Will. "Or have you just forgotten about him?"

The last sentence had the effect of a jab to the stomach. Will gasped, but still he didn't raise his head.

"Suit yourself," Chester snapped at his friend, then retired a short distance, where he lay down. He didn't know how much time had passed when he heard Will talking. It came like words in a dream, and Chester realized he must have nodded off.

". . . you're right, we must keep going," Will was saying.

"Huh?"

"Let's be on our way." Will got briskly to his feet and went directly to the trickling stream to give it a cursory investigation. Then he began to study the opening where the canal passed into the cavern wall, shining his lantern just inside the entrance, in the hard shadows where the gaslight didn't penetrate. Nodding to himself, he focused his attention on the vertical rock face above it.

"We're all right," he announced, returning to where he'd left his backpack and shrugging it onto his shoulders.

"Huh? We are *what*?"

"I think it's clear" was Will's inscrutable response.

"Yeah, clear as mud!"

"Well, are you coming or not?" he harshly asked Chester, who stared at his friend, suspicious of the sudden change that had come over him. Will was already by the side of the canal, clipping his lantern onto his shirt pocket. He faced the wall for a few seconds, then began to heave himself up it. Finding foot- and handholds, he climbed in an arc that took him under the spluttering gaslight but over the entrance of the slow-moving canal, until he was safely on the opposite side.

"Not the first time that's been done," he declared. He called to Chester, still on the other bank: "Come on, don't just stand there. It's a piece of cake — not difficult to get across. Someone's chiseled out some grips."

Chester looked indignant and impressed in equal measures. His jaw dropped, as if he was about to say something, but he thought better of it, muttering only, "Business as usual."

Although Will wasn't following any discernible path, he now seemed to be so convinced they were going in the right direction that it was Chester tagging along after him again. Marching swiftly, they moved deeper into the featureless expanse, not encountering any other landmarks, until they eventually arrived at a place where the floor became looser and began to gradually ascend. Perhaps it had something to do with the fact that the canopy above their heads was also increasing in height but, with every step the boys took, the winds around them seemed to be blowing with much greater force.

"Phew, that's better!" Will said, running a finger around the inside of his sweat-soaked shirt collar. "Bit cooler now!"

Chester couldn't have been more relieved that Will appeared to have pulled himself out of the appalling melancholy into which he'd sunk. In fact, he was chatting away quite normally, although it felt so much quieter without Cal there to badger them. As if his mind were playing tricks on him, Chester had the oddest feeling that the boy was still there with them.

He found himself glancing around in an effort to locate him.

"Hey, this feels sort of chalky," Will noted as they clambered up the slope, slipping and stumbling as the light-colored substrate shifted beneath them. For the last stretch, the incline had become more pronounced, and they had been forced to climb it on all fours.

Will suddenly stopped to pluck a rock the size of a tennis ball. "Wow! A fine specimen of a *desert rose*." Chester saw the pale pink blades that radiated out from a central point to form the strangely shaped sphere of rock. It looked like some sort of cubist flower. Will was intently scratching one of the blades with his nail. "Yep, this is gypsum, all right. Nice, isn't it?" he said to Chester, who didn't have time to answer before Will was spouting forth again. "A fine example." He glanced around. "So there must have been evaporation going on here for the last century or so — unless, of course, this was buried and it's much older. Anyway, think I'll keep it," he said, slipping off his rucksack.

"You're going to do what? It's just a hunk of rock!"

"No, it's not rock. It's actually a mineral formation. Imagine some sort of sea right here." Will opened his arms expansively. "As it dries up, the salts all come out of solution and . . . well, the rest of what you see is sedimentary. You know about sedimentary rocks, don't you?"

"No, I don't," Chester admitted, studying his friend carefully.

"Well, you have three classes of rock: sedimentary, igneous, and metamorphic," Will blathered on. "My favorites are sedimentary, just like we're finding down here, because there's a *story* in them, from the fossils you get in them. They're formed . . ."

"Will," Chester said gently.

". . . formed generally on the surface, mostly underwater. Why would you find sedimentary rocks so deep in the earth? I wonder." He looked mystified at his own question, then answered it. "Yes, I suppose there must have been a subterranean lake or something here."

"Will!" Chester tried again.

"Anyway, sedimentary rocks are cool — I don't mean cool as in *good*, but cool as in cold, as opposed to hot, not *hot* like lava, which are the igneous rocks, which are . . ."

"Will, stop it!" Chester shouted, becoming quite alarmed by his friend's bizarre behavior.

". . . called the *first great class* because they're formed from hot, molten . . . ," Will trailed off in midsentence.

"Get a grip, Will. What the heck are you talking about?" Chester's voice was hoarse with desperation. "What's wrong with you?"

"I don't know," Will replied, shaking his head.

"Well, shut up and concentrate on what we're doing. I don't need a freakin' lecture."

"Right." Will blinked around him as if he'd wandered out of a fog and couldn't quite figure out where he was. He realized the desert rose was still in his hand and he lobbed it away. Then he put his rucksack back on. Chester watched him with concern as he set off again.

They were approaching the high point of the slope, and the floor began leveling off. A ray of light streaked through the air and raked across the ceiling. It looked like a distant spotlight of some sort. As a precaution, Chester turned his lantern down to a mere glimmer and, at his insistence, Will did the same.

They crawled along the last stretch, keeping low, with Chester making sure that Will, in his unpredictable state of mind, stayed tucked in behind him. At the top, they peered over, into a large circular space the size of a stadium. It could have been a moon crater, it looked so barren and dusty.

"Dang, Will, look at this," Chester whispered, waving his friend alongside him and hastily switching off his lantern altogether. "Do you see them? They look exactly like Styx, but they're dressed like soldiers or something."

On the floor of the crater, the boys could make out that there were around ten Styx — although their clothes were unfamiliar, their thin bodies and the way they carried themselves meant they couldn't be anything else — and two of them had stalker dogs. The men were drawn up in a single line, with a further Styx standing slightly forward from them and brandishing a large lantern. Although the base of the crater was illuminated by four large light orbs mounted on tripods, the main Styx's lantern was phenomenally powerful, and he was directing it on something before him.

A tremor went through Chester's body — as he watched the Styx, he felt as though he had stumbled upon a nest of the most evil and poisonous snakes imaginable. "Oh, I hate them," he growled through his clenched teeth.

"Hmmm," Will answered vaguely as he casually examined a pebble with glittering striations that had caught his eye, then flicked it away with his thumb.

It didn't take a clinical psychologist to recognize that something was wrong with him; that his brother's death had knocked a screw loose.

"Hello! Earth to Will! You're acting pretty spacey," Chester said. "Those are *Styx* down there, murderous, mind-warping Styx."

"Yeah," Will said. "Sure are."

Chester was stunned by his total lack of concern. "Well, they make my skin crawl. Let's just get away from here," he suggested urgently, beginning to edge back.

"See the Coprolites," Will said, pointing carelessly at the scene below.

"What?" Chester grunted as he tried to locate them. "Where?"

"There . . . opposite that Styx . . . ," Will replied, pushing himself up on his arms to get a better view. "Right there in his light."

"Where exactly?" Chester asked again in a whisper. He glanced at Will beside him and immediately growled, "You numskull, get your head down! They'll see you!"

"Okey-doke," Will replied, ducking lower.

Chester turned back to the scene and, despite the lancing shaft of light from the Styx's lantern, it wasn't until one of them stirred that he located it (or him or her, for that matter — Chester found it hard to think of the lumbering Coprolites as *people*). The Coprolites' eye-beams were barely noticeable in the well-lit area, and their mushroom-colored suits merged so effectively with the stone of the crater floor that, having found one, Chester still had great difficulty picking out the others. In fact, there were quite a number of them, standing in an uneven row opposite the Styx.

"Just how many are there?" he asked Will.

"Can't say. Twenty or so?"

The main Styx was pacing between the two groups. He would strut up and down and then abruptly wheel to face the Coprolites, thrusting his lantern at them. Although the boys couldn't hear anything he was saying, from the jerking motion of his arms and rapid switching of his head, it was clear he was shouting at the Coprolites. The boys watched for several minutes, until Will became restless and started to fidget.

"I'm hungry. Got that chewing gum?"

"You've got to be kidding — how can you be hungry at a time like this?" Chester asked him.

"I don't know . . . just give me some, will you?" Will whined.

"Pull yourself together, Will," Chester urged, not moving his eyes from the Styx. "You know where the gum is."

In his befuddled state, it took Will forever to undo the flap on the side pocket of Chester's rucksack. Muttering to himself, he rummaged around until he found the green packet of chewing gum. He put it in front of him as he refastened the flap.

"Want a piece?" he asked Chester.

"No, I do not."

Dropping it several times as though his hands were numb, Will finally tore open the packet and pried out one of the sticks. With his fumbling fingers, he was on the verge of sliding the paper casing off the silver foil when both boys let out simultaneous gasps.

They felt a crushing pressure on their backs as knives were thrust against their throats.

"Don't make a sound." The voice was low and guttural, as if it wasn't accustomed to being used. It came from a point very close behind Will's head.

Chester swallowed loudly.

"And don't move a muscle."

Will let the stick of gum slip from his hand.

"I can smell that stinking stuff already, and you haven't even opened it yet."

Will tried to speak.

"I said shut up." The knife dug even harder into Will's neck. He felt the pressure on his back increase, and a mittened hand reached between him and Chester and began to scoop a hole in the loose gravel.

The boys both watched from the corners of their eyes, not daring to move their heads an inch. It was almost hypnotic, a disembodied hand in a black mitten digging itself a small hole, little by little.

Chester suddenly couldn't stop himself from shaking. Had he and Will been caught by Styx? *Or if not Styx, who were they?* His mind filled with panic-ridden thoughts about what might happen next. *Were these people going to slit their throats and bury them here, in this hole?* He couldn't take his eyes off it.

Then the hand very deliberately took the packet of chewing gum between thumb and forefinger, and dropped it into the hole.

"That piece, too," the man's voice ordered. Will did as he was told, throwing the unopened stick in the hole.

Then the hand, in precise movements, scraped the gypsum gravel back into the hole, until the chewing gum was completely buried.

"That'll help, but the smell's still strong," the man's voice came again after the interlude. "If you had opened it, the stalker nearest to us . . ." The voice trailed off, then resumed again. "You can see it down there . . . would've picked up the scent in a matter of . . . what do you think?"

There was a pause during which Will wasn't sure if he was meant to be answering, and then they heard a different and slightly softer voice. This second one came from behind Chester. "They're downwind," it said, "so a couple of seconds at most."

The man spoke again. "Then the Limiters would've slipped the dogs off their reins, and they'd have followed close behind. You'd be dead 'uns, like those poor wretches down there." He drew breath somberly. "You should watch this."

In spite of the threat from the knives at their throats, both Will and Chester made a concerted effort to focus on what was happening below.

The main Styx swung around and barked a command. Three men in clothes of neutral color were each escorted into the center of the crater by a pair of Styx. Will and Chester hadn't spotted them before because they had been huddled in the shadows beyond the scope of the floodlights. They were pushed beside the group of Coprolites, and their escorts returned to the Styx line.

The head Styx barked another order and held his hand high as a number of his men stepped forward and put their rifles to their shoulders. Then, with a staccato shout, the Styx dropped his hand, and flashes exploded from the barrels of the firing squad. Two of the three figures fell immediately. The remaining one tottered for a moment before he, too, went over, collapsing across the other downed men. As the last echoes of the shots reverberated around the crater and an eerie silence filled the place, none of the three moved. It had all happened so quickly.

"No," Will said, not believing his eyes. "The Styx . . . they didn't?"

"Yes, you have just witnessed an execution," came the man's inexpressive voice from close behind his head. "And those were our people, our friends."

With another order, the firing squad passed their rifles to their nearest comrades. Then they each drew some glinting weapon from their sides and took several paces forward. There was a horrible inevitability to it as the advancing Styx each strode up to a Coprolite in the opposing line.

The boys watched as the Styx soldiers lunged at the Coprolites, who simply dropped to the ground like felled trees before them.

The other Coprolites stood in their higgledy-piggledy line, facing in all directions. They made no move to help their fallen brothers and, what was even more astounding, they didn't seem to react to their deaths at all. It was as if, right in the middle of a herd, cattle had been killed, and the rest of them had just accepted it like dumb animals might.

The gruff voice spoke again. "Enough of this. You can feel our knives. We *will* use them if you don't do exactly as you are told. Is that understood?"

Both boys mumbled a "yes," feeling the blades press harder into their skin.

"Put your arms behind your backs," the quieter voice ordered.

The boys' wrists were bound tightly, then their heads were lifted roughly by their hair and blindfolds tied around them.

As hands grasped their ankles, they were mercilessly dragged on their fronts, back down the steep slope behind them. Not able to resist, they tried to arch their heads and keep their faces away from the ground racing beneath them.

Then, with equal roughness, they were manhandled up onto their feet, and both felt something being attached to the bindings around their wrists. They were yanked on by these, each boy hearing the stumbling steps of the other, and led at breakneck speed down the remainder of the slope, leaning back lest they fall. Will guessed that they'd been tethered together, like two beasts off to the slaughterhouse.

At the bottom of the slope, Chester lost his footing and tumbled over, pulling Will with him.

"Get up, you slop bags!" the man hissed. "Or we'll finish both of you, here and now."

Using each other for support, the boys heaved themselves to their feet again.

"Move," the other one snarled, striking Will so hard on his wounded shoulder that he let loose a wail of pain. He heard his captor take a step back in surprise.

Will's hurt and fear, coming on top of the intense feelings of loss for Cal, suddenly made something flip in his head. He stood his ground and spoke in a low, threatening voice.

"Do that again, and I'll . . ."

"What?" the voice said. It was gentler than it had been before, and Will noticed for the first time that it had a youthful and *feminine* edge to it. "What will you do?" it asked again.

"You're a girl, aren't you?" Will said, rather incredulously. Without waiting for a response, he clenched his bound hands together and squared up to her — which was difficult considering he had no idea where she was actually standing.

"I'll call in our backup," he said fiercely, remembering the line from one of his mother's favorite television series.

"*Backup?* What's that?" she asked hesitantly.

"A handpicked team of men are monitoring your every move," he added, with as much conviction as he could muster. "All I have to do is give the signal. You'll be taken out."

"He's bluffing," came the man's voice. It, too, had lost some of its sternness, and there was even a hint of amusement in it. "They're alone. We didn't see anyone with them, did we, Elliott?" He spoke directly to Will. "If you don't cooperate, I'll run your friend through with my knife."

This had the desired effect on Will, bringing him quickly back to earth.

"All right, all right, I'll come quietly, but you'd better watch it. Don't mess with us, or . . . ," Will trailed off. He figured he'd pushed his luck as far as he could and began to move forward again, bumping into Chester, who had been listening to his friend with total bewilderment.

21

"**AND IT IS WRITTEN** in the *Book of Catastrophes* that the people shall return to their rightful place from the Ark of the Earth, at such time that the unholy deluge has withdrawn. And the people will once again plow the unplowed fields, rebuild the leveled cities, and fill the wasted lands with their pure seed. So it is said, and so shall it be," the Styx preacher boomed.

In the confines of the small stone room in the Garrison building, he towered above her kneeling form, his clawlike hands raking the air around him, his burning eyes and his black cloak making him look like some terrible visitation.

His cape flapped open from his thin body as he stepped closer to Sarah, his right hand spearing to the ceiling and his left pointing downward to the floor. "As it is in the firmaments, so it is in the earth below," he crackled in his thin voice. "Amen."

"Amen," she echoed.

"God be with you in all that you do in the name of the Colony." He suddenly thrust his hands at her, grabbing her head and pressing his two thumbs into the ghost-white skin of her forehead, so hard that when he finally released her and stepped back, red marks were visible on it.

He gathered his cloak about himself and swept out of the room, leaving the door open behind him.

Her head bent, Sarah remained kneeling until she heard a stifled cough from the corridor. Looking up, she saw Joseph, a plate of food cradled in his giant hands.

"A blessing, huh?"

Sarah nodded.

"I don't mean to intrude, but my mother made these for you. Some cakes."

"You'd better bring them in quickly — I don't think Doctor Doom would approve," she said.

"No," Joseph agreed, and entered hastily, shutting the door behind him. Then he hovered uneasily, as if he'd forgotten why he'd come there.

"Why don't you make yourself comfortable?" Sarah offered as she moved across the floor to the bed mat.

Sitting by her side, he lifted a layer of muslin from the plate to reveal the cakes, their icing an insipid butterscotch color over the gray fungal fibers used for baking in the Colony. He passed the plate to Sarah.

"Ah, *fancies*." She smiled to herself, recognizing how similar they were to the shapeless but nonetheless delicious cakes her mother would bake for Sunday teatimes. Sarah helped herself to one, nibbling at it without much interest.

"They're wonderful. Please do thank your mother — I remember her well."

"She sends her love," Joseph said. "She's eighty this year and doing—" Without a breath, he interrupted himself, as if he'd been building up to what he really wanted to say. "Sarah, can I ask something?"

"Of course, anything," she said, looking at him attentively.

"When you've done whatever they want you to, will you come home, for good?"

"Have you any idea *why* I'm here?" she shot back, studying him carefully.

He rubbed his chin as if to buy time before giving an answer. "It's not my place to know such things . . . but I'd wager it has to do with what's going on Topsoil. . . ."

"No, I'm headed the other way," she said, tipping her head to indicate the Deeps.

"So you're not involved with the operation in London?" Joseph blurted out, then clamped his mouth shut, clearly regretting that he'd said it. "I don't want to get into disfavor with—" he tried to add hastily before Sarah cut him short.

"No, I'm not part of that. And don't worry, anything you say is safe with me."

"It's not good around here at the moment," Joseph said in a low voice. "People have been disappearing."

As this was nothing particularly new in the Colony, Sarah didn't make any comment, and Joseph also remained silent, as if he was still embarrassed by his indiscretion.

"So, are you coming back?" he asked finally. "After it's done?"

"Yes, the White Necks say I'll be allowed to stay in the Colony when I've seen something through for them." She pushed a crumb from the corner of her mouth, glanced wistfully at the door, and sighed. "Even if you do manage to escape them — to get Topsoil — part of you can never leave. They trap you with everything you hold dear, everything you love, your family. . . . I found that out," she said, her voice thickening with remorse, "far too late."

Joseph heaved himself to his feet, taking the plate from her. "It's never too late," he mumbled as his hulking form made toward the door.

In the ensuing days, Sarah was ordered to rest and build up her strength. Finally, just when she thought she would go stir-crazy from the inactivity, she was summoned to another room by someone other than Joseph. He was dressed identically but was smaller and older, his scalp completely bald and his movements excruciatingly slow as he led the way down the corridor.

He peered back at Sarah, arching his fluffy white eyebrows apologetically. "Me joints," he explained. "The damp's got into them."

"Happens to the best of us," she replied.

He showed her into a sizable room where there was a long table in the center and a series of low cupboards around all the walls. The old man shuffled off without a word, leaving her wondering why she had been brought there. There were two high-backed chairs on opposite sides of the table, and she went over to the nearest of them and stood behind it. Looking around the room, her eyes lingered on a small shrine in the corner where a beaten metal cross about a foot and a half tall was positioned between two flickering candles. Before it a copy of the *Book of Catastrophes* lay open.

Her eyes lit upon something on top of the table: A large sheet of paper with colored patches was spread open, occupying much of its surface. Glancing over her shoulder, she checked the door, at a loss to know what she was supposed to be doing. Then she gave in to her curiosity and, stepping closer, leaned over the sheet.

She found it was a map. She started at the top left-hand corner, spotting two minute parallel lines, meticulously cross-hatched, which, after about an inch, culminated in an area with a series of infinitesimally small rectangles by them. By these was the inscription THE MINERS' STATION, and some symbols which were unfamiliar to her. Then she moved on, noting another inscription that read THE STYGIAN RIVER by the side of a meandering dark blue line.

She began to move away from the corner, scanning the rest of the map, which encompassed a huge light brown area with many connected blobs, some shaded with such different colors as darker browns, oranges, and an array of reds ranging from crimson to deep burgundy. In fact, these colors looked to her exactly like blood in various states of clotting. She decided to see if she could find out what they represented.

Choosing one of the areas at random, she leaned even nearer to examine it. It was bright scarlet and roughly rectangular, with a tiny jet-black skull, a *death's-head*, superimposed over it. She was trying to decipher the legend next to it when there was a sound from close by. The faintest release of a breath.

She immediately looked up.

She recoiled, blundering into the chair and trying not to cry out.

On the other side of the table was a Styx soldier, dressed in the distinctive gray-green fatigues of the Division. He seemed incredibly tall and, with his hands linked in front of him, stood little more than three feet away, scrutinizing her silently. She had absolutely no idea how long he'd been there.

As she raised her eyes, she saw that the lapel of his long coat had a row of short cotton threads protruding from it — they were of many different colors, reds, purples, blues, and greens among them. Like the medals they gave Topsoil, these were decorations for acts of bravery, and he had so many she couldn't count them. She raised her eyes farther.

His black hair was raked back into a tightly bound ponytail. But when her gaze fell on his face, it was all she could do not to take another step away. It was a fearful sight. There was a huge scar, not dissimilar to a cauliflower in both its color and texture, down one side of his face. It engulfed a third of his forehead, extending over his left eye, which was misshapen to the extent that it looked as though it had been rotated ninety degrees on its axis. The scar blossomed out as it spread over his cheek and down to where his jaw hinged. His mouth and the already impossibly thin Styx lips were also stretched wide by the scar, so that his teeth were exposed to the gums and almost as far back as his molars.

It was the stuff of nightmares.

She quickly sought out his unaffected eye, trying not to focus on the damaged, weeping one, which showed blood-red tissues above and below it, laced with a network of blue capillaries. It was like an incomplete anatomical investigation, as if some mad coroner had quit halfway through a dissection of his face.

"I see you started without me," the soldier said. His words were breathy through his distorted mouth, his voice quiet but commanding. "Do you know what the map shows?" he asked.

She hesitated, then leaned over the document once more, gratefully lowering her eyes to it. "The Deeps," she answered.

He gave a nod. "I noticed you'd located the Miners' Station. Good. Tell me . . ." His hand was poised over the drawing of the railway track, and she saw that several of his fingers were completely missing, while others were little more than stumps. He waved this butchered appendage over the rest of the map. ". . . did you know that all of this existed?"

"The Miners' Station, yes, but, no, not *all* this," she answered, truthfully. "But I've heard stories about the Interior . . . many stories."

"Ah, the stories." He grinned fleetingly. The effect was disarming, the glistening margin around his teeth rippling like a lazy sine wave, then straightening out again. He sat down, indicating that she should do likewise. "My job is to ensure you can operate in the Great Plain and its environs. By the time we are finished" — his dark pupils swept toward the items at the very end of the table — "you will be fully versed in our equipment and our weapons, and trained to operate within our strictures. Understood?"

"Yes, sir," she answered, addressing him now as befitted his military manner. He seemed pleased by this.

"We know you are capable — you must be, to have evaded us for as long as you did."

She nodded.

"Your sole objective will be to track down and disable — by any means necessary — the rebel."

The air hung heavy as she stared into his terribly disfigured face. "You mean Will Burrows?"

"Yes, Seth Jerome," he said succinctly. He mopped his weeping eye with the back of his hand, and then snapped his fingers awkwardly, using what remained of his thumb and index finger.

"What . . . ?" She heard a clicking on the stone floor behind her and whipped her head around. A shadow flitted through the doorway.

It was the Hunter, the giant cat that had come to her aid on the surface. Pausing to look around, it briefly sampled the air, and in the blink of an eye it had capered over to Sarah's side and was rubbing itself affectionately against her leg, with such vigor that her chair was pushed sideways.

"You!" she exclaimed. She was both astonished and delighted to see the creature again. She'd assumed that the Styx had had it killed back up in the excavation. Indeed, quite the opposite was apparent: It was a very different animal beside her now, compared to the sorry specimen she'd seen Topsoil.

She could tell from the way it carried itself as it scampered off to sniff at something in the corner of the room that they'd been making sure it was well fed. Its appearance was considerably improved, and the festering wound on its shoulder had been tended to. A lint pad was bound to its shoulder by a copious amount of gray bandaging trussed around its chest. As it was also sporting a brand-new leather collar — not something generally found on these animals — Sarah instantly assumed it had been in the care of the Styx rather than Colonists.

"His name is Bartleby. We thought he might be put to good use," the Styx said.

"Bartleby," Sarah repeated, then glanced across the table at the battle-scarred soldier for an explanation.

"Naturally the animal will be eager to find his old master — your son — employing his keen sense of smell," the man told her.

"Ah yes." She nodded. "How very true." It would be invaluable to have a Hunter when she was tracking in the Deeps, and the fact that it was Cal's scent trail would be incentive indeed.

She smiled back at the man, and then called out, "Bartleby, here!" He obediently returned to her side and sat down, watching her as he waited for another command. She kneaded the scabrous expanse of the cat's wide, flat head. "So that's your name, is it . . . *Bartleby*?" He blinked his saucer-sized eyes at her, a loud purr rumbling from his throat as he shifted from forepaw to forepaw. "You and me together, we'll get Cal back, won't we, Bartleby?"

The smile vanished from her face. "And we'll flush out a big rat in the bargain."

Outside in the rose garden of Humphrey House, several pigeons alighted by the bird table, where the cook regularly left slices of stale bread and other scraps from the kitchen. Distracted from the magazine spread before her, Mrs. Burrows looked up and tried her best to focus on the birds with her red, swollen eyes.

"Blast it! I can't see a bloomin' thing, let alone read!" she grumbled, squinting first through one eye and then the other. "This filthy, *filthy* virus!"

Television news bulletins had begun to pop up a week ago, reporting a mysterious viral outbreak that seemed, as far as anyone could tell, to have originated in London and was now sweeping like wildfire through the rest of the British Isles. It had even reached as far afield as the United States and the Far East. Experts said that although the disease, a sort of mega-conjunctivitis, was short-lived, lasting four or five days at most in the average person, the rate at which it had spread was a serious cause for alarm. The media constantly referred to it as an "Ultra Bug," because it had the unique attribute that its transmission appeared to be both air- and waterborne. A world beating combination, apparently, for the virus that wants to go places.

According to the same experts, even if the government made up its mind to manufacture a vaccine, the process from full identification of a new virus to production of sufficient vaccine for the entire population of England could take many months, if not years.

But the scientific intricacies were of no concern to Mrs. Burrows — it was the sheer inconvenience that made her fume. Dropping her spoon in her cereal bowl, she started rubbing her eyes once again.

She had been perfectly all right the evening before, but, roused by the morning bell outside her room, she'd woken into a living horror show. She was instantly aware of the painful drying of her sinuses and her ulcerated tongue and throat. But all this paled into insignificance as she'd tried to open her eyes and found they were so heavily gummed together that it was impossible to do so. It was only after bathing them with copious amounts of warm water from the hand basin in her room, accompanied by language that would have made a sailor blush, that she'd managed to pry apart her eyelids even a fraction. Despite all the washing, they still felt as though they had a crust over them that could only be removed by scraping it off.

Now, as she sat at the table, she let out a mournful groan. The persistent rubbing only seemed to be making matters worse. With tears streaming down her face, she scooped up a generous helping of cornflakes and, with one bloodshot eye, tried once again to read the copy of *TV Guide* on the table beside her. It was the latest issue, just delivered that morning, which she'd purloined from the dayroom before anyone else had had an opportunity to get their hands on it. But it was no good; she was hard-pressed to make out the titles at the tops of the pages, let alone the smaller print of the program listings below.

"What a stinking, filthy bug!" she complained again loudly. The dining room was uncannily quiet for this time of the morning; on any normal day, even the first sitting for breakfast would have had a healthy turnout.

Grinding her teeth with frustration, she folded her napkin and used an edge to carefully mop each weeping eye. After a series of deep mooing noises as she tried unsuccessfully to ease her sinuses, she blew her nose noisily into the napkin. Then, blinking rapidly, she attempted once more to focus on the magazine pages.

"It's no good, I can't see a sodding thing. Feels like I've got grit in them!" she said, pushing her cereal bowl away from her.

With her eyes closed, she leaned back in her chair and reached for her cup of tea. She put it to her lips and took a sip, then spluttered loudly, blowing it out in a fine mist over the tabletop. It was stone-cold.

"Urgh! Disgusting!" she shrieked. "The service in this place is deplorable." She slammed the cup down on its saucer. "Whole place has come to a standstill," she complained to nobody in particular, knowing full well that most of the staff hadn't shown up for work. "Anyone would think there was a war on."

"There is," came a distinguished voice.

Mrs. Burrows hiked up one puffy eyelid to see who had spoken. At his table, a man in a tweed jacket, perhaps in his mid-fifties, was dunking a finger of buttered toast into his boiled egg with small, deliberate movements. Like her, he seemed to prefer his own company, as he had chosen to sit at the small table in the adjacent window bay. The room was completely deserted except for her and this other diner. It had certainly been a strange couple of days, a skeleton staff with inflamed and seeping eyes doing their best to tend to the patients, who mostly confined themselves to their rooms.

"Hmm," the man said, and nodded as if agreeing with himself.

"Sorry?"

"I said that there *is* a war on," he declared, munching on his piece of egg-dipped toast. From what Mrs. Burrows could see, he had only been mildly affected by the virus.

"What makes you say that?" Mrs. Burrows asked belligerently, immediately regretting that she'd said anything at all.

She ducked her head down, praying that he'd leave her alone and just concentrate on his egg yolk. She wasn't going to be that lucky.

"And we're on the losing side," he continued, chewing. "We're under constant attack from viruses. It could be all over for us before you have time to say *Ring-around-the-rosies.*"

"Whatever *are* you talking about?" Mrs. Burrows muttered, unable to help herself. "What rubbish!"

"On the contrary," he said with a frown. "With the planet so overpopulated, we've got the optimum situation for viruses to mutate into something really lethal, and in double-quick time, too. An ideal breeding ground."

Mrs. Burrows contemplated making a break for the door. She wasn't going to hang around to hear this old fruitcake's prattle, and besides, she'd all but lost her appetite. The upside to this mystery pandemic was that it was very unlikely there would be any activities organized for the day, so she could get in some serious television viewing with little or no opposition to her choice of show. Even if she couldn't see much, at least she could *listen* to it.

"We're all suffering from this rather nasty eye infection at the moment, but it wouldn't take much for it to shuffle a couple of genes and turn into a killer." The man picked up a saltshaker and shook it over his egg. "Mark my words, one day something really nasty will appear on the horizon, and it'll cut us all down, like a scythe through corn," he announced, delicately dabbing the corners of his eyes with his handkerchief. "Then we'll go the way of the dinosaurs. And all this" — he swept his hand expansively around the room — "and all of us, will be a rather short and rather insignificant chapter in the history of the world."

"How very cheery. Sounds like some naff science-fiction story," Mrs. Burrows said sneeringly as she rose to her feet and began to grope her way from table to table, headed for the hallway.

"It's a disagreeable but very likely scenario for our eventual demise," he replied.

This last pronouncement really got Mrs. Burrows's goat. It was bad enough that her eyes were killing her without having to listen to this claptrap. "Oh yes, so we're all doomed, are we? And how would you know?" she said scornfully. "What are you, anyway, a failed writer or something?"

"No, actually, I'm a doctor. When I'm not in here, I work at St. Edmund's — it's a hospital — you might have heard of it?"

"Oh," Mrs. Burrows mumbled, pausing in her flight and turning to where the man was sitting.

"Seeing — so to speak — as you also seem to be something of an expert, I wish I could share your faith that there's nothing to be worried about."

Feeling more than a little humbled, Mrs. Burrows remained standing where she was.

"And try not to touch your peepers, my dear — it'll only make them worse," the man said curtly, swiveling his head to watch as two pigeons engaged in a tug-of-war over a bacon rind at the foot of the bird table.

22

FOR A COUPLE of miles all that could be heard was
the crunch of their feet in the dust. It was hard going for
Will and Chester, trudging along with their silent captors, who
yanked them roughly to their feet if either of them happened to
stumble and fall. And on several occasions, the boys had been
pushed and struck viciously to make them pick up the pace.

Then, without any warning, they were both drawn to a
halt and their blindfolds tugged off. Blinking, the boys looked
around; they were evidently still on the Great Plain, but there
were no features to be seen in the illumination from the miner's light on the head of the tall man who stood before them.
The glare from the light meant they couldn't see his face, but
he was wearing a long jacket with a belt slung around his waist
that had numerous pouches attached to it. He took something
from one of these — a light orb, which he held in his gloved
palm. Then he reached above his forehead and turned off the
miner's light.

He unwound a scarf from around his neck and mouth,
switching his stare between the boys as he did so. His shoulders were broad, but his face was the thing that held their
attention. It was a lean face with a strong nose and one eye

that glinted blue at them. The other eye had something in front of it, held in place by a band around the top of his head, like a drop-down lens.

It reminded Will of the last time he'd had his eyes tested; the optician examining him had worn a similar device. However, this version had a milky lens and, Will could have sworn, a very faint orange glow to it. He immediately assumed that the eye underneath had been damaged in some way, but then noticed a pair of twisted cables attached to the monocle's perimeter that passed around the headband and behind the man's head.

The single, uncovered eye continued to assess both of them, shrewd and quick as it darted from one to the other.

"I don't have much patience," the man began.

Will was trying to guess his age, but he could have been anything from thirty to fifty, and he had such an imposing physical presence that neither boy could fail to be intimidated.

"My name is Drake. I'm not in the habit of picking up outcasts from the Colony," he said, and then paused. "Sometimes, with the wrecks and the broken-down, those that have been tortured or are too weak to last for long . . . I bring about an early release." With a grim smile, he swept his hand around the belt until it came to rest on a large scabbard on his hip. "It's the kindest thing to do."

As if he had made his point, he withdrew his hand from the knife. "I want straight answers. We've been tracking you, and there is no *backup*, is there?" He glared at Will, who remained silent.

"You, the big one, what's your name?" He turned to Chester, who shifted uneasily on his feet.

"Chester Rawls, sir," the boy answered in a tremulous voice.

"You're not a Colonist, are you?"

"Er . . . no," Chester croaked.

"Topsoiler?"

"Yes." Chester looked down, not able to withstand the stare from the cold eye any longer.

"So how did you come to be down here?"

"I was Banished."

"Along with the best of them," Drake said, twisting around to regard Will. "You, the brave — or very idiotic — one. Name?"

"Will," he answered evenly.

"What are you, I wonder. You're more difficult. You move and look like Colonist rank and file, but there's also a touch of the Topsoil about you, too."

Will nodded.

Drake continued: "Which makes you somewhat unusual. You're patently not an agent for the Limiters."

"Who?" Will asked.

"You've just seen them in action."

"I've no idea what *Limiters* are," Will mumbled insolently at him.

"A specialist detachment of the Styx. They've been cropping up all over the place lately. Seems the Deeps have become a bit of a habit with them," Drake said. "So, you don't work for them."

"No, I bloody don't!" Will replied, so emphatically that Drake's eye seemed to flicker marginally wider, with what could have been surprise. He sighed and crossed his arms, tugging reflectively at his chin with one hand.

"Thought as much." He stared at Will, shaking his head. "But I don't like it when I can't understand something right away. I tend to act rashly . . . get rid of whatever it is. Tell me, boy, quickly, *who* and *what* are you?"

Will decided he'd better do as the man ordered and provide him with an answer. "I was born in the Colony and my mother got me out. Got me to the surface," he said.

"So when did you go Topsoil?"

"When I was two, she —"

"Enough," he interrupted, holding up a hand. "I didn't ask for your life story," he growled. "But that smells right. And it makes you an . . . an oddity." He looked past the boys, to the darkness behind them. "I suggest we take them back. We can decide what to do with them later. Agreed, Elliott?"

A smaller figure, no taller than Will, stepped into view with the stealth of a cat. Even in the poor light they could see the curves of her body under the loose-fitting jacket and pants, clothes similar to those Drake was wearing. She had a sandy-colored scarf, a *shemagh*, wound around her face and up over the top of her head, obscuring all her features except for her eyes, which did not once look in the boys' direction.

She was carrying a rifle of some kind. She swung it before her and, digging the butt into the ground, leaned against it. It looked heavy, with a thick pipelike barrel on which, midway along, was attached a chunky sight of some description that glinted dully, like unpolished brass. The weapon was almost as tall as she was, and seemed impossibly cumbersome for a girl of her slight frame.

The two boys held their breath, waiting for her to speak, but after a couple of seconds she merely nodded, then swung the chunky rifle onto her back again as if it weighed no more than a length of bamboo.

"Come along," Drake said to them. He made no move to put on their blindfolds again, but left their hands bound. With just the faintest glow from Drake's miner's light to show them where he was, they followed his broad-backed form as he piloted them through an unremittingly monotonous landscape. Despite the lack of landmarks, he seemed to know unerringly which direction they should be taking. After many more hours of this desertlike terrain, they arrived at the edge of the Great Plain at the mouth of a lava tube. They filed down this at some speed. It was almost, Will thought, as if Drake had the ability to see in the dark.

Now in the enclosed space of the tube, they watched the indistinct outline of Drake's head as he went, but on the occasions when Will and Chester glanced behind to see where Elliott was, there was absolutely no sign of her. And no noise, either. Will came to the conclusion that she must have taken another route, or had remained behind for some reason.

The three of them, Drake, Will, and Chester, took a left fork and very soon arrived at what appeared to be a cul-de-sac.

Drake drew them to a halt. He turned up his miner's light and stood there facing them, his back to the wall, while Will and Chester peered around uneasily. They could see no reason for stopping. Chester held his breath as Drake suddenly reached to his side and yanked his knife from its scabbard.

"I'm going to free your hands," he said before they had time to think the worst was about to happen. "Here." He beckoned with his knife, and then, as they held up their wrists, sliced deftly through the bindings with single strokes.

"Is there anything in those backpacks that'll be spoiled by water? Food, or anything you want to keep dry?"

Will thought for a second.

"Quickly!" Drake pressed them.

"Yes, there's my notebooks and camera, quite a lot of food, and . . . and some fireworks," Will replied. "That's in mine." He looked over at his brother's rucksack, which Chester was now carrying. "In Cal's, there's mostly just food."

Before he had finished speaking, Drake lobbed two folded packages at their feet. "Use these. Get on with it."

The boys each picked up a package and shook it out. They were bags, made from a light, waxed material, with two sets of drawstrings on their openings.

Will tipped out his rucksack, rapidly shoving the things he wanted to keep dry into the bag. He tightened the drawstrings, then turned to look at Chester, who was unfamiliar with the contents of his backpack and, as a consequence, taking more time.

"C'mon, will you," Drake growled under his breath.

"Let me do that," Will volunteered, shouldering Chester aside and finishing off the job within seconds.

"Right!" Drake barked. "Is that everything?"

Both boys nodded.

"A word of advice: Next time I suggest you keep at least a pair of socks dry."

They had been so occupied by the task at hand, neither Will nor Chester had given a thought to what was going to happen next.

"Right, sir," Will said. He was comforted by the words *next time* and the almost paternal advice this complete stranger was giving them.

"Look, I am *sir* to no one," Drake snapped back, making Will feel uneasy all over again. He hadn't intended to say it — it had slipped out as if he had been addressing a teacher at school.

"Sorry, s —" Will began, managing to cut himself off just in time. He caught the momentary sneer on Drake's lips before the man began to speak again.

"You are going to swim through this." Drake thrust his toe cap at the floor by the foot of the wall. Where the boys had thought there was solid ground, they now saw ripples spread sluggishly under a thick film of dust. It was apparently a small pool, some six feet in diameter.

"Swim?" Chester asked, and swallowed nervously.

"You can hold your breath for thirty seconds, can't you, boy?"

"Yes," Chester stammered.

"Good. This is a small sump that comes up in another passage. It's like a U-bend."

"Same as at the back of a toilet bowl?" Chester suggested, his voice brittle with apprehension.

"Oh, nice one, Chester," Will said, grimacing.

Drake gave them both a wry glance, then waved them toward the grimy-looking water. "In you go."

Will put his rucksack on his back and approached the pool, hugging the waterproof bag in his arms. He stepped into the sump without hesitation, each step taking him deeper into the tepid water. Then, with a deep breath, he ducked his head under its surface and was gone.

Feeling bubbles brush his face, he pulled himself along using his free hand. He kept his eyes tightly shut, the noise of the water thundering in his ears. Although the tunnel wasn't particularly wide, pinching down to perhaps three feet at its narrowest point, it wasn't proving too difficult to negotiate, either, even with the dual burdens of the rucksack and waterproof bag.

But despite the fact that he thought he was making good progress, Will didn't seem to be getting anywhere. He opened his eyes in the pitch-blackness, which made his heart beat even faster. The water around him felt thick and resistant.

This was his worst nightmare.

Is this all a trick? Should I turn back?

He tried to keep control of himself, but with the lack of air, his body was beginning to rebel. He felt a wave of panic surge through him and began to thrash around, grabbing wildly for anything that would help him move faster. He had to get out of the inky liquid! He moved with a mad desperation now, driving himself forward through the dark waters in a slow-motion sprint.

He wondered for the briefest of moments if this was how Drake was going to kill both of them. But in the same instant he told himself that Drake wouldn't have needed to go to all this trouble — it would have been simpler just to slit their throats back on the Great Plain, if that had been his intention.

Although it was probably no more than half a minute, it felt like several lifetimes before Will burst out into the air with a huge splash.

His chest heaving, he fumbled for his lantern and switched it to its lowest level. The muted light didn't reveal much about the place he was in, except he noticed that the ground and the walls appeared to glisten a little when his beam caught them. He assumed this was merely due to moisture on their surfaces. Grateful for the air in his lungs, he waited for Chester.

On the other side of the sump, Chester reluctantly hoisted the rucksack onto his shoulders and began mooching toward the patch of water, dragging the waterproof bag behind him.

"What are you waiting for, boy?" Drake said, his voice hard and uncompromising.

Chester bit his lip, dawdling beside the slowly lapping water, which was still agitated from Will's passage through it. He turned to look sheepishly into Drake's single, glowering eye.

"Um . . . ," he began, wondering how he could possibly avoid submerging himself in the grimy-looking pool before him. "I can't . . ."

Drake grabbed his arm, but without any real pressure. "Listen, I mean you no harm. You are going to have to trust me." He raised his chin, looking away from the frightened boy. "It's not an easy thing to put your trust in a total stranger, especially after what you've been through. You're right to be cautious — that's good. But I am not a Styx, and I'm not going to do anything to hurt you. OK?" He brought his singular gaze to bear on the boy.

Close to the man, Chester looked directly into his face and somehow knew that Drake was being straight with him. He was suddenly filled with confidence.

"All right," he agreed, and without further hesitation waded into the dank waters, submerging himself in them. And as he propelled himself through, using the half-swimming, half-running method Will had employed, he didn't allow any doubt to cloud his mind.

On the other side, Will was there to help Chester out.

"You OK?" Will asked him. "You took so long, I thought you got stuck or something."

"No problem," Chester answered, breathing heavily and wiping water from his eyes.

"Now's our chance," Will said quickly, trying to see what lay beyond in the darkness, then glancing back to the pool. There was no sign of Drake, but he wouldn't be far behind. "We should make a break for it."

"No, Will," Chester said resolutely.

"What are you talking about?" Will demanded, already turning and trying to pull his friend with him.

"I'm not going anywhere. I think we're safe with him," Chester replied. He widened his stance to resist Will, who saw he meant what he was saying.

"Too late," Will said furiously as a faint light shone from deep within the water. It was the miner's light on Drake's forehead. Will made a growling noise at Chester just as the man's head and shoulders broke from the surface, and he rose out of it like some apparition, barely disturbing the water at all.

Drake's light was more intense than either of the boys' lanterns and it played on the walls around them. Will could now see that what he had assumed to be moisture was something else altogether. Both the walls and the ground on which the boys stood were streaked with a multitude of fine golden veins, as if a priceless cobweb had been draped over them. The veins glittered with a thousand tiny points of light, suffusing the chamber with a glorious kaleidoscope of warm yellow.

"Wow!" Chester gasped.

"Gold!" Will mumbled in disbelief. He looked down at his arms, noticing they were speckled with glitter, then he saw that both Chester and Drake were covered in it, too. They had all picked up a good measure on their clothes and skin from the shining dust floating on the surface of the water.

"'fraid not," Drake said, now standing beside them. "It's only fool's gold. Iron pyrite."

"Of course," Will said, recalling the shiny cube his father had bought him for his minerals collection back home. "Iron pyrite," he repeated, slightly ashamed that he hadn't known better.

"I can show you places where there's gold, places where you can fill your boots," Drake said as he surveyed the walls. "But what's the point if there's nowhere to spend it?" The coldness had returned to his voice. "Sort out your kit" — he pointed at their rucksacks — "we need to get going."

Once the boys were ready, Drake turned and was off again, an imperious figure taking powerful, long strides down the exquisitely golden galley.

Marching briskly through a confusing maze of rock passages, they eventually came to a ramp leading up to a rough archway. Drake reached through the opening and felt to one side. He pulled out a knotted rope.

"Up," he said, holding the rope toward them.

Will and Chester hauled themselves up the thirty feet or so to the top and waited there, panting from the exertion. Drake followed up with no more effort than it would take a normal person to open a door. The boys found themselves in a sort of octagonal atrium, from which they could see openings leading to other faintly lit spaces. The floor was even and covered with silt, and as Will scuffed his boot on it, he could tell from the echoes that the adjoining rooms were of a reasonable size.

"This'll be home for a while," Drake said, unbuckling the bulky belt around his waist. Slipping off his jacket, he slung it over his shoulder. Then he reached to the contraption in front of his eye and lifted it upward. It was hinged, revealing that his other eye was, in fact, quite normal.

As he stood before them, the boys took in the musculature of his bare arms and how exceptionally lean and honed he was. His cheekbones were prominent, and his face so thin that the muscle groups composing it were almost visible through his skin. And every inch of his flesh, ingrained with dirt and the color of tanned leather, was lined by a mesh of scars. Some were large, bleached-white hyphens that stood proud, while others were much smaller, as if pale filaments had been trailed around his neck and the sides of his face.

But his eyes, overhung by his prominent brow, were intensely blue, and simmered with such an awe-inspiring ferociousness that both Will and Chester found it hard to bear their scrutiny. It was as though their depths divulged a glimpse of some terrifying place, a place that neither of the boys wanted to know anything about.

"Right, wait in there."

The boys began to shuffle toward the room Drake was pointing to.

"But leave your rucksacks here," he ordered and, still facing the boys, added, "Everything OK, Elliott?"

Will and Chester couldn't stop themselves from peering past Drake. By the top of the rope, the small girl was poised, stock-still. It was evident that she had never been very far behind, all the time they'd been walking, but neither of the boys had noticed her presence until now.

"You *are* going to restrain them, aren't you?" she asked in a cold, unfriendly voice.

"Not necessary, is it, Chester?" Drake said.

"No," the boy answered so readily that Will looked at him with barely concealed astonishment.

"And you?"

"Uh . . . no," Will muttered less enthusiastically.

Once inside, they sat unspeaking in the gloom on some rudimentary beds they'd found in there — the only items of furniture in the room. Just long enough to accommodate the boys, there was little width to them, and their surfaces were barely padded at all — like a couple of narrow tables with blankets thrown over them.

As they waited, clueless as to what was going to happen next, the room reverberated with sounds from the corridor outside. There were the muffled tones of a conversation between

Drake and Elliott, and then they listened as their rucksacks were upended and the contents tipped out onto the floor. Finally they heard retreating footfalls, then nothing.

Will took a luminescent orb from his pocket and began to absentmindedly roll it back and forth across the top of his sleeve. Now that his jacket had dried, the action dislodged glittering grains of iron pyrite, which scattered to the ground in a small sparkling shower. "Looks like I've been to a disco," he muttered, and then, without missing a beat, he addressed his friend. "What's the deal, Chester?"

"What do you mean?"

"You seem to have thrown your lot in with these people, for some reason. Why do you trust them?" Will demanded. "You do realize they're just going to steal all our food and then ditch us somewhere? In fact, they'll probably kill us. That's the sort of thieving scum they are."

"I don't think so," Chester replied indignantly, frowning.

"Well, what was all that about out there, then?" Will indicated the corridor with a jab of his thumb.

"I reckon they're rebels of some sort, at war with the Styx," Chester said defensively. "You know, *freedom fighters*."

"Yeah, right."

"They could be," Chester maintained, then looked less certain. "Why don't you ask them, Will?"

"Why don't you ask them yourself?" Will snapped.

He was getting more and more furious. Coming on top of Cal's accident, the traumatic way in which they had been grabbed was really the last straw. He fell into a brooding silence and began to formulate a plan of action in which they would fight their way out and make a run for it. He was just about to inform Chester what he thought their next move should be when Drake appeared at the threshold. He leaned against the doorjamb, eating something. It was Will's favorite — a Milky Way. He and Cal had bought several candy bars in the Topsoil supermarket, and he'd been carefully saving them for a special occasion.

"What are these?" Drake asked, indicating a pair of dun-colored rocks the size of large marbles, which he was cradling in the palm of his hand. He shook them as though they were dice, and then closed his hand and began to grind them, one against the other.

"I wouldn't do that if I were you," Will told Drake.

"Why not?"

"It's bad for your eyesight," Will said, the corners of his lips curling with the hint of a vindictive smirk as the man continued to rattle the stones together. They were the remaining node stones that Tam had given Will, and Drake had evidently found them in Will's backpack. If broken, they became incandescent, releasing a blinding white light. "They'll go off in your face," Will warned.

Drake glanced at Will, unsure whether the boy was being serious. However, taking a large bite of the Milky Way bar, he now held the stones still as he continued to examine them.

Will was incensed. "Enjoying that, are you?" he fumed.

"Yes," Drake answered unequivocally, tucking the last of the chocolate into his mouth. "Look at it as a small price for rescuing you."

"And that gives you the right to help yourself to my things, does it?" Will rose to his feet, his arms bunched at his sides, his face rigid with anger. "Besides, we didn't need to be *rescued*."

"Oh, really?" Drake responded casually, his mouth still full. "Look at the two of you. You're a mess."

"We were doing just fine before you came along," Will retorted.

"Oh, really. So, tell me, what happened to this *Cal* you mentioned? I don't see him anywhere." Drake shot his eyes around the room, then raised his eyebrows quizzically. "Where's he hiding, I wonder."

"My brother . . . he . . . he . . . ," Will started belligerently, but suddenly all the bluster deserted him and he slumped back down onto the bed.

"He's dead," Chester spoke up.

"How?" Drake asked, swallowing the last of the candy bar.

"There was this cave . . . and . . ." Will's voice faltered.

"What sort of cave?" Drake asked immediately, his voice deadly serious.

Chester took over. "It smelled sort of sweet and there were strange plant things. . . . They bit him or something, and then all this stuff—"

"A sugar trap," Drake interrupted, moving in from the doorway and looking quickly from one boy to the other. "And what did you do? You didn't just leave him there?"

"He wasn't breathing," Chester said.

"He died," Will added disconsolately.

"Where and when was this?" Drake pressed them.

Will and Chester shot glances at each other.

"Come on," Drake urged.

"Two or so days ago . . . I suppose," Will said.

"Yes, it was by the first canal we came to," Chester confirmed.

"Then there may still be a chance," Drake said, moving toward the doorway. "A slim one."

"What do you mean?" Will asked.

"We have to go," Drake snapped.

"Huh?" Will gasped, not able to comprehend what he was hearing.

But Drake was already striding purposefully down the corridor. "Follow me! We'll need to take some rations," he yelled back to them. "Elliott! Saddle up! Break out the weapons!"

He halted by their backpacks, where all their belongings had been stacked into ordered piles.

"Take that, that, and that." Drake pointed at the various piles of food. "Should be enough. We'll carry some extra water. Elliott! Water!" he shouted as he turned to them. They were standing rather dumbly as they watched him, confused as to what exactly they were meant to be doing, and why. "Hurry up and stow that stuff . . . that's if you want to save your brother."

"I don't understand," Will said, kneeling and hurriedly shoving the food into his rucksack as Drake had instructed. "Cal wasn't breathing. He's dead."

"No time to explain now," Drake barked as Elliott appeared from another doorway. Her shemagh was still around her head and her rifle slung across her back. She handed Drake two bladderlike containers that slopped with the sound of water.

"Take these," Drake said, shoving them at the boys.

"What's up?" Elliott asked calmly as she began to pass further items to Drake.

"There were three of them. The third wandered into a sugar trap," he answered, casting his eyes in the boys' direction as he took a bundle of cylinders from Elliott, some six inches or so in length. He opened his jacket and slotted them inside it one by one. Then he clipped a pad with shorter versions of the cylinders — each like a thick pencil housed in its own loop — onto his belt and secured it by means of a short cord tied around his thigh.

"What are those?" Will inquired.

"Precautions," Drake answered abstractedly. "We'll be taking a direct route across the plain. We don't have time for subtlety."

He buttoned up his jacket and flicked the weird contraption over his eye again. "Ready?" he said to Elliott.

"Ready," she confirmed.

23

LATER THAT EVENING, Sarah was in her room, poring over the map the Styx soldier had given her. She was sitting cross-legged with it spread open on the floor before her, familiarizing herself with the various place names.

"Crevice Town," she repeated several times, then switched her attention to the northern reaches of the Great Plain, where reports were coming in of recent renegade activity. She wondered if Will was somehow tied up in it — given his past record, she wouldn't have been surprised if he was already causing trouble in the Deeps.

She was distracted by heavy, even steps in the corridor outside. Going to the door, she opened it as softly as she could and saw the massive, unmistakable form lumbering down the corridor.

"Joseph," she called quietly.

He turned and came back to her, tucking some neatly folded towels under his arm.

"I didn't want to intrude," he said, glancing through the partially opened door and past Sarah to the floor, where the map was laid out.

"You should have come in. I'm so glad you're back." She smiled at him. "I was . . . um . . . ," she began, then fell silent.

"If there's anything I can do for you, you only have to ask," Joseph offered.

"I don't think I'll be here much longer," she told him, then hesitated. "There is something I wanted to do before I go."

"Anything," he reiterated. "You know I'm here for you." He beamed at her, delighted that she felt she could trust him.

"I want you to get me out of here," Sarah said in a low voice.

Moving like a shadow, Sarah kept close to the wall. She'd already avoided several Colonist policemen making the rounds of the surrounding streets and didn't want to get caught now. Ducking into a recess behind an ancient drinking fountain with a tarnished brass spout, she crouched down and checked the darkened entrance on the other side of the street.

She lifted her head and gazed at the tall, windowless walls of the outer ring of buildings. It had been from this very spot that, so many years ago, she had seen these buildings through her child's eyes. Then, as now, they gave the impression that they hadn't put up much of a fight against the ravages of time. The walls were shot through with ominous-looking cracks, and there were numerous huge and yawning hollows where the facing stones had simply crumbled away. The masonry appeared to be in such an appalling state of repair that at any moment the whole development might come tumbling down on some hapless passerby.

But appearances can be deceptive. The area she was about to enter had been among the first to be built when the Colony was established, and the walls of the houses were strong enough to withstand anything man, or time, could throw at them.

She took a breath and whisked across the street, slipping into the pitch-black passageway. It was barely wide enough to allow two people to pass abreast at the same time. At once the smell hit her: The stale odor of the inhabitants, a reek of unwashed occupation so intense it was like a physical thing, intermixed with all that went with it, with human effluent and the pungent stench of rotting food.

She came out into a gloomily lit alley. Like all the thorough-fares and runnels that cut through this district, it was barely wider than the passageway from which she'd just emerged.

"The Rookeries," she said to herself, glancing around and realizing that it had changed not one jot, this place where the people who had nowhere else to go ended up. She began to walk, spotting a familiar building here or a door there, still flecked with faint traces of paint in the same color she recalled, and reveling in her memories of the times she and Tam had ventured into this forbidden and dangerous playground.

Basking in the warmth of her memories, she strolled down the middle of the alley, avoiding the open gutter where sewage trickled like heated lard. On either side of her were the ram-shackle old slums, their uppermost stories overhanging to such an extent that in places they appeared to be almost touching.

She paused to adjust the shawl over her head while a rag-gedy bunch of street urchins tore past her. They were so dirty as to be nearly indistinguishable from the backdrop of filth coating every surface.

Two of them, small boys, were shouting, "Styx and stones may break my bones, but names will never hurt me!" at the top of their lungs as they chased after the others. She smiled at their irreverence; if they had done that outside the confines of the Rookeries, the punishment would have been swift and brutal. One of the boys skipped over the open gutter in the middle of the road, past a gaggle of old crones dressed in head shawls similar to Sarah's. They were gossiping intently among themselves and nodding their heads. Almost without looking, one of the women twisted away from the group just as the boy was in reach. Cuffing him with unnecessary roughness, she issued a sharp reprimand. The woman's face was lined and blistered and as pale as a ghost's.

The boy reeled slightly, then, rubbing his head and grum bling under his breath, he hurtled off, undeterred. Sarah couldn't suppress a laugh. She saw in the boy a youthful Tam, recognizing the toughness and resilience she had so admired in her brother. The children were still taunting one another in their high voices, and whooping and screaming with excitement as they hared down a side alley and disappeared from view.

Some thirty feet farther down from Sarah, a pair of brutish-looking men stood talking in a doorway, both with long hair and pendulous, matted beards, and dressed in scruffy frock coats. She caught them eyeing her with vicious sneers on their faces. The larger of the two lowered his head like a bulldog about to attack, and made as if to move toward her. He slipped a gnarled, rootlike cudgel from his thick belt, and she saw the easy way he held it in his hand. This wasn't some vain threat — she could tell he knew how to use the club.

These people didn't take kindly to outsiders straying off the beaten track and onto their patch.

Sarah returned his cold glare but slowed to a crawl. If she were to continue on her original course, it would take her straight by him — there was nowhere else to go. The alternative was for her to do an about-face, which would be perceived as a sign of weakness. If they suspected for even a fraction of a second that she was afraid and shouldn't be there, they'd have a pop at her — that was how things worked in this place. Either way, she knew that she and this total stranger were now locked into a showdown and that the situation would need to be resolved, somehow or other.

Although she hadn't the slightest doubt she could handle herself if it came to it, Sarah still felt a frisson of the old fear, the familiar electric tingle running down her spine. Thirty years ago, this was her and her brother's obsession, the start of the contest. Oddly enough, she found it rather comforting.

"Ay! You!" someone suddenly cried behind her, jolting her from her thoughts. "Jerome!"

"What?" Sarah gasped.

She wheeled around to meet the red-rimmed eyes of the ancient hag. Her face was dappled with the most enormous liver spots, and she was pointing accusingly at Sarah with an arthritic finger.

"Jerome," the old woman rasped again, even louder and more confidently this time, her mouth gaping open so Sarah could see her toothless, livid-pink gums. Sarah realized she had let her shawl drop, and her face had been in full view of the group of women. *But how in the world did they know who she was?*

"Jerome. Yes! Jerome!" another of the women cawed, with mounting conviction. "It's Sarah Jerome, ain't it?"

Although she was in a maelstrom of confusion, Sarah did her best to rapidly assess her options. She scanned the nearby doorways, reckoning that if worse came to worst she might be able to barge her way into one of the half-ruined buildings and lose herself in the rabbit warren of passageways that lay behind them. But it didn't look good. All the doors were firmly shut or boarded up.

She was walled in, with only two ways to go — backward or forward. She was looking at the alleyway beyond the old hags, calculating whether to make a break and get herself back out of the Rookeries, when one of them screamed the most piercing of wails:

"SARAH!"

Sarah flinched with the sheer volume of the squall, and a lull descended on the whole place, an eerie, watchful silence.

Sarah spun around, walking away from the women, knowing it would take her straight past the bearded man. So be it! She would just have to deal with him.

As she neared him, he raised the cudgel to the height of his shoulder and Sarah prepared to fight, slipping her shawl from her head and winding it around her arm. She could have kicked herself for not bringing her knife.

She was almost level with him when, to her astonishment and relief, he began to strike the cudgel against the lintel of the doorway and to shout her name in his gruff voice. His confederate joined with him, as did every one of the group of women behind her.

"SARAH! SARAH! SARAH!"

The entire place was stirring now, as if the timbers of the buildings themselves were coming to life.

"SARAH! SARAH! SARAH!"

The cudgel continued to beat time as people turned out from the houses and into the alleyway, more people than she believed possible. Shutters slammed back from glassless windows and faces peeked out. All Sarah could do was bow her head and keep walking.

"SARAH! SARAH! SARAH!" came shouts thick and fast from all over, and people joined in with the beat of the cudgel, the clattering growing as metal cups or whatever else came to hand were struck against walls, windowsills, and doorjambs. It was like a jailhouse chorus, so loud that the tiles on the roofs began to resonate with the singular rhythm.

Still gripped by panic, Sarah didn't slow her pace, but began to notice the grinning faces, infused with wonderment. Elderly men, bent double from disease, and gaunt women, the used-up people that the Colony had consigned to the scrap heap, were hailing her, shouting her name jubilantly.

"SARAH! SARAH! SARAH!"

Many mouths, with broken and blackened teeth, all yelling in unison. Smiling, wild, sometimes grotesque faces, but all with expressions of admiration and even *affection*.

They were gathering along the way now — Sarah couldn't believe the sheer number of people lining the route. Someone — she didn't see who — thrust a discolored sheet of rough paper into her hands. She glanced down at it. It was a crude etching, the sort of thing the underground press distributed to the people of the Rookeries — she'd seen the like before.

But this one caused Sarah's heart to skip a beat. The largest image, in the center of the sheet, was a picture of her, a few years younger than she was now, although dressed in almost identical clothes. Her face in the picture bore an anxious expression and was looking melodramatically off to one side, as if she was being pursued. It was a reasonable likeness of her. So that explained how she'd been recognized. That and the rumors, which would have most likely spread like wildfire through the Colony, that she'd been brought back by the Styx. There were four other, smaller pictures in similarly stylized roundels in each corner, but now wasn't the time to examine them.

She folded the paper and took a deep breath. Seemingly there was nothing to fear, no threat, so she raised her head, throwing her shawl around her back, as she continued down the alleyway, the masses thronging on either side of her. She didn't acknowledge them, nor look to her left or right, but kept going as the clamor grew even more tumultuous. Wolf whistles and huge cheers and the chanted "Sarah! Sarah! Sarah!" reached the rock canopy above, their echoes falling back to earth and mingling with the uproar all around her.

Sarah reached the narrow passageway that would lead her out through the other side of the Rookeries. Without looking back, she entered, leaving the throng behind her. But their shouts still rang in her ears, and the drumming still resounded deafeningly in the enclosed space around her.

Out in the wider street where the more affluent Colonists' houses stood, Sarah stopped to order her thoughts. She felt dizzy as she tried to deal with what had just happened. She just couldn't believe that all those people, whom she'd never laid eyes on before, had recognized her and had bestowed such adulation upon her. After all, they were the inhabitants of the Rookeries — they neither respected nor admired *anyone* beyond its confines. It wasn't their way. Before now, she hadn't had the slightest inkling that she was a figure of such renown.

Remembering the sheet of paper still clutched in her hand, she opened it and began to scrutinize it. The paper itself was coarse, with frayed edges, but she didn't notice this as her eyes fell on her name at the top of the sheet, spelled out in ornate copperplate letters within a twisting banner, like a flag stirring in the wind.

And there she was, her picture clear as day — the artist had done a good job of capturing her likeness. Around her picture a stylized and wispy fog, or perhaps it was meant to be the darkness, formed an oval frame, and in the four corners of the sheet were the smaller roundels she hadn't had time to look at before.

They were just as accomplished as the main picture.

One showed her leaning over her baby's crib, tears making her face shine. There was a shadowy figure in the background that she assumed was her husband, standing by just as he had done while their child was dying.

The next roundel depicted her with both her sons, stealing out of her house, and another had her grappling valiantly with a Colonist in a semilit tunnel. The last depicted a huge phalanx of Styx, scythes drawn, hot on the heels of a running, skirted figure as it fled down the length of a tunnel. The artist had taken liberties here; it hadn't happened like that at all, but the meaning was clear. She instinctively crumpled up the sheet. It was strictly forbidden to portray the Styx in any way whatsoever — *only* in the Rookeries would they dare do such a thing.

She couldn't get over it. Her life . . . in five pictures!

She was still shaking her head with utter disbelief as she caught the gentle creak of leather and looked up. She froze at the sight that met her.

Stark white collars and long black coats that rippled with the illumination from the streetlights. Styx. A large patrol of them — perhaps as many as two dozen. They were watching her, unmoving and silent, in a casually arranged line on the opposite side of the street. The scene had something of an old photograph from the American Wild West about it — a posse of long riders arranged around the sheriff before the start of a manhunt. But in this picture the sheriff was a teenage girl.

Rebecca, in the center of the front row, took a single step forward. As she stood, proud and commanding in front of her men, the strongest sense of power emanated from her.

Who is she really? Sarah thought, not for the first time.

Rebecca flicked her hand vaguely in the air, the gesture telling the Styx at her flanks to remain where they were. As the chanting continued, muffled now by the boundaries of the Rookeries, she gave a faintly amused smile. She crossed her arms primly and looked askance at Sarah.

"Quite the hero's welcome," she called over, tapping a foot on the cobblestones. "How does it feel to be such a big shot?" she added sourly.

Sarah gave a nervous half shrug, conscious of all the dark pupils of the massed Styx upon her.

"Well, I hope you made the most of it, because the Rookeries, and all the scum rotting inside, will be no more than a bad memory in a few days' time," Rebecca snarled. "Out with the old, as they say."

Sarah wasn't sure how to react to this—was it just an empty threat because Rebecca was angry that she'd dared to leave the Styx compound and venture into the Rookeries?

A bell began to toll somewhere in the distance.

"Enough of all this," the girl announced. "It's high time"—she snapped her fingers and the Styx around her stirred into action—"we were on our way. We've got a train to catch."

24

"**THE PLACE** of Cross Staves," Drake said as he looked at the sign by the letterbox opening in the ground. Will estimated it had taken them ten hours of rapid walking, punctuated by frequent bouts of jogging, to reach the place where — he had thought until now — Cal had died. Both he and Chester were thoroughly exhausted but filled with fragile hope.

At Drake's suggestion, they had taken a couple of breaks on the way, but no one had spoken as they drank water and chewed on some salty sticks with a nondescript flavor that the taciturn man had produced from a pouch.

As they had jogged along, with only Drake's faint miner's light to guide them, Elliott prowled behind, constant yet undetectable in the dark. But she was with them now, as Drake stood by the letterbox opening, a place Will had hoped he'd never again see in his lifetime: a place of fear and dread, a portal into the deathworld.

Drake undid the buckle and slung his belt kit to one side as Elliott handed him a mask, which he fixed over his mouth and nose. "I was given this by a dead Limiter." He smiled drily at the boys. Then he made sure the strange lens was positioned correctly over his eye.

"I want to help," Will declared. "I'm coming with you."

"No, you're not."

"Cal's my brother. He was my responsibility."

"That has nothing to do with it. You stay with Elliott and keep watch. We've broken every rule in the book on the way over, and I don't want to get pinned down when I'm in the sugar trap." Drake gestured toward Chester. "He's the stronger of you two — he's going to help me."

"Sure!" Chester nodded eagerly.

Elliott tapped Will on the shoulder. She was so close to him, he was a bit taken aback. She pointed at the outcrop behind the letterbox opening. "Take that side," she whispered. "If you see anything, don't shout, just tell me. Got that?" She started to hand Will one of the small metal cylinders Drake had been carrying, but he spotted what she was doing.

"No, Elliott, he doesn't know how to use it yet. If it comes to that, just scram and lead them away. We'll regroup at the emergency RV. OK?"

"OK. Break a leg." She smiled under her shemagh as she snatched the cylinder back from a bewildered Will.

"Thanks," Drake said, then jumped in the opening, with Chester close behind.

After they'd gone, Will hunched down low against the rocks, scouring the darkness. The minutes passed.

"Pssst!"

It was Elliott.

Will looked around. He couldn't see her.

"PSSSST!" It came again, louder this time.

He was about to call out to her when she landed right behind him, as if she had dropped from the sky. Evidently she'd been on top of the outcrop.

"Something going on over there," she whispered, pointing off into the darkness. "It's a long way away, so don't panic. Just keep your eyes peeled." She was gone before Will had a chance to ask her exactly what she'd seen. He peered in the direction she'd indicated. As far as he could tell, there was absolutely nothing there.

After several minutes, a distant, deep, rumbling *boom* resounded across the plain. There was no flash, but Will was certain he felt the percussive shock on his face, a faint wash of warm air over and above the constant breezes. He stood up, and Elliott was back in an instant.

"Thought so," she whispered into his ear. "It's the Limiters sending another Coprolite settlement sky-high."

"But why would they do that?"

"Drake thought perhaps *you* could tell us."

Will saw her keen brown eyes flash through the parting in the shemagh.

"No," Will replied hesitantly, "why should I know?"

"This only started — the hunting of our friends and any Coprolites who deal with us — about the time you showed up. Maybe you brought it on. So what did you do to get the Styx so stirred up?"

"I . . . I . . . ," Will stammered, stunned by the suggestion that he was somehow to blame for the Styx's actions.

"Well, whatever you did, they won't let it go. I should know." Her eyes flicked away from him. "Keep alert," she said, making a catlike leap up the sheer incline of the rock outcrop, her outsized rifle balanced in her arms.

Will's mind was whirring. Could Elliott be right? Had he brought down the wrath of the Styx on the renegades and Coprolites? Was he in some way responsible for all of this?

REBECCA!

The thought of his one-time sister made him choke. Could she still be out for vengeance? Her evil influence seemed to follow Will everywhere he went, slithering after him like a poisonous snake. Was she behind what was happening? No, that would be just too outlandish.

He thought back to the moment he and Chester had first entered the underground world, through one of the Colony's air locks and into the Quarter, setting off a chain of events over which he'd had no control. Then he began to think about how many lives had changed for the worse as a result.

For starters there was Chester, dragged into this terrifying mess because, out of the goodness of his heart, he'd offered to help Will search for his father. Then there was Tam, who had lost his life defending him in the Eternal City. And he couldn't forget Tam's men: Imago, Jack, and the others, who were probably on the run right now. All because of him. The burden was way too much to bear. *No,* he tried to convince himself, *this can't all be on me. It can't be.*

A commotion coming from the letterbox opening distracted Will from his tortured thoughts. He saw Drake racing away from the sugar trap, white particles scattering from his head and shoulders like a sprinkling of confetti. He was carrying Cal's limp body. Chester climbed out behind him.

Drake paused for the briefest instant to shake off his mask, then resumed his mad dash, heading directly for the canal.

"Come on," Elliott said to Will as he stood watching dumbly.

The trio followed Drake, pale particles swirling in his wake. But he didn't stop once he'd reached the canal. He hurtled from the bank, straight into the dark river, with a huge splash. Water closed over him, until both he and Cal were totally submerged.

Will and Chester stood on the bank, watching. As the water became calm again, there was only a clutch of air bubbles to mark the spot where Drake had jumped in. Will glanced at Chester.

"What's he doing?"

"Dunno." Chester shrugged.

"Did you see Cal?"

"Not really," Chester replied.

There was a small splash as if, far below, the water was being agitated. Small ripples spread out from the turbulence, then the surface becalmed again. Seconds passed.

Still staring blankly into the canal, Chester spoke in a despondent voice. "He looked pretty dead to me, but I couldn't really see."

"You didn't go into the cavern?"

"Drake made me wait outside. He moved inside it very slowly . . . I suppose he was trying not to set the things off. But then he came out run —"

He stopped speaking as Drake's head broke the surface. The man bobbed up, drawing several deep breaths. They couldn't see Cal's body; Drake kept it underwater. With a few one-armed strokes, he swam to the side, where he braced a shoulder against the crumbling stone bank. He raised Cal out of the water so the upper half of the boy's torso was visible and shook him savagely. Cal's head whipped from side to side as if it might detach altogether from his shoulders. Then Drake stopped, holding Cal still as he peered at his face.

"Shine your lanterns on him," he ordered.

Will and Chester did as they were told. The face was horrible to look at: deathly blue and speckled all over with raised white blotches. There didn't seem to be the smallest sign of life. Nothing. Will began to despair again. His brother was dead and there was nothing anyone could do to change that.

Then Drake shook the boy again and slapped him hard across the face.

Will and Chester both heard a gasp.

Cal's head twitched. He took a tiny breath, and then coughed weakly.

"Thank goodness, thank goodness," Chester was saying over and over again. He and Will looked at each other, wide-eyed with disbelief. Will just shook his head, dumbfounded. This was beyond his wildest dreams — his brother, before his very eyes, seemed to have returned from the dead.

Cal took a couple more wheezy breaths, then coughed again, stronger this time. Then he was coughing nonstop, his throat rasping as though he couldn't get enough air into his lungs. His head jerked around on his shoulders in a spasm and he was violently sick. "C'mon, boy! Good," Drake said, holding him. "That's it!"

He hoisted Cal up as far as he could.

"Take him," he told them. Will and Chester each grabbed Cal under the arms and dragged him out onto the bank.

"No, don't lay him down!" Elliott said. "Get him on his feet. Get his shirt off. Walk him around, keep him moving. It'll work the poisons out."

As they stripped the shirt off his body, they saw Cal's blue-tinged skin in all its glory. Its surface was peppered with raised white welts. His flame-red eyes were open, and his mouth moved in wordless shapes. One on either side, Will and Chester walked the diminutive figure in quick circles. Cal's head rolled loosely as they went, but he was unable to shuffle even a step under his own steam.

Drake had climbed out of the canal and was squatting on its bank as Elliott scanned the horizon with her rifle scope.

But Will's and Chester's efforts didn't seem to be enough. After a while Cal's eyes closed, and his mouth stopped moving as he slipped back into unconsciousness.

"Stop," Drake said, rising to his feet. He came over to where the boys were and, propping up Cal's head with one hand, slapped his face mercilessly with the other. He did this time and time again. Will thought he could see some of the blue color beginning to recede from his brother's cheeks.

Cal's brows twitched, and Drake stopped, watching his face carefully.

"We got to him just in the nick of time. Any longer and the narcotics would've had him in their grip, and the spores begun to take root," Drake said. "In short order they would have digested him. A human compost bag."

"Spores?" Will asked.

"Yes, these." Drake rubbed roughly with his thumb at one of the coarse white welts on Cal's neck. A little of it crumbled away at his touch to reveal even brighter blue skin beneath, oozing with small droplets of blood. "They germinate — like these have — and put down tendrils, which grow into the flesh of the victim, absorbing all the nutrients from the living tissues."

"But he'll be all right, won't he?" Will said quickly.

"He's been out for a long time," Drake answered, shrugging. "Just remember, if any of you are fool enough to make the same mistake twice and blunder into a sugar trap, you have to shock the victim awake. The nervous system almost shuts down and needs a trauma to kick-start it. One way is to shove them underwater. You almost have to drown them to save them."

Cal seemed to be drifting off again, so Drake resumed slapping him, so hard that the noise hurt Will's ears. Then Cal suddenly yanked his head back. He inhaled deeply and screamed the most horrible of screams. Will and Chester shuddered. It was unearthly, like an animal call, reverberating across the dusty desert. But, akin to the primal scream of a newborn baby, it gave Will and Chester such hope. Drake took his hands away.

"That's it. Now walk him around again."

They kept on, in endless circles, and little by little life seemed to be returning to the boy. He began to walk with them, at first with only the feeblest of movements, and then bigger, uncontrolled paces, as his head lolled on his shoulders.

"Drake, better see this," Elliott called, adjusting the sight on her long rifle.

Immediately at her side, Drake took the rifle from her. He looked through the scope. "Yes . . . I see it . . . strange . . ."

"What do you think?" she asked. "There's a lot of dust being kicked up."

He lowered the rifle and looked at her with a bewildered expression. "Styx . . . on *horseback*!"

"No," she said with disbelief.

"They've picked up a light trace from us," Drake said, passing the weapon back to her. "We can't hang around here." He strode over to Will and Chester. "Sorry, boys, no time to rest. I'll carry your kit but you've got the patient." He hoisted both of their rucksacks onto his shoulders and started off without a moment's delay.

Will and Chester lugged Cal between them, Will lifting the boy under his armpits while Chester had hold of his legs. They ran in a half trot, using the muted light from Drake's miner's beam to guide them.

"They can't follow us into the tubes on horseback," he called quietly back to them. "But we've got a long way before we're out of the woods. Move it!"

"This is knackering," Will moaned as yet again his foot caught against a rock and he stumbled, only just managing to keep hold of his brother. "He weighs a frickin' ton!"

"Tough," Drake snapped back. "Pick up the pace!"

Sweat poured from Will and Chester as they struggled along; they were suffering badly from exhaustion and lack of food. Will had a foul taste in his mouth, as if his body was burning its last reserves. He felt dizzy, and wondered if Chester was finding it as hard going as he was. Making matters that much more difficult, Cal kept twitching and writhing. He obviously had no idea what was happening and was trying to push them both off.

They finally came to the perimeter of the Great Plain. The boys both felt fit to drop, their limbs leaden with fatigue. They entered a winding lava tube and, as it turned a corner, Drake turned to them.

"Hold up a second," he ordered, and unhooked one of the packs from his shoulder. "Take some water. We've left the plain earlier than we should have. . . . It's safer, but it'll mean a longer hike home."

They gratefully slumped down to the ground with Cal between them.

"Elliott, rig a pair of trips," Drake called out.

From nowhere she came into the weak beam of Drake's light, stooping down while she positioned something by the rock wall. It was a stubby canister, approximately the size of a soup can and dull brown in color. Once she had anchored it to a small boulder by means of a strap, she backed away, feeding out a taut length of wire, so fine that Will and Chester could hardly see it, across the width of the tunnel. She attached this to a spur on the opposite wall and then plucked it gently: It gave a low twang. "Perfect," she whispered, returning to the canister. Lying on her front, she gently eased a small pin from it and stood up. "Set," she said quietly.

Drake turned to Will and Chester. "We have to move farther down so Elliott can rig the second one," he ordered as he scooped up the rucksack.

Will and Chester got slowly to their feet and lifted up Cal again. By now he had begun to make strange, nonsensical noises, whines and grunts, with the odd drawled word mixed in: "hungry," or "thirsty." But neither Will nor Chester had the time nor the energy to worry about that now. They carried Cal several hundred feet, then came to a halt again as Drake stopped.

"No, don't sit down!" he told them.

So they remained standing as Elliott set up another "trip."

"What do those do?" Will asked, leaning against the wall of the lava tube and puffing, as he and Chester watched Elliott repeat the process.

"They go bang," Drake told him. "They're charges."

"But why do you need two?"

"The first has a delay on the fuse. So the White Necks trigger it, walk into the second charge at about the time the first goes off, and presto, they're sealed in a section of the tunnel. Well, that's the theory, anyway."

"Genius," Will said, impressed.

"Actually" — Drake leaned toward him — "we often set two or more because the Limiters are so bloody good at spotting them."

"Oh, right," Will mumbled, less impressed.

By Will's reckoning, they must have covered quite a few miles before they heard the charges go off in quick succession, like a pair of giant handclaps. Then, after a brief delay, they felt a burst of wind on their sweat-soaked necks. Drake didn't miss a step, continuing at a pace they found difficult to match. By now, Will was holding Cal by one of his arms while the other flailed weakly, sometimes knocking against Will's shins.

They twisted through tube after tube, climbing and descending, sometimes squeezing through series of tight cavities, sometimes wading through semisubmerged, echoing caverns. In these, they were forced to hoist Cal almost to shoulder height, as best they could, so his head wasn't dunked under the water.

The boy appeared to be getting his strength back and, as it returned, he became more and more unmanageable, thrashing around in their grip. At times, it was just too much and they dropped him. On one of these occasions, both Will and Chester were too tired to care anymore as Cal hit the sodden ground with a mighty slap. He loosed off a series of garbled and guttural swear words as they were picking him up again.

"DANG T'Y'USE FIRKS! Y'USE SNECKEN THRIPPS!"

These unrecognizable curses, combined with Cal's ineffectual fury, were so comical that Will couldn't stop himself from chuckling. This infected Chester, who also began to laugh, causing the bizarre drawled invectives to issue from Cal at an even greater rate as he flapped wildly about. The boys' fatigue, and the sheer relief that Cal was alive, were making them both feel a little light-headed.

"Hmm . . . don't think I've ever been called *that* before," Chester said, breathing hard from the exertion. "*Sneck-en-thripps?*" he repeated, enunciating the words carefully.

"I have to admit," Will snickered, "I've always thought you *were* a bit of a thripp."

Both of them dissolved into hysterical laughter, and Cal, who evidently could hear everything they were saying, flailed his arms around even more furiously.

"CRUTS Y'BISHTARDS!" he bellowed hoarsely, then went into a paroxysm of coughing.

"Shut up!" Drake hissed from up ahead. "You'll give away our position!"

Cal became more subdued again, not because of Drake's reprimand, but because he realized that the swearing wasn't achieving anything. Instead, he began to try to grasp hold of Will's leg to trip him up. Will's amusement turned to irritation and he shook his brother. "Cal, enough!" he snapped. "Or we'll leave you behind for the Styx."

Finally they found they were back at the base. Since they hadn't had to go through the sump, Will realized they must have approached it from another direction. They pulled up Cal with the rope knotted around his chest and got him to one of the beds in the end room. Drake told them to sponge some water into the boy's mouth. He coughed and spluttered, most of it dripping down his chin, but still managed to drink a good amount before he drifted off into a deep slumber.

"Chester, you watch him. Will, you're coming with me."

Will obediently followed Drake along the corridor. He felt a rising apprehension, as if he'd been summoned to the principal's office for a telling-off.

They entered a darkened area and then, through a metal doorway, Will found he was in a large room, where a single light orb suspended in the center of the ceiling burned brightly. The room was at least a hundred feet long and only slightly less wide. In one corner was a pair of bunk beds made from thick sections of iron, and every inch of the walls was draped with a mass of equipment. It was like some military treasure trove and, as Will's eyes roamed around, he spotted racks with huge numbers of strange cylinders like the one Elliott had tried to give him at the Place of Cross Staves. There were also some deflated gray suits that Will recognized as the ones the Coprolites wore, and all manner of webbing, coils of rope, and kit bags, all hung in neatly ordered rows.

As he continued behind Drake, Will spied Elliott between the two bunk beds. Her back was to him, and he could see she had removed her jacket and pants and was stowing them in a wall locker. She was dressed in an ivory-colored undershirt and shorts, and he couldn't stop himself from looking at her slim and finely muscled legs. They were smeared with dirt and, like Drake's face, they appeared to have a shocking number of scars on them, which stood out white against the reddish-brown of the dust that coated every inch of her skin. Taken aback at seeing her like this, Will stopped on the spot, but then noticed Drake was watching him intently.

"Sit," he ordered, indicating a place by the wall, just as Elliott emerged from between the bunk beds.

She had a strikingly feminine face, with high cheekbones and full lips below a fine nose. Will saw her eyes flash darkly as she gave him a cursory glance, then she yawned and ran a hand through her short-cropped black hair. Her arms and wrists were so slight that Will couldn't believe he was looking at the same person who toted the long rifle around as if it were merely a stick of bamboo.

His gaze fell on her upper arm, where there was a disturbingly deep indentation in her bicep. The skin lining the hollow was rippled through with jagged pink striations, and its surface was rough, as if melted candle wax had been dripped over it. Will's first thought was that something had taken a bite out of her, and a big one at that.

But everything he noticed about her was dwarfed by the remarkable fact that she appeared to be *young*, perhaps not much older than him. It was the last thing he would have expected, given her intimidating presence out on the Great Plain.

"OK?" Drake asked her as she yawned again and scratched her shoulder absently.

"Yeah. Going to take a shower," she replied, padding barefoot to the door without a second glance at Will, who stared after her, his mouth agape.

As Drake snapped his fingers in front of his face to get his attention, Will realized he had been gawping, and self-consciously averted his eyes.

"Over here," Drake said, more forcibly this time. By the wall were two sturdy-looking metal trunks, and they sat opposite each other on these. Although Will's thoughts weren't quite organized, he started to speak.

"I . . . um . . . wanted to thank you for saving Cal. I was wrong about you and Elliott," he confessed, his eyes flicking automatically to the doorway as he spoke her name, although she'd long since left the room.

"Sure." Drake waved his hand dismissively through the air. "But I'm not concerned about that. Something's going on, and I need to know what you know."

Will was a little taken aback by the question, and looked at the man with a perplexed expression.

"You saw for yourself what the Styx are doing. They're killing renegades by the dozen."

"Killing renegades," Will echoed, and shivered as he thought about the incident he and Chester had witnessed.

"Yes. I have to admit I'm not sorry to see some of them go, but we're also losing friends at a rate of knots. In the past the Styx left us largely to our own devices, apart from when they needed a revenge killing because a trapper overstepped the mark and a Limiter went missing. It's different now; we're being weeded out, and I don't think the Styx are going to stop until every last one of us is dead."

"But why would they kill Coprolites, too?" Will asked.

"To send a signal to them not to trade with us or give us any assistance. But that's nothing new. The White Necks have periodic cullings to keep Coprolite numbers down," Drake said, rubbing his temples as if the matter deeply troubled him.

"What are *cullings*?" Will asked, not understanding.

"Wholesale slaughter," Drake replied brusquely.

"Oh," Will mumbled.

"There's no question that the Styx are hatching something. The Limiters are out in battalion strength, and from what we've seen, there are high-ranking White Necks arriving on the Miners' Train almost by the day." Drake frowned. "We've also got it from a reliable source that the scientists are down here trying something out on human subjects. There are stories they've set up a testing area, although I haven't located it yet.

"This ringing any bells with you?" He paused to scrutinize Will with his striking blue eyes. "You don't know anything about any of this, do you?" he said to the boy.

Will shook his head.

"Well, then, I need to know everything you *do* know. Exactly who are you?"

"Um . . . OK," Will answered, clueless where to start or how much Drake really wanted to hear. He was feeling totally fried, and every muscle in his body ached from hauling Cal, but he wanted to help Drake however he could. So he began to talk in some detail, Drake interrupting with the odd question, and his manner softening slightly and becoming almost convivial as Will went on.

He recounted how his adoptive father, Dr. Burrows, had been observing a group of people up in Highfield who didn't quite seem to fit and had thrown himself into an investigation of them. And how this investigation had led him to excavate a tunnel, which had given him a way into the Colony. Then Will explained, swallowing as his throat tightened, how his father had voluntarily taken the Miners' Train. "And my dad's down here somewhere now. You haven't seen him, have you?" he said quickly.

"No, not me." Drake held up a hand, reacting to the boy's evident agitation. "But — and I don't want to get your hopes up — I spoke to a trapper recently . . ." Drake seemed to hesitate.

"And?" Will said eagerly.

"He heard through the grapevine that there's an outsider hanging around one of the settlements. Apparently this man is neither Colonist nor Styx. . . . He wears glasses . . ."

"Yes?" Will leaned forward expectantly.

". . . and makes notes in a book."

"That's Dad! It's got to be!" Will exploded, laughing with relief. "You have to take me to him."

"I can't," Drake replied bluntly.

Will's elation was immediately replaced by sheer exasperation.

"What do you mean, you can't? You must!" Will implored him, then his frustration boiled over and he jumped to his feet. "He's my dad! You have to show me where he is!"

"Sit down," Drake ordered in no uncertain terms.

Will didn't move.

"I said sit down . . . and calm down, so I can finish what I was saying."

Will slowly lowered himself back onto the trunk, his chest heaving with emotion.

"I said I didn't want to get your hopes up. The trapper didn't give me any details about where this man is, and the Deeps go on for miles. In any case, with all the activity from the White Necks, the Coprolites are moving their settlements. So it's likely he's upped and moved with them, too."

Will was silent for a while.

"But if it *is* Dad, he's OK, then?" he asked eventually, searching Drake's eyes for confirmation. "You think he's going to be all right?"

Drake rubbed his chin thoughtfully. "As long as he doesn't get jumped by a Limiter execution squad."

"Oh, thank goodness," Will said, closing his eyes for a moment.

Even if Drake couldn't tell him where his father was, Will was so comforted by the information he was alive that it gave him a second wind.

He launched into his own story: how, after Dr. Burrows had gone missing, he'd enlisted Chester's help, and how they had gotten into the Colony. He told of their subsequent capture and the grueling interrogations by the Styx. Then he spoke about the first meeting with his biological brother and father, and the revelation that he had been adopted. As he mentioned his real mother, and that she was the only person ever to escape from the clutches of the Colony and survive, Drake interrupted him abruptly.

"Her name? What's her name?"

"Um . . . Jerome. Sarah Jerome."

There was the smallest intake of breath from Drake and, in the silence that followed, Will was sure he noticed a change in the man's penetrating eyes. It was as though they were looking at him afresh.

"So you're telling me you're her son," Drake said, straightening his back. "Sarah Jerome's son?"

"Yes," Will confirmed, surprised by his reaction. "Cal is, too," he added in a mumble.

"And your mother, she has a brother."

Will couldn't tell whether this was a question or a statement of fact. "Yes, she did," he replied. "My uncle Tam."

"Tam Macaulay."

Will nodded, impressed that Drake knew the name. "You've heard of him?"

"Only by reputation. He wasn't a favorite with the powers that be in the Colony . . . they had him down as a trouble-maker," Drake replied. "But you said *did*? What happened to him?"

"He died getting Cal and me away from the Styx," Will answered sadly. As Drake frowned, Will went on to tell him everything he knew about Rebecca, and how Tam had fought and killed her father, the Crawfly.

Drake whistled. "You certainly saved the juiciest part till last," he said, then gazed at Will for a few moments. "So," he pronounced softly, "you've pissed off someone right at the top of the Styx pecking order and," — he was silent for a heart-beat — "and they want your head on a plate."

This knocked Will for a loop and he didn't know how to respond. "But —" he started with a splutter.

Drake spoke over him. "There's no way they'll let you remain at large. Just as your mother, Sarah, is a sort of figure-head, a hero for the insurgents in the Colony, you'll be viewed in the same light."

"Me?" Will swallowed.

"Yeah," Drake said. "You should wear a warning label."

"What do you mean?"

"I mean that you, my friend, are an extremely dangerous person to be around," Drake spelled out for the staggered boy. "It might be another reason why the plain is crawling with Limiters." Then, lapsing into thought, Drake rested his elbows on his long legs and leaned forward to study the floor. "This puts a different spin on everything."

"Why? No, it's not all because of me, it can't be!" Will protested vehemently. "You know how messed up it is in the Colony. . . ."

"No, I don't," Drake rebutted fiercely, jerking his head up. "Haven't been there for a while."

"Well, anyway, why would they still be after me? What can I do to them?"

"That's not the point. You just don't mess with *them* and walk away." Drake gave a snort. "The Styx don't truck with *live and let live*."

"But you said all the important Styx have been arriving in the Deeps. They wouldn't come here just because of me, would they?"

"No . . . that's true." Drake narrowed his eyes, nodding in vague agreement. "They might want to eliminate you, but with all the top brass and scientists turning up, there's no question they're working on something big. And whatever it is, it's obviously important to them."

"What do you think it is?" Will asked.

The man just shook his head and offered no explanation.

"Can I ask you something?" Will ventured, his mind still reeling.

Drake gave a nod.

"Um . . . Chester thinks you're a freedom fighter. Are you?"

"No, not even close. I'm a Topsoiler, just like you."

"You're kidding," Will exclaimed. "How did you — ?"

319

"It's a long story. Maybe another time," Drake replied. "Anything else you want to know?"

Will had been building himself up to ask the question that had been in the back of his mind for some time.

"Why . . . ?" he began, his voice wavering as he wondered if he was pushing his luck.

"Go on," Drake said, flexing his arm.

"Why . . . why did you save Cal? What are you helping us for?"

"That stone you're wearing," Drake said obliquely, as if he was avoiding giving an answer.

"This?" Will asked, touching the green jade pendant around his neck.

"Yes, where'd you get it?"

"From Tam." Probing with his fingertips the three slightly converging lines carved into its polished surface, Will contemplated the pendant. "Is it something important?"

"Legends speak of a fabled race far below, at the bottom of the Pore. It's said they're nearly as old as the earth itself. I've seen that same symbol many times. . . . It's on their ruined temples." Drake stared at the pendant, lapsing into another silence, during which Will felt more and more awkward.

If he hadn't been so utterly exhausted, Will would have launched into a thousand questions about this Pore and the ancient race Drake had mentioned. As it was, his mind was on more immediate matters. He shifted uneasily on the metal trunk, and then spoke up. "You . . . um . . . haven't really answered me . . . about why you're helping us."

Drake looked at him and, for the first time, gave a genuine smile. It seemed a little incongruous with his steely gaze.

"You're a stubborn little sod, aren't you? Can't see your chum Chester being so pushy." He leaned back, a contemplative expression on his face. "Where some lead, others follow," he said under his breath.

"Huh?" Will said, not catching what he was saying.

"In answer to your question," Drake said, straightening up, "life is hard down here, but just because we live like animals doesn't mean that we've lost our humanity. There are renegades a lot less accommodating than Elliott or me, who would kill you just for your boots, or keep you alive for — how can I put it? — their own diversions. I snatched Elliott from a similar fate many years ago." He rubbed his chest as if recalling an injury he'd received on the occasion. "I wouldn't want to see that happen to any of you."

"Oh," Will uttered.

Drake sighed, a long, deep sigh. "You and Chester are not like the walking wounded that are usually Banished from the Colony — you've not been maimed or tortured or broken from years of service." He rubbed the palms of his hands together as he continued. "I didn't count on being saddled with the three of you, I admit." He stared into Will's eyes. "But we'll just have to see how your brother shapes up."

As tired as he was, Will caught the implication.

"And you, sonny boy, could be a big liability with the White Necks after your scalp," Drake said with a yawn, his face becoming expressionless as he glanced around the room. "But I need to find out more about what the Styx are up to before we move from the plain. It'll give some breathing space for your brother to get his strength back. And when we get to where we're going, we could certainly do with some extra hands around the place."

Will nodded.

"The fact that you are Sarah Jerome's son *and* know the ropes Topsoil could be a real asset."

Will nodded again, but then stilled his head as he wondered why this was so important to Drake. "What do you mean?"

"Well, if my instinct is correct, this thing the Styx are working on might have big implications for Topsoilers. And I don't think either of us would just sit by and let them get away with it, would we?" He raised a quizzical eyebrow at Will.

"No way!" Will burst out.

"So, what do you say?" the man asked pointedly.

"Huh?"

"Well, are you in or not? Are you going to join us?"

Will chewed his lip in confusion. He was completely thrown, both by the offer from this formidable man and the suggestion that Cal might not be part of it. What would happen if his brother didn't recover fully? Would Drake just ditch him? And Will wondered what would happen if the Limiters really were out to get him. If it proved too dangerous to have him around, what then? Would Drake simply hand him over? But Will also knew he'd do anything he could to stop the Styx. It would pay them back for Tam's death.

He didn't have any alternative but to accept Drake's invitation. Besides, he, Chester, and Cal were hardly in a position to go it alone, certainly not with the state his brother was in, and not with the Limiters everywhere.

As Drake watched him, waiting for a response, Will knew he shouldn't hesitate — that wouldn't go down well. What else could he do but say yes? At the very least, if he played his cards right, then this man might be the key to finding his father.

"Yes," he said.

They talked some more and then Will was dispatched back to his room, where he found Chester fast asleep on the floor by the bed in which Cal was stretched out.

Will had wanted to say something to Chester, to apologize for being so hasty in dismissing his friend's hunch about Drake and Elliott. But Chester was dead to the world, and there was no way he was going to wake him. Will's fatigue caught up with him, too. He curled up on the unoccupied bed and fell into a dreamless sleep.

25

IN THE DAYS that followed, Will and Chester looked after Cal, serving him the nondescript food Drake and Elliott provided. All he wanted to do was sleep on the narrow bed, but the boys forced him to exercise. Taking fumbling, clumsy steps as if he couldn't quite feel his feet, he glowered resentfully at them.

His speech became less slurred and the blue hue gradually left his skin. Drake came in every day for updates on his progress, then would whisk one of the others off on reconnaissance expeditions so they could begin to *learn the ropes,* as he put it.

When Chester was away on one of these outings, Will took the opportunity to have a word with his brother.

"I know you're awake," Will said to Cal, who was lying on the bed, facing the wall. "What do you think of Drake?"

Cal didn't respond.

"I said, what do you think of Drake?"

"Seems OK," Cal mumbled after a while.

"Oh, I think he's better than that," Will said. "He told me there are others in the Deeps that would cut your throat for the clothes on your back. That's if the Limiters didn't get to you first."

"Hmm," Cal grunted, unconvinced.

"I just thought you should know that if you don't stop moping and get yourself back on your feet, Drake's patience might run out."

Cal spun around to face Will, his eyes filled with a sudden fury.

"Is that a threat? Are you threatening me? What's he going to do, send me packing?" He sat up quickly.

"Yes, something like that," Will answered.

"How do you know? You're just saying that."

"No, I'm not," Will answered resolutely. He stood up and started for the door.

"So you'd just let him dump me?" Cal was staring daggers at his brother by this time.

"Oh, Cal," Will groaned, turning around in the doorway. "What can I do if you won't help yourself? You know that Drake's talking of moving on soon. He and Elliott don't live here permanently. And he says he's going to take us with him."

"All of us?" Cal asked.

"That depends. Do you think he wants to look after three of us, especially when one's a real pain?"

Cal swung his legs over the side of the bed and stared nervously at Will.

"Do you mean that?"

Will nodded. "Just thought you should know," he said as he exited the room.

Cal took Will's words to heart and, in the days that followed, was a changed person. He threw himself into an exercise regime, hobbling around on a dark wooden cane that Drake had given him. The left side of Cal's body seemed to be the problem, the arm and leg taking longer to recover than their right-side counterparts.

On one occasion, disturbed by the constant *tap-tap* of the cane and the abrupt blurting snores of Chester, Will was finding it impossible to sleep. The heat and closeness weren't helping, although they had all pretty much acclimatized to it by now. Eventually Will decided it was useless and got up, scratching as he felt lice on his scalp.

"Well done, bro," he called quietly over to Cal, who gave a mumbled "Thanks" in response, continuing his circuit of the room.

"I need some water," Will decided aloud, and headed out into the corridor toward the small storeroom where the bladders were kept. He heard something and drew to a halt. As he stood in the dim half light, Elliott loomed into sight at the far end of the hallway. She was wearing her usual dark jacket and pants and had her rifle in her hands, but hadn't yet covered her head with her shemagh.

"Oh . . . hello," Will said self-consciously, dressed as he was in just his shorts. He folded his arms protectively across his chest, trying to cover up his lack of clothing.

With an expression of sheer indifference, she looked him coldly up and down. "Trouble sleeping?" she inquired.

"Uh . . . yeah."

She did a double take at the wound on his shoulder.

"Impressive," she said.

Feeling even more uncomfortable under her scrutiny, he slid his hand over the injury he'd received from the Styx attack dog. The heat of the Deeps made it itch like crazy, and Will couldn't stop himself from scratching.

"Stalker," Will said eventually.

"Looks like it was hungry," she observed.

At a loss for words, Will took his hand away to inspect the red patch of newly healed skin, and nodded mutely.

"Want to come on patrol with me?" she asked, in a non-committal sort of way.

It was about the last thing on Will's mind at that time of night, but he was intrigued because he had seen so very little of her and thrilled that she had offered. Drake spoke of her skills with such respect, telling them she had achieved a level of "field craft," as he called it, that Will and Chester would have to work very hard to attain.

"Yeah . . . great," he gushed. "What gear do I need?"

"Nothing much — I travel light," she said. "Hurry up, then!" she urged, since Will showed no sign of moving.

He returned to the room, where Cal hardly seemed to notice him as he continued with his exercises, and got dressed in a mad flurry. A minute later, he went back to Elliott in the corridor. She offered him one of the pads of cylinders that Drake always carried with him.

"Are you sure?" Will hesitated, recalling the incident at the Place of Cross Staves.

"Drake seems to think you'll be sticking around, so you're going to have to learn how to use them sooner or later," she said. "And you never know, we might just bump into some Limiters."

"To tell you the truth, I don't even know what these things are," he admitted, attaching the pad to his belt, then looping and knotting the stay around his thigh.

"They're *stove guns*. Bit more basic than this," she said, lifting up the long rifle. "And you should try this out, too." She handed him something else.

It was a device consisting of a larger and a smaller tube alongside each other, the two looking as though they had been melted together so that the join between them was barely detectable. The whole device was made from a rubbed, dull brass, its surface covered in tiny scratches and dents, and it was about a foot and a half long, with caps on either end of the larger of the two cylinders.

"It's a scope, isn't it?" Will said, glancing at her rifle, which had an identical device mounted on top of the barrel. The only difference was that his version had two short straps attached to it.

She nodded. "Put your arm through the loops . . . makes it easier to carry. OK then, let's go." She turned to face the exit and, in the blink of an eye, had swept into the shadows at the end of the corridor.

Will went after her, shinnying down the rope to find he was submerged in total darkness as he reached the bottom. He listened but could hear nothing. Unclipping his lantern, he turned it up a notch.

He was startled when the light fell on Elliott — she was several feet away, standing still as a statue.

"Unless I say so, that's the last time you use an orb on *my* patrol." She indicated the scope on his arm. "Use the scope, but just remember to shield it from bright light, as it'll frazzle the element inside. Also, be gentle with it — they're rarer than slugs' teeth," she said.

He extinguished his lantern and unhooked the device from his forearm. Flicking up the metal caps at either end, he held it up to his eye, looking around him.

"Wicked!" he exclaimed.

It was amazing. As if illuminated by a pulsing, slightly diffuse amber glow, the scope cut through the pitch-blackness. He could see the tiniest detail of the rock wall across from him, and when he pointed it down the length of the tunnel he could see way into the distance. There was an eerie glow to the floor and walls, making them appear as if they were shiny and wet, even though everything in the immediate area was bone-dry.

"This is so cool. It's like . . . like everything's in a weird daylight. Where'd you get these?"

"The Styx snatched someone from Topsoil who could make them. But he escaped and came down here to the Deeps. He brought a whole load of the scopes with him."

"Oh, right," Will said. "And what powers it? Batteries?"

"I've no idea what *batteries* are," she said, pronouncing the word as if it were foreign. "In each scope there's a small light orb that's been joined to some other things. That's all I know."

Will swiveled slowly on his heels, peering through the contraption toward the other end of the lava tunnel. As he did so, he caught a glimpse of Elliott's face.

In the ethereal amber glow, her skin was smooth and radiant, as if bathed in the softest sunlight. She appeared beautiful and so very young, her pupils shimmering like twin points of intensely sparkling fire. Even more striking was the fact that she was smiling, which he'd never seen her do before. Smiling

DEEPER

at *him*. It filled him with a kind of warmth — a sensation that was new and unfamiliar. He involuntarily took a sharp breath, then, hoping she hadn't heard, managed to control his breathing again. He continued to move the scope in an arc toward the other end of the tunnel, as if he was getting used to the device, but his thoughts were a million miles away.

"Right," she said gently, coiling the shemagh around her head. "Follow me, partner."

They trekked along the lava tube, pausing briefly in the golden cavern to protect their gear in a small waterproof satchel Elliott was carrying before they swam through the sump. Once on the other side, they stopped again to get themselves organized.

"Can I give you a piece of advice?" she asked as he was tying the pad of stove guns back onto his thigh.

"Sure. What?" he replied, not knowing what was coming next.

"It's the way you move. When you tread, you're like the others — even Drake. Try to use the ball of your foot . . . stay up on your toes longer, before you lower onto your heel. Watch me through the scope."

He did as she told him, observing how she took each step, moving like a cat sneaking up on its prey. Through the scope, her pants and boots, drenched from the water of the sump, glimmered with a shifting sheen of pale yellow light.

"It cuts down on the noise and even the tracks you leave, a little."

Will watched her lithe legs as she demonstrated, marveling at what seemed to be second nature to her.

"And you'll need to learn about foraging," she said suddenly, noticing something on the rock wall beside her. "There's plenty of food around if you know where to look. Like this, a cave oyster."

She went over to what he thought was merely a piece of rock jutting from the wall. With the blade of her knife, she began to pry around it. Then she resheathed the knife and put on a pair of gloves.

"The edges are sharp," she explained, tucking her fingers into the gap she had made. Bracing herself, she pulled with both hands and, with a slow sucking noise, the rock gradually came away from the wall. With a final sound like an egg being cracked open, it suddenly came free and she staggered back a couple of paces.

"There!" she said triumphantly and held it up so he could see. It was roughly the size of half a football, and as she flipped it over, Will recoiled. The underside was leathery and pulpy, with a band of small filaments rippling at its circumference. It was an animal of some kind.

"What the heck is it?" he said. "A giant limpet or something?"

"I told you — it's a cave oyster. They feed on the cinder algae around water holes. It tastes disgusting raw, but it's OK boiled." As she poked her thumb into the middle of the pulpy mass, it heaved and the animal began to extend a large, fleshy trunk, like the foot of a snail but many times bigger. Elliott stooped to carefully prop the animal upside down on its shell between two stones. "Should keep it from straying until we get back."

■ ■ ■

Their journey across the Great Plain was uneventful, although they were forced to cross several canals using the narrow lock gates as bridges. Will worked hard to keep up with Elliott, who moved at astonishing speed. He practiced treading as she'd shown him, but it wasn't long before his insteps began to ache so badly that he had to give up.

She slowed as the cavern wall came into sight. Carefully checking the surrounding area with her rifle scope, she led him along the wall and into a low, wide tunnel. She stopped when they'd gone a few hundred feet.

A wall of smell stayed them.

There was the most intense reek of rotten meat — sour blasts of it assailed them. Will tried to breathe through his mouth, but the horrific stench was so strong in the air, he could almost *taste* it.

Then, through his scope, he caught something that made his heart skip a beat.

"Oh no!" he gasped.

On one side of the tunnel, there were the bodies of what, from their clothes, had to be renegades. On the other side, facing them, were Coprolites, still in their bulbous dust suits. Will knew instinctively that the Styx had been responsible, and that the corpses had been decaying for some time. The odor could mean nothing else.

He counted five renegades and four Coprolites. The bodies in both ranks were on thick wooden stakes. The victims' heads sagged forward onto their chests, their feet supported by small timber crossbars nailed to the planks approximately two feet off the ground. This gave an eerie effect, as if the dark and silent bodies were actually suspended in air.

"But why did they do this?" Will asked, shaking his head at the terrible loss of life.

"It's a warning, and a show of their power. They do it because they're Styx," Elliott replied. As she walked down the line of renegades, Will stepped over to the Coprolites.

"I knew this man," Elliott said sadly, standing motionless before one of the bodies.

Holding his breath, Will made himself look at a dead Coprolite. The mushroom color of the suit showed up clearly in the amber of his night scope, but there was a darker texture smeared around the eye holes. The luminescent orbs were missing from them. It was evident that the thick rubber of the suit had been slashed to get the orbs out. He shivered. It brought home the full horror of what the Styx were capable of. "Butchers," he mumbled to himself.

"Will," Elliott said suddenly, breaking into his thoughts. She wasn't looking at the bodies now, but glancing up and down the wide tunnel, as if all her senses were straining.

"What is it?" Will asked.

"Hide!" she hissed at him in a strangled whisper.

That was all. He looked at her, not knowing what she meant. She was standing by the last of the renegades' carcasses on the opposite side of the tunnel. She moved so fleetly that Will could barely keep track of her through his scope. She found a depression in the ground, a small pit, and, tucking the rifle into her body, rolled deftly into it, facedown. Will couldn't see her anymore. She was completely hidden from sight.

He looked rapidly around, desperately seeking a similar hole in the tunnel floor. He couldn't see one. Where could he go? He had to find a hiding place. But where? He ran this way and that, slipping behind the row of Coprolite bodies on his side of the tunnel. No good! The ground was level — it even rose in a slight incline toward the wall.

Hearing a sound, he froze.

A dog's bark.

A stalker!

He couldn't tell where it was coming from.

He was totally exposed.

26

THE ABOMINATION of a dog, the stalker, made the most horrific snorting noises and low, snarling grunts as it pulled on its leash. Its handler was one of four Limiters strolling down the middle of the tunnel. He was struggling to keep the beast under control.

On their heads the Styx soldiers wore dull black skullcaps, and their faces were obscured by large, insectlike goggles and leathery breathing masks. A peculiar camouflage of dun- and sand colored rectangles patterned their ankle-length coats, and the equipment on their belts and in their knapsacks rattled slightly with each stride. It was clear they weren't on active duty — they weren't expecting anyone else to be in the area.

They came to a halt between the two lines of dead bodies, the dog handler hissing an unintelligible command to his animal. It growled and immediately sat on its haunches, still snorting in short, angry bursts as its head craned forward to sample the rancid odor of the rotting corpses. A gush of gluey saliva leaked from its maw, as if it found the stench appetizing.

The Limiters' voices were nasal and reedy, their words clipped and mostly incomprehensible. Then one began to cackle, a vicious, strident laugh, and was joined by the others, until they sounded like a herd of distorted hyenas. They were evidently gloating over their victims.

Will dared not breathe, not just because of the most appalling smell he'd ever encountered, but because he was petrified the soldiers might hear him.

As the Limiters had closed in, he'd been forced to hide in the only place he could think of.

He was clinging grimly to one of the stakes, directly behind a dead Coprolite. In a blind panic, he'd jumped up, pushing his arm into the gap between the Coprolite's body and the rough timber of the stake. And, as he'd tried to hold on, his feet had

scrabbled ineffectually against the stake until the toe cap of his boot had come across the tip of a large nail. Fortunately for Will, it protruded an inch or so through the back of the wood, and at least it gave him some sort of foothold.

But this alone wasn't enough to keep him aloft — as the Limiters approached, he'd needed to find something for his left hand to grip. Desperately feeling around, his fingers came across a gash in the Coprolite's dust suit, just by the shoulder blade. He forced his fingers in, into the thick, rubbery material, touching something damp and soft inside. It yielded as his fingers pushed against it — it was mushy.

His fingers were sinking into the rotted flesh of the Coprolite's body.

Will knew there was no time to find an alternative handhold. *Don't think! Don't think about it!* tore through his mind.

But the stench from the Coprolite's body seemed to intensify, hitting him with the force of a kick in the head.

Oh God!

If it had been strong before, it was simply unbearable now. His fingers had parted the inch-thick rubber suit and opened the gash in it more widely, releasing the foulest of gases from inside. The stench flooded out. Will wanted to drop to the ground and run — it was more than he could endure. It was the reek of warm, putrid meat from the decomposing man.

It. Was. Gruesome.

Will thought he was going to throw up. He felt the vomit forcing its way up into his mouth and rapidly swallowed the acrid fluid down again. He couldn't allow himself to be sick or to slip from his hiding place. He had to stay put, however bad it was. The memory of the stalker attack back in the Eternal City was painfully fresh in his mind — there was no way he was going to be subjected to that again.

He had his eyes tightly shut and was desperately trying to focus all his attention on what the Limiters were saying. As he listened, he willed them to go on their way again. They began by speaking in the Styx tongue, then alternated between it and English. Every so often, he caught the odd smattering of what they were saying. It seemed to be coming from different members of the patrol, but he couldn't tell because they all sounded equally strange.

". . . next operation . . ."

". . . neutralize . . ."

Then, after a lull during which he could only hear the sound of the stalker as it sniffed the dirt and growled:

". . . capture the rebel . . ."

". . . mother . . ."

". . . will assist . . ."

As he kept his body rigid, his arms were aching, and he realized that the very worst thing was happening: His leg, held in a horribly awkward position, was beginning to shake from the strain of supporting his body. He tried to control the trembling, petrified that his boot was going slide from its perch on the nail. Sweat coursed from his temples as he strained to disassociate himself from the sheer discomfort and listen to the Limiters' voices.

". . . sweep . . ."

". . . thorough search . . ."

He still didn't dare open his eyes, praying that he was sufficiently hidden behind the rotund body. It would only take one of the Styx to notice his arm or leg, and the jig would be up. He thought briefly of Elliott lying in the small ditch on the other side from him.

Then it happened. His leg seized up with pulses of agonizing pain. The cramps rippled through his calf and thigh as if someone with an iron grip were mercilessly crushing each of his muscles, all at the same time. He yearned to pull himself up ever so slightly by his arms, but he didn't dare.

His leg spasmed again, as if it had a mind of its own. He fought against its involuntary movements. His whole concentration was upon it, so much so that, for a few seconds, he forgot everything — the stench and the terse babble of the Limiters and the stalker so close by. But the pain and the shaking were growing worse. He had to do something.

Oh Sweet Mercy! He tensed his arms and heaved himself up just a fraction. The weight on his leg was reduced and the relief was instant, but the stake shifted slightly. He realized that the Limiters had stopped talking.

Please, please, please! he prayed.

The Limiters began to speak again.

"Topsoiler," one was saying. "We will find him. . . ."

Immediately there came another sentence, but only a single word registered with Will. It was said with a different intonation, as if the Styx was showing great respect.

". . . Rebecca . . ."

Rebecca? No, no, it couldn't be! His mind somersaulted. But it had to be his sister — the witch he'd *thought* was his sister — they were referring to. Why else would they have happened to use that particular name? It was just too much of a coincidence.

The Limiters fell silent. He detected the dog's snorts, clearly, as if it had moved closer, then heard the sound of boots scuffing in the dust. He half opened one eye and saw lights shifting over the walls and roof. Were the Styx closing around him, encircling him? Had he been caught?

No.

They were moving on.

Their footfalls resumed a single rhythm. They were leaving.

But he had to hold on and wait. Thankful that the Limiters were moving quickly, he clenched his teeth. He didn't think he could tolerate the smell for much longer.

Then something tugged at his ankle.

"All clear," Elliott hissed in a whisper. "Get down."

Will immediately pitched backward from the stake, falling onto the ground and crab-walking away from the Coprolite as fast as he could.

"For goodness' sake, be quiet! What is it?" she asked.

He flexed his fingers, the ones that had been inside the Coprolite's dust suit. There was a sticky wetness to them. Juices from the decaying cadaver. He shivered, shocked to the core. Not looking at his hand, he lifted it gingerly to his face, and caught the rancid stench of old death. Instantly he whipped his hand away, stretching it as far as he possibly could. He felt his gorge rising and took some rapid breaths. He rubbed his hand in the dirt, scouring it again and again with fistfuls of loose sand.

"Gross!" he exclaimed, and sniffed at his hand once more. He recoiled, but not so violently this time, the stench having lessened. "How can anyone live like this?" he mumbled through tight lips.

"Get used to it," Elliott replied in a flat voice. "This is what Drake and I do every day." She raised her rifle to scan down the tunnel, adding in a cold voice, "To survive."

She led him, not back out onto the plain, but deeper into a tunnel. He felt in no condition to go on with the excursion, and was stumbling and exhausted. His skin still crawled at the thought of the dead body he'd touched. He was suddenly angry for himself, and for the men on the stakes, and angry that Rebecca seemed to be somehow linked to what was going on. Would he ever be free of her?

"Hurry it up!" Elliott whispered sharply as he dragged his feet.

He stopped on the spot, spluttering "I . . . I . . ." It may have been an aftereffect of his terror, but he was filled by a sudden fury that needed release. It found a target in the diminutive girl before him.

He wrenched up his scope and tried to focus on her face, his hands shaking. "Why'd you let us get into that back there? You nearly got us caught!" he fumed at her amber outline. "We should never have got cornered like that . . . not with all those Styx so close. We could have both been killed by that stalker. I thought you were good." He became so choked with rage that he could hardly speak anymore. "I thought you knew what you're doing. You . . ."

She stood quite still, unperturbed by his outburst. "I do know what I'm doing. That was unforeseen. If I'd been with Drake, we'd have dealt with the Styx and stashed their bodies under a rockfall."

"But Drake's not here!" he snapped back at her. "I am!"

"We take risks every day," she said. "If you don't, you might as well crawl away somewhere and die," she added coolly and began to walk off, but then paused, swinging her head around to face him. "And if you ever talk to me like that again, I'll ditch you. Despite what Drake thinks, we don't need you that badly, but you bet your life you need us. Got that?"

Will's anger rapidly deserted him and he was left floundering, already regretting his words. Elliott didn't move, waiting for his response.

"Um . . . yes . . . sorry," Will mumbled. He felt deflated, struck by the realization of just how totally dependent he and the other boys were on Drake and Elliott. It was painfully obvious they wouldn't have lasted very long in this wild and lawless land if someone hadn't come to their rescue. He, Chester, and particularly Cal were living on the hard-won skills of others and should have been grateful for that.

Elliott turned and Will got in line behind her as they continued down the tunnel.

"Sorry," he said again into the darkness, but the girl didn't acknowledge him.

An hour later, after taking a confusing warren of interlinking galleries, Elliott stopped and seemed to be searching for something by the base of the wall. There was rubble strewn over the ground, interspersed with large shieldlike plates of rock that she used as stepping stones. Then she stopped.

"Help me with this," she said tartly and began to lift one of the slabs. Will took the other side and together, straining with its weight, they pulled it aside to reveal a small hole in the floor.

"Stay right behind me — there's caves of Red Hots nearby," she advised him.

Recalling that Tam had once mentioned that Red Hots were dangerous, Will didn't think it was an appropriate moment to ask her what they were. In any case, Elliott immediately got down and began to crawl into the hole, and Will followed obediently, wondering where it would take them. Although he couldn't see a thing, he used his hands to feel around and found the tunnel to be roughly oval in shape, and nearly three feet from side to side. He followed the sound of Elliott in front of him, but in places the accumulated gravel and stone chips on the floor made it difficult for him to get through and he had to worm himself along, kicking the shale behind him as he went.

The passage climbed steeply, and Elliott's movements ahead brought down slews of gravel over him. Not daring to complain, he stopped several times to brush the dust and grit from his face.

Then there was no sound from Elliott. Will was at the point of calling out to her when he heard the reverberations of her movements in a larger space. He climbed up a final, almost vertical section of the passage and, using his scope, saw they were in a gallery some ten by fifty yards. Elliott was already lying next to a fissure in the floor. He brushed himself down and then began to cough from all the dust he'd inhaled.

"Shut up," she growled.

He managed to muffle his coughing with his sleeve, and then joined her, lying by her side.

Together they peered down into the jagged fissure. They were looking from a dizzying height into a huge cathedral-like chamber. Far below, he could see the blur of many points of light. He pulled back slightly from the fissure, and, by angling his head, he could get a better view of the area below, where there were the oddest-looking machines. Will counted ten in all, parked in a row.

They were like stubby cylinders, each having a single serrated wheel-like contraption at one end. They called to mind photos he'd seen of the equipment used in the construction of the London Underground. Will assumed these, too, were some form of digging equipment. Then he spotted several groupings of stationary Coprolites and a handful of Styx watching them from a distance. Will looked at the rifle by Elliott's side and wondered if she was going to use it. At this range, it wouldn't have been difficult for her to snipe at the Styx.

After several minutes, there was a sudden burst of activity. Some of the Coprolites began to move slowly along as the Styx strolled threateningly behind them, their long rifles in their arms. The bulbous men looked tiny in comparison to the strange machines as they climbed into them. One of the machines fired up, its engine turning over with a roar and a black cloud issuing from its rear. Then it began to trundle forward, still under the scrutiny of the Styx, and edged out in front of the others.

Will kept watching as it picked up speed. He was able to see the hatches at the rear and the array of exhaust pipes around it, from which steam and smoke were pouring. He also saw the broad rollers on which it was being conveyed forward and could hear rocks cracking under them. The machine steered toward a tunnel that led off the main chamber and disappeared from view down it. He guessed the Coprolites were going off to do some mining, but he had no idea why so many Styx were monitoring them.

Elliott muttered something as she pulled away from the fissure, and he heard her go to a corner of the gallery. Using his scope, he watched as she reached behind a boulder to draw out several dark packages. He went over to her.

"What's that?" he said before he could stop himself.

She didn't answer him for several moments, then said, "Food," as she stowed the packages in her satchel.

She didn't seem to be about to volunteer anything further, but Will's curiosity was piqued.

"Who . . . where's it from?" he ventured.

Elliott pulled out a smaller, tightly bound package from her rucksack and tucked it behind the boulder. "If you really need to know, it was put here by the Coprolites — we trade with them." She pointed at the boulder. "I've just left them some of the orbs you filched from the Miners' Train."

"Oh," Will said, not about to complain.

"They're totally reliant on the orbs. The food's not that important to us, but we try to help them whenever we can." She looked rather scathingly at Will. "After what's been happening around here, they could do with all the help they can get."

Will nodded, but he found it difficult to believe he was responsible for what the Styx were doing to the Coprolites and shrugged off the barbed comment. He was beginning to think that he was being blamed for everything that went wrong.

Elliott twisted away from him.

"We're going back," she said, and together they moved off in the direction they had come from, toward the oval tunnel again.

The journey home went without incident. They stopped while Elliott gathered up the cave oyster — it was still where she had propped it. Its single stumpy leg had evidently been working overtime, whipping around as it had tried to right itself, producing a disgusting white lather that overflowed from the shell in large gobs. But this didn't put off Elliott. She wound a piece of cloth around the bulky shell and stowed it in her satchel. While she was doing this, Will watched her face through his scope. It was grim and unsmiling. Very different from how it had appeared only hours before.

He regretted his outburst. He knew he shouldn't have said what he had to her. He'd made a stupid, arrogant error and wondered how he could patch things up. He chewed the inside of his mouth with frustration, trying to think of something to say. Then, without a word or even a glance at him, Elliott waded into the water of the sump and was gone. He regarded the lapping water, the film of dust swirling in antagonistic circles from her passage through it, and felt as if he might cry. But instead he took a deep breath and followed after her, actually grateful to be totally immersed in the dark, warm water. It was as if it might clear his mind of his troubles.

As he scrambled out of the water, wiping it from his face, he felt somehow refreshed. The moment his eyes fell on Elliott as she waited for him in the golden chamber, the frustration and confusion returned.

He just didn't understand girls — they were completely unfathomable as far as he was concerned. They seemed to say only some of what they were thinking, then they'd clam up, hiding behind a sultry silence and *not* saying the part that really mattered. In the past, when he'd put his foot in his mouth with girls at school, he'd tried to fix it by apologizing for whatever he'd done to offend, but by then it always seemed like they didn't want to hear it.

He glanced at Elliott's back and sighed. Oh well, he'd made a pig's ear of it all, again. What a bloody idiot he'd been. He tried to console himself with the thought that he didn't have to stay with her, or Drake, forever. His single purpose in life remained to find his father. All this was only temporary.

Their water-soaked boots squelched loudly in an otherwise stony silence. They arrived back at the entrance to the base and climbed the rope. There was a stillness in the rooms, and Will assumed Cal had tired of his exercise and gone to sleep.

In the corridor, Elliott thrust her open hand toward him, her eyes averted. He cleared his throat uneasily, not knowing what she wanted, and then suddenly realized she was asking for the return of her scope. He pulled his arm from the loops. She grabbed it from him, but then thrust her hand out again.

After an uncomfortable moment, he remembered the pad of stove guns tied to his thigh, and fumbled at the knot to undo it. She snatched this from him, too, then flicked her head around and was gone. He stood there, dripping water into the dust and struggling with a disorder of isolation and regret.

In the weeks that followed, not once did Will again accompany Elliott. What made it worse was that she seemed to be inviting Chester to go with increasing frequency on her "routine" reconnaissance patrols. While Will and Chester never spoke of this, Will would catch glimpses of his friend chatting with Elliott out in the corridor, the two of them whispering together, and felt a sickening pang that he was being left out. Much as he tried to suppress it, he also felt a mounting resentment of his friend. He said to himself that Elliott should be teaching him, not bumbling old Chester. But there was nothing he could do about it.

Will found he had time on his hands. He no longer needed to tend to his brother, who had progressed from the constant laps of their room and the corridor to the tunnel just outside the base. Here he marched up and down, albeit still with the aid of the walking stick. So, to fill the hours, Will either tried to update his journal or just lay on his bed, mulling over their situation.

He realized, possibly a little late, that even in this roughest and most hostile of environments, where you had to do whatever was necessary, however rank and disgusting it might be, consideration for your friends was still paramount. This consideration, this code of behavior, was the glue that held the team together. You did not doubt Drake's or Elliott's judgment.

You did not question their orders. You did exactly as they told you, because it was for your own good, and theirs.

But Will had to admit that Chester was better suited than he was to following orders. And very early on Chester seemed to have formed an unquestioning and unwavering loyalty toward Drake, which he'd widened to include Elliott.

Cal, too, was now not that dissimilar to Chester in his allegiance to the two renegades. Cal had changed. Perhaps his brush with death had altered him, or he was understandably afraid of being abandoned. There was still the occasional outburst of the old bravado, but, on the whole, his brother was quieter, even *stoic* about their current situation. Will used this very word to describe Cal's changed temperament when writing in his journal — he'd learned it from his father and had thought at first that it implied weakness, a readiness to accept anything, no matter how bad. But now Will was beginning to realize he had been mistaken. A person facing a life-or-death situation needed a certain detachment to be able to think straight and not be panicked into the wrong choices.

Over the course of the ensuing weeks, they had regular instruction from Drake on such topics as finding and preparing food. This had begun with the cave oyster, which, once cooked, tasted somewhat similar to extremely rubbery squid.

Drake would also take them on short patrols and teach them field craft. On one occasion, he woke them at what felt like an early hour, although time did not really have any meaning in the everlasting darkness. He told all three boys to get ready and took them down the tunnel below the base, in the opposite direction from the Great Plain. They knew that it wasn't going to be a very long outing because he'd instructed them each to bring only a canteen of water and some light rations, while he carried a full rucksack.

As they went through a series of passages, the boys chatted among themselves to pass the time.

"Stupid moronic things," Cal had piped up as Will and Chester were discussing the Coprolites. Drake happened to overhear the remark.

"Why do you think that?" he asked quietly. Will and Chester fell silent.

"Well," Cal replied, apparently recovering some of his old cockiness, "they're nothing more than dumb animals . . . grubbing around in the rocks just like worthless slugs."

"So you really think we're *better* than they are?" Drake pressed him.

"Course we are."

Shaking his head as he continued to lead them down the tunnel, Drake wasn't going to let Cal's comment pass. "They harvest their food without fully depleting it and having to continually move on. And wherever they mine, they even refill the shafts. They put it all back, because they have respect for the earth."

"But they're . . . they're only . . . ," Cal dried up.

"No, Cal, we're the ones who are stupid. We are the *dumb animals*. We use up everything . . . we consume and consume until all the resources are gone . . . and then — surprise, surprise — we have to pack up and start somewhere new, all over again. They are the clever ones, in harmony with their environment. You and me . . . our kind are the misfits, the wreckers. Wouldn't you call *that* moronic?"

Now in silence, they traveled about a mile, until Will increased his step, leaving Chester and Cal behind as he caught up with Drake.

"Something on your mind?" Drake inquired before Will was even alongside him.

"Uh, yes," Will faltered, wondering if he should have stayed back with the others.

"Go on."

"Well, you said you were a Topsoiler —"

"And you want to know more?" Drake interrupted. "You're curious."

"Yes," Will mumbled.

"Will, it really doesn't matter what I was back in the world. It doesn't matter what any of us were. It's here and now that counts."

Drake didn't speak for several paces.

"You don't know the half of it," he began, then seemed to stop himself, falling silent for several more paces. "Look, Will, the chances are that I could evade the Styx to return Topsoil, where I'd be forced to live a life much like your mother's, always checking over my shoulder as I passed the shadows. But, not meaning any disrespect to Sarah, I believe living here in the Deeps is more honest. Do you get what I'm saying?"

"No, not really," Will admitted.

"Well, you've seen for yourself it's no walk in the park down here. It's hard: a hand-to-mouth, dangerous existence," Drake said, then grimaced. "If the White Necks don't get you, then there's a million other things that could snuff you out at the drop of a hat . . . infections, rockfalls, other renegades, and so on. But, I can tell you, Will, I've never felt more alive than my years here. Truly *alive*. So you can keep your safe, plastic Topsoil life — it's not for me."

Drake broke off as they came to an intersection with another tunnel. He told them to wait while he proceeded to unpack various pieces of equipment. He did this efficiently, not looking at the boys. Cal held back behind the other two, anxious that he'd annoyed the man, but Will watched with increasing excitement as he saw Drake had brought a selection of the stove guns he and Elliott took with them everywhere.

"Right," Drake said after he'd arranged the cylinders in two groups, each in order of decreasing size, on the sandy bed before them. The boys looked at him expectantly.

"The time's come for you to learn how to use these." He stood to the side so they could see the array of cylinders in the first group, the biggest a stubby tube with a circumference slightly larger than a section of drainpipe and eight inches in length. "All these . . . with the red bands around them . . . are charges. The more bands, the longer the fuse. If you remember, you saw Elliott set a couple of these with trip wires."

Will opened his mouth to speak but Drake held up a hand to silence him.

"Before you ask, I'm *not* going to demonstrate any of the charges here." Drake turned to the other group of items. "But these, as you know," he said, sweeping his hand over a range of smaller tubes, "are called stove guns. This," he said, pointing at the largest one, "is the heavy artillery . . . a stove mortar.

You can see that, unlike the other guns, it doesn't have a trigger mechanism at the base."

He hoisted up the stove mortar and swung it in front of them.

"Simple but very effective for taking out a large number of your enemies, by which I mean the Styx. The casing" — he tapped it with a knuckle and it rang dully — "is made of iron and is capped at both ends." He patted it as if it were an elongated bongo. "This particular version is fired by striking the end." He took a deep breath. "The load can be whatever you want; rock salt, slate pencils, or pig iron are all very effective if you need to wipe out a large number of targets. A *crowd-pleaser*," he said with a wry grin. "Try it for weight, and, whatever you do, *don't* drop it!"

In respectful silence, the boys passed it from one to another, holding it carefully as they inspected the heavier end where the detonator was housed. Cal handed it back to Drake, who laid it down on the sand again.

Then Drake indicated the other cylinders with a wave of his hand. "These are more portable and fired like real guns. They all have mechanical fuses not unlike the cocking arm on a flintlock." He seemed undecided which of the guns to select, and then chose one in the middle of the array. It was almost identical in size to some of the firecrackers Will had set off in the Eternal City, about six inches or so long and an inch in diameter. Its casing shone dully under their combined lanterns.

Drake turned sideways to demonstrate the correct stance.

"Like all these weapons, they are *single-shot*. And watch the recoil — hold it too close to your eye and you'll regret it. As with the others, they're triggered by a spring lever at the rear. They're fired by pulling the cord." He cleared his throat and regarded them. "So . . . who wants to have a go?"

The boys nodded eagerly.

"Right, I'll fire one first to show you how it's done." He went forward and searched the ground until he found a stone with the approximate dimensions of a matchbox. Then he walked another twenty paces to an outcrop in the middle of the intersection, on which he balanced the rock. Returning, he took a stove gun, not from the display on the sand but from the pad on his hip. The boys gathered by his side, jostling for a view. "Stand a little farther away, will you? Once in a blue moon they backfire."

"What's that mean?" Will asked.

"They blow up in your face."

The warning wasn't lost on the boys, particularly Chester, who edged well away — so much so that he was almost standing with his back against the tunnel wall. Will and Cal were less cautious, positioning themselves a few feet behind Drake, Cal leaning with both hands on his walking stick and giving the demonstration his full attention. He looked for all the world like an observer at a golf tournament.

Drake took his time to aim, then fired. To a boy, they flinched as the crack resounded. Thirty feet away, they saw the impact on the rock outcrop and a spray of fragments and dust. The target stone quaked slightly but remained in place.

"Close enough," Drake said. "These aren't accurate like Elliott's rifle. They're mainly intended for close-quarter use." He turned to Cal. "Now you," he said.

Cal was slightly hesitant, and Drake had to position him correctly, nudging his front foot forward and pulling his shoulders around so that his stance was correct. Cal was disadvantaged by the fact that his left leg was still a little weak, and the strain of holding the position showed on his face.

"OK," Drake said.

Cal pulled the cord at the rear of the tube. Nothing happened.

"Pull it harder — the cocking arm needs to be snapped back," Drake told him.

Cal tried again, but in the process moved the tube way off target. The slug hit the chamber wall some distance away and they heard a zinging as it ricocheted down the tunnel beyond.

"Don't worry, it's your first try. You've never shot a gun before, have you?"

"No," Cal admitted glumly.

"We'll have more opportunities to practice when we get to the deeper levels. Nothing like a spot of big game hunting with the wildlife down there," Drake said enigmatically. Will's ears perked up, wondering what sort of animals these might be, but then Drake told him it was his turn.

The gun went off the first time Will yanked the cord, and they saw the spray of dust just in front of the target this time.

"Not bad," Drake congratulated. "You've shot before."

"I've got an air pistol," Will said, remembering his illicit sessions with his old Gat gun on Highfield Common.

"With some practice, you'll get better at judging the distance. Now you, Chester."

Chester stepped forward a little hesitantly and took the stove gun from Drake. He hunched his shoulders over, looking very awkward as he tried to aim the device.

"Rest it on the heel of your hand. No, move your hand underneath more. And, for heaven's sake, just relax, boy." Drake took his shoulders and instead of pulling them around as he'd done with Cal, tried to push down on them. "Relax," he said again, "and take your time."

Chester still looked incredibly awkward, his shoulders creeping up again. It seemed forever before he finally tripped the trigger.

None of them could believe their eyes.

There was no shower of chips this time or whirr of a ricochet. With a crack, the bullet hit the target stone dead on, and it whipped down the tunnel beyond in a blur.

"Atta boy!" Drake said, patting the flabbergasted boy on the back. "Bull's-eye."

"Give that kid a coconut!" Will laughed.

Chester was speechless, blinking at the space where the rock had been. Will and Cal congratulated him profusely, but he clearly didn't know what to say, totally confounded by his success.

They knew the training session was over when, with some urgency, Drake immediately bundled up the charges and the stove guns in the roll of material and shoved them back into his rucksack. However, he left one, a medium-sized cylinder, in the sand. Will was looking at it, wondering if he should bring it to Drake's attention, when a stone flew before them and hit the ground, clattering along until it came to rest in the shale by Drake's feet.

It was the very stone that Chester had hit with such accuracy.

A raspy and lisping voice seeped unpleasantly from the shadows, as if a bad smell had been released.

"Always one fer a bit of showmanship, wasn't yer, Drakey?"

Will immediately looked up at Drake, who was alertly watching the darkness, the stove gun at the ready in his hands. His wasn't a perceptibly threatening or defensive stance, but Will saw the deadly intent in Drake's face just before he flipped the lens down over his right eye.

"What are you doing here? You remember the Rule, don't you, Cox? Renegades keep their distance or suffer the consequences," Drake rumbled.

"Yer didn't keep the Rule when yer gimleted poor old Lloyd, did yer? And took 'is girl."

An amorphous figure emerged from farther down the tunnel, a misshapen and hunched bundle illuminated by the boys' lanterns.

"Ahh, I heard yer 'ad some new lovelies. Some ripe meat."

The shape coughed and continued to move forward, as if it were floating just above the ground. Will saw it was a man, wearing what looked to be a brown and extremely filthy shawl over his head and shoulders, like he was a peasant woman. He was painfully bent over, giving the impression he was seriously deformed. Stopping before Drake and the boys, he raised his head. It was a grisly sight. He had a huge growth on one side of his forehead, like a small melon, and the dirt was rubbed away on it, so they could see grayish skin shot through with a network of raised blue veins. There was another of these growths, slightly smaller in size, on his mouth, so that his lips, black and cracked, were drawn into a permanent O. A constant drool of slick, milky saliva ran from his lower lip and down his chin, where it hung like a liquid goatee.

But his eyes were the worst things to behold: perfectly white, like freshly shelled boiled eggs, with no sign of a pupil or an iris whatsoever. They were the only solid, cohesive area of color on him, and all the more shocking for it.

A gnarled-looking hand, like a sun-dried root, poked out of the shawl and described a circle as he spoke.

"Got anything for yer old mucker?" Cox lisped loudly, with a spray of spittle. "Anything fer the poor old man who taught ya all yer know? How's about one of these choice youngsters?"

"I owe you nothing. Just leave," Drake answered stonily. "Before I —"

"Is them the boys the Blackheads is looking fer? Where are yer keepin' them 'idden away, Drakey?" Like a cobra about to strike, his head jutted forward, the white unseeing eyes sliding over Will and Cal, with Chester lurking terrified behind them. Will saw the thick crosses of darkened scars, one over each eye, and the matrix of many more gray gashes across the coal-black skin of his cheeks.

"Their young scent is so" — the man quickly wiped his nose with a swipe from the gnarled hand — "nice and clean."

"You spend too much time in these parts . . . you look like you're on your last legs, Cox. Perhaps you'd like me to help you along?" Drake said drily as he held up the stove gun. The man's head swiveled toward him.

"No need fer that, Drakey, not toward yer old friend."

Then the shape bowed with great ceremony and instantly vanished from the area of light. Chester and Cal were still staring at the place where he'd been, but Will was looking at Drake. He couldn't help but notice that Drake's hands were gripping the stove gun so tightly that his knuckles were white.

Drake turned to the waiting boys.

"That charmer was Tom Cox. I'd rather have the company of the Styx any time than that twisted abomination of a man. He's as sick on the inside as he looks on the outside." Drake drew breath tremulously. "You could've so easily ended up in his clutches, if Elliott and I hadn't reached you first." His eyes fell to the stove gun in his hand, and, as if he was surprised to find it still poised for use, he lowered it. "Cox and his kind are the reason we don't spend much time on the plain. And you can see what the radiation will do to you, eventually."

He slotted the stove gun back into the pad on his thigh. "We should be on our way." He swung his head to where Tom Cox had been, his gaze lingering on the spot, seeing shadows that the three boys couldn't begin to imagine. Then he led them away, all the time checking to make sure the man wasn't following behind.

On another occasion, Will had spent a night of broken sleep, punctuated by a series of the deepest dreams. He was just drifting off again when he was roused by Elliott's voice from the corridor. It was so faint and unreal, he wasn't sure if he'd really heard it or had been dreaming again. As he sat up, Chester trudged into the room. He was sopping wet, suggesting he had just swum through the sump.

"All right, Will?" he asked.

"Yes, I think so," Will replied groggily. "Been on patrol?"

"Yeah . . . just doing the rounds. All quiet out there. Nothing happening," Chester said cheerily as he took off his boots. He spoke with a casual, soldierly acquiescence, as if he was doing only what he was duty-bound to do, and doing it with a forced heartiness.

It suddenly struck Will how much their friendship had changed over the past two months, as if Cal's brush with death in the sugar trap and the introduction of Drake and Elliott, especially Elliott, had somehow redrawn the geometry of their relationship, all their relationships. As he lay back in his narrow bed with his arms crossed behind his head, the recollection of how his and Chester's friendship once had been flashed through his mind. In his sleep-numbed state, Will was able to take up its warmth gratefully and pretend that nothing had changed. He listened as Chester took off his wet clothes, and felt like he could say whatever he wanted to him.

"It's funny," Will spoke softly, so as not to wake his brother.

"What is?" Chester asked, folding his pants as if he were getting his school uniform ready for the next day.

"I had a dream."

"Right," Chester said distractedly, hooking his drenched socks over a couple of nails in the wall so they would dry.

"It was really weird. I was somewhere warm and sunny," Will spoke slowly, trying hard to remember, since the dream was already growing distant. "Nothing mattered, nothing was important. There was a girl there, too. I don't know who she was, but it felt like she was a friend." Will fell silent for a while. "She was really nice . . . and even when I closed my eyes, her face was still there, smiling and relaxed and sort of . . . sort of perfect.

"We lay on the grass — like we'd just had a picnic in this meadow, or whatever the place was. I think maybe we were both a bit sleepy. But I knew we were in a place where we were *meant* to be, where we both belonged. Although we weren't moving, it was like we were floating on a bed of soft grass, a sort of peaceful greenness around us, under the clearest blue sky you can imagine. We were happy, very happy." He sighed. "It was so different from the damp and the heat and always being sur-rounded by rock like we are now. In the dream, everything was gentle . . . and the meadow was just so very real . . . I could even smell the grass. It was . . ."

He trailed off, basking in what remained of the receding images and sensations. Realizing he'd been talking for quite some time and hadn't heard any activity from Chester's corner of the room, he swung his head around to check.

"Chester?" he called quietly.

His friend was already tucked up in his bed, facing the wall. He gave a heavy snort and rolled onto his back. He was fast asleep.

Will blew out a long, resigned breath and closed his eyes, longing to return to his dream but knowing how very unlikely that was.

27

THERE WAS THE MOST incredible bang as the Miners' Train lurched and skewed from side to side, so dramatically that Sarah was convinced it was going to leave the tracks altogether. Gripping the bench tightly, she shot an anxious glance across at Rebecca, who seemed completely unperturbed. Indeed, the young girl appeared to be in an almost trancelike state, her face perfectly tranquil and her eyes fully open, but not looking at anything in particular.

The train settled back into its previous hypnotic rhythm. Sarah breathed more easily as she peered around the interior of the guard's car. Once again she allowed her eyes to drift over to the Limiters, but quickly looked away, not wanting them to notice her interest.

She had to keep pinching herself to make sure all this was real: Not only was she practically shoulder to shoulder with a four-man Styx patrol, but these were actual Limiters, members of the "Hobb's Squad," as they were referred to in some circles.

When she'd been little, her father had told her terrifying tales about these soldiers: how they liked to eat Colonists alive; how, if she didn't do as he said and go straight to sleep, these cannibals would come calling in the dead of night. According to her father, they lurked under naughty children's beds and if any were to put a foot outside, the Limiters would bite a chunk out of their ankles. He said they were particularly fond of tender young flesh. All that had been quite enough to *stop* her from falling asleep.

It wasn't until she was several years older that she learned from Tam that these mysterious men really did exist. Of course everyone in the Colony knew about the Division — the teams that patrolled the borders of the Quarter and the Eternal City, the regions closer to the surface — any place, truth be told, that Colonists might use as an escape route Topsoil.

But Limiters were a different kettle of fish, and rarely, if ever, glimpsed in the streets. As a result, the Colony was steeped in myth about them and their prowess. Some of the more far-fetched folklore, Tam had told her, was actually *true*: He had it on very good authoriy that they'd actually devoured a Banished Colonist down in the extremes of the Northern Deeps when their food supplies had run out. Tam had also told her "Hobb" was an Old English name for the devil, and a very apt one for these demonic soldiers.

Despite these and many other blatantly outrageous anecdotes that were swapped in whispers behind closed doors, very little was actually known about the Limiters, except for speculation that they were involved in covert Topsoil operations. As for the Deeps, it was said they were trained to survive there for extended periods without support. And now, as she dared to study the Limiters again, she had to agree that they were a most fearsome-looking bunch, with the coldest eyes she'd ever seen, the gray, clouded eyes of dead fish.

There was ample room in the large but rather basic carriage, built on the same chassis as the freight cars, a long line of which preceded it in the train. Its sides and roof were fabricated from timber planking, which had been exposed to intense heat and downpours of water along the route with such regularity that it had become badly warped. Wide cracks had opened up between the planks, letting in the smoke and rushing wind as the train rocketed along, and making Sarah's journey not much more tolerable than the one Will and the boys had experienced in their open car.

Crude wooden benches ran down the interior of the carriage on both sides, and two small, knee-high tables were bolted to the floor at either end, the rearmost of which was occupied by the four Limiters.

The soldiers were clad in their distinctive fatigues, the dun-brown long coats and loose-fitting pants with thick kneepads, so very different from the clothes generally worn by the Styx. Sarah had also been issued a set and was now wearing them, although it made her feel distinctly uncomfortable. She imagined what Tam would have said about it if he'd seen her in the uniform of their archenemies. Feeling the lapel of her long coat, she conjured up the look of mortification on her brother's face. She could almost hear his voice.

Oh, Sarah, how did you get yourself into this? What do you think you're doing?

Not being able to dispel the feeling of unease, she found it hard to keep still, and each time she altered her position on the unforgiving wooden bench, the fatigues made not the slightest sound. It debunked the claim she'd heard that they were made from Coprolite skin; they appeared instead to be cut from exceptionally supple leather, the finest calfskin, perhaps. She assumed this was so that the Limiters could move with greater stealth, free from the trademark creaking of the jet-black counterparts they sported in the Colony.

The Limiters seemed to take turns resting, two sleeping with their feet on the table while the other two remained awake and inhumanly still, sitting bolt upright with their eyes staring straight ahead. There was a sort of fierce alertness about all of them, even the ones who were napping, as if they were ready to go into action in the blink of an eye.

Sarah and Rebecca didn't attempt conversation because of the constant noise — louder than usual, Rebecca had informed her, because the train was moving at twice its normal speed.

Instead Sarah examined what looked like a rather old and battered brown school satchel on the table in front of Rebecca. A wad of Topsoil newspapers poked out from it, and Sarah could make out the melodramatic headline of the uppermost one, which read **ULTRA BUG STRIKES** in bold letters. Sarah had been out of touch with events on the surface for some weeks and had no inkling what it meant. Just the same, she spent many hours during the journey pondering how it could possibly be of interest to Rebecca and the Styx. She itched to take out the newspapers and read more.

But for the duration of the journey Rebecca had not once closed her eyes or nodded off. Lounging back against the side of the carriage, her arms neatly crossed on her lap, it was as if she was in a deep meditative state. Sarah found it more than a little disconcerting.

The only exchange with the Styx girl came later on, when the train eventually slowed to a crawl, then stopped altogether.

Snapping out of her strange state of suspension, Rebecca suddenly leaned forward and spoke to Sarah.

"Storm gates," she said simply, then slipped the newspapers out of her satchel and began to flick through them.

Sarah nodded but didn't reply, since at that very moment there was a low clanking from somewhere up ahead. The Limiters stirred, one of them passing around mess tins filled with strips of dried jerky and battered white-enameled mugs of water. Sarah took hers, thanking the man, and they ate in silence as the train started up again. It had hardly gone any distance when it came to another shuddering halt, and the gates were slammed shut.

Rebecca was studying her newspaper intently.

"What's all that about?" Sarah inquired, squinting at the headline, which read **PANDEMIC — IT'S OFFICIAL**. "Are those recent papers?"

"Yes. I got them this morning when I was Topsoil." Rebecca flicked her eyes heavenward, closing her newspaper. "Silly me! I keep forgetting you know your way around London. I bought them a stone's throw from St. Edmund's — you're probably familiar with it?"

"The hospital . . . in Hampstead," Sarah confirmed.

"One and the same," Rebecca said. "And, boy oh boy, you should have seen the free-for-all outside the emergency room. It's a complete shambles up there — queues a mile long." She shook her head theatrically, then stopped and grinned like a cat that had just devoured a vat of the finest cream.

"Really?" Sarah said.

Rebecca gave a small chuckle. "Whole city's come to a standstill."

Sarah looked askance at her as she shook the newspaper open and went back to reading it again.

But that couldn't be right!

Rebecca had been at the Garrison throughout the morning, preparing for the train journey. Sarah had glimpsed her around the place and heard her voice echoing down the corridors on several occasions — the girl couldn't have been out of the building for more than an hour in any one stretch. That wouldn't have given her enough time to get up to Highfield and back, let alone as far as Hampstead. Rebecca had to be lying. But why? Was the girl toying with her, to see how she would react, or perhaps putting on a show of her power? Sarah was so baffled, she didn't ask anything further about the news reports.

Before the train resumed the journey, Rebecca put aside the papers, and ducked down to yank out a long bundle, wound with sackcloth, from beneath her bench. She held it out to Sarah. Untwisting the sacking, she found it was one of the Limiters' long rifles, complete with light scope. She'd briefly handled a similar weapon in the Garrison when the battle-scarred Styx soldier had given her instructions on how to use it.

Sarah looked questioningly at Rebecca. Receiving no reaction, she leaned forward to the girl.

"Really? For me?" she asked.

With a slow nod, Rebecca smiled demurely back at her.

Sarah brought the weapon to her shoulder. She tested its weight as she pointed it at the unoccupied end of the carriage. It was heavy, but nothing she couldn't manage.

Now it was Sarah who could have purred with satisfaction. The gift of the rifle was a reassuring sign of Rebecca's trust, although she was still a little troubled by the impossible claim that the girl had been in London that morning. Sarah tried to tell herself Rebecca must have gotten her days mixed up, and put the discrepancy out of mind to concentrate on the job at hand.

She ran her fingers down the length of the matt rifle barrel. Now she had the tools, and was ready to do whatever was necessary to avenge Tam's death. She owed it to him and to their mother.

As the train gained momentum, she spent the rest of the journey handling the weapon, sometimes swinging it up into the ready position as she worked the bolt, pulling the hair-sprung trigger and dry-firing it, sometimes just cradling it in her lap, until she was thoroughly familiar with it, even in the subdued light of the carriage.

28

DRAKE HAD TAKEN them out on patrol on the Great Plain and they were making their way through what he called "the Perimeters," where he said the Limiter presence should be minimal.

It was a big day: Cal's first excursion through the water-filled sump and onto the plain since Will and Chester had carried him back to the base as a gibbering wreck all those weeks before. Drake's decision to allow him out was well timed. Cal had been going stir-crazy in the limited space of the base and was truly ready for a change of scenery. Although he was still hobbling slightly, he had recovered most of the sensation in his left leg and was bursting to go farther afield.

As they'd passed through the sump and set off with Drake and Elliott, Will experienced a sense of elation that they were together as a group for the very first time. After several hours of trudging along, with Elliott taking the lead, Drake told them they were shortly going to branch off the plain and into a lava tube. But before they did this, he suggested they have some food, after which he was going to give them a briefing. He stood a dimmed light in a dip in the ground and they gathered around him as they each took their share of the provisions, then settled down to eat.

It wasn't lost on Will that Chester and Elliott had chosen to sit together and were chatting away in secretive tones — even passing a canteen between themselves. Will's high spirits paled and he felt excluded yet again. It rankled him so much that he completely lost his appetite.

He needed to relieve himself. In a fit of pique, he got to his feet and stumped away from the group, grateful he'd be spared the spectacle of Chester and Elliott's cozy little tête-à-tête at least for the time it would take to empty his bladder. As he left, he glanced over his shoulder at all of them sitting around the lantern. Even Drake and Cal were totally engrossed in whatever they were discussing and didn't take any notice of his departure.

Preoccupied by his thoughts, Will just kept walking. It was becoming increasingly evident to him that he was set apart from the rest of them because there was something he *had* to do. All of them — Drake, Elliott, Chester, and Cal — seemed to be entirely caught up with their day-to-day survival, as if this was their sole lot in life, to scrape out a primitive existence in this forsaken place.

But Will knew he had a single, overriding purpose. One way or another, he was going to locate his father, and, once reunited, the two of them would work as a team to investigate what was down here. Just like the good old days back up in Highfield. And then, finally, they would return to the surface with all their discoveries. He caught his step as it dawned on him that, with the exception of Chester, none of the others had any desire whatsoever to go Topsoil. Well, *he* had a greater calling, and *he* certainly wasn't going to spend the rest of his days in this harsh subterranean exile, scuttling away to hide like a frightened rabbit whenever the Styx showed up.

As he reached the perimeter wall, he saw the mouths of several lava tubes before him. He stepped into the nearest of these, relishing the feeling of detachment as the inky darkness enveloped him. When he was done, he emerged from the lava tube, still lost in thought about the future. He took ten or so paces, then stopped stock-still.

Where he thought he'd left the others, there was no movement, no voices, and no light. The group was gone.

Will didn't panic right away, telling himself that he must be looking in the wrong place. But, no, he was pretty certain he wasn't — and, besides, he hadn't wandered that far. Had he?

He scoured the darkness for a few seconds, then lifted his flashlight above his head and swept it from side to side, hoping it would alert them to his position.

"There you are!" he exclaimed as he caught sight of them. From what seemed an alarming distance away, somebody in the group signaled back, letting slip a brief flash of light in answer to his waving beam.

And, as if caught by a camera flash, the picture of them running chaotically like a herd of startled gazelle seared into Will's retinas.

The flash had revealed Drake pointing urgently into the distance. But Will didn't understand what he meant. Then he'd lost all sight of Drake and the rest of them.

Will glanced back to where they'd been sitting. He had left his jacket and rucksack there, only taking with him the small battery-powered flashlight. He had no light orbs, no food or water — nothing!

His stomach felt as if it had been dropped from a tall building. He should have told them where he was going, and he knew with inescapable certainty that whatever was making them flee in such disarray was something threatening. He also knew that *he* should be running. But where to? Should he attempt to catch up with them? Should he try to recover his jacket and backpack? What should he do?

He suddenly felt like a small child again, reliving his first day of school. His father had deposited him at the front doors and, in his usual absentminded way, hadn't thought to make sure Will knew where he was supposed to go. With increasing anxiety, Will had walked aimlessly around the empty corridors, lost and with no one to ask.

Will strained to catch another glimpse of Drake and the others, trying his utmost to figure out where they had been heading. Undoubtedly they would take refuge in one of the other lava tubes. He shook his head. Fat lot of use that was! There were just too many of them. The chances of him picking the same one were slim, to say the least.

"What do I do now?" he said several times in quick succession. He fixed on the dark horizon where Drake had been pointing. It looked innocent enough, but he knew in his heart of hearts that it couldn't be so. What was it? What had made them run?

Then he heard a faraway barking, and the hairs on his neck bristled.

Stalkers!

Will shivered. It could mean only one thing: The Styx were closing in. Again he looked frantically across to where he had left his kit, but he couldn't see it in the gloom. Could he get to it in time? Did he dare? Gripped by a mounting dread, he stood watching as the tiny points of light from the approaching Styx came into view, seemingly so far off, but near enough to send him into a blind panic.

He took a few tentative steps toward where he thought his jacket and rucksack were when there was a sharp noise, like a loud slap, followed quickly by a second. Mere feet away from his head, flakes of rock scattered down. The report of the rifle shots followed, rolling back and forth across the plain like a ripple of distant thunder.

They were shooting at him!

He cowered as another burst of shots flicked the dirt on either side of him. More came, falling uncomfortably close. The air felt as if it were alive, sizzling with the passage of bullets.

Covering his flashlight with his hand, Will flung himself to the ground. As he rolled behind a small boulder, a salvo hit it, and he could smell the hot lead and cordite. They were zeroing in — they seemed to know exactly where he was.

He scrambled to his feet and, crouching so low he was almost doubled over, he ran awkwardly back into the lava tube behind him.

As he passed around a bend in the tunnel, he didn't stop. He eventually came to a junction and took the left fork, only to

373

find a huge crevasse in the way. As he hastily retraced his steps to the fork, he knew that his first priority was to put as much distance as possible between himself and the Styx.

But he couldn't ignore the fact that he would eventually have to backtrack if he wanted to rejoin Drake and the others, and this would be nigh on impossible if he just kept going. The network of lava tubes was complex, each tunnel virtually indistinguishable from the next. Without some kind of feature or landmark, he didn't have a clue how he would find his way back.

Torn between the need to escape and the knowledge that he was going to get lost if he continued, he hung back for a few seconds at the fork. He listened, wondering if the Styx were really on his trail. As the low baying of a stalker echoed down the tunnel, he was spurred into action again. He had no choice but to run.

He covered a reasonable distance in only a few hours. It hadn't entered his mind that he should be limiting the use of his flashlight. But then, to his horror, he noticed it was starting to lose its intensity. He began to conserve the power, switching it off when there appeared to be an uninterrupted stretch ahead, but it wasn't long before the beam began to flicker and dim to a feeble yellow.

Then it failed altogether.

He was submerged in absolute, pumping darkness.

Will frantically shook the flashlight, trying in vain to squeeze more life out of it. He took out the batteries, rubbing them between his hands to warm them up before putting them in again, but this was no use, either. The flashlight was dead!

He did the only thing he could: He kept going, blindly negotiating the tunnels. Not only was he getting himself hopelessly lost, but he could also hear the occasional sound in the tunnels behind him. The idea of a stalker flying out of the darkness and attacking drove him on, his fear of his pursuers greater than that of the unrelenting darkness into which he was sinking deeper and deeper. He felt so lost, and so immeasurably alone.

Idiot! Idiot! Idiot! Why didn't I follow the others? I'm sure there was time! What a fool I am! The self-recrimination came thick and fast as the gloom lapped around him, becoming something tactile, physical, like a viscous black soup.

He was desperate, but a single thought kept him going. He held it in his mind, a beacon of hope to guide him on. He imagined the moment he would be reunited with his father, and how everything would be fine again, just as he'd dreamed it would be.

Knowing how futile it was to do so, but finding it gave him a measure of comfort, he would call out from time to time.

"Dad!" he would cry. "Dad, are you there?"

Dr. Burrows sat on the smaller of two boulders, his elbows propped on the larger one before him, as he nibbled contemplatively on a piece of the dried food the Coprolites had provided. He didn't know if it was animal or vegetable, but it tasted predominantly of salt, for which he was thankful. He had sweated buckets as he'd followed the convoluted route on the map, and could feel cramps coming on in his calves. He knew if he didn't have salt, and lots of it, he'd very soon be in deep trouble.

He twisted around to peer up at the side of the crevice. Lost in the darkness was the tiny track on which he'd just descended — a perilous ledge so narrow he had been forced to flatten himself against the sheer face of the rock, shuffling his way down it, ever so slowly and carefully. He sighed. He didn't want to do that again anytime soon.

He took off his glasses and gave them a thorough wipe with his threadbare shirtsleeve. He'd discarded the Coprolite suit some miles back — it was too cumbersome and restrictive for him to continue to wear, despite the reservations he still harbored about exposure to radioactivity. In retrospect, he might have overreacted a bit about the risks associated with this — it was probably just localized to specific areas within the Great Plain, and it wasn't as if he'd spent very long there. Besides, he couldn't worry about that now; he had more important things to think about. He picked up the map and studied the spidery marks for the umpteenth time.

Then, the food strip gripped in the corner of his mouth like an unlit cigar, he put away the map and, using the large boulder as a book rest, opened his journal to check something that had been nagging him. He flipped through the pages of his drawings of the stone tablets he had chanced upon soon after he'd arrived at the Miners' Station. Locating one of the last drawings in the series, he began to study it. It was a bit rough-and-ready, due to his physical state at the time, but despite this he was confident he'd captured most of the detail. He continued to peer at it for a while, then leaned back again thoughtfully.

The tablet recorded on this particular page had been different from the others he'd found; for a start, it was larger in size, and also some of the inscriptions on it were quite unlike anything else he'd uncovered at the site.

Carved into its face were three clearly defined areas. In the uppermost one, the writing was composed of strange cuneiforms — wedge-shaped letters. Unfortunately these were also the letters used on all the other tablets he'd looked at in the same cavern. He couldn't begin to decipher them. Below was another block of strange, angular, cuneiform letters, very different from those in the first section and resembling nothing he'd ever come across before in all his years of study. The third block of writing was just as bad, but here there was a bizarre succession of glyphic symbols — strange and unrecognizable pictures — all utterly meaningless to him.

"I just don't get it," he said slowly, frowning. He thumbed forward to a page where he'd already jotted some workings in an attempt to translate even the smallest section of any of the three blocks. By looking at repeated symbols in the middle and lower ones on the tablet, he thought he would be able to begin to piece together an understanding of the cuneiform scripts. Even if they were similar to Chinese logographic writing, with a prodigious number of different characters, he hoped that at least some sort of basic pattern would emerge.

"Come on, come on, think, man," he urged himself in a growl, thumping his forehead with his palm. Shifting the food strip from one side of his mouth to the other, he set about his workings again, trying to make more headway.

"I . . . just . . . don't . . . *get* . . . it," he grumbled. In pure frustration, he tore out the page of workings and, crumpling it up, slung it over his shoulder. He sat back and clenched his hands together, deep in reflection. As he did this, the journal slipped from the boulder.

"Blast!" he exclaimed, reaching down to retrieve it. It had fallen open at the drawing that was causing him so much trouble. He placed it back on the boulder again.

He heard a sound. A creaking, followed by a series of small clacks. It ended almost as soon as it had started, but he immediately lifted a light orb and peered around. He couldn't see anything and began to whistle through his teeth in an attempt to comfort himself.

He lowered the light orb, and, as he did so, its illumination fell on the page of the journal that was thwarting his efforts to translate it.

He bent his head closer to the page, then closer still.

"You dunderhead." He began to laugh as he scanned the hitherto meaningless lettering before him. The middle section was now getting his undivided attention.

"Yes, yes, yes, YES!"

He had been in such a bad state when he'd sketched the tablet that he just hadn't recognized the alphabet. Not *upside down*, anyway. "It's Phoenician script, you *stupid* goat! You had it the wrong way up! How could you have done that?"

He began to write hastily on the page and discovered that, in his excitement, he was attempting to use the half-chewed food strip instead of his pencil. He threw it away and, now using his pencil, quickly scribbled in the margin, guessing

at the symbols where he had to because his sketching had
been sloppy in places or because the tablet itself had been
damaged.

"Aleph . . . lamedh . . . lamedh . . . ," he muttered as he
worked from letter to letter, hesitating as he came to those that
were unclear or that he couldn't immediately remember. But
it didn't take him too long to recall them as he was so profi-
cient in Ancient Greek, which was directly descended from the
Phoenician alphabet.

"By Jove, I've cracked it!" he shouted, his voice echoing
around him.

He found that the writing in the middle block of the tablet
was a prayer of some form. Nothing very exciting in itself, but
he could *read* it. Having gotten that far, he began to examine the uppermost block of writing again, which consisted
of a group of glyphics. The symbols immediately started to
make sense, now that he was seeing the detailed pictograph
the right way up.

The symbols were nothing like the Mesopotamian ones that
he'd studied for his doctorate. Knowing that Mesopotamian
pictograms were the earliest known form of writing, dating back
to 3000 B.C., Dr. Burrows was only too aware that what tended
to happen was that the pictographic signs became more and
more schematic as the centuries progressed. So in the beginning the pictures would have been easily understood — such as
a picture of a boat or a bushel of wheat — but with time they
would develop into something more stylized, something more
like the cuneiform letters in the middle and lower blocks on
the tablet. Into an alphabet.

"Yes! Yes!" he said as he saw how the top section repeated the prayer written in the middle one. But it didn't appear as though the writing had evolved directly from the pictographic symbols. All of a sudden, he was hit by the implications of what he'd stumbled across.

"My God! So many millennia ago, somehow, a Phoenician scribe came from the surface . . . he did this . . . he carved a translation from an ancient hieroglyphic language. But how did he get down here?" Dr. Burrows puffed his cheeks and blew out a breath. "And this unknown ancient race . . . who were they? Who in tarnation were they?"

His mind was bombarded with possibilities, but one, perhaps the most far-fetched, loomed far above the others. "The Atlanteans . . . the Lost City of Atlantis!" He caught his breath, his heart pounding with the supposition.

He babbled breathlessly to himself, quickly switching his attention to the lower block of writing, comparing it with the Phoenician words above.

"By Jove, I think I've done it. It is . . . it's the same prayer!" he began shouting. And he immediately spotted the similarities between the hieroglyphs at the top of the tablet and the forms of the letters at the bottom. There was no question in his mind that the pictograms had evolved into the letters.

And, using the Phoenician writing, he should have no trouble translating the lower inscription. He now had the key that enabled him to translate *all* the other tablets he'd found in the cavern and recorded in his journal.

"I can do this!" he announced triumphantly, flipping back through his sketches. "I can read their language! My very own

Rosetta Stone. No . . . wait . . ." He held up his finger as it struck him. "The *Burrows Stone!*" He jumped to his feet and turned to the darkness, holding the journal jubilantly above his head. "The Dr. Burrows Stone."

"You poor schmucks, all you in the British Museum, at Oxford and Cambridge . . . and shabby old Professor White and your cronies from London University who bloody nicked my Roman dig from me . . . I AM VICTORIOUS . . . I WILL BE REMEMBERED!" His words echoed all around the crevasse. "I may even have the secret of Atlantis here in my hands . . . AND IT'S ALL MINE, YOU POOR SAPS!"

He heard the clacking again and snatched up the light orb. "What the . . . ?"

There, where the food stick had landed, something large was moving. His hand shaking, he directed the light at it.

"No!" he gasped.

It was the size of a small family car, with six jointed legs protruding at angles around it and a huge domed carapace for its main body. It was yellowy-white in color and moved ponderously. Dr. Burrows could see its dusty mandibles grinding against each other as it ate the food he had chucked aside. Its antennae twitching exploratively, it advanced very slowly toward him. He took a step back.

"I . . . just . . . don't . . . believe . . . it." Dr. Burrows exhaled. "What in the world are you . . . an oversized dust mite?" he said, mentally correcting himself almost as he spoke. He knew only too well that mites were not insects, but arachnids, the same as spiders.

Whatever it was, it had stopped, evidently a little wary of him, its antennae syncopating like two dancing chopsticks. He could see no evidence of any eyes on its head, and its carapace looked as thick as tank armor. But as he examined this more closely, he could also see that it was battered, with slashlike indentations all over its dull surface, and that there were vicious-looking gouges all along its edges, where it appeared to have been shattered.

Despite the creature's size and appearance, Dr. Burrows somehow knew it wasn't a danger to him. It wasn't attempting to come any nearer, perhaps more apprehensive of him than he was of it.

"You've been through the wars, haven't you?" Dr. Burrows said, holding his light orb toward it. It clattered its mandibles as if in agreement. For a moment Dr. Burrows looked up from the gargantuan creature to peer around.

"This place is just so . . . rich. . . . It's a veritable gold mine!" He sighed, and then delved into his shoulder bag. "There you are, old chap," he said, tossing another food stick at the bizarre creature, which scuttled back a few feet as if afraid. Then, slowly, it moved closer, locating the food and cautiously picking over it. The creature obviously decided the food stick was safe to eat, seized it in its mandibles, and instantly began to devour it with a variety of grating noises.

An awestruck Dr. Burrows reseated himself on the boulder and hunted in his pants pocket for his pencil sharpener. Finding it, he began to twist it on his dwindling stub of pencil. Still chewing, the giant creature lowered itself down on its legs, as if waiting expectantly for another morsel.

Dr. Burrows laughed at the strangeness of the situation as he took up his journal and flicked to a fresh page to make a record of the "dust mite" in front of him. He looked at the blank page, then hesitated, his eyes glazing with indecision. The clacking of the giant creature brought him back abruptly, and he knew what he had to do. He turned back to the drawing of the tablet again. Translating the rest of the Dr. Burrows Stone had to be his immediate priority.

"Not enough time," he muttered. "Not enough time . . ."

29

"**HELP! ANYBODY!** Help me! Is there anybody there?"

Oh, wake up, will you . . . how likely is that? A gruff voice in Will's head wouldn't be silenced. *There's nobody for miles. You're on your own, matey,* it continued.

"Help me! Help! Help!" Will called out, doing his best to ignore it.

What are you expecting . . . that Dad's going to jump out from around the next corner and show you the way home? Dr. "Super Dad" Burrows, who got himself lost on the London Underground? Yeah, right!

"Get lost!" Will roared hoarsely at his nagging self-doubt, his cry resounding in the tunnels around him.

Lost, huh? That's funny! the voice persisted. It was quietly smug, as if it knew exactly how things were going to turn out. *It doesn't get any worse than this,* it said. *You're history.*

Will stopped and shook his head, refusing to accept what it was telling him. There had to be a way out of this.

He closed and opened his eyes, trying to make out something, anything, but there was nothing. Even the blackest night up on the surface had some tiny trace of light, but not down here — this darkness was absolute. And it played tricks on you, giving you hope. False hope.

He moved along the wall, feeling its now all-too-familiar roughness with his fingers, inching forward until he became impatient and tried to move too quickly. His foot snagged against some obstacle and he pitched forward, tumbling down an incline. He came to rest with his face against the loose surface of the ground, breathing hard.

If he allowed himself to think for too long about his situation . . . Here he was, more than five miles below the surface of the earth, alone and frightened and hopelessly lost.

Every new second in this oblivion was as vital and terrifying as the last, and it seemed to him that millions of these seconds now stretched out behind him. He'd been separated from Drake and the others for what he estimated was at least a day. It could very well have been longer. In truth, he hadn't a clue how long he'd been in these endless tunnels, but if his parched throat was anything to go by, then it had to be at least twenty-four hours. The only thing he was certain of was that he'd never been so horribly thirsty before, not in his whole life.

He got up and reached for the wall. His outstretched fingers encountered nothing but warm air. He immediately pictured himself on the brink of a huge precipice and was beset by a wave of vertigo. He took another reluctant step. The floor didn't feel level to him, but he couldn't even be sure of this anymore. He'd reached a point where he was struggling to tell whether the ground was banked or whether it was *he* who was at an angle. He was beginning to distrust even his remaining senses.

His vertigo became worse, and he felt sick. He tried to regain his balance by raising his arms. After a few moments of holding his position, like some lopsided scarecrow, he began to feel a little more confident. He took a few tentative steps, but there was still no sign of the wall. He shouted, listening to the echoes.

He had fallen into a larger space — that much he could tell from the reverberations — perhaps he was at the junction of several tunnels. He tried desperately to contain his rising panic, his shallow, hissed breaths and his heartbeat thumping in his ears in mismatched tempos. Relentless waves of dread swept through his body and he shivered uncontrollably, not sure whether he was hot or cold.

How had it come to this? The question knocked fitfully around his head, like a moth in a killing jar.

He summoned all his courage and took another step. Still no wall. He clapped his hands together and listened to the sound reverberating. The report proved conclusively that he was indeed in something with larger dimensions than just a tunnel — he just hoped it didn't mean there was a chasm waiting for him in the darkness. His head swam again. *Where are the walls? I've even lost the walls!*

A fury rose up in him, and he bit his teeth together so hard they creaked. Clenching his fists, he made an inhuman noise, somewhere between a growl and a scream, but sounding like neither. He tried to order his feelings, finding that he couldn't stifle the anger and self-contempt.

Idiot! IDIOT! IDIOT!

It was as though the gruff voice in his head had won the day, pushing aside any hope that he was going to get through this. He was a fool and deserved to die. He started to blame the others, particularly Chester and Elliott, shouting obscenities at them, at the hushed walls that *must* have been around him, wanting so much to hurt something, to inflict pain. There, in the anonymity of the blackness, he started to thump himself, striking the tops of his thighs with his fists. Then he punched himself on the side of his head, the pain producing a certain stinging clarity, which brought him to his senses.

NO, I AM BETTER THAN THIS! I must keep going. He sank down onto his knees and crawled, probing in front of him with his fingertips for any gap, any void, checking and rechecking that he wasn't about to plunge blindly into a crevasse. He touched up against something. The wall! With a sigh of relief, he stood up slowly and, hugging it, began the tedious slow-stepping again.

30

OVER THE NEXT few hours, the Miners' Train went through several more sets of the storm gates Rebecca had referred to.

The first warning Sarah had that they were coming to their destination was a clanging bell, followed by the loud wailing of the train's whistle. The train began to apply its brakes and screeched to a final halt. The side doors of the carriage were heaved back on their rollers, and there was the Miners' Station, lights burning wanly in its windows.

"All change," Rebecca announced, with a suggestion of a smile. As Sarah leaped down from the carriage and stretched her stiff legs, she saw that a delegation of Styx was hurriedly making its way over.

Clutching her satchel, Rebecca told Sarah to remain by the train and went over to meet the delegation. There were at least a dozen of them, walking with such haste that they raised a cloud of dust in their wake. Sarah recognized one among their number — the old Styx who had accompanied her in the carriage the day she had returned to the Colony.

Sarah's old habits kicked in and she made use of the time to make a mental note of the number and location of the personnel on the ground. She would need to know the lay of the land if the opportunity to escape presented itself.

Other than the various Limiters dotted around the place, there was a troop of soldiers from the Styx Division, immediately distinguishable due to the green camouflage of their uniforms. *But why would they be down here?* she wondered. They were a very long way from home. She estimated that the troop numbered about forty, and around half of them were attending to their weapons, which included mortars and several large-caliber guns. The remainder of the soldiers were mounted on horses and seemed about to leave. *Horses! In the Deeps?*

She turned her attention to the layout of the cavern, scanning the gantries and walkways overhead. She tried to identify ways in or out of the cavern, but soon gave this up — it was impossible to pick out much in the gloomy darkness that cloaked the perimeter.

Already beginning to perspire heavily inside the Limiters' fatigues, she realized how much hotter it was down here. As she drew the dry air into her lungs, everything smelled burnt to her, scorched. The environment was so new and unfamiliar, but she was confident she could acclimatize, just as she'd done when she'd gone Topsoil.

She picked up a movement to the right of the station buildings. She could just about make out six or seven men who were standing still in an untidy line, partially hidden by stacks of crates. She guessed they were Colonists from their civilian clothing. To a man, their heads were bowed as a Limiter stood guard, his rifle trained on them. Sarah found this rather unnecessary, since their hands and feet were shackled together with heavy chains. They weren't about to go anywhere.

Sarah could only think that they must have been Banished. Nevertheless, it was highly unusual for such a sizable group of men to be exiled simultaneously, unless there had been some sort of organized revolt that the Styx had quashed. She was just beginning to wonder whether she was going to be thrown in with these prisoners, when she heard Rebecca's voice.

The Styx girl was showing the Topsoil newspapers to the old Styx, who was nodding imperiously as the delegation stood by. Sarah began to think that all this interest in the headlines — presumably about the Topsoiler disease — had to amount to more than just the Styx's surveillance of current affairs up there. Particularly in light of Joseph's slip of the tongue back in the Garrison about a major operation in London. Yes, there was more to all this than she had first thought.

The newspapers were passed to the rest of the party and, as the meeting went on, the old Styx seemed to be doing all the talking, in their scratchy and indecipherable language. Then Sarah caught Rebecca's voice.

"Yes!" the girl exclaimed quite distinctly and full of youthful glee, raising her forearm in a victorious gesture. Then the old Styx turned to another in the party, who opened a small valise and handed Rebecca something from it. She carefully held it up before her as the entourage looked on.

They all fell silent. Sarah couldn't see precisely what was there, but from the way it glinted briefly in the light, it appeared that Rebecca was looking at two small objects made of a glass-like material.

Rebecca and the old Styx exchanged a significant glance. Then the meeting came to an abrupt end as the old Styx issued an order and, flanked by the rest of the delegation, swept away in the direction of the station buildings.

Rebecca swiveled at the hips to face the lone Styx standing guard over the shackled prisoners. She gave him a sign, spreading the fingers of her hand as if she was shooing someone away. The guard immediately barked at the prisoners, and they began to shamble off, heading toward a far corner of the cavern.

Sarah watched as Rebecca strolled back toward her, holding the two objects aloft.

"What's their story?" Sarah asked her, indicating the prisoners, now barely visible as they moved into shadow.

"Oh, nothing . . . ," Rebecca said, then added a little vaguely, as if distracted, "we don't need any more guinea pigs, not now."

"And I see the Division has brought some pretty heavy-duty hardware with them," Sarah ventured, as a couple of the mounted troops towed away the first of the guns.

But Rebecca wasn't interested in Sarah's questions. Flicking her hair back, she raised the objects to head height.

"For this is Dominion," Rebecca intoned in a low voice. "And Dominion will ensure that justice is returned to the righteous, and the upright in heart will follow it."

Sarah saw that the objects were two small phials filled with a clear fluid, and that their tops were sealed with wax. They both had thin cords attached to them, so that Rebecca could let them dangle from her hands.

"Something important?" Sarah inquired.

Rebecca was distant, her eyes glazed with a kind of dreamy euphoria as she contemplated the phials.

"Something to do with the Ultra Bug in the newspapers?" Sarah ventured further.

The smallest glimmer of a smile played on the Styx girl's lips.

"Could be," she teased. "Our prayers are about to be answered."

"So you're going to use another germ against the Topsoilers?"

"Not just *another* germ. We were only warming up with the Ultra Bug, as they chose to call it. This" — she shook the phials — "is the real McCoy, as they say." Rebecca beamed.

Before Sarah could respond, the Styx girl had whirled around and was striding away.

Sarah didn't know what to think. She had no love for Topsoilers, but it didn't take a great leap of the imagination to figure out that the Styx were brewing up something terrible for them. She knew that the Styx wouldn't think twice before spreading death and destruction if it meant achieving their aims. But she wasn't going to let any of this distract her — there was only one thing she had to do and that was catch up with Will Burrows. She was going to find out if he was to blame for Tam's death. It was family business, and she couldn't let *anything* get in the way of it.

"We're up. Get moving," one of the Limiters snapped at Sarah's back, making her start. It was the first time any of them had spoken a word directly to her.

"Um . . . did . . . did you say *we?*" she stammered, taking a step away from the four Limiters. As she did so, she heard a scrabbling by her feet and looked down.

"Bartleby!"

The cat had appeared from nowhere. Twitching his whiskers, he gave a low, uncertain meow, then lowered his muzzle to the ground and sniffed deeply, several times. He pulled up his broad head sharply, his nose coated with the fine black dust that seemed to be everywhere. He obviously didn't like the dust because he rubbed his face with his paw, making loud snuffling noises. All of a sudden he gave an enormous sneeze.

"Bless you," Sarah said before she could stop herself. She was delighted to have him back. It was as though she now had the company of an old friend on her quest — somebody she could trust.

"Get going!" another of the Limiters scowled, jabbing his thin finger toward the far area of the chamber beyond the stationary engine, which was puffing out copious clouds of steam. "Now!"

Sarah hesitated for a moment, the dead eyes of the four soldiers on her. Then she nodded and took a reluctant step in the direction they had indicated. *Well . . . if you sell your soul to the devil . . .* she thought wryly. She had chosen her path, and she had to stick to it.

So, with the shadowy figures following behind, Sarah resigned herself to her lot and began to walk more briskly, the cat at her heels.

Besides, what alternative did she have, with these ghouls breathing down her neck?

31

THE HOURS PASSED. Will's forehead and the small of his back were sopping with a sticky sweat, from both the heat around him and the unrelenting waves of fear that he fought so hard to stave off. His throat was parched; he could feel the dust sticking to his tongue but couldn't summon up enough saliva to wet it.

The dizziness returned, and he was forced to stop as the floor yawed under his feet. He sagged against the wall, opening and closing his mouth like a drowning man, mumbling to himself. With an immense effort, he straightened up and rubbed his eyes hard with his knuckles, the pressure bringing vague bursts of brilliance that helped to ease his nerves. But it was only a brief respite. The darkness immediately flooded back.

Then, as he'd done so many times before, he squatted down and began to check the contents of his pants pockets. It was an exercise in pure futility, a ritual that would achieve nothing, because he knew by heart precisely what was contained in them — though he kept praying he'd missed something he could use, however insignificant.

First he tugged out his handkerchief and spread it flat on the ground before him. Then he took out the other items and laid them by touch on the cloth square. He arranged his pocketknife, a pencil stub, a button, a piece of string, and some other useless oddments, and, lastly, the dead flashlight. There in the dark, he handled each item, feeling it with his fingertips as if by some miracle it might suddenly prove to be his salvation. He gave a short, disappointed laugh.

This was ridiculous.

What did he think he was doing?

Nevertheless he gave his pockets a last check, just in case he'd missed anything. They were inevitably empty, except for some dust and grit. He hissed with disappointment, then girded himself for the final part of the ritual. He picked up the flashlight, cradling it in both hands.

Please, please, please!

He slid the switch.

Absolutely nothing. Not even a suggestion, not even a glimmer of light.

No!

It had failed him again. He wanted to hurt it, to make it suffer just as he was suffering. He wanted it to feel pain.

With a rush of anger, he drew his arm back to throw the useless object, then sighed and stopped himself. He couldn't bring himself to do it. He growled with frustration and stuffed the light back into his pocket. Then he bundled the remaining items together in his handkerchief and replaced them as well.

Why, oh why, didn't I just take one of the light orbs? I could have, so easily.

It would have been such a small thing to have done, and yet it would have made a world of difference to him right now. He began to think about his jacket. If only he'd had the sense to keep it on. He pictured where he'd left it, draped over the top of his rucksack. His lantern had been clipped to it, and in its pockets had been another flashlight and a box of matches, not to mention several orbs.

If only . . . if only . . .

Those simple objects would have been so vitally important to him now.

"YOU STUPID FOOL!" he began to yell, urging himself on in a rasping croak and cursing the blackness all around him, calling it every name under the sun. Then he fell silent, imagining he could see something creeping slowly across his field of vision. Was that a light, a flicker of light to his right?

What? No, there, yes, in the distance, a glow, yes, a light, a way out? Yes!

His heart racing, he moved toward it, only to trip on the uneven surface and fall once again. Standing up quickly, he searched for it, peering frantically into the velvety blackness.

It's gone. Where was it?

The light, if there ever had been one, was no longer there.

How long can I go on like this? How long before I . . . He felt his legs tremble as his breath deserted him.

"I'm too young to die," he said aloud, realizing for the first time in his life what those words really meant. He felt as if he'd been winded. He began to sob. He had to rest, and dropped to his knees. Then he bent forward, feeling the grit beneath his palms. *This isn't right. I don't deserve this.*

He tried to swallow, but his throat was so dry and swollen that he couldn't. He bent even farther forward until his forehead rested against the sharp grit. Were his eyes open or closed? There was no difference; small spots of colored light, swirling reticulations, massed together into smears, dancing before him, confusing him. But he knew it wasn't real.

He stayed in that position, panting, his head against the ground, and for some reason a vision of his Topsoil mother reared up before him. It was so crystal clear that, for an instant, he felt as if he'd been transported somewhere else. Mrs. Burrows was reclining in front of a television in a sun-filled room. The vision wavered and was replaced by the image of his father in a very different place, somewhere deep in the earth, wandering carelessly along and whistling through his teeth in that high-pitched way he always did.

Next he saw Rebecca, as he'd seen her a thousand times before. She was in the kitchen, preparing dinner for the whole family — a task she'd do every night — a sort of constant in his life that seemed to be present in even his earliest memories.

As if a film had jumped its sprockets, he saw her smiling evilly while she paraded herself in the black-and-white uniform of the Styx.

Witch! Treacherous, lying witch! She had betrayed him, betrayed his family. This was all *her* fault.

Witch. Witch. Witch. Witch. Witch!

In his eyes she was the very worst type of traitor, something twisted and dark and evil, a cuckoo sent from the underworld to wreak havoc on the nest, a quisling.

Get up! The pure hatred he felt for Rebecca galvanized him. He drew in a painful breath and pushed himself up so he was on his knees again. He shouted at himself, urging himself to get to his feet. *Get up, Will! Don't let her win!* Then, standing on his shaky limbs, his arms threshed out in the emptiness around him, in the endless, soul-sucking night land.

"Get going! Get going! GET OUT!" he shouted in a cracked voice. "GET OUT!"

He began to stumble along, calling out to Drake and his father, to anyone, to help him. But he heard nothing except his own echoing voice. Then there was a fall of small stones behind him, and he thought it perhaps too dangerous to continue to shout anymore and fell silent. But he kept going, counting a rough rhythm in his head as he went:

One two, one two one, one, one two . . .

Before long he was seeing horrible things looming out at him from the invisible walls. He told himself they weren't real, but that didn't stop them from coming.

He was losing it. He truly believed he'd go mad if the thirst and hunger didn't get him first.

One two, one two . . .

He rued the day that he had made the decision to take the Miners' Train and come down here to the Deeps. What had he been thinking? To be lost like this, when he could have gone Topsoil! After all, what was the worst that could have happened to him up there? Spending the rest of his life on the run from the Styx didn't seem so bad now. At least he wouldn't have gotten himself into *this* situation.

He fell again, and it was a bad one. He'd tumbled across some jagged rocks and banged his head. He slowly rolled onto his back and stretched out his limbs so he was spread-eagled. Then he lifted his hands in front of his face. Where he should have seen the white of his palms, there was no differentiation from the blankness, the canvas that had become his universe. He did not exist anymore.

He rolled over and felt in front of him, terrified there might be some sort of drop just ahead. But the tunnel floor continued uninterrupted, and he knew that he would have to get back up.

Without anything else to rely on, he'd become highly attuned to the familiar echoes his boots made as he trudged through the gravel and dust. He'd learned to read the minute reports of his footfalls as they reflected from the walls — it was almost like he had his own radar. On several occasions, he'd been forewarned of gaping chasms or changes in the floor level, purely by the nature of these echoes.

He got to his feet and took some steps.

There was a dramatic change in the sounds. The feedback was fainter, as if the lava tube had suddenly ballooned in size. He advanced at a snail's pace, filled with trepidation that he was about to stagger blindly into a vertical shaft.

Within a short distance, there were no more echoes at all — none he could discern, anyway. His boots were encountering something other than the usual debris. Pebbles! Knocking and grinding against one another and giving that unmistakable slightly hollow sound. They shifted under his feet and, in his exhausted state, made it even more difficult to walk.

Then he sniffed, suddenly aware of humidity on his face. He sniffed again. What was it?

Ozone!

He smelled ozone, so evocative of the seaside and trips to the beach with his dad.

What had he stumbled upon?

32

MRS. BURROWS stood by the door to her room, watching the events farther down the corridor.

She'd been roused from her afternoon nap by raised voices and the rapid tap of footfalls over the surface of the linoleum out in the hallway. This struck her as odd. For the past week there had been next to no activity in the place. An uneasy silence had fallen over Humphrey House, the patients largely confining themselves to their beds as, one after another, they succumbed to the mysterious virus that had all of England in its grip.

When she'd first heard the commotion, Mrs. Burrows had assumed it was simply a patient kicking up a fuss. But minutes later, a loud crash came from the area of the service elevator, followed by a woman's voice speaking in urgent tones. It was the voice of someone who was distressed or angry and wanted to shout but was just managing to keep herself in check. Only just.

Her curiosity getting the better of her, Mrs. Burrows had finally decided to take a look. Her eyes were considerably better, but still painful enough to force her to squint.

"What's all this?" she mumbled through a yawn as she stepped from her bedroom into the corridor. She stopped as something by the door to Old Mrs. L's room came into focus, and her red eyes opened wide with surprise. Mrs. Burrows had seen enough TV hospital dramas to identify what was there:

A *paradise cart* — the horrible euphemism for a hospital gurney with stainless-steel sides and top. It was a means of transporting dead bodies without alerting anyone as to *what* was inside or, indeed, if there was *anyone* inside.

Essentially a shiny metal coffin on wheels.

As she watched, the matron and two porters emerged from the doorway to fetch the cart. The porters wheeled it into Old Mrs. L's room as the matron remained outside. Spotting Mrs. Burrows, she walked slowly down the corridor toward her.

"No. That's not what I think —?" Mrs. Burrows began.

With a slow shake of her head, the matron told her all she needed to know.

"But Old Mrs. L was so . . . so *young*," Mrs. Burrows gasped, forgetting herself in her distress and using her nickname for the patient. "What happened?"

The matron shook her head again.

"What happened?" Mrs. Burrows repeated.

The matron's voice was hushed, as if she didn't want any of the other patients to hear. "The virus," she said.

"Not this thing?" Mrs. Burrows asked, indicating her eyes, which, just like the matron's, were still red and puffy.

"I'm afraid so. Got into her optic nerve, and then spread through her brain. The doctor said it's doing that in a number of cases." She took a long breath. "Especially those with defective immune systems."

"I can't believe it. My goodness, poor Mrs. L," Mrs. Burrows gasped, genuinely meaning it. It was a rare moment: She was feeling compassion for someone who really existed, not just for some actor playing a part on one of her soaps.

"At least it was quick," the matron said.

"Quick?" mumbled Mrs. Burrows, frowning with bewilderment.

"Yes, very. She complained she was feeling sick just before lunch, then became quite disoriented and went into a coma. There was nothing we could do to resuscitate her." The matron pressed her lips together and lowered her gaze to the floor. Taking out a handkerchief, she dabbed first one eye, then the other. Mrs. Burrows couldn't tell if this was from the continuing effects of the eye infection or because she was upset. "This epidemic is serious, you know. And if the virus mutates . . . ," the matron started to confide in a low voice.

Just then the porters pushed the paradise cart back out into the corridor, and the matron hurried off to join them.

"So quick," Mrs. Burrows said again, trying to come to terms with the death.

Later that afternoon in the dayroom, Mrs. Burrows was so preoccupied by Old Mrs. L's untimely demise that she wasn't paying much attention to the television. She'd been restless in her bedroom, so decided to seek solace in her favorite chair — the one place that usually brought her a measure of contentment. But when she arrived, she found that there were already quite a few patients lounging in front of the television. Their daily schedule of activities was still disrupted from the lack of staff, so they were mostly left to their own devices.

Mrs. Burrows had been unusually subdued, allowing the other patients to dictate the choice of program, but when an item came on the news, she suddenly spoke out.

"Hey!" she exclaimed, pointing at the screen. "It's him! I know him!"

"Who is he, then?" a woman inquired, looking up from a jigsaw puzzle.

"Don't you recognize him? He was in here!" Mrs. Burrows said, her excited eyes riveted to the report.

"What's his name?" the jigsaw lady asked, holding a piece of the puzzle in her hand.

Mrs. Burrows hadn't a clue what his name was, so she pretended she was so intent on the television that she hadn't heard.

"And Professor Eastwood had been assigned to work on the virus?" came the question from the interviewer offscreen.

The man on screen nodded — the same man with the distinguished voice who had spoken to Mrs. Burrows in a rather disparaging way at breakfast only days ago. He even had on the same tweed jacket he'd been wearing then.

"He's an important doctor, you know," Mrs. Burrows told the handful of people in the row behind her in a self-important way, as if she was confiding in them about a close friend. "He likes boiled eggs for breakfast."

Someone in the room repeated "boiled eggs," as though she was thoroughly impressed by the information.

"That's right," Mrs. Burrows confirmed.

"Shhh! Listen!" a woman in a lemon-yellow bathrobe hissed from the back row.

Mrs. Burrows tipped her head back to glare at the woman, but was too intrigued by the news report to take it any further.

"Yes," boiled-egg-man answered the interviewer. "Professor Eastwood and his research team at St. Edmund's were working round the clock to identify the strain. By all accounts, they were making good progress, although the records were lost."

"Can you tell us exactly when the fire broke out?" said the interviewer.

"The alarm was raised at nine-fifteen this morning," boiled-egg-man replied.

"And can you confirm that four members of the professor's research team also died in the blaze with him?"

Boiled-egg-man's eyebrows knitted together as he nodded somberly. "Yes, I'm afraid that is the case. They were exceptional and highly valued scientists. My heart goes out to their families."

"Do you have any theories what started the fire?" the interviewer posed.

"The laboratory carried a range of solvents in its stockroom, so I suppose the forensic investigation will begin there."

"There has been speculation in the past week that the pandemic may be man-made. Could the death of Professor Eastwood—?"

"I will not be drawn into such conjecture," boiled-egg-man barked disapprovingly. "It is the stuff of conspiracy theorists.

Professor Eastwood was a close personal friend for over twenty years and I will not have —"

"Professor Eastwood must have been getting too close — that's what happened! Someone snuffed him out!" Mrs. Burrows boomed, drowning out the television. "Of course it's a bloomin' conspiracy. It's those no-good Ruskies again, or maybe the lefties, who've got nothing to moan about anymore 'cept what we're all doing to the environment. You see how they're already trying to blame this plague on greenhouse gases and cows' farts."

"I think it escaped from one of our own labs," the jigsaw lady piped up, nodding vigorously as if she'd single-handedly solved the mystery.

Silence returned to the room, with the news report featuring yet another "science correspondent" who was giving the doom-laden prophecy that, at the drop of a hat, the virus could mutate into a far more lethal form, with dire consequences for the human race.

"Ah!" said the jigsaw lady at her card table, pressing a piece of her puzzle home.

Then the television screen was filled with a piece of highly accomplished street art. Graffitied on a section of wall between two shops in north London, it was a life-sized figure wearing a respirator and clothed in a bulky biohazard suit. Apart from the fact that it had a pair of what were unmistakably large cartoon-mouse ears sticking out of the top of its military helmet, the figure was very realistic. At first glance, it looked as though someone was actually standing there. The figure was brandishing a placard that read:

"Too bloody right it is!" Mrs. Burrows bellowed, her thoughts returning to Old Mrs. L's horribly premature death. The woman in the lemon-yellow bathrobe shushed her again.

"Oh, can't you shut up?" the woman complained with haughty disapproval. "Do you have to be so loud?"

"Yes, I do — this is serious!" Mrs. Burrows growled. "Anyway, at least I'm not as loud as your *ghastly* bathrobe, you old trout," Mrs. Burrows threw back at her, wetting her lips as she prepared to do battle. Even if the end of the world was looming, she wasn't going to be spoken to like that.

DRAKE DIDN'T HAVE the faintest idea where Will was.
He kicked himself for not noticing when the boy wandered off in the first place. It was Chester who had spotted him trying to signal to them as they'd all sought refuge in a lava tube. At that moment, pelted by a volley of loosely aimed sniper fire, Drake only had time to return the signal to the stranded boy. His primary concern had been to get the others away from the Limiters, and to safety.

Will didn't know his way around yet, and Drake didn't know him well enough to guess where he might have gone. No, Drake was at a total loss as to where to start looking for the gone boy.

And now, as they crept along the winding tunnel, with Cal lagging behind and Elliott prowling up ahead, Drake attempted once again to blank out all his years of knowledge and experience and adopt the mindset of a complete novice. *Think from ignorance.*

Caught by surprise and completely terrified, the boy's first impulse must have been to try to catch up with them. Realizing that this was impossible, he might have gone for the next most obvious option and left the plain by the closest lava tube. But not necessarily.

Drake knew the boy didn't have anything with him, no food or water, so he might have attempted to brave the sniper fire and get back to his kit. Like that would have done him any good, anyway — Drake had decided not to leave Will's jacket or rucksack behind as souvenirs for the Styx.

So, had he bolted down a lava tube? If he had, bad news. It would have been one of many, with the overwhelming volume of interconnecting tunnels in the network only compounding the problem. Mounting a search-and-rescue operation in so extensive an area — it would take weeks, if not months. Totally out of the question while the threat of Limiter patrols persisted.

Drake clenched his fists in frustration.

No good. He couldn't form any sort of picture.

Come on, Drake urged himself, *what would the boy have done next?*

Perhaps . . .

Perhaps Will *hadn't* entered the nearest tube but had kept to the plain, following the perimeter wall as it curved back — at least this would have given him some cover from the rifle fire.

Maybe he was being overly optimistic, but Drake was gambling on this being Will's most likely course of action. If he had kept to the perimeter, and if the Styx hadn't caught up with him, there was a slim chance he might still be alive.

That was an awful lot of *ifs*. . . .

Drake knew he was grasping at straws.

Or perhaps the Limiters had already trapped the boy and, at this very moment, were torturing him to extract all the information they could. The Limiters would do their usual and wring everything out of him using their excruciating methods. Even the strongest broke, sooner or later. It was a fate ten times worse than death; if it had befallen Will . . .

Cal stumbled behind him, skittering a hail of stones across the floor. *Too much noise,* Drake thought. It reverberated around the space, and he was just about to reprimand the boy when his chain of thought continued, almost stopping him in his tracks. *Three new additions to the team, three new responsibilities . . . all at the same time!* With Limiters popping up all over the place like malevolent jack-in-the-boxes, what the heck had he been thinking?

He wasn't some itinerant saint saving the lost souls the Colony spat out. So what was it? A twisted delusion of grandeur? Did he imagine that the three boys would be his own private army if it came down to a pitched battle with the Limiters? No, that was ridiculous. He should have dispatched two of the boys and kept just the one — Will — because with his infamous mother and knowledge of Topsoil life he might have played a part in his future plans. And now Drake had lost him.

Cal tripped again, falling to his knees with a muffled groan. Drake spun around.

"My leg," Cal explained before Drake had a chance to say anything. "I'll be all right." Cal immediately pulled himself up and began to walk again, leaning heavily on his stick.

Drake thought for a moment. "No, you won't. I'll have to hide you somewhere." His tone was cold and detached. "I made a mistake bringing you. . . . I expected too much from you." His intention had been to station Chester and Cal at strategic points where they could lie in wait for Will in case he chanced by. In retrospect, he should have left Cal and only taken Chester. Or left *both* of them behind.

As he struggled along, Cal was sinking deeper into turmoil. He had caught the tone in Drake's voice, and the implication bounced all other thoughts aside. He remembered Will's words, the warning that Drake didn't carry passengers, and the dread intensified in him that he really would be abandoned now.

Drake surged ahead and, after a final sharp turn in the tunnel, they were back on the Great Plain.

"Keep close and dim your lantern," he told Cal.

Will wondered if he was dreaming. Yet it all seemed so real. To reassure himself, he'd just stooped down to pick up a pebble, feeling its smooth, polished surface, when a faint breeze brushed his face. He stood up quickly. *He could feel a wind!*

He continued down the gradient and then heard a lapping sound. Despite the warm air buffeting him, goose bumps broke out all over his body. He knew what it was. Water. There was *water* out there in the darkness before him.

He moved forward in baby steps until the pebbles gave way to something else — sand, soft and sliding sand. A few steps more and his foot landed with a splash. He squatted down and tentatively felt before him. Liquid. It was lukewarm water. He shuddered. He imagined a huge, dark expanse in front of him.

He needed water so badly. He gently cupped some of the fluid in his hands and lifted it up to his face. He sniffed and then sniffed again. It was flat and lifeless — it had no smell to it. He held it to his lips and sipped.

He spat it out instantly, falling back into the damp sand. His mouth burned and his throat contracted. He started to cough and then retched. If he'd had any food in his stomach, he would have been violently sick. No, it was no good, it was brine, it was salt water. Even if he was able to force some of it down, he knew it would finish him off.

He listened to the lethargic slap of the water and then rose unsteadily to his feet, debating whether he should go back into the lava tubes. But he couldn't bring himself to do that — not after all the hours he'd already spent in them. Besides, there wasn't the remotest chance he'd find his way back to the Great Plain, and even if, by some miracle, he did survive the journey, what would be waiting for him there? A Styx reception party? No, he had no choice but to follow the edge of the water, its sound continually playing on his mind and making his thirst even more agonizing.

Although the sand was level, it shifted under his every step, sapping what little energy he had left as he plodded laboriously across it. He could no longer think straight. He tried to focus. How big was the body of water? Was he simply tracking around its shores, going in one big circle? He tried to tell himself it didn't feel that way — he was pretty sure he was traveling in a straight line.

But with each step, he fell further and further into a state of numb despondency. With a long, drawn-out sigh, he sank down onto the sand and seized a handful of it, thinking he might never get up again. One day far in the future, someone would discover his remains, a dried-out cadaver in the lonely darkness. How ironic: He would die of thirst curled up next to a subterranean sea. Maybe his bones would be picked bare by scavengers, his ribs sticking up from the sand, like a camel's skeleton in the desert. He shivered at the thought.

Will didn't know how long he'd remained there, beaten and drifting in and out of a fitful sleep. Several times he told himself to get back on his feet and walk again. But he was just too tired to resume his aimless wandering.

He nestled his head in the sand and turned to face the direction that he knew he should be taking. He blinked several times, his eyelids rasping against his dry eyeballs, and happened to glance behind him.

He could have sworn he saw the faintest glimmer of light. His vision playing tricks on him again. But he continued to stare at the spot. And saw it for a second time: a tiny, indistinct flash. He scrambled up and began to stumble toward it, leaving the sandy shore behind him as he scrabbled across the rattling pebbles. He tripped and went sprawling. Got up. Swore at himself because he was disoriented. And caught another fleeting glimpse of it. The light.

This was *not* something his tired brain was conjuring up — it was real, and he was so close. Yes, it might be the Styx, but he was past caring. He needed light like an asphyxiated man needs air.

More carefully, he crept up the gravel bank. He could see that the irregular flashes were emanating from a lava tube, its mouth clearly outlined by them. And though the light seemed to flicker in intensity, as he came nearer he could see that there was a constant illumination within the tube itself. He reached the opening, treading softly, until he was able to peer around the corner.

He saw shapes without form, shades without color. It took the most immense effort for him to remember how to use his eyes. He had to keep telling himself that what was before him was not just some hollow manifestation of his own making. Rapidly blinking, he struggled to bring his two lines of sight together and force the click-clack vacillation of the images to come to rest. They fused and made a distance, something certain. . . .

"PIG!" he croaked. "YOU BEAUTIFUL PIG!"

"Wha—?" Chester cried, sitting up with fright and spitting the food from his mouth. "Who—?"

Will could see again. His eyes feasted on the light, luxuriating in everything before him. Not fifteen feet away sat Chester, with a lantern in his hand and his rucksack open between his legs. He'd been helping himself to some food, stuffing it unceremoniously into his mouth, and clearly too preoccupied to hear Will's approach.

Will lurched toward his friend, beyond overjoyed. He half fell, half sat by Chester, who was gawping at him as if he'd seen a ghost. Will snatched the lantern from him and clasped it in his hands.

"Thank God," Will repeated several times in a cracked voice, staring straight into the light. It was so bright it hurt, but all he wanted was to bask in its eerie green flicker.

Chester snapped out of his stupefaction. "Will . . . ," he started.

"Water," Will croaked. "Give me water." His voice was so thin and feeble, it came out as a throaty gush of air. Will pointed frantically. Chester realized what he wanted and hastily passed him his canteen.

Will couldn't remove the stopper fast enough, fumbling at it pathetically with his fingers. Then it was off with a pop, and he rammed the neck into his mouth, gulping the water down greedily and trying to draw breath at the same time. It was going everywhere, slopping down his chin and chest.

"Will, we thought we'd lost you!" Chester said.

"Typical," Will gasped between mouthfuls. "I'm dying of thirst" — he swallowed, the water beginning to rehydrate his vocal cords — "while you're stuffing your face." He felt transformed, elated; the long hours spent in the dark were over, and he was safe again. He was saved. "Freakin' typical!"

"You look really terrible," Chester said quietly.

Will's face, normally pallid from his albinism, now appeared even paler, blanched from the salt crystals that had dried in a crust around his mouth and on his brow and cheeks.

"Thanks," Will eventually mumbled, after another large gulp.

"Are you OK?"

"Awesome."

"But how did you get here?" Chester asked. "Where've you been all this time?"

"You don't want to know," Will replied, still rasping. He looked down the lava tube behind Chester. "Drake and the others . . . where are they? Where's Cal?"

"They're out looking for you." Chester shook his head disbelievingly. "Will, dude, it's so good to see you. We thought you'd been caught, or shot, or something."

"Not this time," Will said and, after a few breaths, he renewed his attack on the canteen, sucking at it until he'd drained the last drop. He belched contentedly, tossing the canteen to the ground, and then, finally, took in the concern etched on his friend's face. Chester's hand, grasping some food, was still poised in front of him. *Dear old Chester.* Will couldn't help but laugh, gently at first, then building to such a hysterical level that his friend edged back slightly.

"Will . . . ?"

"Don't let me keep you from your snack," Will got out before he lapsed into another fit of sick-sounding laughter.

"It's not funny," Chester said, lowering the food. Will didn't show any sign of stopping his strangled guffawing, and Chester's indignation grew. "I thought I'd never see you again," he declared earnestly. "For serious."

There, on his grubby face, his lips covered with crumbs, a big grin began to form. "Whatever. You're stark, raving bonkers, you are." He shook his head. "Bet you're starving. Want some of this?" he offered, gesturing at the open pouch on top of the backpack.

"Gracias, mate. I certainly would," Will said gratefully.

"No problem. It's your food, anyway — this is *your* rucksack. Drake grabbed your kit when we ran for it."

"Well, glad you weren't going to waste it!" Will said, punching him gently on the arm. Will felt close to his friend again, and it felt good. "You know . . . the batteries died in my flashlight. I didn't even have an orb. I thought I was a goner," he told him.

"No way. How'd you make it down here, then?" Chester asked.

"I hitched a ride," Will replied. "How do you *think* I got here? I walked."

"No. Way!" Chester exclaimed, shaking his shaggy head.

Will looked at the inane grin on his friend's face. He'd seen the same big, stupid smile that day when they were reunited on the Miners' Train, and although it had only been two months ago, it felt like several lifetimes. So much had happened, so much had changed.

"You know," he said to Chester, "I think I'd even rather go back to school than do that again!"

"That bad, huh?" his friend asked with mock gravity.

Will nodded, rolling his swollen tongue around his lips, appreciating the novelty of spit once more.

Chester's voice burbled on in the background, but Will was too exhausted to listen any longer. He gently slipped into a languor, his head lolling back against the rock behind him. His legs twitched slightly, as if finding it hard to break from the rhythm of the protracted slog they'd been put through. But their movement became less and less until they were completely still, and Will found a well-earned oblivion, unaware of the horrible chain of events taking place that very moment on the Great Plain.

34

CAL HAD BEEN concentrating all his efforts on walking, and when he looked up, what was before him came as quite a shock.

He and Drake had been tracking around the very edge of the Great Plain, but the usual jagged rock wall wasn't there.

In its place, a vertical and apparently smooth surface ran from the ground to the roof, completely filling the space between the two. It was as if the seam that was the Great Plain had simply been sealed up. The barrier was too perfect to be a natural feature and stretched into the gloom as far as the light from his muted lantern penetrated.

He edged closer to touch its surface. It was solid and gray, but not as perfect as he'd originally thought — in fact it was badly pitted, and in places large chunks were missing, from which reddish-brown stains spread downward, marking the wall.

It was concrete. A huge concrete wall — the last thing he'd have expected to find in this elemental place. And he realized just *how* huge as they continued beside it for another twenty minutes, until Drake signaled him to stop. He pointed at a rectangular opening in the wall, five feet off the ground. Leaning toward Cal, he whispered, "Access duct."

Cal brought up his lantern to inspect it.

Drake grabbed his arm and pushed it down. "Keep it low, you fool! Are you trying to give away our position?"

"Sorry," Cal said, watching as Drake slipped his hand into the shadowy cavity. Then he heard a dull creak as Drake pulled, and a hatch of rusting iron pivoted open.

"You first," Drake ordered.

Cal peered into the grim darkness and swallowed. "You expect me to go in there?" he asked.

"Yes," Drake growled. "This is the Bunker. Been empty for years. You'll be all right."

Cal shook his head. "Be *all right*? I don't want to do this, I do not want to do this!" he muttered, but scrambled unenthusiastically into the duct with a helping hand from Drake and began to crawl.

The light from his lantern licked weakly before him, revealing foot after foot of the regular passage as his hands scrabbled in an inch of dry grit along the bottom of the duct. The sound of his own breathing was intimate and close, and he loathed the feeling of constriction. *Caught like a rat in a drainpipe*, he thought. Every so often he stopped to reach out with his walking stick and knock against the sides to check the way ahead. It gave him an opportunity to rest his leg, which was beginning to ache badly. It felt as though it was going to seize up completely, leaving him stuck in the passage.

Nevertheless, he continued. The duct seemed to go on forever. "How thick are these walls?" he asked out loud. Then, as he stopped to probe in front with his stick again, the tip didn't encounter anything. He inched a little farther forward and checked again. Nothing: He'd come to the end.

He cautiously clambered down from the duct. His feet safely on the ground, he turned up his lantern and swept it in front of him. He nearly cried out as a shape reared up beside him, and he raised his walking stick defensively.

"Quiet," Elliott warned, and he immediately felt like a fool. He'd completely forgotten that she would have been clearing the way ahead, as she always did.

Drake dropped soundlessly from the duct and appeared behind him. He nudged Cal on, and without a further word, they pushed deeper in.

They'd been in a small, gloomy room, empty except for puddles of stagnant water, but now advanced watchfully into a larger space, their footfalls giving short echoes as they scuffed over a linoleum-like floor. It might have once been white, but was now streaked with filth and stained from piles of rotting, acrid-smelling debris.

As Cal and Drake held back for Elliott to scout ahead, Cal's light revealed they were in a pretty large room. Against one of the walls stood a desk, and the walls themselves were mottled with patches of brown and gray damp, with small fungi sprouting in sporadic outgrowths, like little circular ledges. And next to where Cal was waiting, there were some shelves filled with decaying files. The paper had been reduced by the water to a flowing amorphous mulch. It spilled from the shelves to form small mounds of papier-mâché on the floor.

Responding to Elliott's signal, Drake whispered to Cal to move on. They slipped through a doorway and into a narrow corridor. At first Cal assumed the indistinct sheen from the walls was due to moisture, but then he realized he was passing between massive glass tanks. He thought he glimpsed a reflection of his own face in the black-algae-encrusted glass, but as he looked closer, his spine tingled. *No!* It wasn't his reflection at all. It was a leached-white human head resting against the glass, its eyes hollow and its features eroded as if eaten away. He shuddered, moving on quickly, not allowing himself a second look.

They rounded a corner at the end of the aisle, past a final tank, only to find the way blocked by massive slabs of broken concrete. The ceiling had caved in. But just as Cal was thinking they would have to turn back, Drake guided him into the darkness beside it, where the collapsed roof slanted down to a rough stairwell. It was bounded by a twisted, misshapen railing. They squeezed under the slab and, together, crept down the crumbling steps to where Elliott was waiting.

The stench of decay that met them was far from pleasant. Cal assumed they'd reached the bottom when Elliott took a few more steps and waded into dark water. He hesitated, but Drake jabbed him sharply in the back until he reluctantly lowered himself in. The turgid warm water came up to Cal's chest. Dust and oily rainbows circulated as their movements disturbed the surface. Above them were radial growths of fungi, so thick and numerous that they had to be growing one on top of the other, rather like a coral reef.

Tiny filaments hung from the fungi, glittering in Cal's light like a million spiderwebs. But the stench was overwhelming.

421

He tried to hold his breath, but was eventually forced to draw the miasma into his lungs. It caught in the back of his throat, and he began to hack away.

As he struggled to stifle the coughing, he looked down. To his horror, he could see movements just below the water's surface. He felt something tangle itself around his calf. Then it tightened.

"Oh God!" he choked, and in a frenzy tried to dash through the water.

"Stop!" Drake rumbled, but Cal didn't care.

"No!" he shouted loudly. "I'm getting out."

Surging forward, he saw Elliott ascending a set of steps in front of him. He caught up with her, clutching at a rickety iron banister that buckled under his weight. He managed to drag himself out of the fetid water. He was stumbling and tripping up the steps, banging his walking stick against the wall, desperate to get to clean air, when a hand grabbed him by the shoulder. It stopped him in his tracks, pressing agonizingly into his collarbone and spinning him around.

"Don't *ever* pull a stunt like that again," Drake said in a low growl, his face just inches from Cal's and his uncovered eye burning with fury. He shoved the terrified boy up against the wall, still gripping him by the shoulder.

"But there was —" Cal began to explain, hyperventilating from both the foul air and his fear.

"I don't care. Down here, a single stupid action can be the difference between us making it through this or not. . . . It's that simple," Drake said. "Do I make myself clear?"

Cal nodded, trying his utmost to stop his coughing as Drake prodded him on again. They came up into another corridor, with a much higher ceiling than the claustrophobic passage they'd just left. The sides angled outward and then in again toward the top, like an ancient tomb. The ground was damp, and every now and then Cal's boots crunched and cracked as if he was treading on glass.

Soon they were passing openings that led off on either side from this oddly shaped gallery. They went a small distance into one before taking a turning off it into a substantial space that seemed to be divided into smaller areas. A maze of thick concrete partitioning reached halfway up to the ceiling, form ing a whole series of pens. Strewn across the ground at the entrances to these pens were mounds of rubble and heaps of what appeared to be rusting metal.

"What *is* this place?" Cal asked, daring to break the silence.

"The Breeding Grounds."

"Breeding . . . for what? For animals?" Cal said.

"No, not for animals. For Coprolites. The Styx bred them to use as slaves," Drake answered slowly. "They built this com-plex centuries ago."

He ushered Cal on before he could ask any more questions, into a smaller antechamber. It had the feel of a hospital ward. The floor and walls were covered in white tiles, now discolored with years of dirt and damp, and a huge number of beds were heaped haphazardly near the entrance, as if someone had been in the process of removing them but was interrupted halfway through. Strangely, the beds were, without exception, rather small — there was absolutely no way they would have accommodated someone even of Cal's size, let alone an adult.

"Cots?" he spoke aloud. Over each diminutive bed was a circular metal cage of flaking, rusted iron, still locked into position. "Not for babies?" Cal said, horrified. It was like a maternity ward from a nightmare.

"For Coprolite babies," Drake answered as they caught up with Elliott. She pushed through a pair of swinging doors, one of which began to creak loudly from its single hinge. She immediately caught the door, stilling it.

Cal and Drake followed her out into the adjoining corridor, which was lined with warped shelves. On these was a variety of obscure, arcane-looking equipment, corroded to dull browns or bleeding verdigris. Cal's gaze settled on a floor-standing machine with rotted bellows and four glass cylinders protruding from its top. Next to it stood what was evidently a foot pump.

Looking up, he noticed a wooden wall rack housing all manner of lethally pointed instruments, many rusted in place on their rests. Next to this was a chart. Although it was badly affected by mildew, he could make out angular pictures and bizarre writing. He had no idea what it meant and no time to make sense of it.

Tramping through pools of cloudy water, they passed down several more narrow corridors. These were empty except for networks of broad pipes running the lengths of their ceilings, from which old lagging and skeins of cobwebs hung.

And then they turned off into a room. It was L-shaped and stacked floor to ceiling with massive glass cylinders. While he and Drake waited for the signal from Elliott, Cal's attention was caught by the contents of one of the jars.

It contained a man's head in cross section. It had been cut very precisely from the top of the cranium down, so the brain and everything inside the skull was visible. Somehow it didn't look real — it was difficult to imagine it had ever been a person. Cal made the mistake of leaning over to examine the jar from the other side. As the light from his lantern penetrated the yellowy fluid in which the head was immersed, he saw a single staring eye and the growth of dark bristles on the man's bleached-white skin, as if he hadn't shaved that morning.

Cal gasped. It was real, all right.

He turned away, it was so ghoulish. But then his eyes alighted on things just as bad in other jars. Floating, hideously deformed beings, some whole and others partially dissected.

They moved quietly into another area — octagonal and dominated by a single solid porcelain plinth in the very center. Corroded metal bands looped over the plinth, obviously to hold the subject in place.

"Butchers!" Drake muttered as Cal glimpsed scattered tools — scalpels, giant forceps, and other bizarre medical implements — in the shards of broken glass covering the floor.

"Oh no," Cal blurted, a chill spreading through his gut. Although this room didn't have anything like the ghastly specimens he'd just seen, the most awful feeling hung in the air. It was as though echoes lingered on, of the acute pain and suffering that had been perpetrated within its walls, from many years ago.

"This place is full of ghosts," Drake said in sympathy.

"Yes," the boy replied, shivering.

"Don't worry, we're not stopping," Drake assured him, and they pushed through into a larger corridor — it resembled the one they'd been in before, with the oddly slanting sides. They trekked down this until Drake brought them to a stop. Cal caught the suggestion of a breeze on his face again — they must have reached the other side of the Bunker. He leaned heavily on his walking stick, grateful to rest his leg, and tried not to think about what he'd just seen.

Drake listened for a while, peering through the lens over his eye, before turning his miner's light on to a low setting. In front of them was a naturally formed area, circular and about a hundred feet in diameter, with an uneven rock floor. Cal counted as many as ten lava tubes leading off from it in different directions.

"Tuck yourself down one of those, Cal," Drake whispered, pointing randomly at the lava tubes as he wandered out into the open. Elliott had remained behind, crouching low at the exit of the Bunker.

Drake noticed Cal wasn't following him. "Get moving, will you?" The boy groaned and took a few reluctant steps. "Elliott and I are going to split up and look for Will, but you keep watch here. Chances are he could pass this way," Drake explained, adding quietly, "if he hasn't already."

Cal had hardly gone any distance when a hiss came from behind him. He stopped. Elliott was still crouched down, her rifle braced against the side of the opening.

Drake froze but didn't turn to her.

"Come back!" Elliott called to Cal in an urgent whisper, never looking up from her rifle.

"Me?" Cal asked.

"Yes," she confirmed as she panned across the scene through her scope.

Cal crept back to Elliott, who momentarily drew her hand from her rifle to thrust a pair of slim stove guns at him. He took them and backed farther into the corridor behind her, keeping his head down.

Framed by the entrance, he could see Drake standing dead still in the open, his jacket flapping in the slight breeze. He hadn't extinguished the miner's light on his forehead, and its faint beam caught some of the larger boulders and rock outcrops around him, projecting stark shadows against the walls. But nothing stirred.

"Got something?" Drake said quietly to Elliott.

"Yes," she said slowly. "A feeling." Her voice was deadly serious and she looked tense, her cheek pressed hard against the rifle stock. She was rapidly switching her aim from tunnel mouth to tunnel mouth. In a single swift movement she unhooked several more stove guns from her belt and laid them on the ground beside her.

Cal squinted to see what the concern was all about. Nothing was moving in the area beyond Drake. He couldn't understand it.

Seconds ticked by.

It was so silent Cal began to relax. He was certain it was a false alarm, and that Elliott and Drake were both overreacting. His leg ached and he shifted his position a little, thinking how much he wanted to stand up.

Drake twisted around to Elliott.

"I say, I say . . . the invisible man's at the door," he declaimed loudly, no longer making the least effort to lower his voice.

"Tell him I can't see him right now" was Elliott's response, in nothing more than a whisper. As she rapidly moved her aim to another tunnel mouth, she stopped abruptly, as if lingering on something in it, before she finally swung the rifle back on to Drake.

"Yes," she mumbled with a nod of her head, looking at him through the scope. "I should've been on point. It should have been me out there, not you."

"No, it's better this way," Drake said matter-of-factly. He turned his body away from her.

"Good-bye," she said in a strained voice.

There were a few seconds, as long as centuries, then Drake answered her.

"Bye, Elliott," he said, taking a single step back.

Instant pandemonium.

Limiters spilled out from the lava tubes, their weapons raised. The way they moved, they resembled a swarm of malevolent insects. The shadowy dullness of their dark masks and long dun-colored coats seemed to spread from the dark voids of the tunnel mouths, as if they were an extension of the very shadows themselves. Too numerous to count, they lined up in an unbroken semicircle in front of the lava tubes.

"DROP YOUR WEAPONS!" ordered a piercing, reedy voice.

"SURRENDER YOURSELVES!" came from somewhere else.

As a man they began to advance.

Cal's heart had stopped. Drake remained exactly where he was as the line closed in. Then he took another step back.

Cal heard a single shot and saw the fabric at the tip of Drake's shoulder burst, as if a tiny charge had gone off within it. The impact skewed him around, but he quickly righted himself. Elliott answered with rapid volleys, working the bolt of her rifle at blinding speed. Limiters fell one after another as she picked them off. Every shot found its mark. Some soldiers were flung backward as the powerful rifle bucked in her hands, others dropped where they stood. But still they continued to advance. And they didn't seem to be returning fire.

In one smooth movement, Drake bent down. Cal thought he'd been hit again, but then he saw he had a stove mortar in his hands. He struck its base against a rock and a flame erupted, spearing from its mouth. A swath of Limiters was quite literally obliterated. Where they had stood were just a few patches of smoke — the blast had wiped them from existence. Shouts and cries and screaming came from all over. But more Limiters pressed forward, now returning fire at Elliott.

Cal backed down the corridor, away from the opening, the stove guns clutched tightly in his sweating palm. The sole thought crashing through his brain was that he had to get away. Somehow.

Through the clouds of smoke, he thought he saw Drake totter a few steps and fall. At that very moment Elliott seized him by his arm and whisked him away. Then she was running, running and pulling him behind her, so fast he could barely stay on his feet. They'd covered a couple of hundred yards before she heaved him into one of the side rooms.

"Cover your ears!" she screamed.

A bone-shaking explosion erupted immediately. The blast knocked them off their feet. A fireball and chunks of flying concrete hurtled down the corridor past the doorway. Elliott must have primed some charges as she'd moved off. Before the debris had a chance to settle, she picked herself up and yanked Cal back out into a swirling storm of dust. Little patches of fire sizzled and spluttered in the puddles of water on the ground.

As they dashed through thick eddies of choking smoke, a tall shape loomed before them. Elliott shoved Cal out of the way and dropped to one knee. She worked the bolt. The Limiter was coming straight for her, his gun up. She didn't hesitate. She squeezed the trigger. The muzzle of her rifle spat, the flare illuminating the Limiter's surprised face. The shot hit him square in the neck. His head whipped forward onto his chest as he disappeared from sight, back into the billowing dust. Elliott was already up.

"Go!" she howled at Cal, pointing down the corridor.

Another dark shadow plunged at them. The rifle still at her hip, Elliott pulled the trigger. There was a dull click.

"Oh God!" Cal shouted, seeing the look of deadly intent on the Styx's face turn to one of triumph. The man thought he had them cold.

Cal raised his walking stick pathetically before him as if he was going to use it to beat him off. But in the blink of an eye, Elliott had dropped her rifle and grabbed Cal's hand, thrusting the stove guns he was holding in the direction of the Limiter. She pulled at the trigger mechanisms.

Cal felt the recoil and the intense heat as both guns blasted at point-blank range.

He couldn't look at the result. The man hadn't even screamed. Cal was rooted to the spot, his sweating, shaking hand still clenching the smoking cylinders.

As Elliott yanked something from her rucksack, she yelled at him. But Cal was almost dumb with fear. She slapped him with such force his teeth rattled. It shocked him back into action, just as she slung a charge into the corridor where he thought they were about to go. How were they going to get away if she closed off their escape route?

"Take cover, you idiot!" she bawled, kicking him across the passage. He fell into a doorway on the opposite side.

The explosion was smaller this time, and they immediately sprinted through the section of corridor where it had gone off. Cal tripped on something soft — he knew it was a body — and was grateful the dust shrouded everything from sight as he blundered through.

It was as if time had collapsed to nothing. Seconds did not exist. And Cal's body, not his mind, dictated his actions, making him flee. He had to escape — that was the only thing that mattered. Basic instinct had taken control of him.

Before he knew it, they were back in the operating theater with the gruesome ceramic plinth in the center. Elliott hurled a cylindrical charge behind them. They had only gone halfway through the adjoining L-shaped room when the shock wave from the blast caught up.

Horror of horrors, it shattered many of the specimen jars, cracking them open. Their contents slopped out like dead fish as the air filled with the sharp tang of formaldehyde. He glimpsed the semidissected head skedaddling across the floor by his feet, its half-mouth grinning crookedly at him, its demi-tongue sticking out mischievously. Cal leaped over it as he followed Elliott out of the room, and they tore through the ensuing corridors. They took a succession of left turns and then a right — although the dust and smoke weren't nearly as thick here, Elliott halted abruptly and frantically looked around.

"No, no, no!" she ranted.

"What?" he puffed, hanging on to her.

"NO! Wrong way! Back . . . got to go *back*!"

They hurriedly retraced their way around several corners, then Elliott paused to glance down a side corridor. Cal could see the anxiety in her eyes.

"It has to be that way," she muttered uncertainly. "God, I hope it —"

"Are you sure?" he interrupted urgently. "I don't recognize . . ."

She pushed open a door. He was following so closely behind that as she stopped he crashed into her.

Cal blinked and shielded his face. They were bathed in light.

They found themselves in a big white room.

It was startling.

There was absolute calm.

It was completely at odds with everything else Cal had seen in the Bunker: perfectly clean, with a pristine white-tiled floor and newly whitewashed ceiling, down the middle of which a long line of luminescent orbs were suspended.

Along both sides of the room were polished iron doors; Elliott had already gone up to the nearest of these and was peering through the glass inspection window set into it. Then she moved to the next one. The doors all had large check marks daubed on them in black paint, applied so thickly it had run over the buffed metal.

"I can see bodies," she said. "So this is the quarantine area."

It was more than just *bodies*. As Cal went to see for himself, there were two — in some cells three — corpses stretched out on the floor. It was obvious they'd been dead for some time, as they'd already begun to decay. A clear, gelatinous fluid, flecked with yellow and red, had leaked from them and pooled on the stark white tiles.

"Some of them look like Colonists," Cal said, noticing what they were wearing.

"And some were renegades," Elliott said in a strained voice.

"Who did this? What killed them?" Cal asked.

"Styx," she replied.

The mention of that name instantly brought him back to the seriousness of their situation, and he began to panic.

"We don't have time for this!" he shouted, trying to steer her back toward the door.

"No, wait," she said. She was frowning at him but not pushing him away.

"We can't mess around here! They'll be following . . . ," he gasped.

"No, this is important. These cells have been sealed!" Elliott said, examining the edges of the door. Like all the others, it had thick new welds on all four sides, and no handle to open it. "Can't you see what this is, Cal? It's the Styx testing area we heard about — they've been trying out some sort of bio-weapon here!"

Cal was right behind Elliott as she reached the next cell, and he noticed its door didn't have a mark painted on it. As she looked in, a face jumped up at the window. The eyes were bloodshot and swollen. It was a man — in a state of extreme panic. Angry red boils covered every inch of his skin and his cheeks were hollow, his face cadaverously thin. He was shouting something, but they couldn't hear so much as a whisper through the glass.

He began to beat weakly on the window with both fists, but still there was no noise. He stopped, peering at them with his demented, darting eyes.

"I know him," Elliott said hoarsely. "He's one of us."

He was mouthing something, trying to communicate with her by emphasizing the words with his lips.

It was meaningless to her.

"Elliott!" Cal begged. "We have to leave!"

She ran her fingers over a length of the weld that stretched unbroken around the edge of the door in a thick slug, won-dering if she could somehow blow it open. But she knew they didn't have time to try. All she could do was give the man a helpless shrug.

"Let's go," Cal shouted, then screamed, "now!"

"OK," she agreed, swiveling on her heels to run back to the door through which they'd entered.

They were immediately plunged back into the darkened world of the Bunker, the dust-laden air swirling around them. As their eyes readjusted from the clinical brightness of the strange room, they continued down the corridor in the direction she'd originally been taking them.

"Keep close," Elliott whispered as they crept along.

After a short distance, she came to a halt.

"Come on, come on! Which way?" Cal heard her mutter urgently to herself. "Has to be down here," she decided.

Several corridors later, they entered a small hallway from which two doorways led off. She went from one to the other, then paused between the two, shutting her eyes.

By this point, Cal had lost all faith in her ability to get them to safety. But before he could express his doubt, there was a clanging from nearby. A door was being battered down — the Limiters were closing in.

Elliott's eyes flicked open.

"Got it!" she shouted, choosing which doorway to take. "We're in the homestretch now!"

At the end of a sequence of lefts and rights, they were slipping and sliding down the stairs into the submerged basement again. This time Cal had absolutely no qualms about lowering himself into the stagnant water and was clambering up the stairs on the other side in seconds flat. Elliott had held back to set a sizable charge on the opposite stairway just above the waterline. Once she'd done this, she caught up with him, and they were just passing under the sections of collapsed concrete as the charge went off.

The whole place shook and torrents of silt fell over them. A deep rumbling turned into an ominous grinding noise: Everything seemed to be shifting. Huge slabs of concrete crashed down, sending water and dust in all directions, and sealing the way behind.

"That was a close one," he heard Elliott pant as they thundered through the linoleum-floored room and climbed into the duct, scrabbling their way down it.

Emerging from the duct, Cal dropped onto the floor of the Great Plain again with a cry of pure relief. Elliott helped him to his feet and right away began retracing their steps along the wall. They raced on until they were swinging around the corner into a lava tube, away from the plain. And they didn't stop running.

Will didn't know how long he'd been asleep when he was rudely woken by urgent shouting. His head hurt like crazy, a vicious throb stretching across his temples.

"GET UP!"

"Hey . . . !" Will spluttered. "Who . . . ?"

He blinked groggily. Elliott and Cal were standing over him.

"Get up!" Elliott ordered harshly, then kicked him.

Will tried, but then collapsed back. He was shaky and confused, finding it impossible to order his floundering thoughts. He saw her face. Although it was black with filth, he could see she wasn't the remotest bit pleased to see him again. And here he'd thought that she and Drake would be congratulating him for keeping on, for making it against all odds!

Perhaps he'd totally misjudged how they would react, and they were furious with him for becoming separated from the group. Perhaps he'd broken another of their inscrutable rules. Rubbing the salt crystals from his red-rimmed eyes, he studied Elliott's face again. It was set in the grimmest of expressions.

"I . . . I didn't . . . how long have . . . ?" he slurred, noting that Cal's expression was similarly grim, and that both he and Elliott were dripping wet and smelled of chemicals.

Chester had begun gathering the food containers together into his backpack, fumbling in his haste.

"They got him," Cal said, his chest heaving as he lashed his stick demonstratively through the air. "The Limiters got Drake!"

Chester stopped what he was doing. Will shook his head disbelievingly, and then looked to Elliott for confirmation. He didn't need to see the grazes on the side of her face, or the blood welling from a deep gouge on her temple, to know that his brother was telling the truth. The sight of her narrowed, angry eyes was enough.

"But . . . how . . . ?" Will gasped.

She merely turned and marched off in the direction of the subterranean sea Will had spent so long beside.

PART 4

THE

ISLAND

35

THE BOYS had the greatest difficulty keeping up with Elliott, she was moving so swiftly. As if she didn't care whether they kept up or not.

Of the three of them, Cal was struggling the most. He shuffled along and even fell several times as they trekked across the sandy bank. But he always managed to drag himself to his feet and carry on. He was saying something to himself — prayers, perhaps, though Will couldn't be certain and wasn't about to waste his breath to inquire. He had a splitting headache that he couldn't shake, and he was weak from lack of sleep and food. His thirst remained unquenchable — without stopping, he would take gulps from his canteen, but it did little to assuage it.

None of the boys spoke. Questions were burning in their minds. With Drake gone, would Elliott simply abandon them and go off by herself? Or would she continue with the plans that Drake had discussed and keep them together as a team?

Will was pondering this as he noticed a barely perceptible change in the terrain. The punishing, shifting sand had firmed up, becoming a little easier to traverse. He wondered why.

The sea was still to his right. He could hear the odd lugu-brious slap of a wave, but he knew that the cavern wall — to his left and invisible in the darkness — must be quite some distance away by now. They were going deeper and deeper into an area that Will had only touched upon in his hours of blind wandering.

Then, under the dim light shed by his lantern, he saw the pale sandiness had transformed into darker ground. He stumbled over something solid and immovable, his boot strik-ing hard against it. He stooped to explore what it was: It felt exactly like a small stump from a felled tree. Will tried to con-tain his curiosity, but it got the better of him and he clicked up the lever behind the lens of his lantern.

Immediately Elliott swooped back. She stood threateningly in front of him.

"What do you think you're doing?" she growled. "Turn that down!"

"I'm just having a look," he answered, refusing to engage her flashing eyes as he surveyed the area around his feet. It *had* changed. There were several stumps of varying heights, between which were strange-looking plants — succulents, Will guessed — covering the ground so thickly that little of the sand showed through. They were black, or at least a darkish gray, and their leaves, sticking out from stubby central stems, were round and bloated and covered with a waxy cuticle.

"Salt-loving," he proposed, nudging one of the succulents with his boot.

"Turn that light down," Elliott ordered, scowling. She was barely out of breath, while Will and the two other boys gasped heavily, grateful for this small rest stop.

Will looked up at her. "I want to know where you're taking us," he demanded, holding her stare. "You're going so fast, and we're all totally knackered."

She didn't answer.

"At least tell us what the plan is," he persisted.

She spat, barely missing Will's knee. "The light!" she hissed through her teeth as she brought the butt of her rifle up threateningly. Having zero desire to get into a fight, he dutifully clicked his lantern back to the lowest setting. She flicked her head away from him and strode off, passing Cal, then Chester, to take the lead again. It reminded Will of the way Rebecca had treated him back in Highfield. He pondered whether all teenage girls had a similar streak of vindictiveness, and wondered again if he would ever fully understand the opposite sex. In the hours that followed, despite his pleas for her to slow down, it seemed to Will as though Elliott had stepped up a gear and was forging ahead even faster now, purely to spite him.

The succulents grew taller as they moved farther into this new region. When they trod on the leaves, they made squishing noises, as if they were walking over thick mud. Every so often one of the leaves would burst with a loud popping sound, like a punctured balloon, filling the air with the most intense smell of sulfur.

They began to encounter basic-looking plants in wiry tangles, like overgrown banks of brambles. Will thought they resembled the common horsetail, a plant he knew from its rampant growth in Highfield Cemetery. But these had dirty-white stems, some reaching an inch in diameter, around which were collars of black, needle-thin, prickly spikes. The farther the boys traveled, the denser the banks became, until the plants were almost up to their waists and they had a heck of a job wading through them.

Added to this, increasing numbers of thick trees blocked their way. Will could see that their trunks were covered in rough scales and guessed they were huge ferns. The abundance of them made it increasingly difficult to see the person in front. The air had also become intensely humid, and the boys were soon drenched in sweat.

Will was right behind Cal as he labored along, trying to ensure his brother didn't drop behind, when he noticed a change in course. They were going down a slight incline, which would eventually bring them to the beach. He could hear thrashing up ahead as Elliott beat their way through the thick foliage, and he caught a fleeting glimpse of Chester. He and Cal were still on track. But where was Elliott taking them?

They stumbled down the last of the slope and broke from the undergrowth to find themselves on the shore. It was the first time any of the boys had actually seen the sea. Cal and Chester stared at it in silent amazement, a light breeze cooling their sweaty faces. But Will's attention was absorbed by the spectacle of the huge forest from which they'd just emerged. In the penumbra of his lantern, it appeared so dark and impenetrable.

Giant fernlike trees towered high above him.

"Cycads!" Will exclaimed. "These have to be gymnosperms. The dinosaurs ate plants like this!"

At the apex of their gently curving trunks, which had dark rings around them at regular intervals as if they had been built by slotting together a series of increasingly smaller cylinders, grew massive crowns of fronds. Some were fully open, while others were still curled up on themselves. Unlike the green leaves of cycads found on the earth's surface, the fronds of these huge plants were gray.

In between these primordial trees, copses of the bloated succulents and the trailing brambles, so tightly interwoven, gave the impression of the thickest jungle in the dead of night. And Will could see small white fluttering insects dithering between the high branches of the trees. Those nearest to him were clearly the same species of snowy moth he had first seen in the Colony. And Will heard an infrequent, familiar sound — one that evoked the Topsoil countryside so strongly, he smiled. The chirping of crickets!

It was several moments before he wrenched his gaze away from the whole scene.

Cal and Chester, both still trying to get their breath back, were throwing worried glances at the stretch of water before them. Will looked past the two boys to where Elliott was kneeling as she surveyed the shoreline through her rifle scope.

Will went to her side, curious as to what was churning up the water so violently, and found himself standing at the precise spot where a fluxing white line broke its surface. It arced away into the gloom, a mass of shifting white striations of froth and spume on one side.

"This is the causeway," Elliott said in an offhand manner, anticipating his question.

She got to her feet and the boys straggled around her.

"We're going to cross here. If you slip, you'll be washed away. So don't." Her voice sounded flat, telling them nothing about what she was thinking.

"There's some sort of rock outcrop under here, isn't there?" Will pondered aloud, taking a few steps forward to thrust his hand into the bubbling froth. "Yes . . . here it is."

"I wouldn't," Elliott warned.

Will snatched his hand back quickly.

"There are things in there that'll take your fingers off," she continued, and as she did so she turned up her lantern and shone it over the water so they could see the expanse of nothingness, the huge black sheets extending across both sides of the causeway. Each of the boys shuddered despite the warmth of their surroundings.

"Please tell us where you're taking us," Will begged her. "Is there any reason why you're keeping us in the dark?"

His words hung in the air for several seconds before she answered.

"All right," she said, letting out a breath. "We don't have much time, so I want you to listen carefully. OK?"

Each of the boys muttered a yes in response.

"I've never, *ever* seen so many Limiters down here in the Deeps before, and I don't like it. It's crystal clear that they've got something massive going on, and maybe that's why they're tying up loose ends."

"What do you mean, *loose ends*?" Chester asked.

"Renegades . . . us," Elliott answered. Then she tipped her light at Will. "And him." She looked down at the frothing water. "We're going somewhere safe so I can figure out what we should do next. Now, just follow me."

She'd allowed them to turn their lights up several clicks, but the immensely powerful current pushed hard against their boots and threw up a steamy mist around them. The ledge on which they had to walk was uneven and coated with slippery weed. Every so often, it dipped well below the water's surface. Will could hear Chester grunting as he negotiated another of these most treacherous, invisible stretches, muttering with gratitude as he managed to get to where the ledge was more obvious again. Cal babbled up ahead, his voice often rising to a high pitch as if he was pleading for the terrifying crossing to end. There was nothing Will could do to help him — each boy had his own watery tightrope to walk, just trying to take the next step without sliding from the ridge into the roiling nightmare expanse.

They hadn't traveled very far when they heard — they felt — a huge splash.

"Crikey! What was that?" Chester yelped, teetering to a stop on the ledge.

Will could have sworn he caught a flash of a broad, pale-colored tail fin no more than fifteen feet away. They all peered apprehensively at the spot as the choppy water becalmed again.

"Move!" Elliott urged.

"But . . . ," Chester said, pointing a quivering hand toward the water.

"MOVE!" she repeated in a growl, glancing anxiously back at the beach. "We're like ducks in a shooting gallery out here."

It took them about half an hour to reach dry land again. They collapsed onto the sandy foreshore, taking in another wall of thick jungle before them. But Elliott didn't allow a moment's respite, immediately herding them onward through coppices of the succulent plants and tangled clumps of the trailing stems with black prickles, every bit as dense as the bush at the other end of the causeway.

They came to a small clearing, where Elliott told them to wait, and left to scout out the rest of the area. With the jungle on all sides it was impossible to tell where they were, and none of them gave it a second thought. They were all drained, and their clothes wrung through with sweat. As the odd insect fluttered past, Will and Chester shared a canteen of water.

Cal had chosen a spot in the clearing as far away from Will and Chester as he could possibly manage. Sitting cross-legged and staring into space, he began to rock back and forth, muttering monotonously under his breath.

"What's up with him?" Chester said quietly, wiping the perspiration from his brow.

"Dunno," Will replied, taking a large swig from the canteen.

Just then, Cal's voice became louder and they could hear snatches of his ranting: ". . . and the hidden shall not be hidden in the eyes of the . . ."

"Do you think he's all right?" Chester asked Will, who had settled back against the rucksack and closed his eyes with a long exhalation.

"... and it is we who shall be saved ... saved ... saved ...,"
Cal was babbling.

Will opened one eye and called crankily to his brother.

"What'd ya say, Cal? Can't hear you, bro."

"Didn't say anything," Cal replied defensively, sitting bolt
upright with a startled expression.

"Cal, what happened?" Chester asked the boy hesitantly.
"What happened to Drake?"

Cal crawled toward them and launched into a rambling
account, backtracking as he recalled another detail and every
so often stopping completely, in midsentence, to draw a quick
breath before he went on. Then he told them about the white
room with the sealed cells that he and Elliott had stumbled
upon in the Bunker.

"But this renegade — the one who was alive — what was
wrong with him?" Will asked.

"His eyes were all puffy and his face was covered in boils,"
Cal said. "He had some sort of disease."

Will looked thoughtful. "So is that it?" he said.

"What do you mean?" Chester butted in.

"Drake knew the Styx were testing out something down
here. Maybe it's a disease."

With a small shrug, Cal continued, recounting how he and
Elliott had escaped to the lava tubes. His voice broke.

"Drake could have run, but he didn't, so that Elliott and I
had a chance. .... It was like ... like when Uncle Tam made a
stand. ..."

"He may not be dead." Elliott's voice came, silencing Cal.
It was suffused with a mixture of anger and sorrow.

Stunned by her pronouncement, they all looked at her, standing at the edge of the clearing.

"We were careless and they had us, but the Limiters were shooting to maim, not to kill. If they'd wanted us dead, we would be." She spun around to face Will, her recriminatory glare burning into him. "But why would they want to take us alive? Enlighten me, Will."

All eyes were on him as he shook his head.

"Come on, why would that be?" she insisted in a low growl.

"Rebecca," Will answered quietly.

"Not her again!" Chester exclaimed.

Cal started to gibber another monotonous diatribe, wringing his hands together. They could all hear what he was saying now. "And the Lord shall be the savior to those —"

"Stop that!" Elliott turned on him. "What are you doing? Praying?" She reached out and slapped him hard across the face.

"I . . . uh . . . no . . . ," he babbled, his arms up around his head as he cowered, thinking she was going to strike him again.

"Do that and I'll finish you right here. It's all a load of hogwash. I should know, I had *years* of the *Book of Catastrophes* rammed down my throat in the Colony." She grabbed him by his hair and shook his head mercilessly. "Get a grip, kid, because this is all you've got."

"I . . . ," Cal began with a half sob.

"No, listen to me, wake up, will you? You've been brainwashed," she said in a low voice, yanking his hair and jerking his head from side to side. "Do you remember a time before you were born?"

"Huh?" Cal sobbed.

"Do you?"

"No," he stuttered uncomprehendingly.

"No! Why is that? Because we are no different from any animal, any insect or germule."

"Elliott, if he wants to believe —" Chester began, unable to remain silent.

"Keep out of it, Chester!" she snapped, not even looking at him. "We are not *special*, Cal. You, me, we all came from nothing, and that's exactly where we're all going one day, maybe soon, whether we like it or not." She snorted contemptuously and shoved him over onto his side. "Can't you see it's a cult? Your *Book of Catastrophes* is for the birds!"

In the blink of an eye she was in front of Will. He girded himself, thinking he was next in line for the abuse. But she stood silently before him, her arms crossed belligerently over her long rifle. Rebecca had stood before him in this very way so many times back in Highfield, telling him off for tramping mud onto the carpet or some similar petty misdemeanor.

"You're coming with me," Elliott barked.

"What? Where?"

"You got us into this, so you can help get us out," she snapped.

"Help how?"

"We're going back to the base."

Frowning at her, Will couldn't take in what she was saying.

"*You* and *I* are going back to the *base*," she said again, enunciating each word clearly. "Understand? To get equipment and supplies."

"But I can't go all the way back there! I just can't," he pleaded. "I'm wrecked. . . . I need some rest . . . some food . . ."

"Tough."

"Why don't we just go on to the next base? Drake told me . . ."

She shook her head. "Too far."

"I—"

"Get up." She thrust the spare riflescope at him and he slowly rose to his feet. With a helpless glance at Chester, he left the clearing and followed her through the dense foliage back to the causeway.

It was as though he were in the throes of some awful nightmare in reverse, repeating the near-death journey he'd just completed. At least he knew what to expect this time.

Will wasn't really thinking by the end of his second causeway crossing. He followed Elliott mechanically, plodding over the stretch of sand until they came to the edge of the jungle.

"Stop here," she ordered and, under the glow of her lantern, began kicking around, searching for something in the discolored sand packed at the gnarled roots of the succulents.

"Where is it?" she said to herself, moving farther into the undergrowth. "Aha!" she exclaimed, diving down. She unsheathed her knife and used it to trim off the gray foliage of a small rosette-shaped plant, until all that was left was its ragged heart. She continued to cut away at this, reducing it to what looked like some sort of nut. She carefully peeled that, shedding chunks of its woody coat. Then she began to work on the kernel, which was about the size of an almond, slicing it into strips. She sniffed at it before holding her palm out to Will.

"Chew on it," she said, and then sucked a strand herself off the knife blade. "Don't swallow. Just chew slowly."

He nodded dubiously, grinding the fibrous strips between his incisors. They released a sharp sourness that made him stick out his tongue.

She watched, pushing another strand into her mouth with a grimy finger.

"Tastes disgusting," he said.

"Give it a moment — it'll help."

She was right. As he chewed, a coldness spread through his body. It was a pleasurable sensation in the midst of the unremitting heat and humidity, and with it came a surge of energy that blew away the leadenness from his limbs. He felt renewed, strong . . . he felt ready for anything.

"What is this?" he asked, straightening his shoulders, his inquisitiveness returning with a vengeance. "Caffeine?" The only sensation he could compare it with was when his sister had made coffee back at home and he'd tried a cup. "Caffeine?" he repeated, his voice jittery.

"Something like that," Elliott replied with a careless smile. "Come on, let's go."

He now found he could easily keep pace with Elliott as they steamed ahead. Moving with the fleetness of two cats, they traversed the sandy foreshore and then climbed the shingle incline that would take them to the wall of the cavern and the lava tubes.

Will lost all track of time. They reached the base in what seemed like a matter of minutes, although he knew it must have taken considerably longer. It was as if he'd been outside his own body, an onlooker watching someone else sweat and heave for breath at the exertion of traveling so phenomenally fast.

Elliott climbed the rope and he followed. Once they were both inside the base, she tore around like a whirlwind, sorting the various items they were going to take with them. It was as if she'd planned for this very event and knew precisely what to do.

In the main room, which Will had only seen once before, she yanked equipment from wall hooks and swept all manner of things from shelves in the old metal lockers. In seconds flat, the floor was a jumble of discarded items, which she kicked at impatiently when they got in her way. She placed the equipment they were going to take just inside the doorway. Unbidden, Will began to stow it inside a pair of sizable rucksacks and two large bags with drawstring openings.

Elliott suddenly fell silent. Will looked up from where he was kneeling. She was out of sight, behind one of the bunk beds, where she'd been yanking equipment out of Drake's locker. Will stood up as she appeared slowly from around the corner. Whatever was in her hands, she carried it in such a way that Will could sense her reverence.

"Drake's spare headset," she announced. Stopping before him, she held out her hands and offered it to him.

Will regarded the leathery cap with its milky eyepiece and the cables trailing down to a small, flat, rectangular box, which swung gently in the air.

"Huh?" he said, frowning.

She didn't respond but held it farther toward him.

"For me?" he asked as he took it. "Really?"

She nodded.

"Where did Drake get these things?" he said, examining the headset.

"He made them. That was what he did in the Colony. . . . The scientists took him in."

"What do you mean, *took him in*?" Will asked quickly.

"He was a Topsoiler, just like you."

"I know — he told me," Will said.

"The Styx grabbed him. Every so often they go to the surface to snatch people with the skills they need."

"No kidding," Will breathed in disbelief. "So what were Drake's skills? Was he in the army or something? Like a commando?"

"He was a visual optics engineer," Elliott said, pronouncing the words carefully as if she was trying her tongue on an unfamiliar language. "He made these, too." She put her hand to the scope on the weapon hanging from her shoulder.

"No kidding," Will said, weighing the handset in his hands. He recalled Elliott once mentioning that the Styx had abducted someone with the ability to develop devices that allowed them to see through darkness. But *Drake*? Images of him flashed through Will's head: the scarred, lean man who inspired such respect next to stereotypical geeks wearing white lab coats with pocket protectors.

"I really thought he'd been some sort of soldier," Will mumbled, shaking his head. "And that he'd gotten himself Banished from the Colony, like you."

"I wasn't Banished!"

Elliott responded with such passion that Will could only manage an apologetic grunt.

"As for Drake . . . the Styx *made* him work on these. You know what I mean?"

Will was hesitant in his reply. "They tortured him?"

She nodded. "Until he did what they wanted. They'd haul him down here to the Deeps to field-test the devices, but the day came when he saw his chance and made a break for it. They must have thought they'd gotten all they could from him, because they didn't come looking."

"That's so boss," Will said. "So he was a scientist, a researcher . . . a bit like my dad."

Elliott made a face as if she had no idea what Will was talking about and had nothing more to add. She returned to the locker, where she continued to empty out its contents, every so often lobbing the odd item onto the bed.

With bated breath, Will carefully put on the headset. Adjusting the strap so it was tight across his forehead, he made sure the lens was correctly positioned over his eye, testing it by hinging it up and down. As he tucked the rectangular box into a pocket, he realized how incredibly uneasy it made him to wear the contraption. He felt that he wasn't worthy of it.

Maybe at the beginning, when he had first met Drake and wondered at the curious device, there would have been a thrill about wearing it, but not now. It had grown, in Will's mind, into an emblem of Drake's mastery of this underworld, a symbol of the man's standing, like a crown. It spoke of Drake's willingness to go up against the Styx and his supremacy over the motley pack of renegades who roamed the Deeps — and, in Will's estimation, Drake was set apart from these. He was the epitome of all that Will would like to become: tough, practical, and answerable to no one.

Elliott gathered up some further equipment and brought it over to the packs. Dropping it, she passed Will without so much as a glance and disappeared into the corridor. She was back a few moments later with a box of stove guns.

"Pack these and then we're out of here."

Will placed the guns in the backpacks, which, together with the other bags, he ferried over to the entrance of the base. He tied the end of the rope around the whole cargo and managed to lower it to the tunnel floor. He didn't relish the prospect of hauling it all across the causeway and back to the island — it weighed a ton, and he suspected he'd be the one to bear the greater proportion of it.

As he stood by the top of the rope, he noticed that Elliott was walking slowly from room to room. Was she checking to make sure she hadn't forgotten anything or just having a last look, suspecting she'd never see the place again?

"OK, let's go," she said as she joined him by the entrance.

She slid down the rope, and as soon as they were both at the bottom he untied the packs and bags. As he straightened up, he noticed she appeared to be reading a roll of material.

"What's that?" he said.

She snapped at him to be quiet. When she'd finished she looked across at him.

Will just stared back.

"The message is about Drake . . . it was pinned to the rope," she replied. "It's from another renegade."

"But . . . but I only just let the . . . I didn't see anyone," Will stammered, scanning the shadows, terrified that they were going to be ambushed by the likes of that creepy Tom Cox.

"No, you wouldn't have, and anyway, this is from someone we know — a friend. We need to get a move on," she said. From one of the bags, she whipped out the biggest charge Will had seen so far. She anchored the gunmetal-gray canister, the size of a large can of paint, to the rock wall under where the rope hung, then she backed toward the opposite side of the tunnel, feeding out an almost invisible trip wire behind her. Will didn't have to ask: Elliott was setting a powerful explosive in case anyone came looking for the base — so powerful that the whole place would be buried under tons of rubble.

She tested her handiwork, plucking the tautly stretched wire, which gave a threatening twang. After pulling out the pin to arm it, she returned to Will.

"So what now? Do we take this with us?" he said, pointing at the bags.

"Forget it."

"We're not going to the island?"

"Change of plan," she said, her eyes flashing with a fierce determination. He knew then that she had something else in mind, and that they weren't going to go back to join Chester and Cal.

"Oh," Will said as it sank in.

"We've got to get to the other side of the plain, and quick." She looked furtively up and down the tunnel, sniffing several times.

"Why?" Will asked, to which she held up her hand, silencing him.

He heard it, too. A low whine. Even as he listened, the whining grew louder and louder until it became a howl. He felt the gentle breeze on his face and saw it tug at the ends of Elliott's shemagh.

"A Levant," she said, then exclaimed, "the wind's coming: Just our luck!"

Will reeled on his feet as if about to collapse at the thought of facing it, exposed, in the Deeps. Elliott eyed him with concern, then ferreted around in her pocket and offered some more of the root. He took several pieces and chewed on them grimly, tasting the sourness as it spread over his tongue.

"Better?" she asked.

He nodded in acknowledgment, seeing in her eyes not the concern of a friend, but something cold and detached, a clinical professionalism. She needed someone to assist her; she didn't really care about *him*.

"Try the headset," she ordered as he continued to chew.

He nodded, flipping down the eyepiece, then fumbling for the switch on the box in his pocket. There was a faint tone — it began to build, reaching a high pitch and then descending in octaves to a lower sound, so barely audible that he couldn't tell if he was hearing it or just feeling it through his cranium.

"Shut your left eye — just use the one behind the lens," Elliott directed him.

He did as she said, blinking his left eye shut, but could see nothing at all through his right eye, the lens tightly pressed to it. Just as he was beginning to think the device might be faulty, dim points started to swirl, as if ocean waters were being stirred to reveal an eerie phosphorescence beneath their depths. From an initial amber, it rapidly transformed into a brighter yellow, until all the tiny points came together with such startling brilliance it almost hurt. Everything was intensely visible, as if bathed in stark sunlight. He looked around, at his dirt-ingrained hands, at Elliott securing the shemagh over her face, at the wisps of blurry darkness rolling toward them.

"Have you been in a Black Wind before?" Elliott asked.

"Not *in* one," he said, remembering when he and Cal had watched the clouds from behind closed windows in the Colony. Cal's words came back to him: The boy had mimicked a nasal Styx voice: "*. . . pernicious to those that it encounters, it sears the flesh.*"

Will quickly looked at Elliott. "Aren't they, like, poisonous?"

"No." She snorted derisively. "It's only dust, garden-variety *dust*, blown up from the Interior. You shouldn't believe anything the White Necks tell you."

"I don't," Will replied indignantly.

She hefted up her rifle and turned toward the Great Plain. "Let's roll."

He followed behind her, his heart yammering against his rib cage from both the effects of the strange root and anticipation. The X-ray-like vision that the headset gave him, cutting through the darkness like an invisible searchlight, lifted his spirits.

As soon as Will emerged from the water on the other side of the sump, he saw that the landscape was already laced with feathery tendrils of darkness. The spumelike clouds would soon blot out everything. Drake's night-vision device would be of no help whatsoever in these conditions.

"These storms are really thick—won't we get lost?" he asked Elliott as the blackness bled toward them.

"Not a chance," she said dismissively, passing a length of rope around her wrist, knotting it, then giving him the other end to tie around his waist. "Where this goes, you go," she said. "But if you feel me tug twice, you stop dead. Got that?"

"Righto," he replied, feeling a bit removed from the whole situation.

They moved fleetly, sinking into the inkiness so that he couldn't see her even though she was only a few feet in front of him. The smokelike fog clogged his nostrils and coated his face in a fine, dry dust. Several times he was forced to clutch at his nose to stifle a sneeze, and his left eye, unprotected by the night-vision device, was clotted and watering.

He felt two tugs and halted immediately, crouching low while he scanned around alertly. Elliott slipped out of the mist and kneeled down, signaling with a finger pressed to her lips that he should remain silent.

She leaned into him until the shemagh over her mouth brushed his ear. "Listen," she whispered through it.

He heard the faraway howling of a dog. Then . . . a horrible scream.

A man's scream.

Of the most acute agony.

Elliott's head was inclined to one side, and her eyes—the only part of her that he could see—told him nothing.

"We must hurry."

Horrible prolonged wails of suffering wafted backward and forward as if channeled between the palls of smoke, which sometimes cleared to give them a fleeting view of the ground or made strange, shifting corridors down which they moved.

Louder and louder the cries came, accompanying the low howls of dogs, as if some grisly opera of perdition were being sung.

The ground began to rise under Will's feet and his boot crunched on a pink crystal — a desert rose. They were climbing the slope to the large amphitheater-like clearing where Drake and Elliott had first sneaked up on him and Chester. The same place he had witnessed the horrific slaughter of renegades and Coprolites by the Limiters.

There was a high keening — more animal than human — immediately followed by a sudden, soul-searing scream. Will couldn't pinpoint from which direction it had come — it was as if it had hit the stone roof above and was falling and scattering in a rain of noise all around him. The combination of that noise, which made his stomach churn with fear, and the memory of the Styx's murderous actions made him want to fall to the loose surface of the slope and wrap his arms over his head. But he couldn't; the rope between him and Elliott was uncompromising, urging him on, drawing him toward something he knew he didn't want to see.

She tugged twice and he stood still.

She was at his side before he knew it. She waved him forward with a slow gesture of her hand, ending it with a patting motion. He nodded, understanding: She wanted him to advance cautiously, keeping as low as possible.

As they crawled, she kept stopping without warning. He bumped his head against her boots several times. But she never stopped for long. Will assumed she was listening to check for anyone close by.

The Black Wind seemed to be abating. Little stretches of the slope opened before them, fuzzy scenes of the moonscape surface. Will's night-vision device occasionally blanked and then became a static snowstorm before it reset. These blips only lasted for fractions of a second, but they brought back memories of the times his mother — his adoptive mother, as he had to keep reminding himself — flew into a rage because her beloved TV was on the fritz. Will shook his head — those days were so easy and carefree, and so ridiculously inconsequential.

The appalling screaming rose again from somewhere up ahead. They could hear it so much more clearly now. Elliott froze and looked back at him over her shoulder, her eyes furtive and terrified. Her fear was infectious — he felt it wash through him like a cold wave.

Why had they come here? What was it? What was wrong?

He was confused by Elliott's reaction. If the massacre he'd witnessed here before, with Chester, was being repeated, then it wouldn't have warranted such a response. She'd kept cool on that occasion, disturbing as the incident had been.

They continued to crawl on their bellies, arm over arm, across the gypsum, inching up the incline until the wind blew harder on their faces and whipped up tiny dust devils around them.

The carbon pall of the Black Wind was retreating.

They came to the rim of the crater.

Elliott's rifle was already up.

She said something, muffled and indistinct under the layers of cloth covering her mouth. She pulled back the shemagh, pressing her cheek hard into the stock of the rifle. She was shaking, the barrel of the gun quivering unsteadily. *Why? What was wrong?*

Everything was happening too fast.

The lens over his eye crackled with static again, like a machine blink, and then he focused on the scene. There were lights on tripod stands, randomly arranged, and a decent number of figures, too far away for him to make out in any detail. A haze of dust clouds drifted in the intervening distance, like random curtains sweeping across his view, sometimes drawing apart to reveal the scene, sometimes closing to obscure it.

He moved across to Elliott, coiling the rope that connected them as he went.

"What is it?" he whispered, close to her ear.

"I think . . . I think it's Drake," she answered.

"So he's alive?" he gasped.

She didn't answer.

"They've got him prisoner?" he asked.

"Worse," she said, a tautness to her voice. "Tom Cox . . . he's there. He's gone over to the other side . . . he's working with the Styx. . . ." She lapsed into a croak that was swallowed by the howls of the wind.

"What are they doing to Drake?"

As she continued to look through her rifle scope, Elliott could hardly talk. "If it's really him, they're . . . a Limiter is . . ." She lifted her head from the rifle and shook it violently. "They're torturing him on a stake. Tom Cox is ... is laughing ... that evil smear of a —"

Another wail of agony, even more dreadful than the last, cut her off.

"I can't watch any longer ... I *can't* let this go on," she said, gritting her teeth determinedly and staring straight into Will's eyes, her pupils turned to the deepest, darkest amber through his night-vision device.

"I have to ... he'd do the same for me ...," she said as she adjusted the magnification on her scope. Digging her elbows into the dirt and bracing her arms to steady the rifle, she inhaled and exhaled several times in quick succession, then held in the final breath.

Will watched her dumbly. "Elliott?" he asked, his voice quavering. "You're not —?"

"Can't get a shot ... the clouds ... can't see ...," she said, letting out the breath.

The seconds passed, as long as years.

"Oh, Drake," she said, her words lost to the wind.

Then she inhaled again and took aim.

She fired.

The crack of the rifle made Will jump out of his skin. The report echoed around, rolling across the plain and back to him, time and time again, until there was just the whine of the Levant again in his ears.

Will peered into the inky distance, then at her.

She was shivering badly.

"I don't know if I did it ... the bloody, *bloody* clouds ... I ..."

She worked the bolt of the rifle to chamber a new round, then suddenly pushed the weapon at Will.

"You look."

He drew back.

"Take it," she ordered him.

He reluctantly held the rifle just as he'd seen Elliott do and, flipping the lens up over his eye, peered through the scope. It felt cold — and wet — but he couldn't think about that now. He was getting his bearings on the group down in the base of the crater. The scope was set on a high magnification, and in his inexperienced hands he panned it erratically as he tried to locate them.

There! He caught a glimpse of a Limiter!

He panned back. Another Limiter! No, it was the same one, standing by himself. Will held the rifle steady on him, the Styx's terrifying face in pin-sharp focus. Will's stomach fell through the floor: The Limiter was looking up, looking up at the ridge where he and Elliott were lying. Then Will saw other figures, other Styx, running behind him. He moved the scope.

Where's Drake?

The wizened form of Tom Cox came into focus. He was holding a blade — it shone in the light. Then Will saw the stake. On it was a body. He thought he recognized the jacket. *Drake!*

Will couldn't bear to look too closely, and he was assisted in this by the distance and the remaining clouds from the Black Wind. Just as he was getting a grip, he noticed that there was a darkness sprayed around Drake, all over the ground. Through the scope it was not red, but darker, and it reflected the light, like molten bronze. Will broke out into a cold sweat.

This is not real. I am not here.

"Did I get him?" Elliott pressed Will.

Will angled the rifle up so he could see only Drake's head.

"I can't tell. . . ."

Will couldn't see Drake's face; his head was bent forward.

Distant reports of shots echoed toward Will and Elliott. The Limiters were returning fire.

"Will, concentrate — they're homing in on us," Elliott hissed at him. "I need to know I did it."

Will tried to hold the scope steady on Drake's head. Clouds swirled in his field of view.

"Can't see. . . ."

"You must!" Elliott snapped, her voice distorted with desperation.

Then Drake's head moved.

"Oh God!" Will exhaled with horror. "Looks like he's still alive." *Try not to think.*

"Put another round in him . . . quickly," Elliott begged.

"No way!" Will spat.

"Do it! Put him out of his misery."

Will shook his head. *I am not here. This is not me. This is not happening.*

"No way," he gasped again, feeling as though he was going to cry. "I can't do that!"

"Just do it. We don't have time. They'll be coming."

Will raised the rifle and took in a shuddering breath.

"Don't jerk the trigger . . . squeeze it off . . . smoothly . . . ," Elliott said.

He shifted the crosshairs from Drake's head, resting them squarely on the man's chest. Will told himself he would be less likely to miss him there. But this was all crazy, haywire. Will didn't have it in him to actually kill anyone.

"I can't do this."

"You must," Elliott pleaded. "He'd do it for us. You have to. . . ."

Will tried to silence his mind. *This is not real. I am watching a movie. These are not my actions.*

"Help him," she said. "Now!"

Will's whole body tensed, rebelling at what it knew he must do. The intersection of the crosshairs moved unsteadily, but it was roughly on the right place, aiming at the heart of the man he admired so much, now horribly mutilated. *Do it, do it, do it!* Increasing the pressure on the trigger, he shut his eyes. The rifle went off. He cried out as it bucked in his hands, the telescopic sight ramming his brow as it recoiled. He'd never shot a rifle before. Breathing rapidly, he lowered the weapon.

The sharp tang of cordite from the shot filled Will's nostrils. The smell, so reminiscent of fireworks, would mean something completely different to him from that moment on. More than that, it was as if Will was now marked, as if things would never again be the same. *I will carry this with me until the day I die. I might have killed a man!*

Elliott leaned against Will, passing her arms through his, their faces touching as she worked the bolt of the rifle. The

467

intimacy meant nothing in that instant. The spent cartridge spun into the darkness as she rammed a new round into the chamber. Will tried to pass the weapon to her, but she pushed back, wrenching up the muzzle of the rifle. "No! Make sure!" she ordered in a hissed shout.

Will reluctantly put his eye to the scope again, trying to locate the stake and Drake's body. He couldn't. The view zoomed this way and that, a blur. Then he found it, but his supporting arm slipped. He tried again. And saw . . .

Rebecca.

She was standing between two tall Limiters, somewhere to the left of Drake.

She was looking in his direction. Straight at him.

He felt like he was falling.

"Did you get him?" Elliott asked, her voice a croak.

But Will was locked on Rebecca. Her hair was drawn back tightly, and she was dressed in one of the Limiters' long coats with the blocklike patches of camouflage.

It was her.

He saw her face.

She was smiling.

She waved.

More gunshots rang out, spits of lead reaming through what was left of the misty clouds. As the Limiters zeroed in, shots landed nearer to him and Elliott, one so close that shards of rock pelted them.

"Did you?"

"I think so," he said to Elliott.

"Make sure," she pleaded.

He scanned quickly over Drake's body and the stake, but Rebecca was again in his sight, large as life. She seemed to have taken off her coat in the short time since he had first spotted her, and had moved way over to the other side of the stake. Suddenly he thought how easy it would be to shoot her. But even though he might have just killed Drake, he knew he didn't have the stomach to kill Rebecca — despite the intense hatred he felt for her.

"Well?" Elliott said, cutting through his thoughts.

"Yes, I think so," he lied as he pushed the rifle back at her. He had no idea whether he'd hit Drake, and didn't want to know.

He just didn't want to know.

And Rebecca. She had been there while the ghastly torture had been going on.

His little sister!

Her smiling face, her smug, self-satisfied face — the same face that had confronted him time and time again when he was late for dinner or tracked mud onto the carpet or left the light on in the bathroom . . . a disapproving and superior smile that spoke of authority and even domination. . . .

He had to escape, to get away.

He got up, yanking Elliott with him by the rope. They ran wildly down the slope, as fast as they could, Will almost pulling Elliott off her feet.

As they reached the bottom of the incline, there was a flash of light. Amplified by the lens of Drake's device, it filled his eye with a searing, painful brilliance. He yelped. But no, it wasn't the Limiters, it was the electrical storm that always followed a Black Wind. The exposed hairs on his head and forearms bristled with the static.

Massive sparkling balls of electrical discharge bobbed and rolled around them. There came another blinding flash and a deafening whiplash crack. A huge serpentine tongue of blue lightning speared horizontally over the ground, then split in two, each prong multiplying into many more until the tiny forks disappeared into nothing. The air was thick with the reek of ozone, just as if it was a true Topsoil thunderstorm.

"Turn that off!" he heard Elliott call, but he was already fumbling for the brass switch on the box in his pocket. He knew that the intense light might damage the night-vision device. There were so many crackling spheres of angry light spinning out from the remaining dust clouds, rolling around the plain in all directions, that the whole area was lit up like an exploding fireworks factory.

Will heard shots and caught the vicious barking of dogs.

"Stalkers!" he yelled at Elliott.

She snatched a leathery wallet from inside her jacket and ripped off the top. She scattered its contents over the ground as they went, then threw down the empty wallet and kept moving. A small electrical ball of spluttering sparks zipped not inches from her, like some delinquent Tinkerbell, but she didn't slow, almost passing through its circumference.

They came to the edge of the Great Plain.

Then they were in one of the lava tubes, and in darkness again, the glow of the electrical storm flickering faintly behind them. Turning his headset back on, Will saw that Elliott was again taking another of the leathery packets from inside her jacket as she ran.

"What're you doing? What is that stuff?" Will panted.

"Parchers."

"Huh?"

"Stops the stalkers dead in their tracks. Burns them something awful," she told him, pointing to her nose with a malicious grin.

He looked back and caught the sublime glow of pure yellow as some of the powder fell in a pool of water. He knew he'd seen it before . . . it was giving off the same glow as the bacteria that he, Chester, and Cal had come across. *Genius.* If a dog sniffed it up, it would scorch its nasal membranes. He laughed. It would render them useless as trackers.

They ran and ran. He fell, sprawling, knocking his chin against the rough ground. Elliott helped him up. As he leaned against the wall, trying to get back his breath, she rigged a charge across the tunnel.

She shouted him on again.

36

WILL BLASTED into the clearing and skidded to a halt. With his hands on his knees, he bent over, gulping hard to get air into his lungs.

Chester and Cal both leaped to their feet in surprise. Will was an alarming sight: his face filthy from the dust storm and streaked with sweat, Drake's lens over one of his eyes, and the skin around the other smeared with fresh blood from the cut on his brow when he'd fallen.

"Wh-what's happened?" Chester stuttered.

"That's not Drake's, is it?" Cal asked the same time, pointing to the headset.

"I . . . had . . . to . . . ," Will got out between breaths.

Still gasping and swallowing air, he shook his head.

"I . . . ," he tried again.

"We killed Drake," Elliott said flatly, stepping out from behind Will and into the weak light cast by Cal's lantern. "At least we think we did. Will finished him off." The air was thick with insects, swarms of them, the size of malnourished mosquitoes, and she waved her hand in front of her face to shoo them away. Then she glanced down around her feet and plucked a frond from a fern, which she crushed in her hand.

She swiped her palm across her forehead and cheeks. The effect was miraculous, the insects immediately avoiding her as if she were protected by an invisible force field.

"Will did *what*?" Cal asked as Chester, already itching with bug bites, took a frond from the same fern and repeated Elliott's quick ritual. Will seemed to be oblivious to the insects crawling all over his face; his uncovered eye was glazed as it stared into the distance.

"We had to. They were torturing him. That scum bucket Tom Cox was there, too, helping them," Elliott said huskily, then spat on the ground.

"No," Chester said, aghast.

"And Rebecca," Will added, still gazing at nothing in particular. Elliott's head jerked toward him, and he continued, still puffing. "She was with the Limiters." He paused to gulp down more air. "Somehow she knew I was there. I swear she was looking straight at me. . . . She smiled at me. She waved!"

"Now you tell me!" Elliott growled. "With Cox switching sides it was risky enough us going to the base for the equipment. But now there's no way I'm going to take that chance. Not with that Styx out for your blood."

Will bowed his head, still struggling to get his breath back. "Perhaps it would be better if I . . . if I gave myself up. It might put an end to all this. It might stop her."

For an agonizing few seconds all eyes were on Will, and he looked from one face to another, hoping none of them would agree with his suggestion. Then Elliott spoke up.

"No, I don't think it'd make any difference," she said with the bleakest of expressions and, picking a fragment of fern from her upper lip, spat again. "I don't think that would help any of us. This Rebecca sounds like the type who makes a clean sweep of things."

"Oh, she is that," Will agreed despondently. "She certainly likes everything to be tidy."

37

"**W**HOA, BOY!"

Sarah careered around a turn in the lava tube, her feet sending out a slew of gravel as Bartleby tore forward, almost wrenching her over.

"Easy, easy!" she shouted, digging in her heels and using all her strength to try to rein him back. Within a few feet she managed to bring him to a stop. Still breathing heavily from the effort, she grabbed his collar and held him tight. She was grateful for the brief rest; the muscles in her arms were burning, and she sincerely doubted she'd be able to keep the cat in check for much longer if he didn't let up a little.

As he stiffly twisted his head around, she could see a large vein throbbing under the flaking gray skin of his wide temple, and the flickering wildness in his eyes. His nostrils flared wide: The scent was strong now, and he was well on the trail.

She rewrapped the thick leather leash around her chafed hand. Readying herself with a couple of deep breaths, she then released Bartleby's collar. He surged forward, the leash giving a resounding *thwack* as it snapped taut again.

"Steady, Bartleby!" she gasped. This command struck a chord of sorts in the overexcited animal's brain, and he eased up slightly.

As she continued to talk soothingly to the cat, pleading with him to keep calm, she felt the disapproval radiating from the four shadows lurking a little way off. The quartet of Limiters, unlike her and the crazed cat, moved as silently as ghosts. They usually blended in so well with the terrain that they were invisible but, at the moment, they were allowing themselves to be seen, as if they wanted her to feel intimidated. If that was the intention, it was certainly having the desired effect.

She felt profoundly uneasy.

Rebecca had promised her a free hand to track down Will. So why the escort? And why had Rebecca gone to the trouble of involving her at all, when she had absolutely no experience in this environment and when highly skilled soldiers were being deployed at the same time? It didn't add up.

With this thought burning in the back of her mind, Bartleby lurched forward again, dragging her after him whether she wanted to go or not.

Elliott took them out of the clearing and through some dense scrub, Will stumbling and thrashing behind. They found themselves on a strip of shoreline again. She took them along the water's edge and a short distance into what, in the pitch-black, looked like the beginning of an inlet.

Will was in a bad way. The effects of the root had worn off and his fatigue had caught up. He walked stiff-legged, like some sort of Frankenstein's monster, the headset only adding to this impression. Elliott watched him closely.

"He's fried; he needs some shut-eye," she said to Chester and Cal, as if Will wasn't present — and indeed he didn't react to her comment, swaying where he stood. "He's no use to anyone right now."

Chester and Cal exchanged looks.

"No use?" Chester echoed.

"Yes, and that's not good enough." She turned to Cal, running her eye over him. "How about you? How's the leg, kid?"

Chester realized that she was evaluating them and it put him on edge. He didn't delude himself that they all needed to be up to the challenge of escaping from the Styx. But her question was more than a little ominous.

"His leg's much better. He's been resting it," he put in quickly, throwing a sharp look at Cal, who was a little surprised at Chester's intervention.

"Can't he speak for himself?" Elliott glowered.

"Oh, yes, sorry," Chester mumbled apologetically.

"So how is it?"

"Like Chester said . . . much better," Cal replied, flexing his leg to try to put Elliott's mind at rest. In truth it was incredibly stiff, and each time he put any weight on it he didn't know if it was going to support him or not.

Elliott studied Cal's face for a second, then switched her attention to Chester, who wondered whether he would come up to scratch. But before she could issue any judgments, Will mumbled the word *tired* — just once — sat down heavily, and flopped onto his back. Snoring loudly, he immediately fell into the deepest of slumbers.

"He's out. He'll be as right as rain in a couple of hours," Elliott said, then addressed Cal. "You stay with your brother." She handed him the loose rifle scope. "And keep an eye on the foreshore . . . particularly the causeway." She pointed at the sea and the impenetrable blackness. "I need to know if you see anything, anything at all, however small. It's really important you stay alert . . . got that?"

"Why, where are you going?" Cal asked, trying to keep the anxiety from his voice. He'd been worried before that he would be abandoned, and now that Elliott had lost Drake, the fear returned in spades. Was she planning to slope off with Chester and leave him and Will high and dry?

"Not far . . . just need to do some foraging," she told him. "Look after this, too," she said, shrugging off her rucksack and dropping it beside Will's still form. That single action allayed Cal's fears — Elliott wasn't going to get very far without her kit. He watched as she pulled out a couple of sacks from the side pocket and then, accompanied by Chester, slipped into the darkness.

"How are you doing?" Chester asked Elliott as he walked beside her. He was using the lantern on its lowest setting, shielding it with his hand so there was the thinnest strip of light to illuminate the way. As ever, Elliott didn't require any light, seeming to possess a preternatural awareness of her surroundings. They were moving deeper into the inlet, keeping the dense undergrowth to their left and the sea to their right.

Elliott didn't reply to his question, maintaining a brooding silence. Knowing how distraught she must be at Drake's death, Chester felt compelled to say something, but found it incredibly difficult to do so. Although he'd spent a considerable amount of time with her on their numerous patrols together, it wasn't as though they spoke much on these outings. He realized he hadn't actually gotten to know her any better since that day when she and Drake had grabbed him and Will. She kept to herself, as elusive as a faint breeze in the dead of night that you could feel but you couldn't touch.

He tried again.

"Elliott, are you . . . are you *really* all right?"

"Don't you worry 'bout me," came the curt response.

"I just want you to know we're all very sorry about Drake. . . . We owe him for . . . for everything." Chester paused for a few moments. "Was it awful, back there, when Will had to . . . uh . . . to . . . ?"

Without any warning she came to a stop and shoved him hard in the chest, with such unbridled aggression that Chester was completely taken aback. "Don't try to mollycoddle me! I don't need anyone's sympathy!"

"I wasn't—"

"Just drop it, will you?"

"Look, I'm worried about you," he said indignantly. "We're all worried about you."

As she stood there, she seemed to mellow a little, and there was a huskiness to her voice when she finally spoke. "I just can't accept that he's dead." She let out a sob. "He often talked of the day that would come for one or both of us, and that it was just another turn of the wheel. He said you have to be prepared for it but not let it drag you down. He said not to look back, and to make the most of the moment you're in. . . ." She repositioned her rifle over her shoulder, fidgeting with the strap. "I'm trying to do that, but it's hard."

As Chester looked at her, her face hazy in the dim light cast by his lantern, the tough exterior seemed to drop away, revealing a very frightened, very lost teenage girl. Perhaps, for the first time, he was seeing the *real* Elliott.

"We're in this together," he said warmly, his heart going out to her.

"Thanks," she replied in a subdued voice, avoiding his eyes. "We should get going."

They came eventually to a small strip of shoreline that appeared as if a shadow was cast across it. As Chester discovered when he examined it more closely, this had nothing to do with the light: A darker and heavier sediment had collected in these shallow waters.

"Should be rich pickings here," Elliott announced, and handed the sacks to Chester. She walked into the water and, stooping over, passed her hands through it.

Stepping sideways and still searching, she moved along the margin of the water, then suddenly straightened up with an exultant yell. A large animal flapped in her hands. A foot and a half from head to tail, its silvery body resembled a flattened cone with undulating fins down either side, which rippled crazily as if it was trying to swim away through the air. On the top of its head it had a pair of huge, black, compound eyes, and on the underside were two grasping appendages with spines extending from them; these were trying to curl around to reach Elliott's hands as she fought to keep her grip on the beast. She spun around and splashed back to the beach, Chester falling over in an effort to get out of her way.

"Yipes!" he cried. "What's that?"

Elliott swung down the animal, smashing it against a rock. Chester didn't know if she'd killed it or merely stunned it, but it seemed to still be moving, only very slowly now.

She rolled it onto its back, and Chester saw the two appendages still flexing and its circular mouth, lined around its circumference with tens of glistening white needles.

"They're called night crabs. Really tasty."

Chester swallowed, so disgusted he thought he was going to be sick. "I swear it's just a ginormous silverfish," he groaned. He was still lying where he'd fallen. Elliott glanced at the sacks where he'd dropped them, marched over, and pushed the animal inside one.

"That's the main course," she said. "Now let's —"

"Don't tell me you're going to catch another of those things," Chester pleaded, his voice high, bordering on hysterical.

"No, that's not likely," she replied. "Night crabs are pretty scarce. And only the younger ones come this far in to feed. We lucked out."

"Yeah, score," Chester said, only now standing up and brushing himself down.

Elliott was already back in the water, this time shoving her arms deep into the mud. "And *these* are what the crab was looking for," she informed Chester. Thick mud covered her arms up to the elbows as she pulled them out. She held her hand out to Chester so he could see the two curved shells in her palm.

"What a treat: mollusks! I'll see if there are any more."

Chester gave an involuntary shudder at the idea that she actually expected him to eat any of these creatures.

"Go on, knock yourself out," he said.

As they made their way back along the beach, Chester had an intimation that things weren't as they should be. A complete lack of movement; no wave or call of acknowledgment from Cal. Elliott, livid, made straight for the boy. Although he was still in a sitting position, his head hung awkwardly forward as he dozed next to his brother, who was similarly dead to the world.

"Doesn't anyone listen to me around here?" she said to Chester. She was apoplectic — he could hear the breath hissing between her teeth. "Didn't I make it clear he needed to keep on his toes?"

"Yes, you did," Chester answered loudly.

"Shush!" she ordered him as she moved a small distance down the beach, where she raised her rifle to scour the horizon. Chester waited by the two slumbering boys until she returned.

"Drake wouldn't have let this go," she said tensely, pacing up and down behind Cal like a lioness about to strike. Cal remained blissfully unaware of her silent fury, his head swaying gently as he slept on.

"What do you mean?" Chester asked, trying to read the look in her eyes.

"He would've dumped him here. Upped camp and let him fend for himself," she said.

"That's way harsh — how long do you think Cal would last on his own?" Chester objected. "It would be like passing a death sentence on him!"

"Too bad."

"You can't do that to him," Chester spluttered. "You have to cut him some slack. The poor kid's absolutely knackered. We all are."

But she was deadly serious.

"Don't you get it? By falling asleep, he might have dragged us all down with him," she said as she threw a glance over the water. "We don't know what they're going to throw at us next. . . . If it's Limiters, *I* probably won't even see them coming. But it could be civilians — they're often sent in as the vanguard because they're a dime a dozen — pure cannon fodder, collateral. That's how the Styx operate sometimes . . . the soldiers follow in later on to mop up."

"Yes, but—" Chester said.

"No, you listen. You make one mistake and you'll end up facedown in that," she said frostily, thumbing at the sea. She deliberated for a moment, then slung her rifle over her shoulder, stepped behind Cal, and slapped him hard on the back of the head.

"ARGHHHHHH!" he cried, smacked wide awake. He leaped up, his arms waving wildly. Then he realized that it had been Elliott and glared at her.

"S'pose this is your idea of a joke?" he said, huffing resentfully. "Well, I don't think it's funny. . . ."

At the sight of her stony face, his protestations shriveled on his lips.

"You do not fall asleep on watch!" she barked menacingly.

"No," he said, smoothing down his shirt and looking thoroughly abashed.

"Thought I heard voices," Will said drowsily, rubbing his eyes with his knuckles as he sat up. "What's going on?"

"Nothing, just getting dinner ready," Elliott told him. Unseen by Will, she gave Cal a last lingering stare as she swiped her hand across her throat in a cutting motion. He nodded glumly.

Elliott dug a hollow in the sand, then dispatched Chester and Cal to collect some brush, which she placed around its edge. Once everything was to her satisfaction, she lit a small fire deep in the pit. As it grew, she further adjusted the brush as a precaution against any stray light leaking out.

While she was busy tending the flames, Will staggered over to a series of rock pools by the sea's edge. He swung up the lens from over his eye and doused his face with water. Then he seemed to take forever to clean his hands, alternately scrubbing them with wet sand and rinsing them, repeating the process over and over again in a slow, methodical way.

"Do you think I should check on him? He's acting a bit strange," Chester asked Elliott as he watched his friend's compulsive behavior. "What's wrong with his hands?"

"Aftereffects," she said simply, leaving Chester and Cal none the wiser.

Both boys were actually relieved that the opportunity to talk to Will hadn't presented itself. The act of killing had set him apart, putting him in a place they couldn't begin to understand.

So how should they treat him? The question was at the forefront of both their minds. They certainly couldn't pat him on the back and congratulate him. Should they try to commiserate with him over Drake's death, to console him, when he'd been the cause? The reality was that they were more than a little in awe of Will. How did *he* feel about what he'd done? Not only did he have blood on his hands from shooting and killing another human being, it was Drake . . . one of their own . . . their guardian and friend . . . *his* friend.

As Chester gave Elliott a considered look, he wondered again how she was dealing with it. After her brief moment of vulnerability on the beach, she seemed to have reverted to her old self and to be throwing herself wholeheartedly into looking after them. Chester's train of thought was broken as Elliott hoisted the night crab out of the sack and dropped it onto the sand. It was just as lively as when she'd caught it, and she had to place her foot on it to stop it from escaping.

Chester saw that Will was coming toward them. His movements were still sluggish, as if he wasn't yet fully awake. Although dripping with water, he hadn't washed his face very successfully: Large sooty patches persisted under his eyes and across his forehead and neck, and dark smudges dappled his white hair. Under different circumstances, Chester might have joked that Will bore a striking resemblance to a panda.

Will came to a halt a short distance away, refusing to make eye contact with any of them. Instead he bowed his head to look at his feet and scratched at the palm of his hand with an index finger, as if trying to remove something from it with his nail.

"What did I do?" he said. It was difficult to understand him; his speech was slurred as if his mouth was numb, and still he didn't cease picking at his hand.

"Stop that!" Elliott said sharply.

Will quit scratching and let his arms hang limply at his sides, his shoulders sagging. As Chester watched, a droplet detached itself from Will's face and sparkled momentarily as it caught the light. But Chester couldn't tell if it was a tear or merely seawater.

"Look at me," Elliott ordered Will.

Will didn't move.

"I said *look* at me!"

Will raised his head and regarded Elliott groggily.

"That's better. Now let's get something straight . . . we did what we had to," she told him firmly, then softened her voice. "I'm not thinking about it. . . . You do the same."

"I . . . ," he stammered, shaking his head slowly.

"No, don't. . . . Listen to me. You made the second shot because I couldn't. I failed Drake, but you didn't. You did the right thing . . . for him."

"OK," he eventually replied, the word almost lost in a sigh. "Did you mention something about dinner?" he asked after a long pause. The look of despair was still deep in his black-ringed eyes.

"How do you feel?" she asked, remembering the night crab she was standing on — and not a moment too soon, as it rippled its fins in the sand to dig itself out, frantically trying to get back to the water.

"Rough," he said. "My head's stopped buzzing, but my stomach feels like it's been on a roller coaster."

"You need to get some hot food in you," she said, lifting her foot from the night crab as she unsheathed her knife. The appendages under its head were flexing like animated TV antennae.

For a split second of silence, Will took in the creature, then cried out:

"Anomalocaris canadensis!"

To everyone's surprise, his demeanor went through a rapid transformation. He became wildly excited, jumping up and down and waving his arms.

Elliott flipped over the night crab and positioned her knife in the join between two segments on its flat belly.

"Hey!" Will screeched. "No!" He stuck out a hand to stop Elliott from killing it, but she was too quick. She pushed in the knife and the appendages on its head immediately went limp, ceasing their endless waving.

"No!" he shouted again. "How could you do that? It's an *Anomalocaris!*" He took a step toward her, his hand outstretched.

"Keep away from me," she warned him, holding up her knife, "or I'll skewer *you*."

"But . . . it's a fossil. . . . I mean . . . it's extinct. . . . I mean I've seen a fossil of it. . . . It's EXTINCT!" he yelled, becoming even more agitated as none of the others seemed to understand what he was trying to tell them.

"Really? Doesn't look too extinct to me," Elliott said, hefting the dead animal up before him.

"Don't you realize how important this is? You can't kill them! Leave the rest alone!" He'd noticed the second sack and wasn't shouting anymore, just yammering, as if he knew he wasn't going to get anywhere with Elliott.

"Will, chill, OK? The other sack's only got shells in it. And anyway, Elliott says there's a shed load of these crabs out there," Chester tried to tell him, motioning out to sea.

"But . . . but . . . !"

Elliott's expression of pure exasperation was enough to stop him from making any more of a fuss. He bit his lip, looking on in horror at the lifeless *Anomalocaris*.

"It was the biggest predator that swam the seas . . . the T. rex of the Cambrian period," Will mumbled forlornly. "It's been extinct for nearly five hundred and fifty million years."

When Elliott produced the mollusks, as she called them, from the second sack, Will was equally flabbergasted.

"Devil's toenails!" he gasped. "*Gryphaea arcuata.* I've got a box of them at home. I found them with my dad at Lyme Regis . . . but just fossils!"

So, with the impaled *Anomalocaris* suspended above the flames, Elliott, Cal, and Chester sat around the prehistoric barbecue, while Will sketched a living devil's toenail that he had begged from Elliott. Its brothers and sisters (or maybe both — Will couldn't quite recall if they were supposed to have been hermaphrodites) hadn't been so fortunate: Tucked into the hot embers at the edge of the fire, they sizzled softly.

Will was talking to himself and grinning inanely, with the sort of absolute absorption a young child might show when examining a creepy-crawly it has caught in the garden. "Yes, really thick shell . . . look at the growth rings . . . and there's the lid," Will said, tapping the end of his pencil on a flattened circle at the widest end of the shell. He looked up to find all eyes upon him. "This is just so cool! Do you know this was the predecessor to the oyster?"

"Drake mentioned something about that. He liked his raw," Elliott said matter-of-factly as she repositioned the *Anomalocaris* in the flames.

"None of you has the faintest idea how important the discovery of these animals is," Will said, becoming frustrated all over again by their total lack of interest. "How can you even think about eating them?"

"If you don't want yours, Will, I'll take it," Cal piped up. He turned to Chester. "What is an *oyster*, anyway?"

As the food cooked, Elliott brought up the bizarre corridor of sealed cells she had seen with Cal in the Bunker.

"We knew that there was some sort of quarantine area," she mused, "but not where it was or what it was for."

"Drake did say that, but how did you first hear about it?" Will inquired.

"From a contact," Elliott answered, hastily looking down. Will could have sworn he saw a flicker of unease in her eyes, but he told himself it must have been due to her discovery of the sickening cells.

"So all the people were dead," Chester stated.

"All except for the one man," Elliott said. "He was a renegade."

"The others were Colonists," Cal added. "You could tell from their clothes."

"But why would the Styx go to all the trouble of bringing Colonists down here just to kill them?" Chester asked.

"I don't know." Elliott shrugged. "They've always used the Deeps as testing grounds — that's nothing new — but all the signs now are that something big is about to break. Drake's idea was that the three of you might help us throw a monkey wrench into the works and mess up whatever the Blackheads are doing. Especially him over there." She made a face as she glanced at Will, who was still staring in horror at the cooking *Anomalocaris*. "Though I'm not too sure if Drake really thought that one through."

Elliott removed the *Anomalocaris* from the flames and put it on the ground. Then she peeled back one of the segments on its underbelly with the tip of her knife and began to carve up its carcass. "It's ready," she announced.

"Oh, great," Will said hollowly.

Nonetheless, when the food had been divided up, Will capitulated. Putting aside his journal, he began to eat his share, reluctantly at first, but then devouring it hungrily. He even agreed with Chester that the *Anomalocaris* was pretty similar to lobster. The devil's toenails were a different matter altogether, and the boys grimaced as they valiantly attempted to chew them.

"Hmmm. Interesting," Will commented as he finished his mouthful, pondering the thought that he was one of very few people alive who'd feasted on extinct animals. The image of him eating a dodo burger suddenly popped into his head, and he smiled uncomfortably.

"Yeah, really cool barbecue." Chester laughed, stretching out his legs. "It's sort of like being back home again."

Will nodded in response.

The invigorating gusts of wind, the crackles of the dying fire mingling with the crash of waves, and the taste of seafood in their mouths — all this made Chester and Will experience the deepest pangs of homesickness. These elements invoked other, carefree times back on the surface — it could have been a vacation outing or a beach party late one summer's evening (and although Will's family rarely went on such outings — not together, anyway — he was still moved by the notion).

But the more Will and Chester tried to pretend to themselves it was like *home*, the more they realized that it was no such thing, and that they were in a strange and dangerous place in which it was touch and go whether they made it through the next day. Trying to suppress these feelings, they made small talk, but the conversation soon petered out, and each fell to his own thoughts, eating the meal in silence.

Elliott had taken her food with her to the water's edge, and periodically raised her rifle to scour the distant beaches.

"Uh-oh," Cal said, and Will and Chester turned to look as she rose to her feet, letting her food slide from her lap. She held very still, her rifle fixed on something.

"Time to go!" she called over to them, her eye still glued to the scope.

"Did you see something?" Will asked.

"Yes, I caught a flash. . . . I thought we'd have more time before they reached the beaches. . . . It's probably an advance patrol."

Chester swallowed his mouthful in a noisy gulp.

38

"**YOU CRAZY**, crazy animal!" Sarah cried as she skied through the succulent plants, Bartleby pulling as he'd never pulled before. No doubt about it, he was hot on the scent trail of the boys — that was the good news. The bad news was that he was becoming more and more wild and unmanageable, and once or twice Sarah had thought that he was actually going to turn on and attack *her*.

"Slow down!" she shouted.

With a sharp snap, the leash went slack, and she lost her balance and fell flat on her back. The lantern slipped from her hand, spinning away and rebounding off the plants in its path, clicking up to its highest setting as it did so. Blinding rays of light strafed the tall trees behind her, intermittent flashes that would be visible for miles around. If she'd wanted to announce her presence, she couldn't have done a better job.

She was winded and couldn't move for a few long seconds. Then she crawled rapidly to where the lantern had come to rest and threw herself over it to hide its light. She lay on it, panting and cursing blindly. *Talk about rank amateurism!*

Still covering the lantern with her body, she switched it down again before turning her attention to the remains of the

492

leather leash wound around her hand. The end where it had snapped was ragged and torn, and, as she inspected it more closely, she saw teeth marks — Bartleby had been having a quick chew at it when she hadn't been looking. *The crafty so-and-so!* If she hadn't been so infuriated with herself, she might even have admired his guile.

The last glimpse she'd had of him was of his hindquarters, his back legs spinning in a blur and his large paws throwing up foliage as he tore off into the darkness.

"That infernal cat!" she said to herself, calling him every name under the sun. He'd cover quite some distance at the speed he was going, and she'd only be kidding herself if she thought there was some way to get him back. She'd lost her only means of finding Will and Cal. "Infernal cat," she said again, more despondently this time. Her only option now was to stick to the foreshore in the hope that it might still lead her to her quarry.

She picked herself up and broke into a trot, praying that Will hadn't peeled off in a totally different direction from the one Bartleby had been tracking. If he'd chosen a new route through the dense wall of foliage to her left, she didn't have a blind chance of finding him.

Half an hour later the sound of waves was supplanted by that of rushing water. She remembered what she'd seen on the map: some sort of crossing to an island. She cut down toward the sea, and the sound intensified.

She was almost at the causeway when, from out of nowhere, a shape materialized directly in her path. She nearly jumped out of her skin. It was a man. By now she was on the open beach,

with no cover for some distance around her — she had no idea
where he'd sprung from. In a fumbling panic, she swung the
rifle from her shoulder, nearly dropping it altogether in the
process.

She heard a harsh nasal laugh and stood absolutely still, the
rifle held defensively across her body. He was too close for her
to raise it up, anyway.

"Lost something?" he said in a contemptuous voice. He
took a step toward her, and she lifted the lantern a little. In its
dim glow she could make out the rugged face with its shadowed eye sockets.

A Limiter.

"Careless, very careless," he said, and thrust a rope roughly
into her hand. It had a loop on it.

She shook with fear, not knowing what to expect next. It
had been different on the train when Rebecca was with her.
Out here, she didn't relish the idea of being alone with these
monsters — particularly if she'd done something to displease
them. In these dark wilds, they were a law unto themselves.
The thought raced through her mind that handing her the rope
might be a prelude to them *hanging* her. Was this some kind of
game they were playing? Maybe they were going to execute her
because they considered her incompetent, a liability. And she
couldn't really blame them — she'd gotten everything wrong
so far.

But her fear was unfounded. Bartleby edged into view from
behind the Limiter's legs, the other end of the rope tied tightly
around his neck and secured by a slipknot. The cat's whole
deportment was hangdog, his tail tucked between his legs.

Sarah didn't know if the Limiter had given him a beating, but the animal had clearly had the living daylights scared out of him somehow. Bartleby couldn't have been more different; as Sarah pulled him toward her, he came without the slightest resistance.

"We're taking it from here." Another voice came from immediately behind her. She wheeled around to face a row of shadowy forms: the other three soldiers of the Limiter patrol. Although she hadn't seen hide nor hair of them for at least half a day, of course they must have been tailing her the whole time. She understood now why they had such a reputation for stealth; they really did move like phantoms. And she'd thought *she* was good.

Sarah cleared her throat. "No," she began meekly as she glanced in the direction of the splashing water where the causeway began. She held her gaze there, not wanting to meet the dead, staring eyes of the Limiter before her. "I'll take the Hunter on the trail . . . over to the island . . . to . . ."

"No need for that," said the single Limiter who was blocking her way, in a horribly quiet voice that was far more unsettling than a barked order. She could sense his anger that she'd dared to disagree with him. He moved his head sharply to the side and back again — it was a gesture of violence, a foretaste of what might follow if she continued to oppose him. "You've done enough already," he sneered.

"But Rebecca said . . . ," Sarah began, aware that this might be the last thing she *ever* said.

"Leave it to us," one of the Limiters growled from behind, and gripped her upper arm so painfully that she wanted to pull away. But she didn't, and she refused to turn to look at him. All four were standing very close to her now. One of them brushed her other arm, and she could feel their breath on the back of her neck. She was scared witless. A vivid picture swam into her mind, of them slicing her throat and leaving her where she fell.

"All right," she managed to whisper, and the hand crushing her arm eased its vise slightly. She lowered her head, already hating herself for not standing up to them. But better to go along with these savage men, she reasoned, than be executed on the spot. If they captured Will alive, she might yet get the chance to find out the truth about Tam's death. Rebecca had promised Sarah that she'd be able to execute Will herself — at least that meant she'd have some time to interrogate him.

"Go upcoast. The renegades might have some other means off the island," a Limiter hissed into her ear. The hand on her arm gave her a sudden push, and she stumbled a few paces. In the seconds she took to right herself, they had completely vanished. She was alone with just the breeze on her face and the most crushing sense of failure and shame. She'd come all this way only to be pulled off the chase. But she would have been a fool to resist Limiters. A dead fool.

She picked her way slowly along the foreshore, telling herself not to stop as she passed the causeway. But she did allow herself the briefest glance back. Although there was no sign of her Styx patrol, surely one of them was holding back to ensure that she obeyed their orders. She had no alternative but to go where they'd said, which she knew was a total waste of time. Will was on the island — holed up in a dead end with no way out — and she'd been so very, very close.

"Move it!" she snapped at Bartleby. "This is all your fault!"

She tugged hard on the rope. He followed obediently, but pointed his head toward the causeway, whimpering. He knew as well as she did that they were going in the completely wrong direction.

39

IN A CAVERNOUS area, the suggestion of a track. A narrow strip just discernible through the rock field. It could have been naturally formed . . . Dr. Burrows wasn't sure.

He looked more closely and . . . there! . . . yes! . . . he saw the broad flagstones, laid end to end. He used the tip of his boot to scuff away the gravel and expose the gaps between them, which occurred at regular intervals. No question, then, it definitely wasn't a natural feature . . . and as he progressed farther along, a small flight of steps came into view. He mounted them and stopped. Noting that the path continued into the distance, he began to scrutinize the area, and discovered there were squared-off stones standing proud of the ground on both sides.

"Yes! These have been fashioned!" he mumbled to himself. And then he saw they were arranged in lines. He leaned forward to examine them. No, not in *lines*, they were arranged into *squares*.

"Rectilinear structures!" Dr. Burrows exclaimed, his excitement growing. "They're ruins!" Unhooking his blue-handled geological hammer from his belt, he stepped from the track, peering wildly around at the ground by his feet as he went.

"Foundations?" He bent to feel the regular blocks, brushing off pebbles and using the tip of his hammer to heave aside chunks of loose rubble from around them. He nodded in response to his own question, a smile crinkling his dirt-stained face.

"No doubt about it, these are foundations." He straightened up and saw more rectangles, the shapes receding into the darkness. "Was this once a *settlement*?" But as he looked even farther afield, he began to appreciate the scale of what he'd stumbled upon. "No, it was bigger than that! More like a *town*!"

Replacing his geological hammer on his belt, he mopped his brow. The heat was stultifying in here, and the sound of trickling water came from close by. Long ribbons of steam laced the air, slowly drifting past each other like party streamers in slow motion. A pair of small bats flitted by, disrupting the ribbons with the rapid beat of their wings.

The huge dust mite clacked gently as it waited for him like a well-trained dog back on the path. It had followed him for the last mile as he'd made his way along. While Dr. Burrows enjoyed the companionship, he didn't delude himself as to the creature's motives. It was plainly after more of his food.

The breakthrough that he could read the ancient language of the people who had once inhabited these parts had ignited his passion for further knowledge about them. Now, if only he could find some artifacts that would enable him to formulate a picture of how they lived. He was nosing around in the foundations, searching for anything that might help him, when a call resonated through the still heat of the cavern. A strident, low screech that echoed from the walls.

A rushing sound, something like a *whoomf,* followed. It came from somewhere above him.

The dust mite was immediately as still as a statue.

"What the . . . ?" Dr. Burrows looked up but was unable to spot the source of the sounds. It was only then that he realized he couldn't see any roof to the cavern. It was as though he was standing in the bottom of a massive crevasse. He'd been so preoccupied with the discovery of the ruins that he hadn't taken the time to inspect the surroundings.

He slowly moved his light orb so that it was poised above his head. In the gloom he could just make out the sheer stretches of the crevasse sides, gently undulating vertical folds of stone with the texture of a Cadbury's Flake, rising up to darkness. The color wasn't that dissimilar, either, only the rock was a lighter hue of brown. Deprived for so long of his beloved chocolate bar and the daily fixes that were such a part of his life back in Highfield, his mind began to wander and his mouth water. This craving reminded him how phenomenally hungry he was — the supplies the Coprolites had provided were hardly very appetizing or, indeed, very filling.

The rushing sound came again, dispelling any thoughts of food. This time it was closer and louder. He felt the huge volume of displaced air on his face — it was something big, all right. He whipped back his hand with the orb and, cupping it in his palm, huddled down low.

His stomach knotting with fear, he fought the impulse to run, remaining motionless among the rocks. He was in open ground, with nowhere close that would offer cover — a horribly exposed position. He glanced over at the dust mite. It was holding so still that it took him a while to locate it. He told himself that this had to be a defensive behavior — the creature was attempting to conceal itself. Therefore, he reasoned, whatever was circling over them was to be feared. If a monstrously large dust mite, the size of an adolescent elephant and protected by an armored coat, had cause for alarm, then he had to be a prime target. A nice, soft, fleshy human grub, ripe for the picking.

Whoomf!

A huge shadow swooped back and forth.

Closer and closer it came — circling like a hawk, describing increasingly tighter rotations.

He knew he couldn't stay where he was. At that instant, the giant mite moved again, scuttling rapidly off where the path continued. Dr. Burrows hesitated a moment and then bolted after it, stumbling over the foundations and the rough ground. He was barking his shins against the rocks and sliding and tripping on obstacles as he fled blindly, but he did not fall.

Whoomf!

It was almost on top of him. He stifled a cry, flinging his arms protectively around his head as he ran. *What in the world was it? Some winged predator? Coming in for the kill like a bird of prey?*

He couldn't believe how fast the dust mite was moving, propelling itself along on its six legs. He could hardly see it up ahead, and if it hadn't been for the vague track, he was sure he would have lost his way altogether. But where were the path and the dust mite heading?

Whoomf! Whoomf!

"Gah!" he screamed, and dropped to the ground. A draft of warm air from the beat of shadowy wings caught his face. *It was close!* Now on all fours, he frantically twisted his head around for a glimpse of his hunter. He was certain it was wheeling in a circle not far above him and would be swooping down any second now to make the kill.

Would this be it? Snatched from the ground by some subterranean flying beast?

His imagination running riot with thoughts of what the creature could be, he sped off again, crawling like a madman. He had to find a hiding place and darn quick.

Head down, he cannoned straight into something hard. He dropped onto his stomach, half stunned, and tried to see what he'd come up against. He was still on the path, so he guessed it was where the dust mite had gone. He'd reached the cavern wall — and before him was a carved entrance in the face of the rock with a clearly defined lintel perhaps fifty or so feet above.

He cried out with relief, daring to let himself think that he'd found a safe haven. He began to crawl again, keeping close to the ground, scraping his knees and calves and knocking his knuckles raw on rubble as he went. He didn't stop until he realized he hadn't heard the sound for several seconds. All was calm and still. Was he safe?

He sank down onto the ground and curled up in a ball, unable to suppress a severe fit of the shakes. To top it off, he got a serious case of the hiccups, each one making his body spasm as it came. After a few minutes he stretched out and, still hiccupping, rolled onto his side. He drew several deep and tremulous breaths as he slowly relaxed his rigid fingers from around the light orb in his hand.

He cleared his throat and mumbled, "Yes, yes, yes, *hic!*", ashamed of his post-traumatic panic attack, then sat up to look around. He was in an enclosed area with two rows of large columns on either side of him, all carved from the same brownish stone of the cavern outside. His eyes widened in astonishment.

"What the *hic*?"

Elliott was leading the boys inland. In places the undergrowth was so thick she had to use her machete to cut a way through. Following her in single file, the boys helped each other by making sure that the rubbery branches of the tall succulent plants and the lower fronds of the trees didn't swing back into the face of the person behind. It was airless, and the boys were soon dripping with perspiration and missing the open spaces and light winds of the beach.

Despite this, Will's spirits were high. He was pleased that they seemed to be working together as a team again. He hoped that any differences he'd had with Chester were firmly in the past and his friendship with him would revert to how it had been before. And above all else, he was so grateful that Elliott had stepped straight into Drake's shoes as their new leader. He had little doubt she was capable of the role.

Will heard sounds along the way, rasping animal calls and hollow rattling noises. He eagerly tried to locate the source of these, peering all around and up above at the branches of the gigantic trees, but could make out nothing. He would have given anything to stop and conduct a proper search. He was in a primordial jungle, which could be filled with all sorts of fantastic creatures.

The path took them into a clearing, where Will stole glances at the lush vegetation, hoping to catch the merest glimpse of one of these animals. Then, as he peered through the flora, a pair emerged. Will did a double take — he wasn't sure if they were birds or reptiles, but they resembled small, freshly plucked bantam chickens, with stubby necks and mean little beaks. Like two old women complaining to each other, they communicated using both the rasping and rattling sounds Will had been hearing. They turned and scurried back into the brush, flapping stunted wings from which a few mangy patches of fur — or feathers? — sprouted. So much for the exotic creatures he'd been dreaming of!

Elliott led them onto a track, and they continued along until Will heard Chester's voice up ahead.

"The sea," he said.

They gathered around Elliott, crouching down in the bushes. A strip of beach stretched before them and they could hear the sound of waves again.

Cal spoke up. "It looks exactly like our beach. You're not telling me we just came full circle?" he quizzed Elliott indignantly, shaking the sweat from his face.

"This is not the same beach," she informed him coldly.

"But where do we go now?" he asked, frowning as he craned his neck to peer along the foreshore.

She stuck a finger out to sea, out over the rolling waves.

"Well, we're on an *island* and the only . . . ," Will began.

". . . way on and off is the causeway," Elliott finished his sentence for him. "And I'll bet you that at this very moment the Blackheads are sniffing around the remains of our campfire."

An uneasy silence descended over the group until Chester spoke in a small voice.

"So, are we going to swim for it?"

40

HE STAGGERED to his feet, blinking with surprise. He was spellbound by the space around him, his insatiable thirst for knowledge dismissing all other concerns. In that instant, his hiccups ceased, and Dr. Burrows, Intrepid Explorer, was back on duty. His fear of the unidentified beast, and all thoughts of his hysterical rush to escape it, were brushed aside.

"Bingo!" he cried.

He'd stumbled upon some type of edifice, carved into the bedrock of the cavern itself. If he'd been in search of evidence of the ancient race, he'd certainly found it now. He crept forward, his light revealing row upon row of stone seats, many shattered by fallen debris. He was making his way to the front, in the direction the seats were facing, when he happened to look up.

The ceiling high above him was smooth and generally intact, except for a few sections where it had crumbled in. As he shone his orb around, he caught a tantalizing glimpse of something that reflected the light.

"Extraordinary!" he exclaimed, holding his orb higher, its rays only just traveling the distance to a dully glinting circle that was at least fifty feet in diameter.

"Higher . . . have to get higher," he told himself, clambering onto the seat of the nearest of the stone benches, and then up onto the narrow back of the bench itself.

As he moved his light slowly around, teetering precariously, the design became clearer to him. The circle was dull gold or bronze in color and could have been applied by some kind of gilding or possibly even painted on. He spoke out loud as he scrutinized it.

"Let's see, you're a hollow circle with . . . with . . . what's that in the middle? Looks like . . ." He squinted and pushed the orb toward the ceiling as far as his arm would permit, until it was supported by just his fingertips.

In the very center of the circle, also cast in the metallic medium, was a solid disk. Jagged lines that resembled stylized, angular rays extended from its circumference.

"Aha! It's obvious what you're meant to represent . . . you're the *sun*!" Dr. Burrows pronounced, and then furrowed his brow. "So what have we got here — a subterranean race engaged in *surface worship*? A people harking back to a time when they were up above on the crust?"

Something more caught his eye. Simple renderings of humanoid figures were depicted walking around the *inside* of the larger circle — men, evenly spaced, as if treading in a whopping great hamster wheel.

"Hey, what are you chaps doing there? You and the sun are in the wrong places!" he observed, frowning even more deeply as he shifted his light toward the solid disk in the center again. "I don't know who made you, but you're all the wrong way around!"

Despite the topsy-turvy nature of the picture, it wasn't lost on Dr. Burrows that any representation of the earth as a sphere, dating back to the time of the Phoenicians, meant whoever had put it there was incredibly enlightened and advanced.

His arm began to tire from holding the light, so he lowered it and stepped down to the ground once more, baffled by what he'd seen.

"So much for symbolism!" he said, and sniffed dismissively as he resumed his way forward. He passed the front row of seats, and his light beam touched upon what lay before them. He caught his breath as he saw a raised dais, on which rested a solid block of stone. As he came closer to it, he estimated the block was some forty feet from side to side and about five in height.

"What are *you* doing here?" he asked, again speaking aloud into the somber gloom. He glanced back at the rows of seats, up at the roof with the circles, and then contemplated the stone block once more. "You've got pews, a cockeyed mural on the ceiling, and you've also got an altar," he posited to himself. "Absolutely no debate . . . you're definitely some sort of place of worship . . . a church, or a temple, perhaps?"

He trod forward, his light revealing more of the altar as he went. Coming to a halt, he marveled at the craftsmanship: Beautiful and intricate geometric carvings worthy of any Byzantine sculptor decorated its sides.

As he lifted up the orb, an area of wall immediately behind the altar caught the light and shone enticingly.

"Oh my goodness . . . look at you!"

Breathing quickly, he leaned nearer. It was a triptych: three massive carved panels — *bas-reliefs*. He knew they were made of something other than the chocolate-brown rock by the way they were reflecting his light and adding a warmth to it.

His feet found a step at the base of the altar, and then another. As though mesmerized, he climbed up to its top. From one side to the other, the three panels extended the full length of the altar, and each was approximately twice Dr. Burrows's height. His pulse racing with anticipation, he approached the central one and, gently brushing away the dust and cobwebs, began to examine it.

"So very, very exquisite . . . polished rock crystal," he proclaimed as he ran his fingers over its surface. "You are quite beautiful, aren't you . . . but what are you here for?" he asked the triptych, peering closely at its surface. "By Jove, I think you might be gold in there!" he wheezed with disbelief as he saw the shining brilliance behind the transparent layer. "Three huge golden panels, faced with carved rock crystal. What a fantastic artifact! I must make a record of this."

Although his mouth was watering at the prospect of what was on the panels, he resolved to get himself properly organized first, and set about gathering together enough kindling for a fire. It was awkward using his orb as the sole source of light — and besides, a good-sized fire would enable him to appreciate the panels in their full glory. In a matter of minutes, he'd collected enough dry material to start a small blaze on the top of the altar, and the flames took without any hesitation.

As the fire crackled away behind him, he began to sweep the dust from the faces of the three panels using his forearm. For the uppermost sections, he dug out his tattered blue overalls and flicked them upward, sometimes jumping in an attempt to hit the tops.

His efforts raised a cloud of dust and the exertion soon became too much for him in his weakened state. He stopped, breathing heavily, to inspect his progress. With some relief, he realized that he didn't need to clear the dust off completely; when combined with the illumination from the fire, a residual coating of it actually made the panels' carved images easier to see.

"Right, let's have a good old look at the lot of you," he announced and, with his trusty stub of a pencil poised over a fresh page in his journal, he whistled through his teeth in a random, impatient way. "So what are you going to tell me, my pretty?" he said almost flirtatiously to the panel on the far left as he stepped before it.

Amply illuminated by the guttering flames, it depicted a man wearing a headdress that vaguely resembled a squat miter. The figure had a strong jaw and a heavy brow; the long staff he brandished in his clenched fist suggested that he was a person of immense importance.

The figure occupied most of the panel, and Dr. Burrows could see that the man was at the head of a long and meandering procession of people. The procession went on for a considerable distance, trailing away to the horizon and over a large but featureless plain.

"Egyptian influence?" Dr. Burrows muttered, spotting the similarities to objects from that period. He took a step back from the panel. "So what's the message here? This fellow is, undoubtedly, a big cheese . . . a leader, a Moses figure, perhaps taking his people on a journey to this place, or perhaps just the opposite, leading them away in some kind of exodus. But why . . . what was so very important that someone carved you with such consummate skill and left you here at the altar?"

He hummed for a while, uttering the odd random word, then clicked his tongue against his teeth. "No, you're not going to tell me any more, are you? I'm going to have to talk to your friends," Dr. Burrows informed the silent panel. He spun on his heel and made straight for the panel on the far right of the triptych.

Compared with the first panel, the subject matter was more difficult to make out. There was no single predominating image — the scene was altogether more complex and confusing. However, as the firelight fell across it, he began to see what it represented.

"Ah . . . so, *you're* a stylized landscape . . . rolling fields . . . a stream with a small bridge over it and . . . what's this?" he muttered, brushing an area of the panel directly in front of him. "Some form of agriculture . . . trees . . . perhaps an orchard? Yes, I think you might be." He stepped back to peer at the top of the panel. "Curious, very curious indeed. . . ."

Strange columns lanced down from the upper right corner over the rest of the landscape. At the point from which the columns radiated, there was a circle.

"The sun! Oh, it's my old friend the sun again!" Dr. Burrows exclaimed. "Just like the one on the ceiling!" The sphere's jagged rays spread out over the rest of the picture. "So what are *you* telling me? Are you showing me the place where the Moses figure was leading the people? Was this some great pilgrimage to the surface? Is that it?"

He glanced back at the first panel. "A ruler leading his people to some sort of idealized nirvana, to the elysian fields, to the Garden of Eden?" He looked at the panel in front of him again. "But *you're* showing the earth's surface and the sun . . . so what's a nice picture like you doing in a place like this, way down here? Are you just a reminder of what lies up top? A subterranean Post-it note? And who are those people — are they really some forgotten culture, or the forebears of the

Egyptians or the Phoenicians or . . . or perhaps something far more fantastic?" He shook his head. "Evacuees from the lost city of Atlantis? Is that possible?"

He checked himself, realizing he was jumping to conclusions before conducting a full investigation. Lost in thought, he fell silent for a second, then sidestepped to the central panel.

"Maybe *you* hold all the answers," he muttered. In what typically should have been the most important of the three panels, he was expecting to find something impressive — perhaps a religious symbol, a crowning image. But instead, it was by far the least remarkable of the triptych.

"Well, well, well," Dr. Burrows said. The middle panel depicted a circular opening in the ground with craggy rock borders. Its perspective allowed Dr. Burrows to see a little distance down into it, but there was nothing to note besides a continuation of the rock sides.

"Ah!" he exclaimed, bending forward and spying some tiny human figures on the very edge of the hole. "So, you're on a gargantuan scale, I now know that much," he said, reaching over to rub the dust from the little figures, no bigger than ants. He continued to do this for a short while, finding more and more of the Lilliputian people in a procession, until he abruptly stilled his hand, then drew it back.

At the far left of the procession, a number of these tiny human forms had their arms and legs splayed out, as if in free fall, tumbling down into the mouth of the huge opening. Strange winged creatures hovered above them. Dr. Burrows stood on his tiptoes and blew hard to try to remove some more of the dirt from these diminutive flying forms.

"Well, that's a surprise!" he declared. Clad in loose flowing gowns, they seemed to have human bodies, but swanlike wings extending from their backs. "Angels . . . or devils?" he pondered aloud. Then he took several steps back. With his arms crossed and his chin cradled in one hand, he continued to regard the panel, whistling to himself all the while in his erratic, atonal way.

He stopped whistling. "Aha!" he yelled, remembering something. He hurriedly retrieved the Coprolite map from his pants pocket and unfolded it, then held it up before him. "I knew I'd seen you before!"

On the map, at the end of a long line representing what he assumed to be a tunnel or a track, and dotted with various symbols along its path, he saw something similar to the image in the panel. It was sketched in a much more simplistic way, with just a few pen strokes, but it, too, appeared to be some kind of opening in the ground. "Could they be one and the same?" he wondered aloud.

He went closer to the center panel and looked it over again. There was something more at the base, something he hadn't noticed under a crusty coating of a fungal growth. He feverishly scrubbed at it and found that it had been obscuring a line of cuneiform writing.

"Yes!" he bellowed exultantly, immediately flicking his journal open to the Dr. Burrows Stone page. It tallied with the script he'd already interpreted . . . he could translate it!

Squatting down, he wasted no time in getting started. The inscription consisted of five distinct words. He glanced repeatedly between the panel and his notebook, a huge self-satisfied grin forming on his face. He deciphered the first word: "GARDEN . . ."

He clucked impatiently, his eyes rapidly switching from his notebook to the script and back again. "Come on, come on," he urged himself. "What's the next word?"

Then he read, "*TO* . . . no, not *TO*, but *OF*!" And then, "That's an easy word . . . *THE*."

He took a breath and summarized his findings so far. "GARDEN OF THE . . . ," he announced.

The next word stumped him. "Think, think, think!" he said, each time thwacking himself on the forehead. "Get your act together, Burrows, you numskull," he growled, annoyed that his mind wasn't firing on all four cylinders. "What's the rest?"

The remaining words weren't coming so easily, and he was frustrated that it was taking so long to translate them. He scanned the final part of the inscription, hoping that by some stroke of luck he would have a breakthrough.

Just then the fire flared, as a thick piece of kindling began to burn with a loud hiss. Dr. Burrows saw something from the corner of his eye and slowly turned his head away from the panel.

In the brighter light now being cast by the fire, he could see largish hollows, or perhaps holes, all over the side walls of the temple. Many of them.

"That's odd," he muttered, his brow creasing. "Didn't notice them before."

As he looked more closely, his heart missed several beats.

No, they weren't *holes* . . . they were *moving*.

He spun fully around.

He cried out in surprise.

Before him were so many of the enormous dust mites, he couldn't even begin to count them. It was as though the one he had befriended had summoned its brethren, and now hundreds of them had gathered like an outrageous congregation in the interior of the temple. Among them were behemoths easily three or four times the size of the dust mite that had led him in here. They looked as big as Sherman tanks and just as heavily armored.

His cry stirred them into activity, and their mandibles clattered as if they were giving him a genteel round of applause. Several began to lumber toward him with that gradual and inhuman intent that only an insect possesses. It made his blood chill.

He hadn't felt threatened by the original dust mite, but this was an altogether different situation. There were too many of them, and they looked too big, and too darned *hungry*. He suddenly pictured himself as a king-sized food stick, poised invitingly on the altar before them.

Holy smokes holy smokes holy smokes went over and over in his head.

Some of the largest ones, dangerous-looking brutes with dented and holed carapaces, began to advance more rapidly, ramming smaller dust mites out of their way. Their articulated legs thudded on the flagstones. Some reared up, their thick legs sweeping in the air, as they crawled over the backs of the pews, affording Dr. Burrows a flash of their glossy black underbellies.

He snatched up his rucksack, ramming his notebook into it and then swinging it onto his back, his mind racing. He needed a way out, and quick. But he was surrounded. They were everywhere; to his front and sides they were coming, like an advancing armored division of the flesh-tearing variety.

Holy smokes holy smokes holy smokes.

He wondered wildly if he could just make a run for it *over* the dust mites, jumping from back to back as if he were leaping across the tops of cars in a traffic jam. No, nice idea, but he was sure they wouldn't just sit still and allow him to do that — it wasn't going to be that easy. And, anyway, he'd rather not go back out into the cavern, where the swooping creature might still be waiting for him.

He seized a boughlike piece of debris from the fire and waved it at the mite brigade, trying to scare them off with the flames. The nearest were only feet away from the base of the altar now, and others crept steadily toward him from the sides. The flames made no difference — indeed, quite the opposite: They appeared to be attracted by the fire, speeding up appreciably.

In desperation, he slung the bough with all his might at a large dust mite. It bounced harmlessly off its carapace and didn't slow the creature even a little.

Holy smokes holy smokes holy smokes NO!

In an absolute panic, he spun around and tried to scramble up the center panel of the triptych. But he slipped and slod against the dusty face of the carving; he couldn't get a grip. "COME ON, YOU IDIOT!" he yelled at himself, his voice all but drowned out by the clacking of the dust mites — louder and faster now, as if they were aroused by the spectacle of their human food stick trying to make good its escape.

Then his fingers got a hold on the sides of the panel and, with the most immense effort, he lifted himself off the top of the altar. Panting and grunting, his hands and arms strained to their very limits, he held himself aloft, his feet scrabbling ineffectually under him.

"Please, please, please," he begged as his arms began to give out. Miraculously his toes found some sort of foothold in the carving. It was enough. He quickly ran his hands a little farther up, and then, hanging on just by his arms again, he found another foothold. By employing this alternating caterpillar-like locomotion — hands, toes, hands, toes — up he went, climbing for dear life.

He drew on the last of his hysterical strength to reach the top of the panel. Once there, he lodged his right foot in the carving of the huge hole. With this, and his fingers crooked over the top of the panel, he quickly took stock of his situation.

He was in an extremely precarious position, and one that he couldn't hold for much longer; his arms and legs were already exhausted from the effort of climbing. And there was no point in deceiving himself that the dust mites wouldn't be able to swarm up the wall below him — he'd seen them climbing across the sides of the temple. *What could he do to defend himself?* The only thing that occurred to him was that by kicking out with his heel, he might at least be able to impede the onslaught.

He peered around, frantically trying to formulate his next move. He felt the sweat soaking his brow and streaming down his back as, taking deep breaths to try to calm himself, he clung on with grim determination. Then he stiffly twisted his head around to look down at the bugs. As he moved, the orb hanging around his neck slipped out from under his jacket so that its light fell on their massed ranks. This caused a stir among them and they bobbed up and down, their mandibles clattering even louder, as if building to a frenzied crescendo of expectation.

Dr. Burrows thought of chopsticks, many gigantic chopsticks, tearing his body apart, rending him limb from limb.

"Shoo! Go away! Shoo! Be off with you!" he screamed over his shoulder, the same words he'd often used to scare off the next-door neighbor's cat from the back lawn in Highfield. His hands were sopping with perspiration and cramping horribly. What could he do? He glanced up to make sure there wasn't anything he could grab on to and hoist himself higher. As he did so, across the ceiling of the temple he saw a fluxing collage of serrated arachnid body parts, massed and overlapping silhouettes thrown up by the flickering light of the fire on the altar below. They were close now. It was the stuff of horror movies.

"Help!" he exhaled in sheer desperation.

He felt his left hand begin to slither off the ledge as the dust on top of it absorbed his sweat and turned to a slippery paste. He slid his fingers to a fresh position, simultaneously trying to heave himself a little farther up.

Something began to happen.

A low rumble shook his whole body.

Holy smokes holy smokes holy smokes!

He looked around frantically, his light swinging freely from his neck.

"Oh no! What now?" he screamed, an even deeper wave of dread sweeping through him.

He had the strangest sensation that he was moving. But his hands, now almost completely numb, still retained some measure of grip, and his foot was still securely anchored. No, he wasn't sliding down the panel to the ravenous arachnids below.

The juddering stopped, and he again attempted to hoist himself farther up the panel.

Immediately the rumbling resumed, more violently this time.

His first thought was that it was an underground tremor, some type of subterranean earthquake. But it was *he* who was moving, not his surroundings.

The middle panel of the triptych, which he was hanging on to for dear life, was slowly tipping over. Under his weight, it was swinging *forward*, into the wall of the temple.

"Help me!" he wailed.

Everything became a blur. He immediately assumed that the panel had broken loose from its fixings and was falling. What he couldn't see was that the panel was pivoting halfway down its length, just below his foothold.

And like it or not, he was going with it.

The panel continued to rotate, with him still clinging doggedly on until he found himself horizontal, effectively lying on top of it. It rotated to its limit and came to a sudden halt with a jaw-rattling thud of stone against stone.

Dr. Burrows was catapulted forward, haphazardly flipping head over heels through the darkness. The flight ended almost as soon as it began. He landed flat on his back, the wind knocked out of him. Gulping and coughing, he tried to catch his breath as his hands clutched at the soft sand beneath him. He'd been lucky — it had cushioned his fall.

There was a loud thud behind him and a spray of something wet across his face, accompanied by a sharp hissing sound.

"What the —?" Dr. Burrows heaved himself into a sitting position and turned to see what was there, fully expecting the arachnid hordes to be bearing down on him. But his spectacles had been knocked off in the fall, and without them he couldn't discern anything at all in the near-darkness. He felt around in the sand until he found them, and quickly replaced them on his head.

He heard a scrabbling by his side and whipped his head in its direction. It was a jointed leg from one of the dust mites, as big as a horse's, severed at what was probably its equivalent of a shoulder. He watched as it suddenly snapped open and shut again, with such force that it flipped itself over in the sand. It was moving as though it had a mind of its own — and for all Dr. Burrows knew, it probably did.

He backed away from the limb and got to his feet, swaying groggily and still wheezing and coughing as his breathing slowly returned to normal. At any moment the arachnids would swarm over him.

But there was no sign of the giant dust mites, or, indeed, the interior of the temple; just an unbroken silence, and darkness, and plain stone walls.

It was as though he'd been transported to a completely different place.

"*Now* where am I?" he muttered, resting his hands on his legs. After a few moments he began to feel better and straightened up to inspect his new surroundings. Within several seconds he'd pieced it all together. Realizing how incredibly fortunate he'd been, he began to babble.

"Oh, thank you, thank you." He joined his hands together in a brief prayer, weeping tears of gratitude.

Another spray of warm fluid filled the air. It reeked, a bitter stench that made him choke. He cast about to see where it was coming from.

Six feet or so above the ground, the shiny and mangled remains of a dust mite protruded from the wall. It had been trapped by the swinging panel as it slammed shut again. A bluish transparent fluid oozed and pumped from several sheared-off tubes, some the diameter of drainpipes, in the midst of the mashed wreckage. As he looked on, another shower of fluid spurted out, making him jump back in alarm. It was as though the valves of some bizarre machine were opening to release the pressure and flush themselves out.

It struck him that the decapitated head of the dust mite might not be very far away, most likely with an active set of mandibles, if the severed limb that was still snapping open and shut was anything to go by.

He wasn't about to stick around to find out.

"You silly old fool, you nearly cashed in your chips back there," he told himself as he stumbled hurriedly away from the scene. He mopped his face with his sleeve and, still a little dazed, saw that sweeping down through an arched corridor were wide steps . . . many steps, which he now began to follow, still muttering incoherent prayers of gratitude.

41

SARAH WAS SITTING dejectedly on the beach, her knees drawn up to her chin as she hugged her legs. She'd abandoned any attempt at concealing herself: The lantern was on full beam and, with Bartleby at her side, the two of them gazed at the rolling waves as they broke on the shore.

She'd done as the Limiters ordered and followed the shoreline, but she'd have been kidding herself if she thought it was anything more than a tactic to get her out of the way. There was no possible reason for her to be here.

As they'd been walking, she'd noted that the spring had gone from Bartleby's step now that there was no scent trail to sniff out. She couldn't remain angry with him for the way he'd behaved; there was something touching about the tenacity he'd shown in tracking his master. She kept reminding herself that this Hunter had been Cal's companion — the truth was that the animal had spent more time with her son than she had, and she was Cal's mother!

With a rush of affection, she'd watched Bartleby's huge shoulder blades rising and falling hypnotically, first one side, then the other, as he slunk along. They stuck out at the best of times under his loose-fitting and hairless skin, but they were even more prominent now with his head hanging so low. The aimless way he was carrying himself spoke volumes — he looked exactly the way she felt.

And now, as they sat on the beach, she couldn't contain her frustration.

"Wild-goose chase," she grumbled to the cat. He was scratching his ear with a paw. "Ever tried goose?" she asked, and he stopped, his hind leg still poised in the air, regarding her with his huge shining eyes. "Oh, I don't know what I'm saying!" she admitted, and lay back against the white sand as Bartleby resumed his scratching. "Or doing," she confessed to the stone roof far above, invisible in the darkness.

What would Tam make of all this? What would he think of her if he'd seen the way she'd acted? She'd kowtowed to a patrol of corpse-chewing Limiters! She was supposed to be finding out whether Will was really to blame for her brother's death, and also getting Cal safely back to his home in the Colony. She was a long way from achieving either of those aims. She felt she had failed miserably. *Why didn't I stand up to them?* she asked herself. "Too weak," she said aloud. "That's why!"

If the Limiters took Will alive, and she were to come face-to-face with him after he'd been captured, what would she do? The Limiters would probably expect her to kill him in cold blood. She couldn't do that, not without knowing whether he was really to blame for her brother's death.

But if she didn't, the alternative for him would be worse . . . unthinkably worse. Death would be a picnic compared to the tortures he would endure at the hands of Rebecca and the Styx. As she pondered her dilemma for the umpteenth time, she realized how strong her feelings were for her son, despite everything he supposedly had done. She was his mother! Could he be capable of betraying his own family? Not knowing the truth was driving her mad.

She suddenly became so angry that her brother had lost his life. Rage boiled up inside her, and she arched her back, pressing her head hard into the sand.

"TAM!" she cried.

Alarmed at her outburst, Bartleby scrambled to his feet. He watched as she sank back onto the beach in a sullen, helpless silence. Her wrath had no outlet, nowhere to go. She was like some clockwork toy that Rebecca and her cronies had wound up, letting it run only so far before stopping it short.

Bartleby finished washing himself and made several dry, hacking sounds as he spat grains of sand from his mouth, then yawned exuberantly. He sat back fully on his haunches and, as he did so, broke wind with the volume of a bugler trumpeting an urgent retreat.

It came as no surprise to Sarah; she'd noticed the cat had been supplementing his diet by chewing on the moldy remains of unidentifiable things he found along the way. Evidently at least one of them hadn't agreed with him.

"Couldn't have put it better myself," Sarah mumbled through her clenched teeth, squeezing her eyes shut in frustration.

42

FOLLOWING THE FLIGHT of stone steps wherever they took him, Dr. Burrows had eventually emerged into another vast space. Here he found that the path of regularly laid slabs continued, and he went with it, moving down a gentle incline. For as far as he could see, menhirs peppered the ground. Dumpy, teardrop-shaped boulders up to twelve feet high, with rounded tops — it was a bizarre sight, as if some semideity had been randomly chucking large dollops of dough all over the place.

Given the uniformity of the menhirs' shapes, though, Dr. Burrows began to ask himself if they had been positioned not by nature but design. He muttered various theories about their origin as he went, every so often jumping when his light, falling across the nearest boulder, cast shadows on those behind, giving the impression that something was lurking in wait. After his close calls with the winged creature and the hungry bug army, he wasn't going to take any more chances with the local fauna.

But another part of his brain was also whirring away on the images he'd seen in the triptych, trying to make sense of them. He cursed his luck that he hadn't been able to fully decipher the inscription on the center panel in time. At least he had *seen* the letters that formed the remaining words. Now he was trying his hardest to recall them.

Using the technique that usually worked, he forced himself to think about something unrelated, hoping this would unlock the images in his memory. He directed all his attention to the Coprolite map, much of which was still an enigma to him.

All that he'd encountered so far, the chocolate cavern and then the temple, was on the map, clear as day, once he'd examined it again. The problem was, the rather strange icons that represented them were so small as to be almost microscopic, and he'd misplaced his magnifying glass somewhere along the way. It probably wouldn't have made much difference even if he did still have it, because there was no legend on the map to tell him what any of the features were. Interpreting them came down to pure guesswork.

Nevertheless, at least the Coprolite map gave him some notion of the sheer scale of the Deeps. It had two major features on it: the Great Plain and its surrounding areas to the left, and to the right something that could very well be a huge hole in the ground — he didn't need a magnifying glass to determine that! The same hole as portrayed in the triptych, he assumed.

Numerous tracks radiated from the Great Plain, and many of these eventually converged at the hole, as if it was a street map of the center of some large conurbation back up on the earth's surface. And he was on one of those tracks right now.

Quite a number of routes led off the hole and over to the far right of the map, where they all seemed to terminate in dead ends. Whether this was because the Coprolites never used them, or because they had never explored them, he didn't know. But this race had lived in these parts for how many generations he could only guess, and given that they were master miners, he would have been mightily surprised if they'd left any stone unturned or quarter unexplored. The Coprolites, from what he could gather, were not only master miners but master *prospectors* — the two went hand in hand — so they would have surveyed all the outlying areas in case precious stones or something similar were to be found there.

Dr. Burrows wondered if his expedition, his "grand tour" of the subterranean lands, was going to culminate in him going up and down a series of these cul-de-sacs. Provided he could find some food and, more crucially, some clean water, his time would be occupied with exploring all the areas marked on the Coprolite map, combing them for ancient settlements and any artifacts of note.

If this was the case, his journey had a finite end, and there was no way he would be reaching deeper levels in the earth's mantle, where untold archaeological treasures might lie or past civilizations beyond anyone's imagination might have once lived — or still live.

He knew he shouldn't be disappointed. Despite all the danger he'd faced, he'd already made some of the most remarkable discoveries of the century, probably of *any* century. If he ever made it back home, he'd be lauded as one of the greats of the archaeological fraternity.

When he'd set out from Highfield on that day so long ago, heaving back the shelves in his cellar to begin down the tunnel he'd dug, as if he'd been a character from some farfetched children's story, he'd had absolutely no conception of what he was getting himself into. But he had got this far, and in the course of his journey he'd overcome everything that had been thrown at him, surprising himself in the process.

And now, as he thought about it, he realized he'd developed a taste for adventure, for taking risks. As he strolled down the dark path, his shoulders straightened and he allowed himself a swagger.

"Move over, Howard Carter," he declared in a loud voice. "Tutankhamen's tomb is nothing compared to *my* discoveries!"

Dr. Burrows could almost hear the thunderous applause, the accolades, and imagine the many television appearances and the . . .

His shoulders suddenly slumped again, and the swagger evaporated.

Somehow it wasn't enough.

Sure, he had a mammoth task ahead of him. Just documenting everything on the Coprolite map would be enough to keep him busy for many lifetimes — and require a huge research team — but still, he felt a profound sense of disappointment.

He wanted more!

The hole shown on the map . . . what could it be? All the routes wouldn't converge there, it wouldn't be so prominent in the ancient temple's triptych, if it was just some geological feature!

He halted on the path, muttering animatedly as he began to point in the air at an imaginary blackboard.

"Great Plain," he announced, pointing at the left of the blackboard with a thrust of his hand as if he was addressing a lecture hall full of students. He swung his other arm up to the right, outlining a ring in the air with his light. "Big hole . . . here," he said, jabbing repeatedly into its center. "What are you, mystery hole?"

He lowered his arms to his sides, exhaling through his tea-stained teeth. Yes, that hole *had* to be important.

The triptych flashed before him. There was a message in those three panels. And he needed to recall the last letters of the inscription so that he could complete the translation and put the whole thing together. But it remained just out of his grasp!

He sighed.

He had to get to the hole and find out for himself.

Maybe it was what he was yearning for . . . *a way down.*

Maybe there was still hope.

He started off again with a burst of enthusiasm.

About twenty minutes into his new journey, Dr. Burrows heard a scratchy noise ahead of him and immediately looked up.

The noise came again, clearer.

Within seconds his light revealed that two forms were gliding toward him on the path.

He couldn't quite believe what he was seeing — two people, walking together.

As they drew closer, he saw that it was a pair of Styx: the soldiers known as Limiters, from the look of their long coats, rifles, and backpacks. He'd seen a couple of them before at the Miners' Station when he'd first gotten off the train. The scratchy noise was their voices.

He couldn't believe his luck. He hadn't so much as glimpsed a single living soul for days and thought how bizarre it was to bump into another human being down here, never mind two, in this network of thousands of miles of passageways and interlinking caverns. What were the chances?

When they were no more than fifteen feet from him, he hailed them, calling out "Hello!" in an expectant, friendly voice.

One of them glanced at him, with ice-cold eyes and a face devoid of expression, but there was no effort at any sort of acknowledgment. The other soldier didn't even raise his eyes from the path ahead of him. The two of them continued marching purposefully and talking to each other, not paying him any heed whatsoever as they moved on.

Dr. Burrows was flummoxed but didn't stop, either. Their total lack of interest made him feel like a street beggar who'd had the effrontery to ask a couple of businessmen for money. He couldn't believe it!

"Oh, well, suit yourself," he said with a shrug, turning his thoughts back to more important matters.

"Where are you, what are you, hole in the ground?" he inquired of the silent menhirs around him, his mind again churning with endless theories.

43

"**STROKE!** Stroke! Stroke!" Chester called as he and Will pulled the oars. Chester had said he'd done some rowing with his father, and Elliott had let him take control the moment they'd clambered into the rickety-looking boat. In fact, *boat* was too grandiose a word for the canoe-cum-coracle, which had creaked ominously as they all climbed aboard. It was about fourteen feet long and had a wooden frame over which a hidelike material was stretched and stitched.

It clearly hadn't been designed to carry four passengers, particularly not with all their gear. Scrunched up in the prow of the boat, Cal grumbled quietly to himself as he tried to nurse his bad leg. He was attempting to position himself so he could straighten it out, which was nigh on impossible with Will pressed so close by.

"Oi! Watch it! There's no way I can row if you keep doing that!" Will protested when Cal dug into his back yet again as he shifted himself around. Cal finally found that the optimum position was for him to lie in the bottom of the boat with his head crammed into the V of the prow — by doing this, he could hook his bad leg up on the side and extend it fully.

"This isn't some pleasure cruise, you know!" Will joked in between breaths when he caught the curious sight of a foot sticking up in the air from the corner of his eye.

"Stroke . . . str — concentrate, Will!" Chester ordered as he endeavored to get his friend to row in time with him. It quickly became evident that Chester didn't really know what he was doing, either, despite his earlier claims. All too often his oars skimmed ineffectually over the surface with a spray of water.

"Where did you say you learned to do this?" Will asked.

"Wilderness camp," Chester admitted.

"You're kidding!" Will exclaimed.

"Shaddup, will you?" Chester retorted with a broad smile.

Their syncopation was chaotic, to say the least, but Will decided that traveling by boat had to be the best way to get around. The physical exertion from the rowing was blowing the cobwebs from his mind; he felt more clearheaded than he had in days. And the light breeze gusting over the water was just enough to whisk the perspiration from his brow as he heaved on the oars. He felt invigorated.

They seemed to be making good time, although Will couldn't see the shore — or anything else, for that matter — to judge how fast they were going. The endless darkness and the invisible stretch of water all around them were a little daunting; the only light was from Chester's lantern, dimmed to its lowest setting, in the bottom of the boat.

Perched at the helm, Elliott, true to form, watched alertly behind them, although the island had long since been shrouded from view. Facing her as they rowed, Will and Chester were just about able to make out her dim silhouette. They were waiting for her to issue instructions, but it seemed like an interminably long time before she spoke.

She suddenly told them to stop, and Will and Chester rested the oars, although the boat seemed to coast along surprisingly quickly by itself, as if caught in a powerful current. Will hung his head over the side — he could see faint, indistinct shapes deep within the water. They appeared to intensify and then fade away just as fast. Some were small and darted rapidly, while others, more substantial forms, moved ponderously and gave off a much stronger light.

As he watched with rapt fascination, the broad, flattened face of a fish, maybe as much as a foot and a half across from gill to gill, bobbed up just below the surface. Between its large eyes there was a long stalk, which had at its tip a greenish, pulsating light. Its mouth gaped open to release a gush of bubbles, closed again, and then the fish submerged. With a frisson of excitement, Will immediately spotted the resemblance to anglerfish, which inhabit the deep recesses of Topsoil oceans. *There must be a whole ecosystem hidden under these waves,* he thought. *Living creatures that generate their own light!*

Much as the fish had just done, he opened his mouth to say something to the others about his discovery when he was silenced by a tiny splash, like a stone hitting the water, perhaps some fifty feet off the port side.

"It starts," Elliott whispered cryptically.

A distant bang followed, maybe as much as a second later. More of these splashes and subsequent bangs ensued, but they were too far away for Will to see what was causing them.

"Now would be a good time to turn off that light," Elliott suggested.

"Why?" Chester asked innocently, still peering into the darkness.

"Because the Limiters are on the beach."

"They're shooting at us, dimwit," Cal spoke up. On the starboard side, no more than fifteen feet away, Will noticed a small tick of water flick up from the sea's surface.

"Shooting at us?" Chester repeated, slow to take in what he was being told. "Shooting?!" he exclaimed as he figured it out at last, immediately fumbling to extinguish the lantern. The light off, he sat up and swiveled around in the direction of Elliott. He was flabbergasted at how calm she was. The volley continued, with further splashes around them — they seemed to be coming closer. Chester flinched each time.

"If those really are shots . . . ," Will began.

"Certainly are," Elliott confirmed.

". . . then shouldn't we be rowing like mad hooligans?" Will asked, tightening his grip on the oars in readiness.

"No need, we're well out of range . . . they're taking potshots." Elliott allowed herself a small laugh. "We must've really ticked them off. But it would be one in a million if they hit us."

Will heard Chester grumble something to the effect of "With my luck," as he tucked his head protectively into his shoulder, simultaneously trying to get a view of the island in the pitch-black.

"I've got them exactly where I want them," Elliott said quietly.

"*You've* got them exactly where *you* want them?" Chester's voice wheezed with incredulity. "Surely you —"

"Slow fuses," Elliott interrupted. "My speciality."

The tone of her voice told them nothing, and they all waited, with just the sounds of the creaking boat and the swirling water around them, and the odd splash from the continuing gunfire.

"Any second now . . . ," Elliott said.

A flash lit up the stretch of beach from which they had set out to sea. It looked deceptively tiny to the boys over the distance. Then the sound of the blast reached them, making them all jump.

"What the —" Cal exclaimed, sitting up.

"No, wait . . . ," Elliott said, holding up her hand. Her outline was thrown into sharp relief by the far-off flames. "If any of them lived through that, they'll be falling over themselves like scalded rats to get inland and away from the beach." She began to count, inclining her head ever so slightly with each number.

The boys held their breaths.

A second explosion, far mightier than the first, erupted with massive red and yellow starbursts that streaked high into the cavern, their plumes leaping over the tops of the tall fern trees. It seemed to Will that the whole island must have been blown to smithereens. They all felt the force of the blast on their faces, and pieces of airborne debris were already falling into the water around them.

"Blimey!" gasped Cal.

"Awesome!" said Chester. "You totalled the island!"

"What the heck was *that*?" Will asked, wondering if there'd be anything left of the wildlife, or whether it would all be engulfed by fire — though he had to admit that if a few shabby primordial chickens got their tail feathers singed, then he wasn't overly concerned.

"That was the clincher," Elliott said. "The perfect ambush . . . and the first explosion drove them straight into it."

It was as if the flames were floating on the surface of the sea itself, sending long reflections across the inky waters. For the first time Will could gauge the vastness of the space they were in: The far-off coastline to his right was dimly lit up, but there was absolutely nothing visible in the direction they were heading nor any sign of land at all to his left.

With the sound of the explosion still resonating around the immense cavern, debris continued to fall close to the boat, much of it burning until it hit the water and sizzled out.

"Did you set all that up?" Chester asked Elliott.

"Drake and I did. He called it his 'party trick,' although I never understood what he meant," Elliott admitted. She twisted away from the spectacle, her features hidden within the impenetrable blackness as the nimbus of fiery tongues silhouetted her. She slowly bowed her head as if in prayer. "He was so good . . . a good man," she said, in not much more than a whisper.

As Will, Chester, and Cal marveled at the inferno on the island, none of them uttered a word, sharing her sense of loss for Drake. It was as though the burning island was a funeral pyre, a fitting send-off for him — not only was there a glorious light extravaganza in this unlikeliest of places to honor his death, but also some of his enemies had been brought to justice.

After the sober moment of reflection, Elliott spoke up.

"So, how do you like your Limiters done?"

She began to laugh jubilantly.

"Rare," Chester replied, quick as a flash. The boys joined in with her laughter, hesitantly at first, but then roaring so loudly the boat rocked.

Sarah was shocked from her torpor by the first explosion, and by the second she was on her feet and racing down to the water's edge, with Bartleby following close behind her.

She whistled at the sheer size of the blast and immediately brought up her rifle, wrapping the sling around her arm to hold the weapon steady. Through the scope she scrutinized the fiery point, so small over the waves. Then she slowly moved the rifle away from the island, combing back and forth over the watery horizon. The glow radiating from the fire enabled the light-gathering scope to function highly effectively, but it was still some minutes before she spotted anything. She adjusted the magnification on the scope, trying to clarify the image.

"A boat?" she asked herself. In the extreme distance there was no way she could tell who was in it, but she knew instinctively that it wasn't the Styx. No, in her gut she knew that what she sought was in that boat bobbing on the waves.

"Looks like we're back in business, my old friend," she said to Bartleby, who was flicking his bony tail as if he already knew what they were going to do. Sarah took a last glance at the burning island, and her lips curled into a malicious smile. "And I suppose Rebecca will need to draft some new Limiters."

44

"GET IT TOGETHER," Elliott urged from the helm as Will and Chester pulled on the oars, still not in sync with each other.

"Where exactly are we going?" Cal called out to her. "You said you would take us somewhere safe."

There was a splash as Will misjudged his stroke, his blade skipping across the water. Elliott gave no response, so Cal tried again.

"We want to know where you're taking us. We have a right to know," he insisted. He sounded peeved; Will knew that his leg must be bothering him.

Elliott turned her face from her rifle. "We're going to lose ourselves in the Wetlands. If we make it that far." She paused for several uneven oar strokes, then spoke again. "The White Necks won't be able to track us there."

"Why?" Will asked, wheezing from the exertion of rowing.

"Because it's like . . . like one big, never-ending swamp. . . ." She sounded uneasy, as if she lacked conviction in what she was saying, and this didn't give the boys much confidence, since they hung on her every word. "No one in their right mind *ever* goes into those parts," she continued. "We can lie low until the Styx give us up for lost."

"These Wetlands, are they deeper? Below where we are now?" Cal said, before Will had the breath to ask.

Elliott shook her head. "No, it's one of the outlying areas of the Great Plain that we call the Wastes. Some of the fringes are just too dangerous because of hot spots. . . . Drake never let us spend more than a few days there. It'll suit us for a while, then we'll move on to some other places in the Wastes. They're a lot easier to survive in."

The boys remained silent after that, each left alone with his thoughts. Her words rang in their heads — the Wastes didn't sound very promising, but none of them felt terribly inclined to ask any more questions.

"We're in the pull of currents from a band of whirlpools a couple of miles east," Elliott eventually said. She jabbed a finger over their heads to the starboard side. "And if you don't want to see them up close, I suggest you both put your backs into keeping us on course."

"Aye-aye, Captain," Will grumbled, his earlier enthusiasm for the boat journey all but gone.

Several hours later, after a marathon rowing session, Elliott told them to stop again. Will and Chester welcomed the rest, their arms so tired that they trembled when they raised their canteens for a drink. Elliott instructed Cal to keep watch with the loose rifle scope and Will to put on his headset.

Will flipped the lens down over his eye and turned it on. The view sizzled with orange snow until it settled into a cohesive image, and he saw that they weren't far off the coast. The boat was drifting toward what Will took to be a headland.

As they drifted farther in, silken fingers reached over the surface of the water. A wispy mist crept toward them, the hazy layer thickening to such an extent that it began to spill in over the sides of the boat. The lantern at Chester's feet sent a diffuse illumination through the mist, conferring on it a milky translucence and making their faces glow eerily. Before long they couldn't see anything below their waists. It was a strange sensation to sit there, with the unbroken blanket all around them, as they cut a path through it in the now invisible boat. The fog seemed to absorb all sound, damping even the lapping of the waves.

The air temperature grew warmer as they went, and although none of them said a word, the boys felt as if there was a physical pressure forcing itself down on each of them. Whether it was the gloominess of the mistscape or some other phenomenon, they were all experiencing identical sensations of melancholia and desolation.

They drifted for another twenty minutes. They seemed to be entering a cove or bay. The forlorn silence was broken as the keel of the boat bumped against rocks and ran aground. It was odd. It felt as though the dark spell had been broken, as though they had all woken from an uneasy dream.

Elliott wasted no time in jumping out of the boat. They heard the splashes as she landed, but there was no indication of how deep the water was because the fog reached just over her thighs. She waded to the front of the boat and, guiding it around, heaved it along behind her.

Will turned his attention to the stretch of coast. They had indeed arrived in a bay, its two promontories jutting out to sea on either side. The slow-moving mist tumbled out from the creek, parted in places by peaks of jagged-looking rocks. He, Chester, and Cal stayed put while Elliott drew the boat behind her for a short distance. Then she ordered them to disembark, and, one after another, they clambered reluctantly out of the boat, taking their kit with them.

The water was no more than three feet deep, although currents pulled powerfully against their legs. Taking care not to slip, they trod toward the rocky foreshore while Elliott tugged the boat up a small inlet to hide it. It made a hollow scraping sound as she dragged it ashore.

Will and Chester splashed through the last of the shallows. "Shouldn't we help? She . . . ," Chester was suggesting to Will, just as they both noticed a change in the foreshore. The noise from the boat seemed to bring about a muted rumble, although the cloak of mist prevented them from seeing its source. Cal, scrambling over the rocks some twenty paces ahead of them, had also realized something was up. All three of them stopped on the spot.

The low rumble continued. There was a stirring and a movement, as if the rocks themselves were coming to life, and, all at once, scores of small lights glowed just above the misty blanket, flickering dimly like pairs of candle flames fanned by a draft.

"Eyes!" Chester stuttered. "They're eyes!"

He was right. They caught the light from Chester's and Cal's lanterns and reflected it back, just as surely as if they were deers in a car's beams. Looking through his headset, Will saw that what he'd assumed was the craggy rock formation of the promontories and the foreshore was much more: It was a living carpet, and in a fraction of a second the whole area was rife with activity.

As the streaming mist parted, Will made out what appeared to be birds — storks with long legs — flexing open their wings. But they weren't birds; they were lizards, the likes of which Will had never seen before.

"What do we do now?" Chester said, pulling closer to Will in his panic.

"Will!" Cal called out, hovering uncertainly, then beginning to step backward into the water again.

"Where's Elliott?" Chester asked urgently. They spotted her striding across the foreshore. Showing no concern whatsoever, she cut a furrow straight through the creatures. With a rubbery beating sound, they unfolded their wings and moved out of her way, making the most miserable wails, like young children crying out in terrible pain.

"That's really spooky," Chester said, a little more at ease now that he saw that the creatures didn't seem to pose any danger.

As their wings flapped, wafting aside the mist, Will observed that the creatures were angular and each had a single prehensile claw on its leading edge. Their bodies were bulbous, with tapering thoraxes and dumpy abdomens, and, like their wings, they had a gray sheen to them, similar to polished slate. Their heads were the shape of flattened cylinders with rounded ends, supported by spindly necks, and their jaws, as they gaped open and shut again, were smooth and toothless.

Elliott's passage through the flock disturbed the creatures so much that they began to take wing. But before they could lift off from the ground, they needed a running start — a few strangely stiff and mechanical steps.

In seconds the air was thick with the creatures, their wings beating and thrumming in an unbroken hum. The strange unsettling calls continued, spreading down the colony as if they were communicating their alarm to each other. Once all the creatures were airborne, they gathered into a single flock over the water. Entranced, Will watched them through his lens, a continually shifting orange smear that disappeared into the distance in a mass migration.

"Get a move on!" Elliott shouted. "We don't have time for sightseeing." She waved impatiently to them to follow her up the foreshore.

"Weren't they just wild? Wish I'd gotten a photo of them," Will babbled excitedly to Chester as they hurried to catch up with Elliott, who was making a beeline for the cavern wall.

Chester didn't seem amused. "Yeah, right. How about if we made it into a postcard to send to the folks back home?" he snapped in a loud voice. "Wish you were here . . . having a wonderful time . . . in the land of the freakish talking dragons."

"You've read too much of that fantasy stuff. They're not *freakish talking dragons* at all," Will retorted sharply. He was so caught up with this latest discovery that he hadn't sensed his friend's frame of mind. Chester was simmering and about to blow. "What they are, Chester, is *freakin' amazing* . . . some sort of prehistoric flying lizard, like pterosaurs," Will continued. "You know . . . pterodactyls—"

"Listen, matey, I don't give a stuff what they are." Chester cut across Will belligerently, his head down as they negotiated their way through the craggy rocks. "Every time this happens, I tell myself there can't be anything worse, and, sure enough, just around the next corner . . ." He shook his head and spat, as if disgusted. "Perhaps if *you'd* read those books and been into *normal* stuff, instead of grubbing around in tunnels like some troll or something, we wouldn't be in this mess. You're the freak . . . no, you're worse than that, you're an egghead and a jerk and a danger to anyone around you!"

"There's no need to throw a wobbly, Chester," Will said, trying to smooth things over.

"Don't you tell me what to do. You're not in charge," Chester seethed.

"I was only . . . the lizards . . . I . . . ," Will tried to respond, his voice failing with indignation.

"Oh, just shut up! You just can't get it into your thick bonce that nobody else gives a stuff about your grotty fossils or animal mutants, can you? They're all gross and should be squashed, like insects," he ranted, stamping his foot down and grinding it in the dust to emphasize his point as he spun around to face Will.

"I didn't mean to upset you, Chester," Will said apologetically.

"Upset me?" Chester shouted hysterically. "You've done worse than *that* to me. I'm fed up to the back teeth with all of this! And, most of all, I'm sick of the very sight of *you!*"

"I told you how sorry I was," Will replied weakly.

Chester threw his hands open in an aggressive gesture. "So it's as simple as that, is it? D'you really think you can blag your way out of this with a *sorry,* then I'm expected to let you off . . .

I'm supposed to forgive you for everything, am I?" He gave Will such a look of scorn that it struck him speechless. "Words are cheap, especially yours," Chester said in a low, shaking voice and strode off.

Will was shattered by his friend's remarks. So much for the spirit of camaraderie that he had felt before. He'd so hoped their friendship was back on sound footing again, but he saw now that their jokey exchanges on the beach and in the boat meant nothing at all. Will had been laboring under an illusion. And however much he tried to shrug it off, he was cut to the quick by his friend's outburst. He didn't need to be reminded that he was to blame for everything. He'd wrenched Chester away from his parents and his life in Highfield and gotten him embroiled in this nightmarish situation, which was getting worse by the second.

He started walking again, but his guilt had returned and it weighed heavily on him. He tried to tell himself that Chester's sheer fatigue must be the cause of his outpouring — tempers were bound to be frayed when they'd all had so little sleep — but he didn't find this a very convincing reason for Chester's behavior. His former friend was speaking his mind; it was as clear-cut as that.

Not helped one bit by Chester's outburst, Will himself felt pretty ropy. He would have given anything for a hot bath and a clean bed with crisp white sheets — he felt like he could sleep for a month. He sought out his brother a little way ahead and saw that with each step Cal took he was leaning heavily on the walking stick. His gait was awkward, as if his leg was about to give out at any moment.

No, none of them was in good shape. He hoped that before long they'd have an opportunity for a well-earned rest. But he wasn't about to delude himself that this was in the cards, not with the Limiters on their heels.

They gathered around Elliott by the cavern wall. She was standing before an open seam, a slitlike gap at the base of the wall that was several feet in height. It seemed to be the main source of the mist, which poured out in an unceasing flow. Will kept his distance from Chester, pretending instead to devote all his attention to the seam, although the thick mist prevented him from seeing very much of it.

"We've got a long haul ahead of us," Elliott warned as she unwound a length of rope, which they tied around their waists. She was at the head of the chain, then Cal, Chester, and lastly Will. "Don't want anyone to wander off," she told them, then paused before looking from Will to Chester.

"You two OK now?"

She heard it all. . . . She must have heard everything Chester said, Will thought uneasily.

"Because this isn't going to be easy, and we all need to stick together," she continued.

Will grunted something approximating a yes, while Chester didn't offer any sort of response, studiously avoiding Will's eyes.

"And you," Elliott said, singling out Cal. "I need to know . . . are you up to this?"

"I'll manage," he replied, nodding sanguinely.

"I sincerely hope so," she said, and turned to give them all a last look before she ducked into the seam. "See you on the other side."

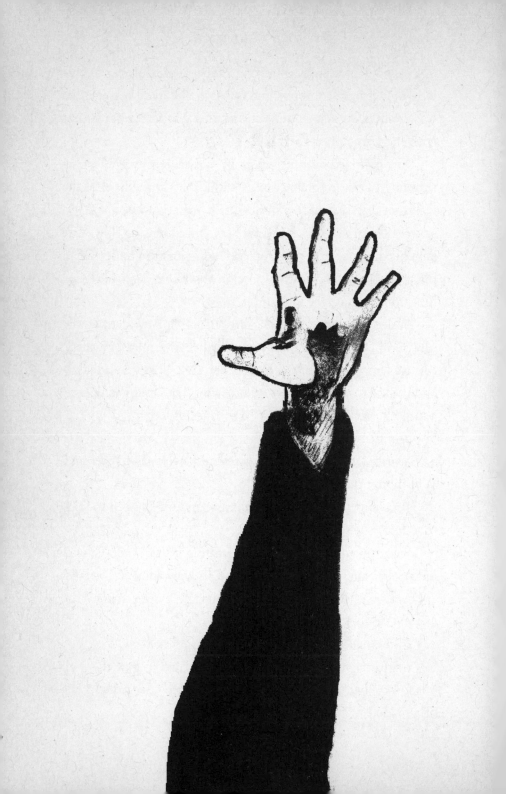

PART 5

The

Spore

45

"**REMARKABLE!**" Dr. Burrows cried, his voice echoing over and over, then fading until all that could be heard was the splatter of water. It fell in occasional showers as he stood before two large stone columns at what appeared to be the conclusion of the path.

He turned this way and that as he tried to take in everything at once.

For starters, the keystone at the apex of the arch had a three-pronged symbol cut into it. He'd seen it several times before on sections of masonry throughout his travels in the Deeps, and it also cropped up on the stone tablets he'd recorded in his notebook. The symbol didn't correspond to any of the glyphics on the Dr. Burrows Stone, so the question of what it meant vexed him considerably.

But this paled into insignificance as he took a few paces under the structure and the path broadened out into an area laid with large flagstones.

With mounting disbelief, he laughed, then stopped, then laughed again as his eyes fell upon the jet-black void before him. It was the most colossal hole in the ground. And he was standing on some sort of pier that overhung it.

A wind gusted from above as he took small steps over the worn flagstones to the very brink of the precipice.

The sheer scale of the opening caused his heart to pound with excitement. He certainly couldn't see any evidence of the other side — it was completely shrouded in darkness. He wished he had a more powerful light source so he could make an informed estimate of its size, but from his reckoning a pretty substantial mountain could have been dropped into it, with room to spare.

Slowly raising his head, he could also see that there was a correspondingly large opening in the roof — whatever this feature was, it seemed to continue above and was the source of the wind and the sporadic torrents of water. His lips moved, but made no sound, as he began to speculate on where this incredible natural feature might end — maybe it had once been open at the earth's surface and at some point become capped off by a shift in the tectonic plates or perhaps by volcanic activity. . . .

But he didn't dwell on any of that now as he was once again compelled to look down into its depths. It was as if the blackness of the vacuum was mesmerizing him, drawing him closer. From the corner of his eye he spotted some steps leading off the edge of the platform.

"Is this it?" he asked himself with bated breath. "Is this my ticket even deeper?"

He started down the cracked stone stairs.

"Blast!" he said, his shoulders hunching as he found that the stairway hardly went any distance. He kneeled, peering in the gloom to see if a section had collapsed.

"No joy," he sighed despondently.

There was nothing he could see to suggest that the stairs did indeed extend farther down — there was just the small vestigial flight, consisting of seven steps, on which he was perched. Maybe, farther around the rim of the opening, there might be a similar set of steps that was intact. Another way down.

He returned to the top, still trying to make sense of everything. So this was the hole on the Coprolite map, and it had to be the same hole depicted on the central panel of the triptych in the ugly bug temple.

He could see why the ancient people had considered it so significant. They — the civilization that had built and used the temple — clearly believed it was something holy, something worthy of worship. He massaged the nape of his neck as he began to think.

Were those ant-sized people in the main picture of the triptych throwing themselves into the hole as part of some ritual act? Were they simply sacrificing themselves? Or was there more to all this?

These questions built in his head, swirling around his cranium as if they were caught in a tornado, every one of them demanding his attention, calling for him to solve them, when all of a sudden his whole body convulsed as if he'd been struck by lightning.

"Yes! I've got it!" he cried, just falling short of shouting out *Eureka!*

He tore open his rucksack and yanked out his notebook, literally dropping onto it as he dived to the ground and began to dash off what he was remembering. The remaining words from the central panel in the temple had at last surfaced in his memory — he could visualize very nearly all of the detail, not quite photo-perfectly, but enough so that he could use his Dr. Burrows Stone to attempt a translation once he'd gotten the letters down.

After ten minutes of furious scribbling, a big smile formed on his face.

"Garden of the . . . *Second Sun!*" he cried. Then the smile evaporated and his brow creased. "Garden of the Second Sun? What the heck does that mean? What garden? What *Second Sun?*"

He rolled onto his side to regard the hole.

"Facts, facts, facts, and only the facts," he said, quoting an oft-used mantra that kept him in check whenever he felt he was about to be swept away by a wave of wild speculation. He tried to think in logical sequences, knowing he had to discipline himself to construct a foundation from all the things he'd discovered. Then, and only then, could he start to build some theories on top of it and set out to test their veracity.

One thing he could quite categorically assume was a revelation in itself: All the geologists and geophysicists back home had gotten it completely wrong. He was many miles below the earth's surface, and by their reckoning he should be cooked to a crisp by now. While he'd run into areas of intense heat, where there was very possibly the presence of molten rock, it certainly didn't correspond to the generally held belief about the composition of the planet and the increasing temperature gradient.

That was all well and good, but it didn't help him get closer to any of the answers he was seeking.

He began to whistle through his teeth, thinking, thinking . . .

Who were the people of the temple?

It was clear that they were a race who, many millennia ago, had taken refuge under the surface of the planet.

But, as depicted in the "Garden of Eden" triptych, they'd made a pilgrimage back to the surface of the earth; what had become of them there?

With an expression of utter bafflement, he let out a final high-pitched squeak of a whistle and rose to his feet. He went back through the arch, then picked his way down the steps again.

Maybe he had been mistaken. Maybe the steps did continue somewhere down below, but he hadn't seen them. He took the blue-handled geological hammer from his belt and, squatting on the bottom step, lodged its tip into a fissure in the wall. He thumped it with the palm of his hand to make absolutely sure it was firmly anchored. It seemed secure enough. Then he gripped it with one hand and, with the light orb suspended by its lanyard in the other, he leaned out as far as he dared, attempting to see more of what lay below.

As he peered into the pitch-blackness, the light orb swinging and his brain still whirring away on the triptych, an idea popped into his head.

By jumping into this hole, did the people of the temple truly believe they'd reach some promised land? Was this the way to their Garden of Eden, or their nirvana, or whatever you chose to call it?

Suddenly, like a second bolt from the blue, he was hit with a bombshell of a concept.

Maybe he'd been looking in the *wrong direction* all this time. He'd been so intent on looking *up*, he'd never considered looking *down*!

Maybe there was a very good reason why the ancient people had had nothing to do with the cultures on the surface for so many millennia. Even if they had originally fled *from* the surface, bringing their ability to write and their enlightened ways with them, maybe they'd never *returned* there. This could be why he could recall nothing in the historical record of all the earth's civilizations that picked up their story.

So . . .

He came up from his thoughts for a quick breath before diving straight back into them again.

. . . did they have the secret of what lies below, in the center of the earth? Was there really a "Garden of the Second Sun" to be found there? And did they really believe that they could get there by throwing themselves into a whopping great hole? Why would they believe that? Why? Why? Why?

Perhaps they were right!

The whole notion was too fantastical for him, but, just the same, the primitive people quite evidently believed the act would take them to their idyllic paradise — believed it with a fervor.

Certainly Dr. Burrows was overtired and suffering from a lack of food, but a nonsensical suggestion popped into his head.

Should I chance it all and jump into the hole?

"You've got to be joking!" he immediately answered himself out loud.

No, it was lunacy! What was he thinking? How could he, a man of considerable learning, subscribe to a pagan belief that by some miracle he'd survive the fall and find wondrous groves of fruit trees and a blazing sun waiting for him?

A sun in the center of the earth?

No, he was being exceedingly foolish. Talk about rational scientific deduction!

Roundly dismissing the suggestion, he pulled himself back onto the step, and then turned around.

He screamed with fright.

The giant insect was there right behind him — his oversized dust mite — its mandibles swishing in his face.

Dr. Burrows recoiled, scrabbling away from it in complete and utter panic. He lost his balance, his arms cartwheeling as he tipped backward from the step.

There was no heroic yell as he fell, just a brief squawk of unwelcome surprise, and he was gone, a tiny figure corkscrewing through the air, down into the dark oblivion of the Pore.

46

FROM UP AHEAD Chester pulled the rope with such force that it caught against Will's wrist and yanked his arm from under him. He dropped into the hot, sticky mud. He heard Chester's voice, muffled and indistinct, as it uttered what Will took to be curses, most likely directed toward him. Chester yanked the rope again, even more fiercely this time. In light of their earlier exchange, Will knew without a doubt that Chester would be blaming him for this unpleasant leg of their journey, just as he did for anything else that came along. Will's resentment grew — wasn't he suffering just as much as the others?

"I'm coming! I'm freakin' coming!" he shouted back furiously as he began to haul himself along again, spitting and swearing as he went.

He thought he was closing the gap on Chester, but he still couldn't see him through the mist. It was only when Will pulled on the rope that he discovered it must have snagged on something. It was stuck fast.

Chester was shouting again at the delay. Whatever he was saying sounded pretty disagreeable.

"Shut up, will you? The rope's caught!" Will screamed back as he lay on his side and used his lantern to try to see what

557

was causing the problem. It was hopeless; he couldn't see a thing. Guessing it had become hung up around a piece of rock, he flipped the rope several times until it eventually came free. Then he crawled up the slope like crazy until he caught up with Chester, who, once again, had stopped — presumably because Cal, in front of him, had also come to a standstill.

Right from the start the seam had climbed at a constant gradient of thirty degrees. The lack of headroom meant there was no choice but to go up the incline on all fours. The underlying substrate was smooth and ran with copious amounts of water as it drained down the slope and into the sea below. As they climbed, the water was replaced by warm mud. With the consistency of crude oil, it was incredibly slippery and made the going that much more difficult.

A little farther up they came to a stretch where the rock became quite hot to the touch, and Will could see little pools of the mud bubbling. Then they passed through an area in which small jets of steam puffed around them like miniature geysers — clearly these were the source of the ever-present mist.

It wasn't dissimilar from being in a sauna turned up to its full setting — it was intolerably hot and humid. Will was breathing quickly and pulling at the collar of his shirt in a futile attempt to cool himself down. And every so often, the stench of raw sulfur permeated the air, so much so that Will felt quite dizzy and wondered how the others were dealing with it.

Elliott had allowed them to have their lanterns on full beam, saying that the light was unlikely to be detected within the confines of the seam, especially since the mist masked everything. Will was grateful for this; it would have been horribly claustrophobic without any illumination to show the way.

On a couple of occasions, Will heard his brother's voice up ahead. From his curses, he sounded distinctly unhappy. Indeed, all three boys were giving vent to their frustration, interspersing their grumbling and groaning with some pretty choice language. Chester was the most vociferous, letting rip and swearing like a sailor. Only Elliott was her usual taciturn self, remaining silent as they went.

With a yank on the rope from Chester, Will realized he'd almost fallen asleep, and he quickly started off again. In no time at all, he had to stop and, as he wiped the mud from his eyes, he observed a nearby mud pool in which bubbles formed and popped with a noise that was best described as a steady *glop glop*.

Yet another unnecessarily savage tug of the rope came.

"Gee, thanks, friend!" he yelled up the slope at Chester.

The frequent tugs were a constant reminder of who Will was roped to. With nothing but the grueling climb to occupy him, he began to dwell on what Chester had said.

"Words are cheap, especially yours!"

"I'm sick of the very sight of you!"

The sentences rang loud and clear in Will's mind.

How dare Chester say those things?

Will hadn't intended for any of this to happen. He'd never in a million years dreamed they'd end up in such danger when he and Chester had set out to discover what had become of Will's missing father. And months ago, as they had walked together along the railway track on the approach to the Miners' Station,

Will had apologized to Chester from the bottom of his heart. Chester had given every indication then that he had accepted Will's apology without reservation.

"Words are cheap, especially yours!"

Chester had thrown it all back in his face, and what could Will possibly do to make amends?

Nothing.

It was an impossible situation. It started Will thinking about what would happen when he was reunited with his father. It was clear that Chester had formed a strong allegiance to Elliott — maybe partly to spite Will. But whatever his motivation, the two seemed very close, and Will was soundly excluded.

But if his father appeared on the scene, how would Elliott react to him joining up with them? And how would his dad react to her? Would they all stay together: he, his father, Chester, Cal, and Elliott? Will couldn't imagine them somehow all getting along — Dr. Burrows would be far too cerebral and absentminded for Elliott. In fact, Will couldn't think of two more different people — worlds apart.

So, if they split up, then what about Chester? The lines had been drawn and Chester definitely wasn't in Will's camp any longer. Will admitted to himself that things had gotten so bad between them that he really wouldn't mind if Chester went off with Elliott. But it wasn't as easy as that: Will and his father would need Elliott, too, especially with the Styx after him.

His thoughts ground to an abrupt halt as the rope snapped taut again, and Chester's guttural, grumpy voice urged him to hurry up.

They continued to climb, and Will noticed that the air seemed to be clearing of mist and steam. A faint breath of cold air percolated around them. This didn't help matters any; they were all plastered with thick mud, and as it began to dry it caused their stiff clothing to chafe against their skin.

The breeze grew into a strong wind and, with a final tug of the rope, Will found that they had reached the top. At last he was able to stand up and stretch the kinks from his back. He rubbed the mud from around his eyes and saw that the others were already on their feet and doing the same as him, easing the fatigue in their cramped limbs. All of them except Cal, who had found a rock to perch on and was massaging his leg with an expression of pure agony. Will peered down at himself and then at the others. The foursome looked like mud people, so thick was the dried crust on them.

As Will stepped into the center of the space, the wind blew with such steady force that it whisked the breath from his mouth. He cleaned his lens of mud and turned on his headset to discover they were in a large tunnel with a roof that was probably fifty feet high. At its edges multiple smaller tunnels led off — so many that their dark openings immediately made him uneasy, as he imagined Styx lurking inside.

"You don't need the rope now!" Elliott shouted to Will. He tried his best to undo it, but the knot was so stiff with mud that she had to help him. Once the rope was untied, Elliott coiled it up again, and then she beckoned them all over. Will noticed that Chester still wouldn't make eye contact with him as he joined the group.

"You go that way," she said, pointing down the large tunnel. Her voice was snatched away by the wind, making it difficult for the boys to hear her.

"Sorry?" Will asked, cupping a hand behind his ear.

"I said, *you go that way!*" she yelled, already backing toward a side tunnel. Apparently she wasn't going with them.

The boys looked at her questioningly, their faces anxious.

Sarah was close — so close she could almost smell them herself, despite the jets of sulfurous steam.

The Hunter was well and truly in his element — this was what he'd been bred for. The scent was so fresh here that he was in a crazed rush to get to his quarry. Strings of milky saliva hung from his muzzle, and his ears twitched as he kept his head to the ground. His body was a blur of scrabbling legs, which slewed mud in their wake as he raced up the seam. He was literally pulling Sarah behind him, and it was all she could do to keep hold of the cat. As he paused to clear his nostrils of mud with rapid piglike snorts, she called out to him.

"Bartleby, where's your master?"

Although he didn't need the slightest encouragement, she called to him once more, goading him on in a crooning voice.

"Where's Cal, then? Where's Cal?"

With a flying start, he shot off again at full tilt, taking her by surprise. She slithered along on her stomach and shouted at him to ease off for a full fifty feet before he finally slowed long enough for her to get up on all fours again.

"When will I learn to keep my big mouth shut?" she mumbled, blinking through her mud mask.

After she'd seen the flying lizards on the wing, knowing full well what had disturbed them, she and Bartleby had sped along the remaining stretch of beach to the cavern wall. Then, on the rocks, he'd soon picked up the trail that led to the seam, raising his head and loosing a victorious, deep-pitched meow.

Now, as they made good headway up the seam, she spotted tracks the group had left — the odd palm print told her that there was someone else with Will and Cal, someone who was smaller. A child? She wondered.

47

THE WIND didn't let up as it swept down the main passage, funneled sometimes by the narrower stretches into a gale, which pushed so hard at the boys' backs that it helped them along. After the heat and steam they'd endured in the seam, it was a welcome change, although the air itself still felt warm on their faces.

The roof ran high above them, and all the surfaces they could see were smooth, as if they'd been scoured by the wind-borne grit that even now compelled the boys to keep their heads tucked down, lest any particles catch them in the eye.

After Elliott had left them to their own devices, they'd started out at a brisk pace. But as time passed and she didn't reappear, the boys began to lose their sense of purpose, ambling along lackadaisically.

Before she'd gone, she had explained that they were to stay on the main track while she scouted the route up ahead for what she called "Listening Posts." Chester and Cal seemed to accept her explanation, but Will was distrustful.

"I don't understand. . . . Why do you need to go off on your own?" he'd asked her, studying her eyes carefully. "I thought you said the Limiters were way *behind* us?"

Elliott hadn't answered immediately, quickly looking away from him and cocking her head, as if she could pick out some sound over the wail of the wind. She listened for a second before turning back to him. "These soldiers know the lay of the land nearly as well as Drake and I do. As Drake *did*," she corrected herself with a wince. "They could be anywhere. You don't take anything for granted."

"You're saying they could be lying in wait for us?" Chester asked, glancing around the passage uneasily. "So we might wander straight into a trap?"

"Yes. So let me do what I do best," Elliott had replied.

Now that they were without her as a guide, Chester took the front position with Will and Cal following closely behind. They felt extremely vulnerable without their catlike protector to watch over them.

While the relentless gale helped keep them cool, it also dehydrated them, and there were no objections when Will proposed they stop for a break. They leaned against the passage wall, gratefully sipping water from their canteens.

Neither Will nor Chester made any effort to speak. Cal, with his bad leg, had his own problems to deal with and was similarly silent.

Will glanced at the other two boys. He knew he was not alone in wondering if Elliott had deserted them. He believed she was eminently capable of leaving them stranded here. If she was unencumbered by the three of them, she'd be able to move at much greater speed to the Wetlands or wherever she intended to go.

Will wondered how Chester would take it if she'd really left them high and dry. He trusted her without reservation, and it would come as a terrible blow. Even as Will looked at him now, he could see Chester was squinting into the gloom for any sign of her.

All at once, over the howling of the wind, there came the unholiest of noises, a low-pitched whining. It was a sound Will hoped he'd never hear again. Seized with dread, he screamed out in alarm.

"Dog! Stalker!"

Cal and Chester both regarded him with dazed bewilderment as he dropped his canteen and leaped toward them, pushing them to move.

"Run!" he yelled in a blind panic.

Several things happened within a single heartbeat.

There was a low whimper, and a dark blur flew from out of the blackness. It leaped low from the ground, soaring straight up at Cal. If the boy hadn't been so close to the passage wall, it would have bowled him over. Will caught a glimpse of the sinuous animal and was even more certain it was a Styx attack dog. He thought all was lost until he heard his brother's shouts.

"Bartleby!" Cal cried with delight. "Bart! It's you!"

Simultaneously two distant cracks flashed farther down the tunnel.

"There she is!" Chester exclaimed. "Elliott!"

Will and Chester watched as the girl departed the shadows and stepped into the middle of the tunnel.

"Stay back!" she shouted to them as she crept down the main trail.

Cal was in raptures, completely oblivious to anything but his beloved cat. "Who put this silly thing on you?" he asked the animal. He immediately unbuckled the leather collar and slung it away. Then he hugged the oversized feline, who repaid him by licking his face.

"I don't believe I got you back, Bartleby," Cal said over and over again.

"I don't believe it, either. Where the heck did he come from?" Will said to Chester, forgetting their differences for the moment.

Despite her instructions to the contrary, they both began to walk slowly toward Elliott. Will turned on his headset and saw that she had her rifle trained low on something. But he didn't begin to grasp what had happened until Chester spoke.

"Elliott took some shots at somebody," he said flatly.

"Oh no," Will exhaled. The two light bursts must have been the muzzle flash as Elliott had fired. He halted on the spot.

Down the tunnel, Elliott had kicked the weapon away from the body and was squatting down to examine it. No need to check for a pulse — she saw the pool of blood spreading through the dust — if the Styx wasn't already dead, it was only a matter of time.

Her first shot had been aimed at the lower body, to stop the attacker in his tracks, quickly followed up by a second shot to the head, which had clipped him on the temple. *Incapacitate . . . then kill.* Her aim had been a little off, not as clean as she would have liked, but the end result was still the same. She allowed herself a satisfied grin.

The Styx had dried mud all over him — so he must have followed them up the seam. With her fingertips, Elliott felt the waxed leather surface of the long coat striped with blocks of brown camouflage, a pattern painfully familiar to her. Well, that was one less Limiter — he wouldn't be bothering them again.

"For you, Drake," she whispered, but then a frown creased her brow.

Something didn't make sense. The would-be assassin had been storming toward the boys with his weapon at his shoulder. Elliott was sure he had been about to take a shot "on the wing," but . . . he hadn't fired. And he hadn't demonstrated any of the precision or stealth she'd have expected from a soldier of the Limiter division. Their combat skills were legendary, yet this man had been in a mad rush. But it was academic now — he was down — and this was no place to hang around. More likely than not there'd be more Limiters on the way; and she wasn't about to be caught in the open like some sitting duck.

She began to scavenge what she could. No rucksack — that was disappointing. The Limiter must have dumped it back on the trail so he could advance more quickly. At least he still had his belt kit, which she stripped off, lobbing it over by the rifle.

She was searching through his jacket pockets when she came across a folded piece of paper. Thinking it was a map, she shook it open, staining it with crimson smudges from the blood on her hands. It was a broadsheet celebrating some sort of event — she'd seen them before in the Colony. The main picture was of a woman, with four smaller images, vignettes of different scenes, around it. Elliott scanned them quickly before something caught her eye.

There was a sixth picture at the bottom that looked as though it had been added later, since it was sketched in pencil. She looked askance at it.

It was the spitting image of Will — although he looked all cleaned up in the picture, with neatly cropped hair.

She peered more closely at it, bringing her lantern to the paper. It *was* Will, but there was another detail that caused her to suck in her breath. He had a hangman's noose tight around his neck. The other end of the rope curled up above his head to form what was very clearly a question mark.

And there was also a shadowy, less clearly defined figure behind him, which vaguely resembled Cal. While Will had the desperate look of the condemned, this second figure smiled serenely. The expressions on the two faces were totally out of sync, and the combination quite unsettling.

She studied the rest of the page, lingering on the central picture of the woman, then read the name in a swirling banner at the very top.

Sarah Jerome.

Elliott immediately bent over the body, pulling the head around so she could examine the face. Despite copious amounts of blood from the head wound, she could tell right away it wasn't a Limiter.

It was a woman!

With long brown hair that had been swept back.

There were no female Limiters. That was unheard of — Elliott, of all people, knew this.

She realized who was before her. Who she had killed.

Will and Cal's mother. Sarah Jerome.

She pushed the head to the side again, thinking she should hide it in case any of the boys wandered over.

"Need any help?" Will called out.

"No," Elliott replied, "just stay put."

"It's a Styx, isn't it?" Will shouted, his voice a little tremulous.

"I think so," Elliott called back after a slight pause.

She hesitated, looking at the blood-soaked head, weighing up whether she should tell Will. With a pang of recollection, she thought of her home back in the Colony. She remembered the heartbreaking moment when she'd been forced to leave her own mother, knowing in all likelihood she would never see her again.

Filled with indecision, Elliott regarded the piece of paper once more. She couldn't keep this secret to herself. She couldn't live with it on her conscience.

"Will, Cal, over here!"

Will came jogging over, with Chester following behind. "You really nailed him," Will observed, eyeing the body with some trepidation.

"You might want to look at this," Elliott said quickly, thrusting the bloodied broadsheet into his hand.

He scanned the sheet as it flapped in the wind. Recognizing the sketch of himself at the bottom of the page, he shook his head in disbelief. "What *is* this?" Then his eyes alighted on the name at the top. "Sarah . . . Sarah Jerome," he read out loud. He turned to Chester. "Sarah Jerome?" he said again.

"Not your mother?" Chester asked as he leaned in to see the broadsheet.

Elliott kneeled down beside the body. Without saying a word, she very gently turned the head, pushing the damp hair aside to reveal the face. Then she stood up. "I thought it was a Limiter, Will."

"Oh! It's her! It *is* her!" Will exclaimed, glancing between the broadsheet and the body on the ground. He didn't really need the picture; the similarities between his own face and hers were remarkable. It was as though he was seeing his reflection in a dusty mirror.

"What's she doing down here? And why was she carrying that?" Chester asked, pointing at the rifle.

Will shook his head, overwhelmed. "Get Cal," he said to Chester as he stepped closer to Sarah. Squatting down by her shoulder, he put out a hand to touch the face that was so very much like his own.

He drew it back as she gave a small moan.

"Elliott, she's alive!" he gasped.

Then her eyelids flickered but remained shut.

Before Elliott could react, Sarah's mouth opened and she drew a breath.

"Will?" she asked, her lips moving weakly, her voice so quiet that he could barely hear it over the desolate howl of the wind.

"Are you Sarah Jerome? Are you really my mother?" he asked in a cracked voice. His emotions were in a complete tumult. Here he was meeting his biological mother for the first time, yet she was dressed in the uniform of the soldiers who were after him. And in the picture she'd been carrying, he had a noose around his neck. What did that mean? Had she been about to shoot him?

"Yes, I'm your mother," she groaned. "You must tell me . . ." Then her voice failed her.

"What? Tell you what?" Will asked.

"Did you kill Tam?!" Sarah screamed, her chest heaving and her eyes flicking wide open as she stared at Will. He was so shocked that he almost fell backward.

"No, he didn't," Cal answered from beside Will, who hadn't even noticed he was there. "Is it really you, Mother?"

"Cal," Sarah said, tears spilling from her eyes as she squeezed them shut and began to cough. It took her several seconds before she was able to talk again. "Just tell me what happened in the Eternal City. . . . Tell me what happened to Tam. I need to know."

Cal found it difficult to speak, his lips trembling. "Uncle Tam died saving us . . . both of us," he said finally.

"Oh my God." Sarah wept. "They were lying to me. The Styx were lying to me all the time." She tried to sit up.

"You need to keep still," Elliott told her. "You're bleeding badly. I thought you were a Limiter. I shot —"

"That doesn't matter now," Sarah said, rolling her head with the pain.

"I can dress your wounds," Elliott offered, shifting uneasily on her feet as Will looked up at her.

Sarah tried to say no but broke into another coughing fit. When it had passed, she continued. "Will, I'm sorry I ever doubted you. I'm so very, very sorry."

"That's . . . that's OK," Will stammered, not really knowing what she meant.

"Come closer, both of you," she urged them. "Listen to me."

As they leaned in to hear what their mother wanted to tell them, Elliott set about applying some gauze pads to Sarah's hip, tying them in place with bandage strips.

"The Styx have got a deadly virus and they're going to spread it Topsoil." She stopped talking, clenching her teeth together with a moan, then resumed. "They've already tested a form of it there, but . . . but it was only a trial run. . . . The full-strength virus is called Dominion . . . going to cause a terrible plague."

"So that was what we saw in the Bunker," Cal whispered, looking at Elliott.

"Will . . . Will," Sarah said, staring at him with an intense desperation. "Rebecca carries the virus around with her . . . and she wants you out of the picture. The Limiters" — Sarah tensed her body, then relaxed again — "won't stop until you're dead."

"But why me?" Will's head reeled — here was the confirmation he was dreading. The Styx *were* out to get him.

Sarah didn't answer but, with the greatest effort, looked at Elliott as the girl put the finishing touches to a bandage on her temple. "They're coming for all of you. You've got to get away from here. Are there others you can call on for help?"

"No, there's only us," Elliott answered her. "Most of the renegades have been rounded up."

Sarah was silent while she tried to steady her breathing. "Then, Will, Cal, you have to dig yourselves in deep . . . somewhere they can't reach you."

"That's what we're doing," Elliott confirmed. "We're going to the Wastes."

"Good," Sarah croaked. "And then you must go Topsoil and warn them what's coming."

"How . . . ?" Will began.

"Oh, it hurts," Sarah groaned, and her face went limp as if she'd blacked out. Only the occasional flutter of her eyelids told them she was hanging on to consciousness.

"Mum," Will said hesitantly. Addressing a complete stranger in that way felt so incredibly foreign to him. There were a thousand things he wanted to ask her. "Mum, you've got to come with us."

"We can carry you," Cal said.

Sarah's response was resolute. "No, I'd only slow you down. You've got a fighting chance if you get going."

"She's right," Elliott said, picking up Sarah's rifle and belt kit and handing them to Chester. "We have to leave now."

"No, I'm not going without my mother," Cal insisted, seizing Sarah's limp hand.

As Cal talked to his mother, tears flowing freely down his cheeks, Will took Elliott aside.

"There's got to be something we can do," he pressed her. "Can't we take her with us some of the way and hide her?"

"No," Elliott replied emphatically. "Besides, moving her isn't going to help her any. She's probably going to die, anyway, Will."

Sarah called Will's name, and he immediately rejoined Cal by her side.

"Never forget," Sarah said to the boys. She was really struggling now, her face contorted with pain. "I'm so proud of both of . . ." She didn't finish the sentence. As Will and Cal watched, her eyes slid shut and she was still.

"We've got to go," Elliott said. "The Limiters will be here soon, very soon."

"No!" Cal shouted. "You did this to her. We can't —"

"I can't undo what I've done," Elliott answered him evenly. "But I can still help you. It's your choice whether or not you let me."

Cal was about to object again when Elliott began to walk away, with Chester close behind.

"Just look at her, Cal. We wouldn't be doing her any favors if we tried to shift her," Elliott added over her shoulder.

Despite Cal's continuing protests, both he and Will knew in their hearts that Elliott was right. There was no way they'd be able to haul Sarah with them. They, too, began to move away. Their mother might stand a better chance if another renegade were to find her and tend to her injuries, as Elliott had told them. But both Will and Cal knew just how unlikely this was and recognized that Elliott was trying to give them what little comfort she could.

As they rounded a corner in the tunnel, Will stopped and turned to look back at Sarah where she lay. With the mournful, unremitting howl of the wind all around him, it was such a forlorn and chilling thought — that she could die there in the dark, with no one by her side. Maybe his fate would be the same, to breathe his last in some far corner of the earth, alone.

Maybe he should have been suffering the most intense sorrow that his real mother was bleeding to death there in the tunnel. But all he felt was just a cloud of confused emotions. To Will, Sarah was little more than a stranger who had been gunned down due to an unfortunate mistake.

"Will," Elliott urged him, pulling him by the arm.

"I don't understand. What's she doing down here?" he said. "And why did they give her Bartleby?"

"The Hunter belonged to Cal?" Elliott asked.

Will nodded.

"Then it's simple, really," Elliott said. "The White Necks knew you and Cal were together. So what better than to let Sarah use the animal to track its master and lead her straight to you?"

"I suppose that's right," Will said, frowning. "But what did the Styx think —?"

"Don't you see? They wanted her to find you and kill you," Chester cut in, his voice measured and dispassionate. He had remained silent until now and was thinking more clearly than Will. "They obviously tried to make her believe you were responsible for Tam's death. It's another of their vile little schemes. Just like this Dominion thing she spoke about."

"Now can we just hurry it up?" Elliott said, sprinkling some Parchers on the trail behind her.

They continued along the main track with Cal walking apart from them, his prancing and overjoyed cat by his side.

And before long they emerged out onto a thin strip of a ledge, the wind still blowing hard. They stopped. They could see nothing before them, and no way down.

48

"**WHAT NOW?**" Will asked, trying to put all thoughts of Sarah out of his mind and focus on their current situation. Elliott had brought them to the edge of a crevasse, but what lay beyond or below, he couldn't tell.

Will was aware of Chester's cold stare upon him, and it made him extremely angry. It still felt as though his old friend was silently blaming him for everything. Considering what Will had just been through, he'd have expected Chester to cut him some slack. Clearly he was expecting too much.

"So, are we going to jump for it?" he said, peering at what he assumed was a sheer drop.

"Sure, be my guest. It's several hundred feet down, as the stone falls," Elliott replied. "But you might want to try over here instead."

At the very edge of the ledge they saw two prongs. They went as near as they dared, the combination of the high wind and the sheer drop making them move with caution, and discovered that it was the tip of an old iron ladder.

"A Coprolite ladder. Not as quick as jumping, but much less painful," she said. "This place is known as the Sharps — you'll see why when we get down."

"What about Bartleby?" Cal suddenly piped up. "He can't climb down this ladder, and no way am I leaving him here! I only just got him back!"

Cal was kneeling with his arm around the cat, who was rubbing a huge cheek against the side of the boy's head and purring so loudly it sounded like an overcrowded beehive.

"Send him along the ridge. He'll find his own way down," Elliott said.

"I'm *not* going to lose him again," Cal stated resolutely.

"I think I got the message," Elliott barked. "If he's any sort of Hunter, he'll seek us out at the bottom."

Cal humphed indignantly. "What do you mean? He's the best Hunter in the whole Colony! Aren't you, Bart?" He ran his hand affectionately over the creased, hairless pate of the cat's domed head, and the beehive sounded as if a riot had broken out.

Elliott went first, followed closely by Chester, who pushed past Will to the front. "Excuse me," he said brusquely.

Will chose not to say anything, and as soon as Chester disappeared from view, he went next. He found it disconcerting as he took hold of the two rusty uprights and edged his legs over the brink until he found a rung with his foot. But once he'd started to move, it wasn't too bad. Last to follow was Cal, who had dispatched Bartleby on the longer journey down via the ledge but was having huge misgivings himself as he descended the ladder, stiffly and deliberately.

It was a long climb and the ladder trembled and creaked ominously with their combined movements, as if some of the fixings had broken loose. Their hands soon became coated with rust and so dry that they had to be extra careful not to lose their grip. The wind gradually dropped off the lower they went, but after a while Will noticed that he couldn't see or hear Cal above him.

"Are you OK?" he shouted up.

There was no reply.

He repeated the question, louder this time.

"Fine," came the begrudging reply from Chester below.

"Not you, you dork. It's Cal I'm worried about."

As Chester mumbled something in response, Cal's walking stick swished past Will, spinning end over end as it fell.

"Cal!" Will exclaimed, thinking for one awful moment that his brother had slipped and was going to follow after it. He held his breath and waited, but still there was no sign of the boy. Reversing his direction, Will began to climb. He soon came across Cal, who was completely stationary, both arms wrapped tightly around the ladder.

"You dropped your stick. What's up?"

"I can't do this . . . ," Cal gasped. "Feel sick . . . just leave me alone for a minute."

"Is it your leg?" Will asked, concerned. "Or are you still upset about Sarah? What is it?"

"No. I just feel . . . feel dizzy."

"Ahh," Will said, remembering. There'd been signs of it before when they were Topsoil. Cal wasn't used to heights after spending his whole life in the Colony. "You don't like being up here; it's the height, isn't it?"

Cal swallowed a yes.

"Well, just trust me on this, Cal. I don't want you to look down, but we're almost at the bottom. . . . I can see Elliott there right now."

"Are you sure?" Cal said skeptically.

"Absolutely. Come on."

The deception worked for about a hundred feet, until Cal again came to a standstill.

"You're lying. We should be there by now."

"No, really, not far now," Will assured him. "And don't look down!"

This went on several times, Cal becoming more and more distrustful and angry until Will really did reach the bottom.

"Touchdown!" he announced.

"You lied to me!" Cal accused him as he stepped from the ladder.

"Yeah, but hey, it worked, didn't it? You're safe now," Will replied with a shrug, happy that he'd been able to talk his brother down, even if he'd resorted to deception to achieve it.

"I'm never going to listen to you again," Cal threw huffily at him as he began to hunt around for his walking stick. "You're a lying slug."

"Oh, sure, feel free to take it out on me . . . just like everybody else around here does," Will replied, more for Chester's benefit than Cal's.

Will turned from the ladder, his feet making a glassy noise as if he were treading on pieces of broken bottle. Indeed, as they all moved around, the ground produced a grinding and vitreous ringing. From what little Will could see, before them seemed to be a colonnade of closely packed pillars spearing up into the darkness, each one more than 200 feet in girth.

"I'm only going to do this because the Limiters should be far enough behind that it doesn't matter, and I want you to know what we're getting into," Elliott said, turning up her lantern and holding it on the area before them.

"Wow!" Will exclaimed.

It was like looking into a sea of dark mirrors. As the beam from Elliott's light struck the nearest column, it was reflected onto another. The beam crisscrossed around them, creating the illusion that there were scores of lanterns. The effect was staggering. He also caught sight of his and the others' reflections from all angles.

"The Sharps," Elliott said. "They're made of obsidian."

Will began to study the nearest column. Its circumference wasn't rounded after all, but composed of a series of perfectly flat plains that ran vertically up its length, as if it had been formed by many longitudinal fractures. It didn't seem to taper in the slightest toward the top.

Scanning around, Will came across a different style of column. The flat plains along its length were gently curved, like some gargantuan licorice twist. Indeed, as he looked further, there were more like this in between the straight columns, and a small number that were extremely pronounced in their curvature.

His mind was awhirl as he started to speculate on the factors that could have produced such a unique natural phenomenon. Although he was bursting to say something about the columns, he checked himself, remembering only too painfully the reaction from Chester when he'd waxed lyrical about the flying lizards. But if ever anything resembled a setting for one of Chester's precious fantasy stories, these crystalline monoliths had to be it. *The secret lair of the dark fairies*, Will thought wryly. No, better still: *the secret lair of the dark and extremely vain fairies*. He suppressed a chuckle at this, keeping the notion firmly to himself. It wouldn't be wise to antagonize Chester any further; relations with him were at an all-time low as it was.

Chester picked that moment to speak up, sounding distinctly unimpressed with their surroundings, most likely in a bid to tweak Will.

"Uh-huh. The Sharps. So now what?" he asked Elliott, who turned her lantern down again, dousing the confusion of light beams and multiple images. Will was actually relieved because it was so incredibly disorienting.

"It's a maze in here, so do exactly what I tell you," Elliott replied. "Drake and I set up a cache halfway through, where we can replenish our food and water and also stock up on our munitions from the arsenal. It's not going to take us long, and then we're heading on to the Pore. Once we're past that, it's a couple of days' haul to the Wetlands."

"The Pore?" Will asked, his curiosity piqued.

"What about Bartleby?" Cal demanded, bringing the exchange to an end. "He's not here yet."

"Give him a chance. You know he'll find us," Elliott said in an understanding tone, attempting to mollify the boy.

"He'd better," Cal said anxiously.

"Let's do this," Elliott said, sighing as her patience wore thin.

There was no way that the boys could move quietly with the clinking and crunching of the glassy gravel underfoot, although Elliott managed it effortlessly, as if she were gliding over the surface.

"All that noise you're making will carry for miles. Can't you *rock apes* tread more lightly?" she implored them, but it was useless. However much care they took, they still sounded like a herd of rhinoceros stampeding through a glazier's. "The cache isn't far from here. I'm going to check it, then you can follow me in. Understood?" Elliott stated, then slipped away.

As they hung around, waiting for her return, Cal suddenly spoke.

"I think I hear Bart. He's coming."

Leaving Will and Chester, he edged slowly forward, hugging the side of the column.

His dimmed lantern fell on something.

It wasn't Bartleby.

It wasn't his own reflection in the glossy obsidian, either.

A Limiter stood before him in all his dark glory.

He had been skirting around the column from the opposite side, his rifle at his waist.

For the briefest moment, he looked as surprised as Cal, who squawked an urgent, unintelligible warning, alerting Will and Chester.

Cal's eyes and the Limiter's locked. Then the Limiter's upper lip pulled back into a brutal sneer, his teeth bared in his hollow-cheeked, hideous face. It was animal and insane. The grimace of a killer.

Cal's instincts kicked in and he used the closest thing he had to a weapon. He brought up his walking stick and, by some freak stroke of luck, the handle hooked the Limiter's rifle before he could raise it, yanking it clean from his hands.

It clattered across the obsidian gravel.

For another moment, the Limiter and Cal simply stood there, even more surprised than before. It didn't last long. In less than a heartbeat, the Limiter's hand snapped in front of him, gripping a gleaming scythelike dagger. It was standard issue for the Styx military, with a slightly curved and lethal-looking blade about ten inches long, and Cal had seen it used to deadly effect when the Crawfly cut down Uncle Tam. Brandishing it, the Limiter dived at the boy.

But his big brother was already there, tearing in from the side. Grabbing the Limiter's arm, Will crashed into him, sending the man flying. Will followed him down, landing on top of him. Still holding the soldier's arm, Will used all his weight to keep him from using his knife.

Cal followed suit and launched himself onto the soldier's legs, wrapping his arms around the man's ankles as tightly as he could. The Limiter punched at Will's back and neck with his free arm, trying his utmost to get at his face. But Will's rucksack had ridden up around his shoulders, making it difficult for the Limiter to land his heavy blows. Shouting to Chester, Will kept his head well tucked down.

"Use the gun!" Will bawled over and over again, his voice muffled because his mouth was pressed against the Limiter's upper arm.

"Chester, the gun!" Cal shouted hoarsely. "Shoot him!"

As the boys' discarded lanterns sent a flurry of random beams glancing off the columns like a confusion of small spotlights, Chester, poised several feet away, had lifted the rifle and was trying to take aim.

"Shoot!" Cal and Will screamed in unison.

"I can't see!" Chester screamed back frantically.

"Do it!"

"Just shoot!"

"I can't get a clear shot!" Chester shrieked in absolute desperation.

The man thrashed wildly under Will and Cal, and Will was just about to shout again when something large slammed up against him. He swiveled his head around, lifting it just enough to see that Chester had also piled on. He'd evidently given up trying to take a shot with the rifle and decided the only thing he could do was join the fray. He'd dropped to his knees, pressed one into the Limiter's abdomen, and was raining punches on his face with both fists. As Chester made an attempt to pin down his free arm, leaning forward to grab hold of it, the Limiter saw his opportunity. He tensed his neck and, with a sickening thump, head-butted Chester hard.

"YOU SCUM!" Chester screamed. He immediately resumed the beating, dodging the Limiter's loose arm every time it took a swipe at him.

"DIE! DIE, YOU JACKHOLE! DIE!" Chester raved as he intensified his punches, his fists pummeling the Limiter's face.

If Chester had happened to catch sight of his reflection in one of the columns, he wouldn't have recognized himself.

His face was a distortion, twisted into a crazed, determined mask. All the resentment and fury from his imprisonment in the Colony had found a release and was pouring out in one unstoppable torrent. He kept pounding the soldier, pausing only to fend off the Limiter's fist when he tried to retaliate.

The four of them writhed in the deadly struggle, swearing in breathless desperation as the man grunted stentorously like a wild boar, trying anything and everything to get free. Chester was still hammering away at the soldier, but it seemed to be having little effect. The boys' combined weight constricted his movements, but he was still able to use the elbow of his free arm to deliver the occasional weak counterstrike. And he tried to gouge at their faces with his clawed fingers, again unsuccessfully.

"KILL HIM!" Cal yelled from lower down the Limiter's body.

The boys fought on, knowing only that they had to restrain the soldier by whatever means necessary. There was simply no alternative. It was him or them.

As their bodies strained and pumped against each other, there was an obscene intimacy to the struggle. Chester could smell the sourness of the man's sweat and his vinegary breath in his face. Will felt the man's thick muscles knotting underneath him as he used all his strength to try to free his arm.

"NO. YOU. DON'T!" Will shouted, doubling and redoubling his efforts to restrain the man's bucking form.

The Limiter changed his tactics, perhaps as a last resort. He raised his head as far as he could and spat and snapped, attempting to bite them while making noises not unlike the stalker that had mauled Will so horrifically in the Eternal City.

But these small acts of savagery were only a distraction: He'd identified a chink in their combined onslaught. He screeched victoriously as he brought up his knees and dislodged Cal just enough to be able to wrest free a leg. He drew it back and drove his heel hard against Cal's stomach. The kick sent Cal sprawling across the glass gravel, his breath knocked out of him. He curled up, gasping air back into his lungs.

Now the Limiter had more leverage. He swung his legs and began to twist and thrash with such force that Chester was finding it impossible to hang on. As Chester fought back, the Limiter caught him with a resounding clout to the head. Stunned, he slumped to the ground.

Will had no idea of the others' plights. He didn't dare look up for fear of being beaten or gouged, stubbornly clinging to the Limiter's arm and spreading his body weight the best he could to keep the man down. Will was going to do his utmost to stop the soldier from using his scythe, even if it was the last thing he did — and he knew it might well be.

Less constricted now, the Limiter repeatedly drove his fist into Will's head and neck. Will cried out with pain. He couldn't withstand much more of this punishment.

Fortunately Chester had regained consciousness. Snatching up a large shard of obsidian, he began to slam it against the Limiter's skull.

The Limiter cursed Chester in the nasal Styx language, then reached up and clapped his hand around Chester's jaw. He hooked his thumb into the corner of Chester's mouth and used the painful hold to yank the hapless boy aside.

His legs scrabbling, Chester had absolutely no alternative but to follow where the Limiter was pulling him. Once Chester was on the ground and in easy reach, the Limiter gave him a tremendous blow on the cranium. This time, there would be no quick recovery. Chester lay in a groggy confusion, a Milky Way of spinning stars interlacing with the matrix of reflected light beams all around him.

With both Cal and Chester out of contention, only Will remained. The Limiter got a grip on Will's neck and was digging his fingers into it, closing off his windpipe. The soldier babbled something exultantly in the Styx tongue. He thought he'd won.

Choking from pain and lack of air, Will saw that the end was near. Somehow it didn't come as a great surprise. After all, this was a *trained soldier* they'd taken on. They were just three kids. What chance had they ever had?

Click! As if the Limiter had snapped his fingers, a second scythe materialized from nowhere in his free hand. The blade flickered in the light of a nearby lantern as, in one fluid and easy movement, the Limiter switched his grip on the weapon.

"No!" Will croaked in alarm, his stomach sinking as he caught sight of the scythe. The killer had him cold. The blade glinted as the Limiter sucked in a breath through his battered lips and began to lower the weapon. Will's neck was now totally exposed. Will clenched his teeth, all hope deserting him as he waited for the knife to find its mark.

There was an earsplitting bang.

The bullet passed so close to Will, he felt its heat on his skin. The Limiter's raised hand hovered for what seemed to be an eternity, then opened. The knife slipped from its grasp.

Will stayed exactly where he was, numb with bewilderment, the sound of the shot still ringing in his ears. He wouldn't look at the soldier directly, but could see enough to know he was a grisly mess. He heard a long exhalation as the man's lungs emptied. Then came a wracking paroxysm, the whole of the man's body tightening, and a wet gurgle as a pink mist filled the air. Will felt droplets on his face. That was enough to snap him out of his paralysis. In a mad rush, he scrambled back, away from the Limiter, and leaped to his feet, spewing out a stream of unintelligible words and horrified gasps.

Panting rapidly, wiping his face over and over again with his sleeves, he stopped and turned. Cal stood stock-still, holding Chester's rifle. He stared at the dead man.

"I got him," he said quietly, not lowering the rifle, or his gaze.

Will went to him, as did Chester.

"I got him in the face," he said again, even more faintly. His eyes were empty and his expression blank.

"It's OK, Cal," Will said, easing the rifle from his brother's rigid hands and passing it to Chester. He put his arm around Cal's shoulders and slowly guided him away from the grim sight of the dead Limiter. Will was still shaken, but his concern for Cal outweighed any he had for himself. The boy dumbly complied when Will told him they should both sit down. He felt Cal tremble against him. This was not the moment for his brother to go into shock.

"You got him good! You bagged him! You bagged yourself a Limiter!" Chester was babbling excitedly and laughing, his words slurred and poorly formed because of his swollen face. "Got him smack in the kisser! Bull's-eye! Serves him right! Hahahaha!"

"For goodness' sake, shut up, Chester," Will growled at him. His brother began to gag, then was violently sick. He was crying and mumbling something about the Limiter.

"It's OK, it's OK," Will said, not letting go of him. "It's over."

Elliott rushed in.

"Idiots! Do you think you could make any more noise?"

She saw the dead Limiter and gave a single approving nod. Then she looked over at the boys. Still twitchy from the adrenaline, Chester jigged from foot to foot, while Will and Cal sat comatose.

She scanned the glass columns.

"The White Necks are even closer than I thought."

"You can say that again," Will muttered.

She turned to Chester, who was now dabbing at his nose, trying to stem the flow of blood from it. She smiled. "You shot him. Nice work."

"Um . . . I . . . no . . . ," Chester stammered. "I couldn't get . . ."

"Cal did it," Will cut in.

"But you had the rifle?" she said to Chester, looking perplexed and a little disappointed. Chester didn't offer any further explanation, glowering sullenly at Will. Then Elliott twisted to Will and Cal. "Get up. We have to go now . . . right now. Anyone hurt?"

"My jaw . . . my nose . . . ," Chester began.

"Cal needs a second. Look at him," Will interrupted urgently, leaning back so Elliott had a view of his brother's dazed, out-of-focus eyes.

"Not a chance. Not after all that racket," she said.

"Can't he —?" Will begged.

"No," she growled. "Listen!"

They did as she said, and heard a baying in the distance.

"Stalkers!" Will exclaimed, the hairs on the back of his bruised neck standing up.

"Yes, a pack of them," Elliott nodded. She looked at the boys with a small smile. "There's another reason I think *now* would be a good time to hit the road," she said.

"What's that?" Will asked quickly.

"I've lit a fuse in the cache. The whole arsenal's going to blow sky-high in sixty seconds."

This last piece of information galvanized Cal into action. Elliott scooped up the Limiter's rifle as they thundered past his body, and then they ran like they'd never run before. Will stayed close to Cal, who started off the best he could on the glass shards with his weak leg. But once Bartleby rejoined the crew, the boy raced along as fast as the rest of them.

Like firecrackers going off, there was a volley of gunfire. A hail of lead peppered the columns around them, the impacts sometimes sending plate-sized fragments gyrating into the air. Will instinctively bent his head and began to slow down.

"No! Keep going!" Elliott yelled.

Bullets ricocheted and whined from the mirror surfaces as they fled. Will felt tugs on his pants legs, but couldn't stop to see the cause. .

"Get ready!" Elliott shouted over the barrage.

It came.

The explosion was huge. A blinding light scorched around them, sent in a thousand different directions by the reflective surfaces, and then, as soon as the reverberations of the initial blast subsided, a tremendous crashing began.

Broken columns came toppling down, colliding one into the other, like dominoes in a chain reaction. A goliath section of fractured column slammed into the ground directly behind them, sending up a dust storm of powdered glass that sparkled like black diamonds in their lights. It clogged their throats and stung their eyes. The ground itself rocked with each impact.

The bedlam and crashing continued unabated, and before any of them knew it they were speeding after Elliott into a tunnel. Will jerked his head around just in time to see a column collapse against the entrance and completely seal it off. They were submerged in a miasma of glass sleet for several hundred feet. Then the air cleared and Elliott brought them to an abrupt halt.

"We have to go, we have to go," Chester urged her.

"No, we have a few minutes' grace. They can't follow us in here," she said, picking fragments of glass from her face. "Drink some water and get your breath back." After taking a large swig from her canteen to rinse out her mouth, she swallowed several gulps and then passed it around. "Anyone hurt?" she asked as she set about checking each of them over in turn.

Chester couldn't breathe through his nose, but Elliott told him she didn't think it was broken. His mouth was also badly swollen and split at the corner where the Limiter had crooked it, and his head tender from the catalog of punches. As Elliott used her lantern to examine him, he saw his knuckles were red and bruised, and his forearms soaked through with blood. She examined them carefully.

"It's all right. It's not yours," she said after a quick inspection.

"The Limiter?" Chester said, giving her a wide-eyed look and shivering as he recalled how he'd pummeled the soldier with the chunk of obsidian. "That's terrible . . . how could I have done that . . . done that to another person?" he whispered.

"Because he would have done worse to you," she said curtly, before moving on to Cal.

The boy appeared to be unhurt except for some very tender ribs. But he was slow to respond when Elliott spoke to him, still shocked that he'd shot the Limiter.

She took him by both shoulders, her voice sympathetic.

"Cal, listen. Drake gave me some advice once, after a horrible thing happened to me."

The boy looked vaguely at her.

"He said that our skin has a dead layer on it."

She had his attention now — he frowned quizzically at her.

"It's the cleverest thing. It dies and the top layers flake off, to protect us from infection." Straightening up, she lifted her hands from his shoulders and brushed one over the back of the other to illustrate what she was saying. "The bacteria — or germules, as you call them — they settle, but can't get a hold."

"So?" Cal said, intrigued.

"So right now, part of you is dying, just like your skin. It might take a while — it did with me — but it will die to save you. And next time you'll be tougher and stronger."

Cal nodded.

"So let it go and just move on."

Cal nodded again. "I think I see," he said, his face losing its rigidity and his eyes regaining a measure of their vitality. "Yes, I see."

Will had been listening and was impressed with the way Elliott had been able to comfort the boy. Cal already seemed to be back to his old self, chatting enthusiastically to his beloved cat.

Elliott checked Will next. Considering what he'd been through, he was relatively unscathed except for some angry red bruises and grazes on his neck, a number of abrasions on his face, and a mountain range of bumps on the back of his head. As he gingerly touched them, he thought of the tugs he'd felt when they'd been running and, probing his calf with his fingers, discovered a couple of small tears in the fabric of his pants legs.

"What's this?" he said to Elliott. He knew they hadn't been there before.

Elliott inspected them.

"They're bullet holes. You should count yourself lucky."

The shots had punched straight through the material, and he could stick a finger in the holes to show where they'd landed. Relieved that he hadn't been hit, that he'd indeed dodged another bullet, he broke into laughter. Cal gave him a curious look, while Chester just clicked his teeth dismissively. Elliott regarded him with quiet disapproval.

"Keep it together, Will," she rebuked him.

"Oh, I'm together all right," he came back at her, breaking into a fresh peal of laughter. "Against all odds."

"OK, to the Pore!" she announced. "Then the Wetlands."

"Where we'll be home and dry?" Will asked with a chuckle.

49

"**IS THAT YOU**, Will?" Sarah moaned as she felt some-one gripping her wrist. Then she remembered that he, Cal, and the others had long gone, just as she'd urged them to do.

She opened her eyes to darkness and the most excruciating agony she'd ever experienced in her life.

Every single pain and ache, every single toothache and headache and discomfort that comes during a lifetime, all accumulated together into a single moment of unendurable agony: This was how it felt. A thousand times worse even than childbirth.

She cried out, battling to stay conscious. Her eyes remained open despite the fact that she couldn't see who was there. She didn't know how long she'd been out for — it was as if she'd pushed her way between a pair of heavy curtains and some-thing ineluctable was pulling her back through them so they could draw together again. It was the most tremendous strug-gle, because the pain was forcing her back behind the curtains, a place so tranquil and warm and welcoming. It was all she could do to resist the temptation to go there. But she wasn't going to allow herself that final bow, and with each labored breath she fought against it.

The grip on her wrist tightened, and as she heard the rasping sound of the Styx language, her heart fell. A light appeared somewhere in the very periphery of her vision, and there were more Styx voices as she saw shadowy forms flitting around her.

"Limiter," she said, recognizing the camouflage on the arm that was now checking over her body.

In confirmation, a harsh voice snapped at her.

"Stand up!"

"I can't," she said, forcing herself to focus in the dim light.

There were four Limiters there. She'd been found by a patrol. Two of them hauled her to her feet. She felt the crippling pain in her hip and screamed — it reverberated through the tunnel, but it was as though someone else was crying out. She came close to losing consciousness again, the curtains parting a little to allow her through.

The Limiters forced her to walk, suspended between them. The pain was unbearable. She felt her hip grinding, fractured bone upon fractured bone, and nearly blacked out. Sweat trickled down her forehead and into her eyes, making her blink, making her close her eyes.

She was dying and she knew it.

But she wasn't going to die yet.

As long as she was breathing there was still a chance she could help Will and Cal.

Drake slipped through the tunnel as fleetly as the winds that swept around him. He paused every so often to search the path for any sign that it had been used recently. The constant gale ensured the sand and grit didn't lie undisturbed for long, so he knew he was unlikely to be confused by any old tracks along the way.

Without stopping, he touched the tip of his shoulder, which had been clipped by a bullet. It was only a flesh wound — he'd had worse. He dropped his hand to the knife at his hip, and then to the pad of stove guns on his thigh. He felt distinctly vulnerable without his rifle and rucksack full of munitions, which he'd lost back at the entrance to the Bunker. And his hearing was slightly impaired from the blast of the stove mortar, an unremitting whistling present in his ears.

Still, all that was a small price to pay for getting out with his life. It had been a close call — the closest yet — and it didn't make sense to him. The Limiters had him cold, and yet they'd held back. It was as if they *wanted* him alive — but that wasn't their modus operandi at all. After the mortar had caused mayhem among the droves of approaching Styx, he had taken advantage of the chaos and the whirling dust to duck back into the Bunker.

From then on it was child's play. He could navigate the complex with his eyes shut, although Elliott's explosions had blocked several of the fastest routes through. And there were numerous patrols of Limiters, many with stalkers, to contend with. For a while he laid low in a dugout he'd prepared for this very eventuality. He was fortunate that the dogs were hampered by the aftermath of Elliott's handiwork; the fumes and dust still carried in the air made it impossible for them to pick up his scent trail.

He used a drainage duct to exit the Bunker, but even when he was back on the Great Plain he found he wasn't out of the woods yet. To shake off the mounted troop of Styx and the packs of stalkers snapping at his heels, he'd had to lay some false tracks. He'd used every trick in the book to finally elude them.

Now, as the sound of the wind joined with the whistling in his ears, he squatted down to study the ground. He was concerned that he hadn't found anything yet. Elliott could be taking one of several routes, but this was the most likely.

He got up and continued for another hundred feet until he came across what he'd been looking for.

"Here we are," he announced, evaluating the impressions in the dust. They were fresh footprints, and it was easy enough for him to tell to whom they belonged.

"Chester, and . . . and this must be *Will*! So he made it!" he said, with a shake of his head and a tight smile, relieved. He reached his hand over to the left, tracing around another print, and then lowered himself down onto his chest to assess the profile in more detail.

"Cal — your leg's acting up, isn't it?" he muttered, seeing the unevenness of one of the boy's footprints.

Another set of tracks caught his eye in the dust next to Cal's.

"Stalker?" he posed aloud, wondering if there was any evidence of a struggle, and maybe even traces of blood, in the area. He crawled closer to scrutinize the prints.

"No, this is no dog, this is feline. This must be a Hunter."

Mulling over what this could mean, he stood up and searched a wider area. "Elliott, where are you?" he was saying to himself as he attempted to locate her prints, knowing it would be more difficult due to the manner in which she moved.

A quick search yielded nothing, and he decided he couldn't afford to spend any longer checking. Every second meant that Elliott and the boys would be that much farther away. He set off again along the tunnel.

Several hundred feet farther on, he squatted down to inspect the ground again, then cried out.

"Ow! Dang it!"

He felt the Parchers burn his hand and saw the faint glow they were beginning to emit. He immediately wiped his hand on his pants to remove the bacteria before they sucked the moisture from his skin and flared fully into life. A moment too late and the reaction would have been as painful as if his hand had been immersed in acid. He'd witnessed enough stalkers yelping and bucking in agony, their noses shining as brightly as a tail light on a Topsoil bicycle, to know how it went.

But he'd removed the bacteria in time and, aware that Elliott wouldn't have used them unless she'd thought it absolutely necessary, he began to run.

That was when he heard a massive explosion from somewhere up ahead.

"That sounds suspiciously like my Sharps munitions store going off," he said to himself.

There followed a deep rumbling that could have been mistaken for rolling thunder, although it lasted for considerably longer than any Topsoil storm. The wind in the tunnel faltered, then reversed direction.

If he had been moving rapidly before, he now flew through the tunnel, terrified he was going to be too late.

50

"**GOT SOMETHING?**" Chester asked Elliott as they studied the horizon through their rifle scopes.

"Yes . . . activity to the left," she confirmed. "Do you see them?"

"No," Chester admitted. "Nothing."

"There are two Limiters, maybe a third," Elliott said.

They'd already had several sightings of Styx along the way, and each time had been forced to change direction. This had been the pattern since they'd emerged into a goliath space with odd-looking, dough-shaped rock formations scattered throughout it — menhirs, Will had called them.

"We'd better make ourselves scarce," Elliott said. Although the Limiters were a considerable distance away, she and Chester kept low and used the menhirs for cover as they stole back to where Will and Cal were waiting.

"What's up?" Will asked.

"More of them," Chester replied curtly, keeping his eyes averted.

"Doesn't look promising," Elliott said, shaking her head. "We can't go the way I wanted, so we're going to cut down the slope closer to the Pore, and then . . . then on to . . . ."

She hesitated as the distant sound of a howl carried through the arid air, followed by barking.

Bartleby let out a small meow, and his ears pricked up like radar dishes as he spun his whole body around to where the noises were coming from.

"They've got the stalkers in here," Elliott said. "Come on."

They kept on the move, filled with a sense of urgency, but Will and the others found they weren't as panicky as they might have been. For one thing, the soldiers were far enough off that it didn't feel as if they posed an immediate threat. But more significantly, the fight with the Limiter had had a profound effect on each of them. Elliott's words of reassurance to Cal back at the Sharps resonated within all three boys; it was as though they had been partially anesthetized from the constant fear and dread that they'd been living with. Elliott was right — the experience, horrible as it was, had toughened them up.

And they'd found out their opponents weren't the invincible warriors they had once thought. They could be beaten. Besides, the boys had Elliott on their side. As they tramped down the slope, Will dreamingly began to imagine her as some new kind of superhero. *The incredible exploding girl,* he mused, *with fingers of dynamite and nitroglycerine for blood.* He chuckled to himself. She always rose to the occasion with something up her sleeve to help them out of a tight corner. *Long may it continue,* he thought.

So it came as a surprise when, after another stop to reconnoiter the horizon, Elliott grew increasingly agitated. She was always so calm and collected that her behavior began to infect the boys, setting them on edge. She was seeing Limiters everywhere.

"This isn't good. We've got to head even farther down," she told them, making a brisk quarter turn and lifting her rifle to her shoulder for a final check before setting off on the new course.

Will didn't grasp the importance of this change in direction until they eventually came upon the Pore itself.

Water drizzled down on them in sporadic, wind-tossed showers, as Will gazed into the seemingly infinite cavity.

He whistled in astonishment.

"That's one humongous hole!" he exclaimed, immediately going to the brink and peering down.

His vertigo affecting him, Cal maintained a wide margin between himself and the edge of the enormous drop.

Will was examining the curvature of the Pore through his headset. "Man, this is big. *Really* big."

"Yes," Elliott said. "You could say that."

"Can't even see to the other side," Chester muttered to no one in particular.

"It's about a mile at its widest," Elliott said, taking a swig of water. "And who knows how deep it is? Nobody who's ever fallen in has come back to tell the story — except, a long time ago, they say a man hauled himself out of it."

"I heard about him. Abraham someone," Will said, recalling that Tam had talked about him.

"Many people thought he was a fraud," Elliott went on. "Either that or his brains were cooked by fever." She stared deep into the Pore. "But there's a heap of old legends about some sort of"— she hesitated, as if what she was about to say was ludicrous —"sort of place below."

"What do you mean?" Will asked, quickly turning to her. He had to know more, regardless of how Chester might react. "What place?"

"Oh, here we go again with his twenty questions," murmured Chester, right on cue. Will ignored him.

"They say there's another world, but Drake thought it was a load of old codswallop," she said, screwing on the top of her canteen.

As they passed around the edge of the Pore, there were no further signs of any more Limiters. Within a few minutes of fast marching, Will noticed the outline of some sort of regular structure. Through his lens it became clear that it wasn't a building but a massive arch.

Although crumbled and eroded, the arch had an icon on its keystone that he recognized. Carved into it were three divergent lines: the same symbol that was on the jade pendant Uncle Tam had given him just before his final showdown with the Styx Division in the Eternal City.

While pondering this coincidence, Will was distracted by the peculiar sight of papers strewn all over the ground on the far side of the arch. Chester and Elliott had already picked up a few of these pages and were examining them.

"What's all this?" Will asked as he joined them.

Chester put some pages in his hand without comment.

One glance was all it took.

"Dad!" Will exclaimed. "My dad!"

A number of the sheets contained pictures of stones, on which were painstakingly drafted sketches of strange and complex symbols. Densely penciled notes filled other pages. The unmistakable handwriting of his father littered the margins.

Will scanned the ground, pushing through the loose pages with his boot. He found a rather ratty pair of brown wool socks knotted together, with large holes in the toes, and then, bizarrely, a Mickey Mouse toothbrush, well used from the looks of it.

"I wondered where that had gone!" Will smiled, pushing against the grimy and worn bristles with his thumb. "Silly old Dad . . . he took my toothbrush with him!"

But any cheerfulness evaporated as he came across the blue-and-purple-marbled cover of a notebook. It was clear then where all the pages had come from. He snatched it up and studied the label stuck on the front, a bookplate with a bespectacled owl at the side and *Ex Libris* printed in swirly copperplate lettering across the top.

"*Journal Three . . . Dr. Roger Burrows,*" Will read out loud.

He dashed back to the arch. Passing under it, he didn't pause as he moved out onto the platform, immediately spotting a weather-worn flight of stone steps that led off from it. Reaching the last one, he stooped to peer below. He couldn't see anything. But as he raised his eyes, blinking as the rain fell on his face, something caught his attention.

Straight in front of him was his father's blue-handled geological hammer, its tip lodged in the rock. He leaned over to retrieve it. It came loose after several tugs, and he regarded it for a few seconds before renewing his efforts to try to see farther down the walls of the Pore. Even through the lens of his headset, he saw nothing there.

Deep in thought, he rejoined the others.

"What happened here?" he said, his voice brittle with apprehension.

Elliott and Chester were silent — neither of them able to give him an answer.

"My dad . . . ?" Will said to Chester.

Chester looked into the space between them, his face expressionless and his lips tightly clamped as if he was disinclined to say anything.

"He's probably all right," Elliott said. "If we keep going, we might . . ."

"Yes, we might catch up with him," Will completed her sentence, grabbing at the suggestion to give himself some comfort. "I bet he just left these things behind by accident . . . dropped them. . . . He's a bit forgetful sometimes . . ." His mind churned with explanations for his father's absence as he looked back at the arch. "But . . . not . . . careless," he added slowly. "I mean . . . it's not as if his rucksack's here, or . . ."

A terrified yelp from Cal yanked him from his thoughts. The boy had been lounging against a sizable boulder a little way back from the edge of the Pore, and leaped up as if he'd been stung by a bee.

"It moved! I swear the stinking rock moved!" he shouted.

The rock *had* moved, and was still moving. Like some miracle, it had risen up on jointed legs and was rotating. As it came to a stop, they all saw the huge, vacillating antennae. The machinelike mouthparts gave a single clack.

"Ohmygosh!" Chester shrieked.

"Oh, do shut up!" Elliott rebuked him. "It's only a *cave cow*."

The boys watched as the insect — Dr. Burrows's gargantuan "dust mite" and one-time traveling companion — clacked again, and then trundled cautiously forward. Bartleby scampered around its circumference, venturing forward to sniff at it and then retreating back again, as if he didn't quite know what to make of the creature.

"Shoot it!" Chester exhorted Elliott as he shielded himself behind her, petrified. "Kill it! It's horrific!"

"It's only a *baby*," Elliott said, quite unconcerned as she went up to it and slapped its thick exoskeleton with a dull thud. "They're harmless. They graze on algae, not meat. You don't need to be . . ."

Something speared on the cave cow's mouthparts silenced her. Patting the insect again, she leaned forward to retrieve it.

It was Dr. Burrows's backpack, badly torn and turned inside out.

Will approached her slowly and took it from her.

His eyes said it all.

"So this thing . . . this cave cow . . . you say it's harmless, but could it have hurt my father?"

"Not a chance. Even the adults wouldn't harm a hair on your head, unless one of them sat on you by accident. I told you, they don't eat flesh." She put her hand over Will's as he continued to clutch the rucksack, and pulled the bag toward her face so she could sniff at the ruined canvas. "Thought so . . . it had food in it. That's what the cow was after."

Will wasn't reassured as he glanced repeatedly between the stationary cave cow and the arch. His brow creased with concern.

It didn't look good and everyone knew it.

"Sorry, Will, but we can't hang around," Elliott said. "The sooner we get clear of here, the better."

"No, you're right," he agreed.

As Elliott, Chester, and Cal set off again, Will rushed around, gathering up as many of the pages as he could and stuffing them inside his jacket. Then, fearing he might be left behind, he ran to catch up with the others, the Mickey Mouse toothbrush clasped firmly in his hand.

"These . . . boots . . . are . . ."

Lines of the song ran through Sarah's befogged head. She was half grunting, half gasping odd snatches from it as the Limiters on either side forced her to keep walking, each step causing the most terrible pain in her hip, as if barbed wire was being slowly twisted deep in her flesh.

Little by little, Sarah was dying, and the Limiters knew it. So much for emergency medical attention. They didn't give a jot about her. They would probably get a pat on the back from Rebecca even if they delivered a dead body.

But Sarah knew she had to stay conscious and was fighting the darkness that threatened to swamp her.

". . . made for walking . . . one of these days . . ."

One of the Limiters grunted something guttural at her, but she defied him, carrying on with the song.

"... these boots are gonna to walk all over you...."

Sarah's blood left a broken, splattered trail behind her. Quite by chance, once or twice it spilled across patches of Parchers that Elliott had sprinkled in her wake as she and the boys had fled the very same way. Brought to life by Sarah's blood, the bacteria flared with such brilliance it was as though light was blazing directly out of the very ground itself, like flashlights from the outermost circle of hell.

But Sarah was oblivious to her shining path. She had fixed her mind, completely and absolutely, on a single, overwhelming purpose. As far as she could fathom, the Limiters were taking her in the same direction Will and Cal had gone.

That was good and bad.

It probably meant that further Styx were also on their trail, so her sons were in danger.

But it also meant that she might still be able to help them. Even if it was the last thing she did.

51

WHEN HE CAME up behind the Limiter patrol, Drake had to slow down. He swore silently. There was nothing he could do to get ahead of them.

Chancing his luck, he crept closer, to assess the situation. They were dragging someone with them, but he wasn't going to jump to any conclusions about the captive's identity. Maybe it was some unfortunate renegade the soldiers had caught, he thought as he kicked his heels, impatient to get going again. He touched the stove guns strapped to his thigh — it would be pushing it to use them against four soldiers in the first place, and he also didn't want to risk hitting their prisoner.

So he was forced to bide his time until finally the patrol lugged the prisoner out onto the ledge at the drop to the Sharps. From there, they took the longer ridge path down. As soon as they were out of sight, Drake rapidly descended the rusty Coprolite ladder, taking cover the instant he touched bottom. The air glittered with millions of tiny, slow-moving glass particles, which rimed his eyes and lined his throat. As he weaved between the massive glass stumps and the fractured sections of column left in the aftermath of what clearly had been a devastating explosion, he repeatedly had to stop and hide. He spotted a number of dead Limiters around the place, but it was swarming with quite a few live ones, too, conducting a search of the area.

He came to the passage he knew Elliott would have taken, but its mouth was completely blocked by a collapsed glass column. His only option was to skirt farther around the perimeter and take the next available route.

In the process, he spotted the patrol with the prisoner again as they stormed down the last section of the ridge. Two of the four Limiters immediately peeled off, probably to check in with their comrades deeper in the cavern. The remaining two allowed their captive to drop to the ground. He heard a woman's scream as the figure fell.

Whoever she was, Drake couldn't just leave her to their mercy.

He picked up a shard of obsidian and slung it fifty feet to the left of the Limiters' position. The pair of soldiers reacted immediately, raising their rifles and stalking toward where it had landed. Drake chose his moment and threw another large shard to draw them even farther away, then stole across to where the woman lay. Cupping a hand over her mouth lest she cry out, he lifted her in his arms and made for the exit tunnel.

Once he'd run far enough, he put her down.

She was wearing a Limiter's uniform, but, even stranger than this, the woman's face was somehow familiar to Drake. She tried to say something, but he told her to stay quiet as he assessed her injuries.

"These bandages . . . who did this?" he asked, noticing with surprise that the dressings were identical to ones he and Elliott carried.

"You're a renegade, aren't you?" Sarah threw back at him.

"Just tell me — did Elliott do this?" he pressed.

"Small girl, big rifle?" Sarah managed in reply.

Drake nodded, still trying to figure out where he knew her from.

"A friend of yours?" Sarah asked. She saw Drake raise his eyebrows. It was uncanny; for an instant it could have been Tam before her: a leaner version, maybe, but the quizzical expression was identical. At once she felt she could trust this total stranger, this grizzled man with hard blue eyes and an odd-looking device around his head.

"Well, she's a lousy shot." Sarah chuckled grimly.

Drake was taken aback; the woman was showing the most incredible bravery despite the magnitude of her wounds. But he was wasting precious seconds.

"I've got to go," he said apologetically, standing up. "My friend Elliott, she needs my help."

"And I need to help my sons, Will and Cal," Sarah said.

"Ah, so that's who you are," Drake realized with a start. "The legendary Sarah Jerome. I thought I recognized your—"

"And if you want to know what the Styx are up to," Sarah interrupted, "we can talk along the way."

Elliott led the boys to another arch, although it hadn't withstood the ravages of time as well as the first one. Only a single pillar was still standing, the rest lying in pieces across its flagged platform.

Will and the others had just stepped off the giant flagstones when the baying of stalkers rolled toward them again. They sounded alarmingly close. Elliott had been going at full speed but came to a dead stop, spinning around to face the boys.

"How can I have been so incredibly stupid?" she burst out in a fierce whisper.

"What do you mean?" Chester asked.

"Can't you see it?" she said, her voice cracking with exasperation.

Crowding around her, Will, Chester, and Cal exchanged blank looks.

"They've been harrying us for miles . . . and I didn't spot it." Elliott gripped her rifle with such aggression that one of her knuckles cracked. "What a fool!"

"Spot what?" Chester said. "What are you talking about?"

"The pattern. . . . We've run into Limiters at every turn, and we've gone exactly where they wanted us, like hens in a roundup! They've corralled us, time after time."

Will thought she was about to break into tears, she was so livid with herself.

"I've played straight into their hands. . . ." She let the stock of her rifle slide to the ground until it rested in the dirt, then she leaned against the barrel, her head bowed. She was visibly crestfallen, as if all her sense of purpose had suddenly left her. "After everything Drake taught me. He wouldn't —"

"Oh, don't even, we're doing just fine," Cal cut her off, trying to remain calm but sounding far from it. Spent to the point of collapse, he just wanted to get wherever and finally rest. "Can't we just go along there?" he appealed to her, pointing at the perimeter of the Pore.

"No way," Elliott replied wanly.

"Why not?" he pressed her.

She didn't answer for a moment, her eyes on Bartleby. The cat's head was up and his ears cocked alertly; as they watched, he raised his head even higher and sniffed. Elliott gave a resigned nod as she finally answered Cal.

"Along there, somewhere, is a bunch of Limiters, all with rifles trained and ready." At the boys' continued refusal to accept what she was saying, she seemed to pull herself together, her eyes flashing angrily at each of them in turn. "And out there"— she jerked her thumb to the left —"will be enough White Necks to fill a stinking church. Why don't you ask your Hunter? He knows."

Cal glanced at his cat and then regarded Elliott dubiously, as Will and Chester took a few paces in the directions she had indicated to scrutinize the barren landscape.

Pulling down his lens, Will could see a considerable distance up the slope where the menhirs lay in haphazard arrangement. "But . . . but there's absolutely *no one* there," he insisted, his voice whining with the implausibility of it all.

"Nothing this way, either," Chester added. "You're getting jumpy, Elliott, that's all. We're fine, really," he pleaded as he and Will wandered back to rejoin her.

"If *fine* is being shot to shreds, boys, then I'd have to agree with you," Elliott said tersely as she swung up her rifle in a single deft movement, readying it against her shoulder.

52

DRAKE BOMBARDED Sarah with question after question as they went, grilling her about what she knew. She was finding it increasingly difficult to concentrate and often answered disjointedly, sometimes getting the sequence of events in the wrong order as she told him about Rebecca and the Dominion plot.

Eventually they lapsed into silence, Drake because he was trying to conserve his energy to carry Sarah, and Sarah because the spells of light-headedness were coming with greater frequency. Like a leaking bucket, she felt the lifeblood seeping from her. The odds were stacked heavily against her ever seeing her two sons again.

"These boots are gonna . . . ," she wheezed as Drake carried her along. The pain from her shattered hip was so vast and all-consuming that at times she saw herself as a cork bobbing on the surface of a shiny red-hot ocean, which, at any moment, might fold over her and suck her into its depths. She fought and fought to stay afloat, to stay focused, but her whole head throbbed with a searing pain from the gunshot wound to her temple, as if her brain had been cleft in two.

"You keep lying when . . ."

And finally, Drake's chest heaving with the exertion, they came to the gradient leading down to the Pore.

Despite his fragile cargo, he broke into a run.

A singsong shout rolled over the expanse toward them.

"Oh, Will!"

He went rigid.

"I know you're there, Sunshine!" it called gleefully.

Will recognized the voice without a moment's hesitation. He locked eyes with Elliott.

"Rebecca," he gasped.

For an instant none of them moved.

"I think we're in trouble," Will said helplessly.

Elliott nodded. "You're so right," she agreed, her voice devoid of any intonation.

Will felt exactly like a rabbit caught in the blazing headlights of a huge juggernaut that was thundering down on it.

It was as if, deep in his bones, he'd always known this moment would come, that it had been inevitable right from the start. And yet he'd led all of them straight into it. His befuddled gaze fell on Chester, but his old friend gave him such a glare of bitter recrimination and contempt that Will had to turn away.

"Well, don't just stand there! Take cover!" Elliott barked.

They scattered, Elliott and Chester flinging themselves behind one menhir as Will and Cal took another.

"Oh, Willlllll!" the voice came again, spiked with little-girl sweetness. "Come out, come out, wherever you are!"

"Do nothing," Elliott mouthed at him with a rapid shake of her head.

"Hey, big brother, don't jerk me around!" Rebecca shouted. "Let's have a little chat, for old times' sake."

As Elliott had commanded, Will didn't respond. He stuck an eye around the side of the boulder, but saw only darkness.

Rebecca went on, unamused. "OK, if you're going to play silly games with me, let's get the rules straight."

There was a lull. In the ongoing absence of any reply from Will, Rebecca continued.

"Righty-o . . . the rules. One . . . as you seem a little bashful, I'll come down to you. Two . . . if anyone gets it into their head to take a pop at me, the gloves are off, and this is how it'll go. First I'll let slip the stalkers; my little darlings haven't been fed for days, so, trust me, you *really* don't want that. Or in the unlikely event the dogs don't do you in, my squad of crack riflemen will. Last, I've got the Division with some heavy ordnance up here . . . their guns will smash anything in their path, you included. So, pull any stunts and you'll suffer the consequences. Got that?"

There was another pause, then her voice came, more strident and imperious this time. "Will, I want your word I've got safe passage."

Will quit trying to see up the slope and slumped back behind the huge menhir. He felt that Rebecca would be able to look right through even that, solid rock, as if nothing more than a pane of glass separated them.

A chill sweat trickled down the small of his back, and he found that his hands were shaking. He closed his eyes and, banging his head against the rock behind him, moaned, "No, no, no, no, no."

How could it have gone so wrong? They'd been making good progress toward the Wetlands, with wide-open spaces before them and an abundance of routes to choose from. Now they were in this appalling predicament, hemmed in with a colossal black hole behind them. *How could it have come to this?*

And in Rebecca, they were up against somebody so utterly merciless and brutal; somebody who *knew* him like the back of her hand.

He shot a glance over to Elliott, but she was remonstrating with Chester. Will couldn't catch anything of what they were saying. As he watched, they appeared to reach agreement and their frantic exchange finished. Elliott quickly shucked off her rucksack and began to delve around in it.

"Hey, Mole-face," Rebecca called down. "I'm waiting for your answer."

"Elliott!" Will hissed urgently. "What do I do?"

"Buy some time. Talk to her," Elliott snapped, not looking up as she began to play out a length of rope.

Encouraged that Elliott seemed to have settled on a course of action, Will took several deep breaths and poked his head around the edge of the menhir. "Yes! OK!" he yelled back to Rebecca.

"That's my boy!" Rebecca answered cheerfully. "I knew you'd be up for it."

In the ensuing seconds they heard nothing more from Rebecca. Elliott and Chester each tied the rope around themselves, then Chester slung the other end of it across to Will as Elliott crouched down behind her rifle.

Will shrugged at Chester, who just shrugged back. Will could only think that, as a last resort, Elliott had decided they were going to attempt to climb down the Pore. He couldn't see any other way out. He turned to Cal. His brother was whimpering quietly to himself, his face nestled in Bartleby's neck as he clasped the agitated animal to his chest. Cal had lost it, and Will couldn't blame him. Will secured the rope around himself, then knotted it around Cal's waist. His brother passively allowed him to do so, without questioning why.

Will glanced back at the Pore. It *was* their only way out. But was it much of a solution? What *was* Elliott thinking? Will had seen for himself that the hole consisted of a sheer rock face, with nothing to cling to. It looked pretty grim for them all.

Will heard Rebecca whistling in the darkness as she approached.

"*You are my sunshine,*" he murmured, recognizing the tune. "I really hate that song."

When she spoke again, she was much closer.

"Right, this is as far as I'm coming."

Massive searchlights blasted on from farther up the slope.

"Whiteout!" Elliott exclaimed, raising her head from her rifle as the blazing light hit the scope. She squeezed her eye shut several times, recovering from the glare. "That's just freakin' great!" she fumed. "I can't get a fix on *anything* now!"

Dazzling beams of light swept back and forth over the area where Will and the others were hiding, sending solid black shadows slashing across the ground.

Will stuck his head a little farther around the edge of the boulder. He'd had to turn off the headset to protect it, and the blinding intensity of the lights made it difficult to see, but he could make out someone — it certainly looked like Rebecca. She was standing in the open ground between two menhirs. He pulled back and glanced at Elliott, who was still lying prone, an array of explosives and stove guns within easy reach on the ground. She adjusted the position of her arms, ready to fire on the figure, even without the use of the scope.

"Don't! Don't shoot her," Will begged in a whisper. "The stalkers!"

Elliott didn't reply, her focus fixed on her target.

"Will! Got a little surprise for you!" Rebecca called out. Before she'd finished speaking, her voice came again, like some ventriloquist's trick. "Quite a surprise!"

Will frowned, and couldn't stop himself from taking another look.

"Meet my twin sister," Rebecca's voice announced. Or, rather, *two* voices announced, in unison.

"Careful!" Elliott warned as Will got to his feet and stuck his head even farther around the side of the menhir.

As he watched, the solitary figure appeared to split into two, revealing that a second girl had been standing immediately behind the first. The two turned to face each other, and Will saw identical profiles. They were mirror images.

"No!" he choked in disbelief, pulling back a little, then leaning out again.

"How's that for a bombshell, bro?" the Rebecca on the left shouted.

"All the time, there's been *two* of us, completely interchange-able," the Rebecca on the right cackled.

His eyes *weren't* deceiving him.

There were two Rebeccas, side by side!

It had to be a trick — an illusion of some kind, or maybe a second person wearing a mask. But no. As the twins moved, as the twins talked, it seemed as though they *were* absolutely identical.

They continued to chatter in such a quick-fire way that he couldn't tell which of them was saying what.

"Your worst nightmare — two irksome little *skin and blisters*, two little sisters!"

"How else do you think we worked it when one of us had to be Topsoil at all times?"

"We took turns babysitting you at the Highfield home."

"One on, one off, one up, one down, doing tours of duty for all those years."

"We both know you *so* well. . . ."

"We've both cooked your lousy food . . ."

". . . picked up your filthy clothes . . ."

". . . washed your soiled, stinking underpants . . ."

"You dirty dog!" one sneered in disgust.

". . . and listened to you blubber in your sleep, crying out for *Mammy* . . ."

". . . but *Mammy* don't care . . ."

Despite the dire situation he found himself in, Will squirmed with acute embarrassment. It would have been bad enough if there was only a single Rebecca saying all this, but *two* of them, knowing every little intimate detail there was to know about him — and discussing it between them! It was more than he could bear.

"Shut up, you foul cow!" he screamed.

"Oooh, touchy, touchy," one of the twins cooed mockingly.

Temporarily oblivious to the legion of Limiters surrounding him, Will was suddenly transported back to his home in Highfield, to how it had been for all those years before his father went missing. He and his sister continually clashing over the most trivial of things. This felt exactly like another of their outrageous spats when she would wind him up with her interminable needling and well-aimed taunts. The outcome was always the same — he would eventually blow his top, and she would stand back to gloat, a smug smirk on her face.

"And I think you mean foul cows," the Rebecca on the right suggested with a sibilant "s," while the other continued to harangue him.

"But Mammy didn't have time for her little Will . . . he wasn't in the program guide . . ."

". . . he wasn't Must-See TV."

Two belly laughs.

"What a sad, sad boy," a twin cawed.

"Joe Nobody digging his stupid holes, all on his lonesome."

"Digging for Daddy's love," sneered the other, and they both cackled uproariously.

Will closed his eyes — it was as if they were poking around inside his head, picking out and cruelly exposing his innermost fears and secrets. Nothing was inviolate — the twins were putting everything on show for all to see.

Then the twin on the left spoke out, her voice deadly serious.

"What we wanted to tell you, Will, and that lumbering oaf Chester, is that very soon now there won't *be* any home to go back to."

"No more Topsoilers," the second twin warbled gleefully.

"Well, not *quite* so many," the first corrected her in a sing-song voice.

"What are they saying?" Chester demanded. He was sweating profusely, his face an ashen white under the patches of dirt.

Will had had enough.

"Lies! It's all a load of lies!" he shouted, his whole body shaking with terror and anger.

"You saw for yourself, we've been busy bees in the Eternal City," a twin said. "We've had the Division prospecting there for years."

"And they finally isolated the very bug we were looking for. Our scientists did some work on it, and here are the fruits of their labors."

Will watched as the twin on the left took something that hung around her neck and held it up into the searchlights. It glittered as the beams caught it: a small glass phial, or so it appeared.

"Choice little number, this . . . bottled genocide . . . the big daddy of all pandemics from centuries ago. We call it Dominion."

"Dominion," the other repeated.

"We're going to let it rip Topsoil and —"

"— the Colony will reclaim its rightful home."

The twin with the phial proffered it to her sister as if she was proposing a toast.

"To a new London."

"To a new world," the other one added.

"Yes, *world*."

"I don't believe you, you witches! It's all trash talk!" Will protested. "You're lying!"

"Why would we bother?" the twin on the right countered, waving a second phial. "See this? We've got the vaccine, old chap. You Topsoilers won't be able to produce it in time. The whole country will be crippled, and there for the taking."

"So don't flatter yourself that we're down here just on *your* account."

"We've been doing a spot of spring-cleaning in the Deeps, ridding it of rotten old renegades and traitors to the cause."

"As well as running some final trials on Dominion — but then, some of your new buds have seen that for themselves."

"Ask Elliott. She knows the story."

At the mention of her name, Elliott jerked her head up from behind the rifle. "The Bunker," she mouthed at Will, recalling the sealed cells she'd blundered across with Cal.

Will's mind raced. He knew in his gut that Rebecca — the Rebeccas, he had to keep reminding himself — were capable of the most abject cruelty. Did they really have a plague? His thoughts were brought to an abrupt end as the twosome started up again.

"So, to business, bro," the Rebecca on the left said. "We're going to make you a one-time offer."

"But we're going back first," added the other.

Will watched as the doppelgängers both spun daintily on their toes and began to skip their way up the slope.

"I might be able to nail one . . . ," Elliott whispered. She was behind the rifle again.

"No, wait!" Will pleaded with her.

". . . but not both," Elliott went on.

"No. You'll only make it worse. Hear what they've got to say," Will begged, the blood in his veins turning to ice as he imagined the pack of stalkers descending on their gang of four, ripping each of them limb from limb.

As he watched, both figures slipped from view among the menhirs. *What were the twins up to? What was this offer going to be?*

He didn't have to wait long to find out. The twins yelled down at him in quick succession.

"People have a habit of *dying* around you, Will, don't they?"

"Fun-loving Uncle Tam, sliced to shreds."

"And that fat fool Imago. A little fish told me he got sloppy —"

"— and now he's stone-cold dead," the other twin chimed in.

"By the way, have you bumped into your real mother yet? Sarah's down here, and she's looking for you."

"Somehow she got it into her head that you're to blame for Tam's death, and —"

"No! She knows that's not true!" Will cried, his voice cracking.

For a beat the twins were silent, as if they'd been taken by surprise.

"Well, she won't get away from us a second time," one Rebecca promised, not sounding quite so confident anymore.

"No, she won't. And while we're playing family reunions, sis, do tell him about Grandma Macaulay," the other Rebecca suggested with a harsh edge to her voice. This twin was clearly not fazed in the slightest by Will's interruption.

"Oh, yes, I forgot about her. She's dead," the first Rebecca answered bluntly. "From unnatural causes."

"We spread her on the pennybun fields." They both shrieked with laughter, and Will heard Cal murmur, his face still pressed against Bartleby.

"No," Will croaked, fearing for Cal. "It's not true," he said weakly. "They're lying." Then, in an anguished shout, he asked them, "Why are you doing this? Can't you just leave me alone?"

"Sorry. Not possible," one answered.

"An eye for an eye," the other added.

"Out of curiosity, why did you put a bullet in that trapper we were 'questioning' back on the Great Plain?" a twin continued. "It *was* you, wasn't it, Elliott?"

"Did you get him mixed up with Drake?" the other said, then gave a full-bodied guffaw. "Bit trigger-happy, aren't you?"

Will and Elliott exchanged confused looks, and she mouthed "Oh no," at him.

"And as for that silly old goat, Dr. Burrows — we left him to putter around . . ."

Will stiffened as he heard his father's name, his heart missing several beats.

"— like bait in a trap —"

"— and we didn't even have to finish him off."

"Looks like he did the job for us."

The twins' high-pitched giggles echoed around the dark stones.

"No, not Dad," Will whispered, shaking his head as he pulled back behind the menhir. He slid down its rough surface and slumped to the ground, his head hung low.

"So this is what we're putting on the table," a twin shouted, her voice deadly serious once more.

"If you want your little gang to live —"

"— then hand yourself over."

"And we'll be lenient with them," her sister piped in.

They were toying with him! Just as if they were playing some childish game, only this was sheer torture.

They went on in persuasive tones, telling him that his surrender would help his friends. Will could hear what the Rebeccas were saying, but it was all just noise. As though a dense fog had descended on him, he felt disoriented, and it was all he could do to sit upright against the menhir. He examined the ground around him, listlessly lifting a handful of dirt and crushing it in his fist. As he raised his head, his eyes alighted on Cal's face. Tears were streaming down the boy's cheeks.

Will had no idea what to say to his brother — he couldn't begin to express what he himself felt about Grandma Macaulay's death — so he just turned away. In the opposite direction, he noticed Elliott had left her position behind the menhir. She was snake-crawling through the arch by the edge of the Pore, almost at the first of the stone steps that led nowhere. Connected to her by the rope, Chester had begun the same short journey.

Trying to pull himself together, Will flung aside the fistful of dirt. He glanced again at Chester. He knew he should be following him, but he couldn't bring himself to — move. He was in a maelstrom of indecision. *Should he give up the game and just hand himself over? Sacrifice himself in a bid to save the lives of his brother, Chester, and Elliott? It was the least he could do. . . . After all, he'd gotten them into this. And if he didn't surrender, then they were probably all doomed, anyway.*

"So what's it to be, big bro?" a Rebecca twin prompted him. "Going to do the right thing?"

Elliott was now completely hidden from sight down the flight of steps. "Don't, Will! It won't make any difference," she called to him.

"We're waiting!" shouted the other Rebecca, without any hint of her former humor. "Ten seconds, ready or not!"

The sisters began to count down, their alternating voices proclaiming each second.

"Ten!"

"Nine!"

"Oh God," Will mumbled, throwing another glance at Cal. "Eight!"

Sobs wracking his body, Cal babbled incomprehensibly at Will, who could only shake his head hopelessly in response.

"Seven!"

From behind the edge of the Pore, Elliott was urging him and Cal to get moving.

"Six!"

Chester, at the top of the steps, was jabbering at him rapidly.

"Five!"

"Come on, Will!" Elliott snapped, her head bobbing up above the lip of the Pore.

"Four!"

Absolute confusion reigned as they each tried to speak to him at the same time, but through it all Will only heard the seconds as the twins coldly announced them, nearing the end of the countdown.

"Three!"

"Will!" Chester yelled, yanking at the rope in an attempt to pull him closer.

"Will!" Cal was screaming.

"Two!"

Will staggered to his feet.

"One!"

"Zero!" the twins said simultaneously.

"Your time's run out."

"The deal's off."

"More needless deaths you've notched up, Will!"

Will heard Cal shouting and spun around.

"NO! WAIT!" his brother was shrieking. "I WANT TO GO HOME!"

He'd jumped out from behind the menhir and was waving his arms, in plain view of the Limiters and bathed in the full beams of the spotlights.

Right in the firing line.

Cracks of multiple rifle shots came from all around the upper reaches of the slope. So many in such a short space of time, it sounded like a speeded-up drumroll.

The barrage struck Cal all over his body with a messy, deadly precision. He didn't stand a chance. As if swatted by a huge invisible hand, the bullets' impact swept him off his feet, leaving a momentary red trace airborne in his place.

Will could only watch as his brother flopped in a broken heap by the very edge of the Pore, like a puppet whose strings had all been cut. It was as if it had happened in grisly slow motion. The bounce of his brother's arm as it hit the damp ground, the fact that he was only wearing one sock — Will absorbed even the smallest details.

Then Cal's body simply tipped over the edge. The rope around Will's waist snapped tight, the sudden tension yanking on him and forcing him several steps forward.

Bartleby, who had been waiting obediently where Cal had left him, scrabbled up in a whir of long limbs and burst after his master, vanishing from sight over the lip of the Pore. The drag on Will from the rope increased, and he knew that the cat must be hanging on to Cal's body.

Shots sizzled through the light beams, which switched back and forth so rapidly that they gave a stroboscopic effect. The bullets fell all around him, like a metal rain, whining and ricocheting off the menhirs and flicking up sprays of dirt at his feet.

But Will didn't make any attempt to hide. With his hands pressed against his temples, he screamed with every last drop of air in his lungs, until all that was left was a rasping croak. He swallowed down more air and screamed a second time: The word *Enough!* was just discernible through it. As his howl came to an end, a deathly hush filled the place.

The Limiters had ceased firing.

Chester and Elliott were no longer yelling to get his attention.

Will swayed where he stood. He was numb, oblivious to the rope as it bit sharply into his waist.

He didn't feel a thing.

Cal was dead.

This time there was no question in Will's mind. And he might have saved his brother's life if he'd surrendered to the twins.

But he hadn't.

Once before, he'd thought Cal was gone for good, and Drake had performed a miracle and resuscitated him. But now there were no reprieves, no happy endings. Not this time.

The intolerable weight of responsibility he bore crushed him. He, and he alone, had been responsible for destroying so many lives. He saw their faces. Uncle Tam. Grandma Macaulay. People who had given everything for him; people he loved.

And he couldn't help but believe his father, Dr. Burrows, was lost to him, too. He would never see him again, not now. Will's dream was finished.

The lull was brought to an abrupt end as the Limiters opened fire again, the barrage even fiercer than before, and Chester and Elliott resumed their panicked shouting as they tried to get through to him.

But, as if the sound had been turned down, Will wasn't hearing anything. His glazed eyes drifted over Chester's stricken and desperate face, mere footsteps away, as his friend yelled with all his might. It had no effect — even his friendship with Chester had been taken from him.

Everything he'd relied upon — the certainties underpinning his uncertain life — had been knocked out from under him, one after another.

His brain burned with the horrific image of his brother's death. That last moment blotted out everything else.

"Enough," he said, quite steadily this time.

Cal had lost his life because of *him*.

There was no avoiding it, no room for excuses, no quarter.

Will knew it should be him hanging there, punched full of holes, not his brother.

It was as if something was being stretched and stretched in his mind, creaking and bellying from side to side, until it was so close to the breaking point that it would fracture into tiny, sharp fragments that might never be pieced together again.

He struggled to stay upright as Cal's deadweight pulled at him. The Limiters continued to fire, but Will was somewhere else, and none of it mattered anymore.

He took a single stiff stride toward the Pore, allowing the weight to draw him on.

From the top of the stone steps, Chester came toward him, holding out his hand and hoarsely shrieking his name.

Will looked up and saw him as if for the first time.

"I'M SO SORRY, WILL!" Chester yelled, then his voice became strangely calm as he realized Will, at last, was listening. "Come here. It's OK."

"Is it?" Will asked.

Just for that second, it was as if they were insulated from all the horror and fear that surrounded them. Chester nodded and smiled briefly back at him. "Yes, and so are we," he replied, his words heavy with meaning. "I'm sorry."

A tiny germ of hope was born within Will.

He still had his friend — all was not lost, and they would get themselves out of this somehow.

Will took another step, reaching out his hand toward Chester.

Faster and faster, closing the distance between them, the rope pulling him forward. By the very edge of the Pore, he was just about to take hold of Chester's hand.

At the top of the slope, the Rebecca twins shouted simultaneously.

"Good riddance to him!"

"Bust out the big guns!"

The heavy artillery bucked into life. The Limiters' bank of howitzers spat massive shells that swerved like fireballs, leaving flaming red trails behind them. The whole slope was lit up with their blazing light, and the sound was deafening.

The shells struck, splitting any menhirs in their path and throwing up huge curtains of dirt, smashing into the paved platform and lifting the flagstones like a gust of wind scatters a pack of playing cards.

Will was thrown forward, knocked senseless by the blasts. He sailed straight into the pitch-black, clean over his friend's head.

If he'd been conscious, Will would have seen Chester's flailing arms and legs as he grabbed at anything he could in a last-ditch attempt to prevent himself from being dragged over by the rope that bound him to Will.

And he would have heard Elliott's screams as she, too, was yanked into the Pore after Chester.

If Will had been capable of thought, he would have felt the dark air rushing around him as he plummeted down and down, his dead brother somewhere beneath him, and the other two, still howling and screaming, up above. And he would have been terrified by the odd sections of masonry and the rubble from the pulverized menhirs that were falling all around them.

But there were no thoughts, just a black nothingness in his mind, identical to what he was plunging through.

Will was in free fall, his ears popping mercilessly and his breath stolen every so often by the rush of air as he shot through it, reaching terminal velocity.

On occasion he collided with Elliott, Chester, and even Cal's limp corpse, the ropes twisting around their limbs and torsos in random arrangements to bind them together, and then untwisting as they floated apart, as if they were dancers in some macabre aerial ballet. Every so often Will's trajectory took him to the side of the seemingly endless Pore, where he either crashed against the unforgiving rock or, curiously, hit softer matter — which, had he been conscious, would have caused him a great deal of surprise.

But in his insensible state, he was unaware of any of this; in a place beyond caring.

If his mind hadn't been disconnected, he would have noticed that although he continued to fall through the black vacuum, his rate of descent was slowing.

Imperceptibly at first, but definitely slowing . . . slowing . . . slowing . . .

53

ONCE THEY WERE in sight of the Styx floodlights, Drake hadn't risked remaining on his feet for the final distance. Instead he had dragged Sarah with him to a vantage point midway between where the Limiters were concentrated and, at the bottom of the slope, where Elliott and the boys had apparently been run to ground.

As Drake crouched behind a menhir, Sarah just lay there. She was too shattered to do anything but listen. With her head propped on a boulder, and her clothes soaked through and stuck to her with her own blood, she caught some of the shouted exchange between Will and the twins. The fact that there were indeed two Rebeccas didn't come as any great revelation. There'd long been rumors in the Colony that the Styx dabbled in eugenics — genetic manipulation for the advancement of their race — and that twins, triplets, and even quadruplets had become the norm as they multiplied their numbers. Yet another myth that had been borne out to her. She should have twigged that there were two Rebeccas when the one on the train claimed to have been at the Topsoil hospital that same morning — the Styx child had been telling the truth.

Sarah heard the twins taunting Will, then their threat to kill Topsoilers using Dominion.

"Did you get that?" Drake whispered over to her.

"Yes," she said, nodding grimly in the darkness.

The shouted exchanges came to her as if she was at the bottom of a well, echoing and swirling and often too indistinct to grasp in their entirety. But despite her deteriorating condition, some part of her brain retained enough functionality to process the snippets.

She heard her name mentioned and what the twins said about Tam's and Grandma Macaulay's deaths. Sarah's body locked up with fury. The Styx were wiping out all the members of her family, one by one. Then she heard the threats to kill Will and Cal and everyone with them.

"You've got to help them!" she said to Drake.

He looked helplessly at her. "What can I do? I'm hopelessly outnumbered and I've only got stove guns. There's a whole Styx army over there."

"But you have to do something!" she exhorted him.

"What do you suggest? I chuck rocks at them?" he said, his voice uneven with anguish.

But Sarah had to at least try to go to her sons' aid. Unnoticed by Drake as he continued to watch events from behind the menhir, she began to haul herself over the ground. She was determined to get to where Will and Cal were, even if she had to stop often to rest.

She heard the Rebecca twins counting, and the shouts of desperation down at the end of the slope.

Squinting through the glare, she glimpsed a small figure as it stepped into the light. She knew with a mother's intuition that it was Cal. Her heart pounded feebly as she extended a hand to where he stood, so far away. She watched him frantically waving his arms and heard his hopeless cries.

Then the shots came.

She saw his death. She dropped her hand to the ground.

There were terrible screams, then a cacophony of sound, and the air was filled with what appeared, to her jumbled head, to be flaming comets. The ground shook as she'd never felt it shake before, as if the whole cavern was collapsing around her. Then the noise and light were gone, in their place an awful quietness.

She was too late, too late for all of them. She'd wanted to call out to Cal, but hadn't.

She wept dusty tears.

She realized what a fool she had been. She should never have doubted Will! The Styx had tried to trick her into making the biggest mistake of her worthless, sorry excuse of a life. They'd even convinced Grandma Macaulay that Will was to blame. The poor, deluded old lady had believed their lies.

It was so obvious to Sarah now that the Styx were purging their domain. Once she had served her purpose, she'd have been next in line for the chopping block.

Why hadn't she trusted her instincts? She should have taken her life in the excavation back in Highfield. It had felt so wrong when she'd lowered the blade from her throat and allowed that little snake to persuade her to work with the Styx. From that moment of weakness onward, Sarah had unwittingly committed to a misguided manhunt for her own sons. A dumb cog in the Styx's grand plan. For that she could never forgive herself — or them.

She closed her eyes, feeling her fluttering heartbeat, as if there were a hummingbird trapped in her rib cage.

Maybe it was better this way, to let it end at last, right here and now.

She flicked her dull eyes open.

No!

She couldn't allow herself the luxury of death, not quite yet. Not while there was the faintest chance she could put some of this unholy mess right again.

She retained a sliver of hope that Will was still alive. She might be able to get to him. These thoughts pierced her brain like skewers, causing her as much pain as her injuries, and spurring her on.

Using her arms, she dragged herself toward the place where Will had been trapped, but every action became more and more labored, as if she was clawing her way through molasses. She didn't let up. She'd covered a significant distance when she blacked out again.

She came to, not knowing how long she'd been unconscious. There was no sign of Drake, but she heard voices nearby. She lifted her head and caught a glimpse of the Rebecca twins. They were issuing orders to a squad of Limiters at the very edge of the Pore.

She knew then that she was too late to save Will. But could she exact revenge for Tam, for her mother, for her sons?

Dominion!

Yes, there was something she could do. She was willing to bet that one or both of the Rebeccas still had the Dominion phials on them. And she'd seen how vitally important the virus was to their plan.

Yes!

If she could at least stymie the Styx's schemes, and maybe save some Topsoiler lives in the bargain, it would go a little way toward absolving her. She had doubted her own son. She had done so much wrong. It was time to get something right.

Using the side of a shattered menhir, she managed to get to her feet. Her irregular pulse thumped through her head, as loud as a kettledrum. The landscape swayed and pitched as she stood hunched over in the hard shadows, a different form of darkness amassing and beginning to engulf her; a darkness that light would not affect.

Pointing and looking down, the Styx girls stood at the rim of the Pore.

With a Herculean effort, Sarah dredged every remaining drop of vitality from her wrecked frame. Her arms outstretched, she flew at the twins, covering the remaining distance as fast as her broken body would propel her.

She saw the identical looks of surprise on their faces as they turned, and heard their identical screams as she swept both of them over the brink with her. It hadn't taken much to dislodge them, but it had taken all Sarah had left.

In her last moments of life, Sarah was smiling.

EPILOGUE

IN HUMPHREY House, Mrs. Burrows sat alone in the dayroom. It was well past midnight and, now that her eyes were rid of the mystery virus, she had no problem watching television again. But she wasn't engrossed in one of her many soaps; there was a grainy black-and-white picture on the screen in front of her. As she'd done many times before, she stopped the tape, rewound it, then played it back again.

The video recording showed the door to the reception area bursting open and a figure rushing through it. But before the figure went out of view, a face was visible; it looked up and then hastily down, as if it was aware that it was being caught on the security camera.

Mrs. Burrows froze the tape with a decisive press of the remote and moved closer to the television, leaning in to see the face with its flustered eyes and flurried hair. She touched the screen, tracing around the woman's features, which, flipping between two frames on the tape, were smeared and blurry, as if a ghost had unwittingly been captured on film.

"For your delight and delectation, the one and only Kate O'Leary, Woman of Intrigue," Mrs. Burrows mumbled as she made slits of her eyes and clicked her tongue against her teeth,

DEEPER

still scrutinizing Sarah's face. "Well, Ms. Kate *Whoever-You-Are*, there's nowhere on this earth you can hide that I won't find you." She fell into thought as she whistled in an atonal and random way, a habit of Dr. Burrows's — curiously, one she had often upbraided him for. "And I'm going to get my family back from you if it's the last thing I do."

An owl hooted and Mrs. Burrows turned to the windows, glancing at the darkness of the gardens outside.

As she did so, a man in a flat cap and a large overcoat stepped neatly back from the window so she wouldn't see him. It was highly unlikely that the Topsoiler woman, with her crude night vision, would be able to make him out in the gloom, but he wasn't about to take the chance.

The owl took to the wing and glided between the trees, while the heavyset individual waited patiently before resuming his vigil at the window.

As he waited, another man on a small hill a short distance away focused in on him, his light-gathering scope mounted on a tripod.

"I see you," Drake said, pulling his jacket collar around his neck as a wind rose up. Making another small adjustment to a furled ring on the scope, so that he had a pin-sharp image of the man in the shadows, he muttered under his breath, "Who will watch the watchers?"

From a nearby road, the undipped beam of a car's headlights briefly fell across the rear of Humphrey House. At that distance, it amounted to nothing more than a glimmer, but, processed by the light-intensifying electronics of the scope, it was bright enough to make Drake blink. Taken by surprise at the unexpected interruption of his surveillance, he drew in a sudden breath. The flash triggered memories of the blinding arcs when Elliott and the boys had been shelled by the Limiters, those last moments at the Pore when all he'd been able to do was watch as the ghastly events unfolded.

Drake stood up from the scope. Stretching his back to ease the stiffness in it, he stared into the depths of the night sky above.

No, he hadn't been able to save Elliott or the boys, but he was going to do everything in his power to stop the Styx. If they thought they could still resurrect their plan to use Dominion, they were in for a rude awakening. He took a cell phone from his pocket and dialed a number, strolling back toward the parked Range Rover as he waited. Waited for the answer to the call . . .

NOTE TO ENTOMOLOGISTS

To avoid any confusion: Dr. Burrows's dust mite is an arachnid (hence, related to spiders) and not an insect. But it is evident that evolutionary pressures down in the Deeps have been responsible for a number of specific adaptations: The so-called cave cows possess three pairs of legs (not that uncommon with mites), while the fourth pair of legs may have evolved into what Dr. Burrows perceives to be its "antennae" and "mandibles." The authors will be attempting to capture a specimen for further study, and their findings will be posted on **WWW.TUNNELSTHEBOOK.COM** in due course. Thank you.

Special Sneak Preview Of

Coming Soon!

FreeFall

RODERICK GORDON **BRIAN WILLIAMS**

The Third Book in the *New York Times*
Bestselling **TUNNELS** Series

"**CHESTER,**" Will said, becoming more like his old self again, "there's something you should know."

"What?"

"Notice anything weird about this place?" Will asked, giving his friend a quizzical glance.

Wondering where to start, Chester shook his head, his full head of curly, oil-drenched hair whipping around his face and a strand catching in his mouth. He plucked it out immediately with a look of disgust and spat several times. "No, except this stuff we landed in smells, and *tastes,* bloody awful."

"My guess is that we're on a dirty great fungus," Will went on. "We've ended up on some sort of ledge of it that sticks out into the Pore. I saw something like this once on television — there was a monster fungus in America that stretched for more than a thousand miles underground."

"Is that what you wanted to—?"

"Nope," Will interrupted. "This is the interesting thing. Watch carefully." He casually tossed a light orb a few feet into the air. Chester looked on with stunned amazement as it seemed to float back down to Will's hand again. It was as if he was witnessing the scene in slow motion.

"Hey, how'd you do that?"

"You have a go," Will said, passing the orb to Chester. "But don't throw it too hard or you'll lose it."

Chester did as Will suggested, lobbing it upward. But he applied too much force and the orb shot up some fifty feet, illuminating what appeared to be another fungal outcrop above them, before it floated eerily down again, the light playing on their upturned faces.

"How—?" Chester gasped, his eyes wide with surprise.

"Don't you feel the, um, weightlessness?" Will said, grasping for the right word. "It's low gravity. My guess is that it's about a third of what we're used to on the surface," Will informed him, pointing a finger heavenward. "That, and the soft landing we had, might explain why we're not as flat as pancakes right now. But be careful how you move around or you'll send yourself spinning off this shelf and back into the Pore again."

"Low gravity," Chester repeated, trying to absorb what his friend was saying. "What does that mean, exactly?"

"It means we must have fallen a *very* long way."

Chester looked at him uncomprehendingly.

Will smiled. "Ever wondered what's at the center of the earth?"

ACKNOWLEDGMENTS

On the publication of **DEEPER** and for the success of **TUNNELS** in the United States, we would like to thank Chicken House publisher Barry Cunningham and editor Siobhán McGowan, as well as Ellie Berger, Suzanne Murphy, Charisse Meloto, Rachel Coun, Jackie Harper, John Mason, Elizabeth Parisi, Kevin Callahan, Starr Mayo, Jess White, and all our other many friends at Scholastic in New York.

Lastly, we would like to thank our respective families, who are still waiting for us to emerge into the light. One day soon . . .